To Linds
ex-wife ever!

Mind Control Empire

Andrew Garvey

Mind Control Empire

Andrew Garvey

GREENPOINT PRESS
NEW YORK, NY

Mind Control Empire by Andrew Garvey

ISBN 978-0-9966912-0-8

Library of Congress Cataloging-in-Publication Data

Book Designer: Robert L. Lascaro
LascaroDesign.com

Greenpoint Press
A division of New York Writers Resources
greenpointpress.org
200 Riverside Blvd.
Suite 32E
New York, NY 10069

New York Writers Resources:

- newyorkwritersresources.com
- newyorkwritersworkshop.com
- greenpointpress.org
- ducts.org

Printed in the United States on acid-free paper

For Jack

PROLOGUE

I AWOKE IN THE MIDDLE OF THE NIGHT to a call in my ear tattoo telling me that a Chinese national had just gutted a passenger on a Trailways bus in the wilds of the former state of Wyoming and was still playing with the organs like toys, throwing them around like baubles and lassos when he wasn't eating them.

The scene was playing out like something from most people's nightmares, but to me it sounded like a comprehensive mental rewrite by one of the bigger players in mental stewardship (mind control) operations in the world.

So I arose from my bed without waking my wife, Janet, and walked downstairs in my coveted high-rise townhome so I could speak freely. After getting an overview, I told my groggy team through the tattooed microphone in my neck that the incident constituted an offensive into our regional and mental power base. We needed to leave for Wyoming within the hour.

It wasn't that the presumably Chinese active was killing; we could always get our own puppets to kill. But to play in the offal and eat it was a gesture meant to be striking.

In this war of mental customization, insanity was the warhead, and the populace, the delivery mechanism. This was an especially brutal payload. Nations show off this way. We've tempted each other with new, depraved, or ingenious acts, implicitly daring the other to top us. It's a game we've played to show the control we can have over our people and others when we want it. In this case, we were topped.

We needed to both try to replicate their results and respond proportionally, but not necessarily in that order.

A two-legged killer drone had been deployed on the soil of the former United States of America, and as I quickly showered and dressed, I knew I would have to figure out a way to keep this case out of the news. The programmed killer needed to be interrogated and tested someplace away from public scrutiny where time limits weren't imposed. He also needed to be tested in a Corporate Person Community that allowed the legal application of the methodologies we use.

My name is Dr. Donald Isaacson. I'm the Chief Science Officer on the board for all mental stewardship operations in the American Community of Corporate Persons (ACCP). We have satellite offices all over the world—usually in war zones—but my boss, Dr. Robert Gushlak, is ultimately in charge of every mind control operation on this continent, from the flash rates of digital graphics to the surreptitious deradicalization of terrorists before they can strike, among other varied and strange assignments. But a job is a job, and controlling the sentiments of one hundred and fifty million people is an impossible one, which makes the work less morally questionable, to my mind.

While we do our best, a blanket solution is not yet available to lead the various populations of the American Community completely in the trajectory of personal and domestic betterment, which is the purpose, after all.

We're the good guys. ▪

CHAPTER 1

THREE HOURS LATER, my team of five plus my boss, Dr. Gushlak, were unloading our equipment from the aging black Bombardier BD-700 we kept gassed up for events just like this one. Even though money had been tight since the USA had become a group of corporate micro-nations ten years previously, the Mental Stewardship section was flush and could afford these luxuries.

We were first responders of a different sort than most, and we always kept our identities as hidden as we could. Fake badges usually worked.

We had done this sort of thing over the years when we needed to, pretending to be BATF or Homeland Security to gain access to evidence, so the roles felt natural enough and the terminology was not so difficult. We were not, after all, an investigative agency except when someone's brainwashed drones had been released to shoot up schools and set off bombs. That's when we were called to action.

Usually, the subject in question initiated a self-termination program, but this one had been captured alive. We assumed he was a mind control subject in the first place because no one really went psychotic anymore. There'd generally be too much dope in the water no matter where on the continent anyone lived.

"Dr. Gushlak," I said to the doctor as he leaned over in the hangar at Casper Inter-Community Airport and inspected his bag. He turned and stood up slightly. "Should I figure out a place for the interview?"

"I'll find somewhere," he said, waving a liver-spotted hand off toward the general distance where there were presumably hotels and aging federal buildings.

"Yes, Doctor," I replied, and set about my business coordinating men, equipment and vehicles for the drive across the barren stretch between Casper and Cheyenne, where the psychotic was waiting.

It was not so odd that Dr. Gushlak would, himself, go to the front lines of an operation; he often liked to see the "specimens," as he called them, firsthand. But why he would want to come all the way out here from the comfortable, safe Intelligence Community that made up most of the former northeastern United States was beyond me. All that was in this new place were prairies and the wet cold of late winter, swept by the smell of a feedlot somewhere upwind.

I wondered briefly if Dr. Gushlak got a thrill from seeing the gestalt of a mental stewardship attack, or if it was just professional interest. It was hard to tell. Dr. Gushlak was inscrutable, really. A recent widower who had also lost his only daughter to an infection from a minor cut, the doctor likely hid his pain behind his fluffy white beard, a mass of white tangled eyebrows, and a now commonly downturned head. But the piercing intensity that surrounded him like an aura was the same as ever and he kept up with his never-abating workload. Since his wife's death I had admired his ability to maintain watch over such a massive network of advancement-facilitation projects. It's not easy to control a population in the first place, but after *two* personal tragedies... I respected the doctor's endurance and style.

He had been my boss for the past ten years, since the end of the Great Rebuilding, when the states had split into territories and major employers within them had paid to become their own micro-nations with their own laws and cultures and housing, while still paying property tax and protection money to what had been deemed the essential parts of the federal government.

During those years, I'd seen him give nervous breakdowns to terrorists from afar, pull deeply-buried information from the minds of the unwilling, and control human bodies to make them do anything in the realm of possibility, and I'd never seen him appear out of place or as if he didn't know what to do in a tough situation. Decisive and deeply familiar with the functions of the mind, Dr. Gushlak was a presence to whom people listened. Not a small part of that was the fact that he was a professional hypnotist, so coercion by way of his intonation and commands was frequent and professionally applied. He was a wizard.

Soon enough, my team and I were on the highway going south toward a gruesome transport bus somewhere in the dark. We zipped through the borders of a sovereign Caterpillar® Community between the airport and the highway by remote key that opened the gates. A badge held to the window for the guard, and another silent group of nondescript people in a black federal vehicle made their way into the dark.

After many miles of nothing and just before the Agricultural Community of Wheatland, we saw a series of emergency lights, visible from quite a distance over the hills, cutting frenetic swaths of blue and red through the early morning fog. When we closed in, I saw that the numbers of law enforcement on scene were impressive for such a rural spot; but, then again, a man had awakened a bus full of nighttime travelers by harvesting human sweetbreads with a hunting knife and playing with his food. It was gross; it *would* get a huge law enforcement response. And I would have to do damage control and make everything go away. Or not.

"Grab your shit and play along," I said to the rest of my group in the SUV. Technically, if we were caught pretending to be FBI, we'd be arrested and eventually released on national security grounds, but the arrests were so...restrictive...and the waiting in jails so tedious that I always knew my script going into a new situation. However, I was going to have to play jazz on this one since some pretty big technical details had been overlooked: namely, that we should be pretending to be CDC, not FBI.

My team lumbered with the bags and cases, following me toward the mass of badges, weapons, and black fabric surrounding a long-distance passenger bus, and looked for whomever the most people revolved around. I honed in on a Wheatland law enforcement officer who took long strides through the chaos of passengers, vehicles and first responders, directing order that seemed to sprout from his footsteps.

Remembering the gun-hand rule, I held my fake FBI ID in my left hand and walked briskly up to the hulk of a man.

"I'm Special Agent Isaacson with the FBI. You're in charge?" I asked.

The man paused, nodded his head barely perceptibly, and clenched his jaw.

"Yep. I'm Mike Nader, the constabulary head of the Wheatland Community, and seeing as this happened within the second concentrism of our territory, I've been in charge up to this point and wasn't expecting the FBI to take over...." He sighed.

"Oh, no, not at all," I replied dismissively. "You keep doing what you're doing. This is your investigation and your Community. We're just here to make sure there's no Schizovirus involved, get some blood samples from the suspect, and probably just disappear. We shouldn't be too long. That work?"

A distrusting expression flitted across the officer's face, but he shrugged.

"If you guys want to come all the way out here to my investigation without taking over, just make sure you don't get in my way. That maniac ate one of *our* citizens on his way home from the Oil Communities up north, and the locals are taking it personally. He'll be hung in a couple of days; that's our way. Get your blood and photos. Just stay scarce."

"Well, officer," I said, stopping him with a touch before he could return to the mess of witnesses and lights behind him. "We need to see the suspect. Can you point the way?"

"Yeah," said Community Officer Nader, extending a long arm toward a BAT van near the edge of the parking lot of aging official vehicles. "We got him out of the bus a half-hour ago with tear gas, so he's probably not feeling so good, but have at him."

I thanked the officer and walked through the flashing vehicles to the back of the white van that was guarded by two serious-looking young men. I flashed my credentials and waved at the group behind my back: my heavies, Rob and Derek, and my comms officer, Jack.

"We're FBI. We need to make sure the suspect isn't a carrier of the Schizovirus."

The two officers looked at each other and, nodding, one of them produced a pair of keys he used to unlock the outer doors of the sealed BAT van.

Through the holes in the second security door, I could see a bloodied, hairy, hogtied mess lying face down on the floor of the compartment. There was clearly no sympathy for this man, as I knew that particular stress position would become quite painful after a while. In a torture scenario, a rope would be placed around the neck and tied to the leg shackles securing the legs to the handcuffs, forcing the torturee to defy resistance on the noose, which was impossible once the victim became tired. Inevitably leading to strangulation, that was from a slightly less evolved time and place in the continent's history—roughly, a handful of years ago.

But this was the recently formed Community of Wheatland, in the Federated Wyoming Territory, where the folk were firm but abided their own laws, and it was a testament to these people's sense of humanity that the man had not "committed suicide" via dozens of bullets or been crushed under the pile of arresting officers bearing down on a well-placed knee on the neck. He was shackled and bruised and oozing mucus and saliva that drained down through the small holes in the BAT van floor normally used to drain the urine of drunks, but he was alive and seemed responsive.

I asked the officer with the keys to open the inner security door so I could get a closer look and perhaps talk with the man. The officer eyed me warily and appeared about to say something, but quietly he did as told.

The steel door was opened, and I hopped into the compartment. Various fluids leaking from the man and his clothing smeared the floor. The suspect craned his neck to look at me.

"You're in a lot of trouble," I said, putting on a pair of surgical gloves and looking at this normally unforgivable man. With a thought, I directed the exocortex attached above my eye to start recording. "You're probably carrying Schizovirus. What's your name?"

Somehow through the bubbles coming out of his mouth and the heavy accent, he muttered a name.

"Jin Ming?" I asked, signaling one of my men with a gesture.

The man nodded, and Jack, my communications coordinator, immediately performed a database search on his pad. After a few moments, he shook his head.

"Where are you from, Ming?" I asked.

"Bakken Community," he replied.

Jack raised a finger, signaling he had a hit. A moment later, he looked up and gave me a thumbs-up. I thanked him and he gave a quick nod, intently focused on the task before him.

"Okay, Jin Ming, I'm going to do a simple test to check for the nodules of the virus, so that means I'm going to touch you. Do you understand?"

The man nodded his head.

I knelt down beside him and began to comb through the tangle of hair and dried blood covering his head, looking for the indicator that he had been reprogrammed. After noticing several unusual burns at various places on his scalp, I found it behind his right ear: a small bump the Chinese always used as a signature on their work. Whenever these bumps were biopsied, they inevitably turned out to be a cyst or a fibroma or something the body could naturally produce, but this small physiological feature was ubiquitous among those confirmed as unknowing operatives from China.

"There's an infection," I said to my team convincingly. As my photographer jumped into the back with me, and the two local law men backed away warily, I surreptitiously pulled a micro-needle from my pocket and jabbed it half a dozen times in the neck of the drone. He didn't even notice. By the time my photographer documented the bump behind Jin Ming's ear from several angles, pustules were already rising from his neck due to the blister agent I had injected. Given several moments to present themselves, the already discolored lesions were then photographed in closer detail, along with the mysterious burns.

My photographer and I jumped out of the van, and I told the guards to lock it up.

"We'll be right back," I told them. "It's not contagious, yet, so you'll be fine."

The two breathed a sigh of relief.

We made our way back to the center of activity to find Nader talking with the crime-scene technicians by the bus. He saw us and, perhaps noticing the determination of our walk, let his head slump as we approached.

"Lemme guess," he began, crossing his arms and looking at the ground in front of him. "He's got the Schizovirus and you're going to take him somewhere else. You know, a lot of folks think you cooked up this whole Schizovirus yourselves, and you're just trying to contain it..."

As I looked at him, the boredom in my eyes was purposeful and clear.

"And while we're at it," he continued, readjusting his testicles for emphasis, "wouldn't they send the CDC out to check for Schizovirus, not the FBI? What the hell are *you* doing here?"

"CDC has budget cuts, we were closer, we got called," Jack interjected.

I grabbed the digital camera from my photographer's hand and showed the screen to Nader closely enough to make the point. The abscesses changed depending on their location; their sizes and the amount of fluid leaking from them varied but always made a horrible picture.

"Does *this* look like a conspiracy to you?" I asked him angrily, flipping from frame to frame. My photographer's tradecraft required that he include pictures of "afflicted" children in the roll after the ones he had immediately taken. "The number of people who have died from this disease is *devastating.* I *hate* this stuff. But I do it every day so we can try to contain it and keep casualties to a minimum. And your conspiracy theories—which I hear *every day*, by the way—don't help my job a whole hell of a lot."

Nader stood silent.

"So yeah," I continued decisively, "I'm going to put that stage 2 viral incubator in a big cold bag of hydrogen sulfide and take him to a federal facility where the CDC can deal with this sort of thing; we're just a first response team. I have a paper here..." I produced a signed letter from a high authority, "that allows me to take the suspect, but I'd much rather you give me permission so that the federal government and the Communities of Corporate Persons can continue to live and not just intone their spirit of cooperation. It's so much better now, isn't it, after all? No more of the fighting? Just rapport and respect between average people?"

"Whatever," said Nader, and he picked up his radio. "Freeman," he said.

An officer called Freeman responded.

"I want you to know that the FBI's taking the suspect, so don't stop them."

"B-b-b-but why?" Freeman stammered on the radio.

"I'll tell you later, but you might want to wash your hands, if you get my meaning."

The radio was silent. Everyone on scene who had a radio immediately began looking for hand sanitizer. I thanked Officer

Nader for his cooperation and told him that I respected the job he was doing for his Community, among some other appropriate phrases I always had in reserve for use in these occasions. He nodded and continued on his way, unchanged by our encounter.

So we piled the drone into a clear, body bag-like plastic duffel wrapped in plastic cooling tubes, piped in the 80 ppm hydrogen sulfide in air to ensure an effective suspended animation, and headed back to the airport, our little deception accomplished. I didn't even have to deal with the media.

DR. GUSHLAK SECURED an aging telecom company warehouse that had been absorbed by the federal government during the Great Rebuilding. Cobwebbed and filled with old wooden cable spools and dust, it was far enough away from neighbors that nothing would be heard if odd sounds needed to be made.

My men Rob and Derek, a married couple, unloaded the bag containing the Chinese drone from the car and took it inside to a table where Dr. Gushlak was waiting. He unzipped the bag and instructed that the man be shackled to an old office chair.

With this completed, Dr. Gushlak used a wet rag to wipe the blood off the unconscious man's face and hands. He took a photo of the face, scanned the eyes, registered his chips, fingerprinted him, and took a couple of vials of the man's blood before deftly excising the abnormal tissue from behind the man's ear and setting it aside for later analysis.

Deciding it was time for the drone to wake up, Dr. Gushlak attached an oxygen mask to the man's face and left to use the restroom. I had seen him rush out enough times that I was certain he must have prostate or bladder issues.

A woman from logistics started collecting the FBI badges from my team. As I handed mine to her, I asked if we could get CDC badges next time we faked a Schizovirus outbreak since it made more sense if we were going to kidnap the drone. I saw her get nervous, and I turned dismissively away to look at the soiled creature who was about to have his mind opened up like a can of herring.

I wondered what the doctor would use. Because of its size, we couldn't bring the GOD machine with us, so I supposed it would be a scopolamine derivative or a microbe we called Bloodhound because it helped us hone in on hidden or adaptive secrets. So far, the Chinese drone hadn't talked that much, so there would probably be an amphetamine mixed in somewhere, too. We would have to find out where he came from, if he was the only one of his kind, and what had triggered the event. Not that he would necessarily consciously know, but we could get the subconscious mind to cooperate when we needed it to, and that often involved chocolate, which lay alongside several bottles and syringes on a dusty desk next to the drone.

Jack, my best officer, set up shop next to the Chinese man and was in the process of attaching a cap of electrodes to his skull, which he then hooked to his tablet. From my position, I could see the brainwave activity monitor and blood pressure and pulse rate pop up on the screen, and Jack declared to me that he was ready.

"Does this specimen speak English or do any of you speak Chinese?" Dr. Gushlak asked the men assembled as he came out of the restroom, rubbing his hands with an alcohol wipe.

"I speak English," Jin Ming said through his oxygen mask, his eyes still closed and his chin on his chest.

"Well, good," replied Dr. Gushlak happily. "That'll save us the trouble of finding an interpreter." The doctor smiled broadly at him, reached forward, removed the oxygen mask carefully, and sat in a chair facing him, about five feet away.

"Go ahead, then," said the doctor, urging the man to talk. "Where are you from?"

Jin Ming looked confused.

"I don't remember," he said, shaking his head. "I only remember ticking."

Dr. Gushlak scowled.

"Do you remember where you were before you heard ticking?" he asked Jin Ming.

"Do *you* remember where *you* were before *you* were born?" Jin Ming replied.

"No, I don't. That's very interesting," the doctor replied, and made a note on his legal pad. "So you were born hearing ticking? What exactly are you saying?"

Jin Ming declined to respond.

"Why did you do what you did?" Dr. Gushlak continued, switching subjects. "Why did you kill that man and eat him?"

Again, Jin Ming looked confused.

"I wanted to eat," he replied, as though it were the clearest thing in the world.

"And why did you throw his parts around?"

"I wanted to play."

"And did it make you happy to eat and play like that?" Dr. Gushlak asked intently.

"Yes. I wanted to be happy because I know I must die."

Dr. Gushlak slowly set down his pen and regarded Ming warily.

"Why must you die?" he asked the man.

"Because I'm the countdown clock. I'm counting down to the end of the world."

"When is the end of the world—" began Dr. Gushlak, but he was interrupted.

"I have to be stopped for the world to live," Jin Ming said, his eyes suddenly opening wide and staring at the ceiling. The pulse rate on Jack's monitor instantly spiked.

Right then, Jin Ming seemed to access the phenomenon of hysterical strength to break the bones in his right hand and pull his hand through the handcuff. It was so quick, the snapping of bones happened all at once, that no one had time to react before he grabbed an overlooked linesman's knife on the floor by his chair with the fingers that weren't broken, switched it to his cuffed left hand, leaned his neck down to his hand and sliced open his carotid artery.

A massive amount of blood began to spurt across his chest and hand, and panic immediately set in. Rob and Derek scrambled to try to plug their fingers in the wound, but Jin Ming fought them off with the same strength that helps grandmothers lift cars off children. It had to have been a programmed response because he fought like an animal with that one broken hand until he didn't have the strength to continue. By the time we had him under control, he had cut through not just his carotid, but his wrist as well.

"He needs a hospital ASAP," I shouted to the doctor, who by this time had retreated a safe distance and been looking on with bemused interest.

"What does it hurt in the long run to lose this man?" declared Dr. Gushlak above the panting and anxiety of my men. We all stopped what we were doing and looked at him in surprise. He had our attention.

"Mr. Jin Ming!" Dr. Gushlak called. "Do you want to die?"

"No," Jin Ming murmured, "but at least I will save the world."

"Let the man think he died a hero," Dr. Gushlak said to us all with a nod.

No one moved.

"That's an order."

Jack, who had been a military medic during the Collapse, took his fingers out of Jin Ming's neck wound and walked away looking for a sink. One by one, each man left the side of the Chinese mind-control subject and let him bleed out onto the floor of the old warehouse. I was the last near him, and I noted the time of his death rattle in my logbook from just beyond the dark pool cooling beneath him.

ON THE RIDE BACK to the airport, I knew better than to ask the doctor why he had let the man die. I didn't feel right about it, but empirically speaking, it was likely more humane than the other options. Wheatland wanted him dead, his mind was clearly oatmeal, and the public (as well as we ourselves) were definitely in danger with him around. Plus, his wounds were far too severe to give him any real chance of living had we gotten him to a hospital; so, in all, I stayed silent and accepted this as the way things were sometimes done.

"The countdown clock for the end of the world..." mused Dr. Gushlak to himself. "That's a new one."

I nodded.

"I've never heard it before," I replied. "If they have a self-termination program, it's usually that they blow their brains out to let the voices free, or that aliens want them to fly away with them but they have to leave their bodies behind. A countdown clock? That's different."

"I wonder," Dr. Gushlak said, suddenly turning and looking at me in the back of the black SUV. "Carnage and chaos programming aside, what if his suicide trigger was the time?" What if he was programmed to believe in a specific end-date for the world, and he needed to kill himself before it happened?"

"What's today?" I asked.

"March second," he replied.

"April second is in a month," I intoned.

On another April second ten years prior, we had accidentally caused a problem for the Chinese.

It had been totally accidental.

We had known for a while that the Chinese had been putting compounds coated in specific enzymes into their public water supplies. These compounds, when ingested, collected in specific parts of the brain and formed crystalline growths that resonated to external radio frequencies and converted them into an electrical charge to alter neural behavior on cue. One day there was a power surge in a province where we were experimenting with the radio signals that triggered the reaction, and we lobotomized two dozen Chinese people in the vicinity. China found out it was us and they apparently had not forgotten.

"So we can expect more of this, I'd imagine?" Dr. Gushlak asked me.

"Probably, Doctor," I said, nodding and looking out at the early morning sun coming over the rolling hills of desolate southern Federated Wyoming.

It might just be a busy month. ■

CHAPTER 2

IN ONGOING MILITARY CONFLICTS, one will often be able to watch the news media reports on allied deaths and enemy kills that day. If it's a well-put-together report that we had a hand in, the wording will always be the same. Allies "die" and enemies are "killed." After all, you can kill a colony of ants, but you rarely say the ants "died." Die is a human word, usually reserved for humans and things that humans can identify with. You can kill anything from a deer to a virus, but nothing other than a human dies except something anthropomorphized… at least in most cases of common usage.

This type of thing is well-planned, secretive social programming, and language is an extremely important way of securing the sentiments of the population—in this case, in a war. There are so many little tricks in the way events can be not just portrayed, but talked about, that approval percentages can be coerced and tickled out of the underbelly of the average mind.

"New direction" in politicians' speeches is a subliminal sexual cue. Sound it out. "New direction." "Nude erection." "The sky is so beautiful" becomes "This guy is so beautiful." Even the selective use and pronunciation of "happiness" has a bit of "penis" in it. Male Community leaders use this sort of thing the most, and it sways the numbers of their women and gay supporters.

The best choice for a Corporate Person Community wanting to control people is to come to us through our private front corporations that ostensibly sell advertising but offer additional services to those able to afford them. We can prerecord audio commands and messages for insertion into the grid, and, since we have a great deal of control over the telecom hubs, we can digitally, in real time, put those messages in the background noise of crowded scenes of entertainment media streaming across the network. When interspersed with a regular three- to five-second visual shot rate, we can trigger a brain state somewhere between alpha and theta. The murmuring in bars and whispering at funerals will be made up of "soda" and a "fizz" and "thirsty," then something that sounds like the name of one of the sodas of the Coca-Cola® Community that hired us. It's all very subtle, but if anyone complains that the TV is talking to them, they get visited and tested for the Schizovirus. If they keep complaining, they'll be found to have the Schizovirus and hospitalized.

The cop dramas that still entertain the masses help boost the authority of law enforcement by including commands in the background noise of substation scenes, like "We know what you did" for those who feel guilty about something, "You're dead" to subliminally intimidate those who might fight authority, or "You're a hero" to those who always wanted to fight crime and inform on their neighbors or whatever. Subliminal commands are selective, after all. Your subconscious usually just pays attention to the commands that are relevant to you, so the shows lump them together in the audio background and let the brain subconsciously select the appropriate ones to associate with the scene.

It's better to keep these things secret, because it's not just for advertising; we're reprogramming entire societies, often one person at a time, to follow the laws and be contributing citizens on the continent. The size and vision of the operation is massive: trying to contain aberrant behavior and set everyone in generally the same direction.

For instance, the way we train news personalities to deliver the financial market reports—keeping them upbeat, optimistic, and false when necessary—has sustained markets at times when they faced oblivion, all because the media understand their part in keeping the country running predictably.

That's why they work with us, we work with them, the machine runs for another day, and everyone stays fed.

Everyone stays alive that way.

The continental numbers on unemployment, CPI, inflation, and GDP are all rigged, but it's our job to make sure that no one questions them and upsets the apple cart. My organization makes sure media personalities issue commands with words like "trust" and "believe" surrounding the new numbers for those financial indicators, as in, "I trust these numbers are better than last quarter," and "You'd better believe it, Karen. Now back to you." You'd be surprised how well it works.

People and institutions trade in the markets based on appearances. The positive appearance we put forward of our small nations is really all that matters, since everyone agrees on the reality of their information and trades accordingly. It's Dr. Gushlak's job to intercept and redefine that reality before it drifts down to street level and builds for itself the emotional supports the continent ultimately needs to survive. What's termed a "lie" is not always such a bad thing if it reinforces the greater truth of life and its constancy.

Isn't it better to live and love and eat and work than it is to realize that your entire reality is a simulation that can be—nay, is—run many times over? Honed to work with their particular personality type, most people's reality in this new dawn is the one we secretly give them, from streaming news to calm them if their metrics say they're excitable, to pop-up ads encouraging childbearing among young women in underpopulated communities. The Intelligence Community, as well as the other Communities on the continent, has added a "filter bubble" to the exocortex or implanted chip each citizen is required to wear that strategically and subliminally adds words like "trustworthy" and "loyal" and other preferred qualities to the information streamed through these devices. These individualized filter bubbles help keep families together, crime in check, and markets positive, as do the rest of our technologies. We're trying to make people happy most of the time and angry when they need to be outraged at foreign aggression or overpriced wheat.

In ten years of official operations, we've taken the population by the hand and led it through storms and sunny meadows and kept things interesting and ordered. We are an effective force.

In the typological system we keep, every person on the continent is assigned a color, a number, and a letter. Mine, for instance, is yellow14L. The yellow identifies me as a necessary continental asset, the 14 represents my personality type, and the L signifies a low likelihood of needing to be mentally influenced by our array of technologies.

Others have colors that indicate their expendability, numbers that cover all personality types, and letters that basically show if they need fine-tuning. I, however, won't be fine-tuned, given my position. It is I and those like me who do the fine-tuning of others.

I remember watching a young red02H—an independent-minded hothead with a need to be stewarded—turn into a productive, nose-to-the-grindstone citizen who stopped going to rallies and talking politics not long after we started work on him. Through our application of pressure and chains on his media alone, we made him grow wiser in less than two years. Then he found a girlfriend and a decent job and he's since fallen off of our radar.

That's usually how the process works. It's very subtle, but with the degree of constant info-stream connectivity in everyone's daily life, it meshes soundly with reality and makes pronounced and effective alterations to the map of the mind. It's a necessary service that we provide and it helps everything function how it's supposed to.

I don't worry much about my role in it, for that very reason. Most people are happy to just be happy. What differentiates me from the rest is that instead of being happy, I'd rather be informed. That's why I'm grateful to occupy my position.

This office holds the secrets of the land. You can't beat that.

WHEN I WAS YOUNG, I didn't know explicitly about mental stewardship and the engineering of reality. Every little manipulation and coercion I did, I did by feel and intuition. Perhaps it was being brought up by alcoholic foster parents that made me watch the subtle cues and micro-expressions on their faces so I could avoid being beaten or... whatever. This, in turn, evolved into changing entire situations with my tone, doing funny things, or saying an appropriate word to escape the abuse.

Eventually, after I earned my way to college, there was a moment when I realized I should probably do something in a field related to psychology, since I knew I was operating a step above the more general coercive level.

For years I wore a hint of women's perfume to clubs and bars because it seemed to confuse the girls enough to make them linger those few extra seconds that make the difference between sex and failure. I don't know where I got the idea, but it certainly did the trick, and later I performed an fMRI experiment that proved the science of it.

One particular night, while out with my roommate, Joe, I was wearing my perfume and I spotted a girl across the bar. She had red hair, a dark complexion, good-looking friends, and an air about her that indicated she was single. I wanted to meet her but didn't want to use any tired old phrases.

I kept her in the corner of my eye as I sat at the bar with Joe, and, as an experiment, I started mirroring her movements. If she put her hand through her hair, I put my hand through mine a second later. If she crossed her legs, I crossed mine. On this went as I pretended to ignore her until she definitely caught on to something and began unconsciously mimicking my movements. That's when I intuited I could offer myself for review.

I jerked my head ever so slightly and seemingly unconsciously in the direction of the bathroom and started walking there. From my peripheral vision, I saw her watching me until I passed, and she followed.

I met her in the bathroom hallway and nodded to her as she passed, briefly searching her eyes for intention. She shyly walked past while I checked my cell phone, then paused hesitantly, as though wanting to say something, but I beat her to it.

"Are we on the same wavelength?" I asked her, inquiringly.

She glanced at the floor for a moment and tucked a hair behind her ear.

"I suppose we might be," she said, looking up at me in a happy way.

As she was putting her number in my phone, I realized that she was wearing the same perfume as I, and that I had just experienced "mirroring," which was heavily referenced within the topic of my PhD dissertation and attracted the attention of Dr. Gushlak, leading to my career. (And the girl was great, by the way. Her name was Jenny. I dated her for a few months and we split well. No regrets.)

I guess I always tried out things on people. Not *mean* things, just things that were a bit *off*, in order to glean what I could from people's reactions. I'd randomly wave to people on the roads and highways to see what they'd do. I faked a nervous tick to see what kinds of responses I would get. I once committed character suicide to get out of a relationship, telling a girl I had a particularly nasty STD so I'd never have to see her again. (She was stalking me and it was a mess I couldn't resolve any other way.)

In a completely different and committed relationship, I knew the woman had cheated on me, so I began to pour declarations of trust on her until she eventually shattered from the pressure and confessed to the affair after a couple of weeks.

People have told me that was cold, but *cheating* is *cold,* is it not? Life is often Old Testament, as am I.

So, I have always been kind of an observer of human behavior and I also spent a lot of time reflecting on my own nature in my grandfather's isolated Massachusetts cabin, away from my foster parents, where I'd sometimes stay alone for weeks at a time in summer. Almost immediately after the Hooding Ceremony at MIT, I was off to that cabin again, where I spent the next six months mostly alone except for the people I'd see at the grocery stores on the monthly drive into town.

I spent those six months reading and writing about my experiences in solitude, and there was a great amount there. From the Russian startsy to the Desert Fathers of Egypt to the medicine men of various tribes worldwide, truth-seekers have always known that solitude is a place where one can find out what is and what is not a part of oneself. With that differentiating of self from other comes the knowledge of oneself that crafts its own divinity for long moments of sunshine and breezes. It's this communion with the solitary condition of God that teaches the most honest lessons, primary of which is that we are all our own gods in one form or another.

When we react to external stimuli or form thought patterns when alone, we create a neural cascade that flows down both brain hemispheres and creates a sort of delta of reality. Merely observing—a fundamental component of consciousness and something even newborns do—is a creative act in this basic way. And so we become small gods of our own making.

After those six months, I came to the conclusion that it was not such a bad thing to play god, because everyone plays at being their own god anyway, whether they realize it or not. Why not hand over the reins to the people who really know what's going on and how to do it best? ▪

CHAPTER 3

THE SCHIZOVIRUS was a necessary invention when the free media—before we had everyone's filter bubbles worked out—began to pay so much attention to the bizarre behavior and sometimes grizzly effects of the onslaught of foreign human drones sent to our shores. The supposed virus was a good cover both for the actions themselves and the resulting disappearance of the individuals in question when we got our hands on them.

Disposal of the drone was, frankly, often necessary. During the course of their original brainwashing, the drones had their lives ripped away, were made to watch unwatchable things, believe unbelievable things, think unthinkable thoughts, and were subjected to any number of other depravations that led them to being so unpredictable that it always seemed more humane for everyone involved to have them overdose on a barbiturate and slip into nothingness.

This is a real war we're fighting, and it has suffered its share of unfortunate losses. Since the time of the sun first rising and setting on the amoeba, one creature has taken the life of another to sustain itself, and we are not so different from all life in this particular program. We fought if we had to, and sacrificed the lives of many for a cause we believed saved more. Time will show that we were on the right side of history, just as we were on the right side of the Collapse.

Jin Ming's life was one that Wheatland Community's safety would have required be taken from him.

After several hours of headwinds to the Intelligence Community of the northeast—the largest Community in the American Community of Corporate Persons, the center for many remnants of the former government, and my home country—Dr. Gushlak, myself, and my team touched down at the Techton IC Airport and exited the Bombardier with the chilled corpse of Jin Ming in a special box that would look like large luggage to anyone who might glimpse us rolling it along the tarmac to yet more black SUVs. But in these, the Intelligence Community airfields, the shadows kept themselves hidden if they were there at all. It was roughly noon, anyway.

In terms of rank in our Community, Gushlak was at the top of the list with a handful of others who made up the Intelligence Chiefs. We rolled past checkpoint after checkpoint and easily sped through X-ray portals with the vehicles' identifiers reading only "DNFW" against a red background instead of blue. It stood for Designated Not For Withholding, but the soldiers guarding the transportation routes referred to the designation as Do Not Fuck With. It was nice traveling with Gushlak because he could always get through without a problem. The unlucky individual who caused one would get a swift tongue-lashing from a powerful man with a Total Clearance Badge, a temperamental prostate, and Jedi mind tricks, basically.

The Techton IC Airport was in the exact center of a huge circle of warehouses and windowless office buildings with so many ordinary and bizarre routes among them that even an intelligence newbie could find a way to shake a limited tail. The civil engineers had planned this new city to accommodate secrets and their carriers, so when one left the airport, one could emerge in any part of the city he/she wanted. In addition, due to the miracles of materials science, a complex maze of frictionless vacuum tubes—yes, vacuum tubes—throughout the city helped shuttle workers anywhere they needed to go with great speed and anonymity. The massive amount of air that was used for the tubes was channeled into most buildings to control the climate of both human space and computer space, so things were efficient and self-contained.

The inland boundaries of the Community were marked only by a 60-foot-wide swath cut through the forests and former neighborhoods of what used to be the states of Maryland, Virginia and Delaware. Occasionally, one would come across a tower at the border hosting surveillance equipment of every variety, and if one were to dig in the right places, motion sensors would be found close enough together to cover footfalls along the whole border. Unmanned Aerial Vehicles using perpetually airborne blimps as docking stations patrolled the border day and night in infrared, and we had a satellite sucking up real-time video of the entire Community. With this standard surveillance, we could rewind time for an entire city in the Community to find a point of origin and destination for anyone within the borders. From what I knew of it, the Atlantic border was a sophisticated system, as well, but seeing as I had nothing to do with border security, I didn't know much about it. I just knew the whole thing had been used to great effect to keep out the "zombies"—the roving tribes of starving individuals who had ended up without Communities to settle in and had been a nuisance during and after the Collapse. That's when they had been in the news every day… but it had been some time since I had heard of any coming around.

It seemed that everyone in the Intelligence Community had a standard look, depending on his or her position. Most office workers usually wore dark suits and suit pants, sensible shoes, and sunglasses even on cloudy days with the light filtering in through tinted windows. The custodial services had a standard Community jumpsuit, and they were treated with as much respect as anyone else because they also had to pass stringent background checks to be employed in this Community. Most everyone kept to themselves, never picked up anyone else's dropped papers, ate at the great local restaurants a couple of times a week, and maybe scored some quickly-metabolized synthetic drugs on the weekends in a SCIF. It was rumored that the diplomats of the other micro-nations made many of their illicit drug purchases in these SCIFs, but no one knew for sure, as secrecy was their purpose.

Every corner bar in the city—and we had many—had its own Sensitive Compartmented Information Facility, which any patron with any clearance could use for completely private and secure conversations... or for the occasional sexcapade or drug binge. Isolated and protected from all forms of external tapping, and recertified regularly, the SCIFs were impervious to scrutiny and hid anything one wanted to hide. In a Community determined to know everything, great effort was exerted to keep its compartmented knowledge well away from its other compartments.

Our little convoy of vehicles stopped at a shrouded bank of vacuum tubes near a railway station. We unloaded Jin Ming from the back, and everyone left their gear with the vehicles and drivers. I would ride back with them to our building.

Rob and Derek quickly loaded the crate into one of the vacuum tube's capsules, and Dr. Gushlak scanned a destination for it on the interior screen, stepping in to accompany the drone back to the security of our headquarters himself.

"Are you sure you want to send it back in the tube?" I asked the doctor hesitantly. Years before, I had gotten stuck in a vacuum capsule for two hours in a deserted sub-basement parking garage and it made me suspicious of most things related to the rotating, roller-coaster nightmares.

"It'll be fine, Donald. It's faster anyway," Dr. Gushlak smiled at me. He knew my phobia but was kind enough to not hassle me about it. "Taking a car?"

I nodded.

"All right, then," he replied nonchalantly. "See you back at base. The day's just started. And what a nice one, at that. Enjoy the drive."

Dr. Gushlak extended an arm into the air to punctuate his point about the weather before deftly slipping all the way into the capsule and shutting himself in with the corpse of Jin Ming.

The capsule began to spin slowly, getting the rotation that would hold its contents against the interior walls. After its momentum was set, the vacuum would pull the still-spinning, frictionless vehicle through the three-dimensional maze of randomized connection points, forks in the tube, and realignment stations to its ultimate destination at the Hayden Center: the home of our operation to save the minds of the continent.

The rest of the men except Jack settled into a handful of the other capsules, inserted their inner-ear stabilizers and sent themselves to the Hayden Center.

As I watched them spin and shoot away, I was grateful that Dr. Gushlak hadn't brought attention to my fear in front of the team. I was their direct boss, sure, but we joked around a bit and I didn't want them to get any more ammunition than I had already given them by having four ex-wives. It's a real prejudicial thing people can and have pointed at me for, like *I* was the wrong person in the equation, or something.

I got in the vehicle with Jack and reclined the passenger seat, telling him I'd try to grab a twenty-minute nap on the way back to the office.

As I closed my eyes, I remembered there had been something about being stuck in that vacuum tube that I'd never been able to shake. A sense of loss, almost. Maybe a bit of despair mixed with shame. Certainly it had elements of helplessness in it… and perhaps that's all it was. Maybe it was the loss of control that had stuck with me. Loss of control is a powerful feeling and leaves deep scars on a person's soul. I, myself, carried around a deep, unmentioned fear from that moment that I tried not to resent.

Shaking my head to clear it of the memory, I realized how tired I was and commented on it to Jack.

"You're getting old," Jack said.

"Uh-huh," I replied. I had also been awake for a full workday plus overtime, but old was an adequate way to describe it, too. I was almost fifty-three and felt it some days, although a regular workout schedule kept me in decent shape and I could keep my head when overworked. Plus, being a boss meant I could lock my office door every once in a while and keep visitors from witnessing my aging professionalism reclining across my couch.

My beautiful wife, Janet, my fifth wife, had a lot of sympathy for me; she knew it must be a hard job in mental stewardship operations (that was all I was allowed to tell her). She had sympathy because she was, after all, a coworker; she was an R&D technician about ten corridors down for some sort of augmented sensing technology, but that was her business and she wasn't allowed to tell me, which I also understood. I certainly couldn't tell her much of what I was doing, but Janet was a sharp woman and deduced from my salary that I likely was doing something important for the continent, or at least the Community, and that I helped everything run smoothly. We had a fair understanding of each other and, so far, there had been very few fights or words of disagreement.

I only tested her one time. From my other marriages, I had learned the importance of seeing what kind of person a woman is when she's angry. (It's a good idea to see a man angry, as well, before making any sort of lasting commitment to each other.) Some can be violent, some can be crude. Some can be classy and witty, others can collapse a lifetime of hidden unhappiness into a dark moment sparkling with rage, suspended in time, unleashed at whomever's closest. I clearly didn't want her to be like my second wife, who would have shot me in my sleep if my gun hadn't been keyed to my personal sweat signature. But my fears with my fifth wife turned out to be ungrounded, as Janet didn't even respond to the little swipes and bitter comments I constantly made during a long weekend. She just told me, "If you're going to be an undercutting prick, then I get the bed.

Hope you're better tomorrow."

She put me in my place and told me what to do. No one ever told me what to do, except for Dr. Gushlak. So I guess that's why I loved her so much. Janet was tough and she'd call me out on my bullshit. She passed the anger test, at any rate.

It was nice. We'd have lunch in the Hayden Center's cafeteria only every so often, as she thought seeing each other every day during the day would make our three-year marriage sour quickly. She was still young. Thirty-six. Lots of ideas about how the world could be a single place with all its peoples getting along fine and exploring the stars hand-in-hand and speaking with synthetic telepathy that was already popular with so many. So, really, she was thinking in the way I probably should have thought about my job, with global peace and oneness being the goal, and technology the method to get us there. Idealistic and hooked on whatever her filter bubble streamed in the off-hours, her mind was always somewhere great and wonderful and so very much Janet.

I had met her a few years earlier in a major hallway in our building when she dropped a pile of papers next to me from a folder labeled "TOP SECRET."

Far from leaning down to help her, I stopped dead in my tracks, turned my back on her and, more specifically, her papers and yelled, "Info Drop!" I watched as many of the other commuters in the crowded hallway also stopped dead in their tracks and turned the other way, or, if they were in a hurry, kept their heads turned away as they walked past. The cameras were watching, after all, and the footage was scrutinized in real time by the Artificial Intelligences, or the AIs as we call them.

I think maybe I had a quicker reaction time than she did, but then again, who wants to be embarrassed by yelling to a crowd that they just fucked up and everyone should pay attention to it by ignoring them?

I don't blame her for being reluctant to announce her momentary butterfingers. Most of the material in the "TOP SECRET" folders doesn't matter much anyway—the important stuff is transported in envelopes—but we follow the protocols in every corridor, and if I hadn't, everyone around her would have been written up for not shouting about a spill of classified documents.

As I walked with her to the closest security office to report the incident, she was red in the face and her hair was a mess from her hands-and-knees scramble.

"I never thought I'd be the one in my office to do it," she exclaimed, out of breath and trembling slightly. "And now I owe them a dinner, dammit. Why the hell do we have folders in this day and age anyway, huh? They fall open *far* too easily... and I'm *so* sorry to interrupt your day, sir. I've been off balance ever since a cat or raccoon hopped onto my balcony at three a.m. and I thought it was a burglar and I couldn't sleep. Aaah! This is terrible. I'm *so* sorry."

"No problem," I replied, smiling slightly at the awkwardness she obviously felt. I was still smiling to myself when two security guards met us coming the other way from the security office.

"The footage was reviewed and no information was compromised, Dr. Cross," said one of the security guards to the embarrassed woman. "You and Dr. Isaacson can go about your business. Please be careful in the future with your papers. Have a nice day."

"Tha...thank you. Thank you so much," said Dr. Cross, whom I noticed was quite a good-looking woman behind her exocortex and disheveled hair. She turned to me and offered her hand.

"Dr. Isaacson," she began, with a shy, beautiful smile, "Thank you for protecting our secrets, and I apologize for the inconvenience."

I took her soft hand in mine, returned her handshake, and for a moment—I'm sure it was pheromones or our immune systems sensing extraordinary compatibility—I intuited the clear impression that we should mate.

Now, I'm not *trying* to sound stupid, but I had a very basic, animalistic desire to take this woman because every gene in my body probably sensed that our offspring would change the world. Yes, I'm guessing a bit, but it was a very powerful attraction. I think that's why I held on to her outstretched hand.

"What's your first name, Dr. Cross?" I asked in a voice that had to restrain its sexual stress from showing up on the voice stress application many people had installed on their exocortexes.

"I'm Janet," she said, continuing to shake my hand.

I introduced myself and, perhaps recognizing that she would rather disappear and never see me again because of the embarrassment of the situation, I dropped her hand a beat too late and bid her adieu, knowing secretly that I would bother her in the cafeteria from then on if I saw her. Sitting at her table and that sort of thing. Forcing a laugh or two out of her, if I could. Flirtation, basically.

Over the weeks, she eventually succumbed to my honest attempt to get her attention, and, determined that this relationship would be better than my others because of a better knowledge of Janet, I waited two whole months before proposing to her. It was difficult—what with the fifteen years of yoga she had under her belt—but I managed to keep those words off my lips for quite some time.

"Man, I could use more time with my wife," I said to Jack in the vehicle on the way into Hayden, shaking my head and readjusting my seat to a sitting position. "She's the best thing that ever happened to me."

"Yeah, she's great, Doc," Jack agreed. He continued. "And smart, too. She married a guy who's had wedding-night sex four other times, so she obviously knows she wants an experienced man, am I right?" Jack held up a hand in expectation of a high-five.

I left him hanging.

"Where are you from, Jack?"

"Uh, originally Kansas. Why?"

"There's no place like home, huh? Ever met Toto?"

Jack scrunched his face and shook his head.

"Everyone says shit like that..." he began, but I interrupted.

"Exactly. How often do you hear people talking about my previous wives?"

"All the time."

"So do you think I like hearing about it all the time?"

"No, I guess not, Doc."

"So you understand what I'm saying, right, Jack?"

"I think so."

"I'm telling you to shut the fuck up, Jack."

"Roger that, Doc."

We pulled up to the Hayden Center entrance, and as we still had a red-tagged vehicle, we proceeded through the checkpoint without stopping.

It was so nice not being stopped. I couldn't imagine being one of the low-level couriers I watched stuck in the line and subjected to the scrutiny of human questioning, remote temp and pulse, biometric and vocal lie detection, just to gain access to one of the Center's many smaller compartments and their ever-smaller security lines. Much better to have a red tag and not spend time at the mercy of another's whims.

We drove around the massive complex to the loading docks on the far side from the entrance, always within sight of razor wire and tall fences beyond the sea of vehicles.

I could see where the vacuum tubes all came together like bundled drinking straws shoved in a conical maw in the side of the big building. The only people who could come directly in that way were those who had been precleared, like Dr. Gushlak, our team, and myself, if I wanted. But I didn't.

We pulled into a huge hangar of sorts that could accommodate transportation vehicles and large trucks. Driving all the way to the back, we arrived at a tunnel we drove down for another few minutes until we reached a grid of house-sized storage units that stretched as far as we could see.

I certainly wasn't aware of what was in the ones that weren't ours. In *ours*, we kept our tactical and response gear and spare hardware to do things like whisper into the mind of a potential terrorist or shoplifter without anyone else hearing. (It's possible to modulate microwaves and infrasound that demodulate when they come into contact with a skull, making manmade voices in the head a very real technology with very real and effective outcomes.) We kept that equipment there, entire racks of speaker hijackers, our mobile command vehicles, weapons, and various amounts of chemicals and microbes that could assist us in getting the truth out of people.

On other shelves inside the storage unit were blast dispersion grenades with substances that make everyone peaceful and puppetlike. There were miniature EMPs that could knock out any expensive electronic upgrades in people's heads that might be a threat to our stewardship. There were neural disruptors that paralyzed the body when applied to the neck, chemicals that took away most inhibitions (for harvesting information), remote brain denaturing equipment, quick-track implants, lie-detection equipment programmed to pick up on micro-expressions and voice stress, chocolate bars (for kids and those with nothing to hide), and just about every other type of technology one might need to master a mind. Except for the GOD Machine. That was up in Dr. Gushlak's lab since it was too finicky and large to be deployed on missions.

I helped Jack unload the bags from the rear of the SUV, and after checking the inventory of each, we put them back on the shelves by the door for easy access in the future.

"Why do you still do inventory?" Jack asked me when we were done. "You don't have to do this stuff, Boss."

I thought about it for a moment.

"I don't ask you guys to do anything I wouldn't do," I replied. I was sincere about that. "I've done this a million times over the last fifteen years, but it's still part of the job. It humbles a man to do this next to people making half his salary."

I smiled at Jack slyly. He finally understood.

"You make twice what I make?!" he asked me.

I shook my head and smiled.

"No," I said with a sigh, "but it's true that we all need some humility, especially when we're the stewards of the population. It goes for me, just like it goes for anyone."

Jack nodded and that seemed to satisfy his curiosity.

We left the SUV in the storage unit with a half-dozen others that were for our exclusive use. Jack locked the door with a series of safety mechanisms and we made our way to the nearby mobile walkways that would take us to the office. Even with the walkways, it would take another ten minutes to get all the way across the building and to our section in Mental Stewardship operations.

We passed corridor after corridor in the massive building, all coded differently, with random words there, colors here, and there were even dark corridors marked merely by symbols, likely to make deciphering their meanings and designations more difficult for anyone who wanted to know.

And the people were busy, trained to not make eye contact, focused on where they were going and not their surroundings, which were very much like an airport terminal without windows. Full-spectrum lighting made up for the lack of sun, though, and there were tastefully put-together little alcoves with rock gardens and green plants and chairs for sitting. Usually these alcoves were adjacent to coffee and snack kiosks along the main corridor, so one might pass an unofficial office meeting being held at one or random workers trying to escape the cubicle environment by doing office or personal work next to a small fish pond or the rare aviary. White noise was provided over the loudspeakers in the form of a bubbling brook to prevent overhearing conversations.

The whole Intelligence Community operated on the idea that happy workers made loyal workers, and loyalty was clearly of the utmost importance, so while much of the Community looked bland and boxy on the outside, it had everything on the inside that would foster Community-wide contentment. In addition to piping in scents like peppermint to increase productivity or vanilla to induce calmness, during office parties and near holidays we pumped in pheromones like oxytocin to foster a family-like feeling among the office workers. Free gyms operated twenty-four hours a day, a ten-minute massage usually required no more than a five-minute walk, and every employee received a paid month off from work every year. Workers took advantage of the free classes at the Learning Center to paint or sculpt or write or even get an additional degree or two. And, of course, nearly everyone's filter bubbles kept out digital information of any sort that might make their day less enjoyable or productive.

Jack and the rest of the team had their filter bubbles intact, set at various levels of access to the fullness of the info-stream. My filter bubble had been removed seven years before, when I had stepped into my position and been deemed stable enough to deal with any sort of news or information without negative repercussions for my psyche. While that was deemed to be the case, I have learned things I did not like one bit.

My life was very different from the lives of my peers, as far as I could tell, for this very reason. The only other person I personally knew who didn't have a filter bubble was Dr. Gushlak, and we rarely talked about forbidden topics in public except in generalities. It wasn't so much that it was difficult keeping knowledge of the Intelligence Community's mistakes to myself as it was difficult to find a mental compartment into which to stuff those bits of knowledge without corrupting my primary and secondary goals. Betrayal of fundamental principles was still a foreign concept for me, so it stood illuminated and alone—like a museum piece—every time I took a look around my mind.

As a steward, my first job was to control my own thoughts, and I dutifully did so by not interacting emotionally with the terrible knowledge I had. Oh, I let it exist all right, in stark relief against everything else I knew. But I would pass by it, exert no force against it, become nothing if it came for me through the subconscious, and allow it its place out of phase from my ego. It was only by way of great effort and knowledge of mental judo that I kept my job, mission, and mind intact. I wasn't sure how Dr. Gushlak kept his convictions in the face of glaring Community hypocrisies, but over the years I realized he dealt well with them.

As Jack and I rounded a red corridor attached to the primary corridor, I began to remember what it was like before all the upgrades and behavioral modifications had been mandated and adopted. I remembered from my college days that young men engaged in fights at bars, and cell phones were all on the *outside* of the body. I remembered what it was like reading people's behaviors before voice stress analytics and micro-expression monitors took the mystery and the game out of it. I remembered the silence of the cabin in Massachusetts and the immense calm that came from having no strong electromagnetic fields nearby. I remembered the horrible emotional noise the news made when there were no filter bubbles, and then the grip of terror everyone felt when the Collapse was announced and panic immediately ensued. I remembered all those things on that brief walk because my subconscious knew I hated this hallway, hated the color, and was actively trying to distract me from it.

I allowed my subconscious to do this to me.

Soon enough, though, the color of the hallway changed to a light gray and the ceiling suddenly arched, much like a chapel. The additional area was completely full of full-spectrum lighting and the hallway sprouted evergreens and birch arranged at random throughout it, giving the impression of being outside and inside at the same time. Seemingly from all around there came sounds of water in motion, as though one was walking somewhere with a brook nearby. Fresh air from outside was piped in, along with the aroma of jasmine, because it was one o'clock.

We came to the end of the hallway and, using the synthetic telepathy function of my exocortex, I opened the doors to our section with a thought and walked into the facility.

Soaring ten stories high beyond a black-marbled atrium floor was a wall made entirely of glass overlooking the city. Green trees with the various trunks of different species framed the view on every level, and the vines that closed the gaps between them grew green and purple. Flowers of every color were abundant in recessed planters all across this first floor, and six pairs of robotic doves flew around the atrium, cooing and looking as graceful as the real thing. (They were robotic because no one wanted to deal with dove shit.) This magnificent first impression was intentional and implied financial resources that made this area recognizable as an important place.

Jack and I took a LIM shuttle to the top floor in a matter of seconds. I didn't mind the LIMs, because they were direct-route, vertical shuttles that one didn't have to spend much time in due to the speed of being catapulted by electromagnets. There was no chance of being spun and flung by vacuum tube into an empty parking garage with these; I could see the beginning and I could see the end and that was all I needed to know.

When we reached the top floor, I saw Dr. Gushlak standing in the lobby, excitedly giving instructions to the guards. One of them saw us and pointed, saying something to Dr. Gushlak. The doctor turned, smiled and walked hurriedly toward us.

"You'll never believe what we found!" he said, his eyes wide with excitement.

"Do the guards need to know?" I asked, eyeing them.

It was out of character for Dr. Gushlak to forget his discretion, but he remembered it, and nodding, walked swiftly back the way he had come and urged us to follow.

We strode past laboratories and offices, passing mine on the way, before arriving at the doctor's laboratory with the GOD machine in one corner. On a dissection table lay the body of Jin Ming, and next to the table, a strange machine.

"You can leave, Jack," said Dr. Gushlak when we entered the room. Looking dismayed but knowing his place, Jack acknowledged the order and walked out to return to his cubicle where he might or might not hear from his coworkers what was going on.

"So what's going on, Doctor?" I asked.

"That mole we excised from behind the subject's ear, Donald, it had a message in it!" he said excitedly, taking off his glasses and wiping a brow with his sleeve.

"A message?" I asked, not immediately understanding.

Dr. Gushlak started chuckling and then he began to laugh as he walked toward the strange-looking machine, picked up a small dark square with his tweezers, and held it out to me for my inspection. He was practically crying with laughter by the time he managed to blurt out his words.

"They sent us a message on microfiche!"

CHAPTER 4

THE COLLAPSE DESTROYED SO MUCH, it's no small feat that the Corporate Person Communities were able to pull themselves together at all, and it's a miracle that no major international wars broke out. Due directly to the OPEC nations discontinuing oil trade in dollars, along with serious European debt issues, the economic fallout was swift and devastating.

Inflation of the currency made cash in a wheelbarrow a reality and RFID bank cards became the primary form of exchange. Government debit cards helped buy groceries for the unemployed for a while, but even with direct emergency CFTC manipulation of the commodities markets and vastly expanded social programs, the government could not supply the millions going without.

At the height of the economic crisis, a new influenza strain emerged and decimated the elderly, which some economists noted lessened the burden on Social Security. It also killed many of the very young, as flu is prone to do, and shrunk a new generation. I remember there were plenty of questions at the time as to where this particular flu had originated and how it had appeared across the country and around the world simultaneously, but there were never any claims of a foreign viral attack.

As a novice social engineer at the time, I merely noticed that people tended to stay inside and were generally peaceful during a pandemic in order to lessen the chance of exposure. Because of this, rioting was limited, people relied on the system's "news" outlets for their news, and the military guarded grain silos and cattle feed lots and took charge of the distribution of food from that point on with few complaints.

The popular rhetoric in the media at the time was that we had overspent ourselves and we could only blame our own debt for our misfortune. This morphed into the eventual delineation between debt-free zones and indebted zones that split the population into producers and mere eaters. Individuals who had no or negligible personal debt and useful skills were moved to the debt-free zones that functioned much like normal cities, to whose sustainability they contributed. Those who were dependent on the federal government and/or had no usable skills went to indebted zones and emergency camps that were fenced not only with chain link and barbs, but with the guilt of being a burden on a suffering society.

Eventually, revolutionaries put up a fuss, and various populations around the country found out that the Air Force didn't mess around when it wanted to quell unrest. The iron fist of Uncle Sam smashed power plants and municipal water utilities into rubble and mud, and there were trade blockades against entire states that wanted to secede from the USA.

The repercussions were tremendous. Masses died of disease, crime, dehydration, and starvation. The suffering wandered the roads and highways aimlessly, eating what they could, killing each other over scraps, and dying everywhere. They became known as "zombies," because someone realized it was a good label to use to desensitize people to other people's humanity. Millions perished. All in a few years.

Then the government seemed to *decide* to collapse from internal, non-public pressures, and the first Community, the Intelligence Community, was created as its own state since it had powerful reasons and resources to stay intact. An archipelago of freestanding Military Communities surrounding existing military bases was formed with IC support shortly thereafter to house the peacekeepers and ensure that there would be no foreign attempts at invasion during a time of continental weakness.

The human world went through terrible turmoil as a whole. Once foreign aid stopped being issued to the Third World because of budget cuts, nations and ethnic groups worldwide died in huge numbers only lessened by cannibalism. Small nations were expanded or absorbed while the strong took from the weak, as nature itself became the only law. There was no national, ethnic, or religious monopoly on suffering; everyone suffered tragically and deeply for long years.

And people grew tougher, like the sapling battered by the wind. They were more firm in their stances, both ideologically and physically. Pounds were shed quickly, laboring outdoors became the new play, and a sterner approach to life and hardship was adopted by more than just the generation that had lost their parents all at once in the pandemic. Smiles were less common, but something of the old America remained in the offering of aid to family and neighbors alike and doing of occasional good deeds for strangers. Certain Communities revived old traditions while others were entirely progressive in their outlooks. Security was nearly universally tighter because *all* had seen violence, and the Intelligence Community, from its early days, was able to supply UAVs and surveillance equipment to the new, growing system of corporate micro-nations and the sovereign satellites that began to fill the land of the former USA.

The Intelligence Community quickly acquired enough raw materials from trading partnerships with these entities to forge a new, albeit *smaller* nation that felt a lot like the old country. Although most people still ate from their gardens and cans, we already had a gourmet restaurant operating in the first year we were up and running. Occupying most of Maryland and Virginia, we had our own fishing off the coast and our own farming inland; and while we clearly needed both basic and complex materials and goods from the rest of the continent, we could mostly take care of our own.

And we began to watch again after a period of disjointed leadership, miscommunication, and attention lapse. We began watching our global neighbors again, and we again watched the left coast. We used our ears to hear deep into oceans and we used our silver voice to pacify the souls of men. We called for a new order and showed the way by example.

We sold some of our intelligence but kept the majority to ourselves. We bought what others knew about our allies and enemies and, more often than not, paid in pharmaceuticals made by the many drug factories within our borders. We enjoyed a lot of advantages living in such long-settled land. The huge variety of employers living under our banner allowed for an economic diversity naturally denied to, say, Wheatland in the former Wyoming Territory. While our main business was intelligence, the Community's GDP came from many diverse sources, although there was a definite geographic and architectural difference between the intelligence areas and elsewhere.

Remnants of the old federal government continued to perform certain functions. Taxes were collected each year from every Community, based on GDP, to pay for intelligence and military and ensure protection and recognition as a legitimate continental partner. The law of the land stated that the military wouldn't intervene if a recognized Community mounted a contained offensive against an unrecognized Community to absorb the area into its own territory. This kept all Communities paying their fair share into the collective pot. Other monies went to pay for various departments that provided necessary services in a loose alliance of only 150 million people. With the population more than halved in five years, the government's job changed in innumerable ways.

Now, twenty years after the formation of the Intelligence Community and our Military Community partners, we had developed a pretty good system of governance, established a currency after great effort and resistance, and installed the filter bubbles in *all* citizens' personal media and communication connections. Really, the only thing we had to do now was take care of the outliers within the human condition. Most everyone else just fell in line after the easier path was made apparent.

I'll admit, I don't have many coworkers—who are usually military—with my level of access or perspective of time, so I've felt I've had little in common with them or their regimented and still-filtered perspectives. I'm a scientist. It's part of my position to be able to order them around, but for the most part, I avoid any personal closeness because of the difference in the fundamental mindset.

To better explain: In military basic training, *first* comes shock and the removal of the familiar. Shouting, nakedness, violence, threats of violence, absence of traditional comfort spheres, nothing unique about one's person, and so forth. *Simultaneously* comes forced exhaustion, both physical and mental. *Then* the repetition of simple ideas to drown out one's own thoughts and deeply embed new messages. Marching chants create a detached but reactive mindset. After a certain amount of time, we've machined ourselves a device that does what we want.

This patterning has proven its usefulness throughout history in the training of soldiers, and has been adapted and used to recruit converts within cults, and we use similar immersion technologies on many different types of people to turn particular neural pathways into neural expressways for a conditioned automated response. It's one of the most time-tested things we do.

So, in other words, as a co-writer of the programming used to govern the thoughts and actions of so many of my underlings and peers, I cannot in good faith be a genuine friend to them. I just know too much about them, which is strange and not a little sad. Wearing my exocortex, I see their personality quotient in augmented reality hanging in the air next to them. I see the changes in the temperature of their faces. Truthful language sings in my ears while lies sound discordant. I remember the things my position has allowed me to know, I remember that I have the burden of remaining silent about them, and I realize that these people are not, in fact, my peers, but the agents of a knowing nation of unknowing.

And *I* should know.

For my wife I've made an exception, because love is not stopped by filter bubbles and a worldview insufficient for maintaining equal footing. Love is something innately biological, yes, but there is also what you might term a spiritual equivalent you can see dancing in eyes gazing on perfection. Love ignores faults; it gets over resistance and works cooperatively. Even though I probably know my wife better than she's aware—*no*, I have not read her file—I consider her my equal in all the ways that matter. Her ignorance of the machinations that form her opinions for her becomes less of an issue when everything exterior to our relationship is ignored and we enjoy our love and oneness in the quiet times. My wife is my peer. My wife is my love.

Doctor Gushlak is also something of a peer, and I believe he perceives me similarly. We share in common the absence of military servitude, and, in fact, I think that's perhaps a significant reason he advanced me to the position I now occupy. Sometimes he mutters disparagingly about inside-the-box thinkers, and I get the impression he enjoys having someone around who knows many of the things he knows, although certainly not all of them. It is indeed lonely in a tower of knowledge with room for one. I feel that loneliness often, and I cannot imagine containing the secrets the doctor must hold inside his own structured mind.

I remember the days when nobody was hooked into the broader electronic world most of the time, when my classmates in high school and college could laugh and joke about anything without being monitored or required to pre-edit what they were going to say, when many friendships were completely genuine and open, when the lies being told *to* you weren't being told *into* you, and when the Collapse had not yet happened. Things had been pleasant and fun, even.

It was an innocent time. But then, that's youth, isn't it? I suppose everyone has to grow up, and the Collapse did that to just about everyone.

This new American Community of Corporate Persons was an infant; its populations, a remnant of a nation's adolescence before being cut down. We became the phoenix rising from the char and ash and realized that in order to be many, we must become one. So the many Communities came together under a new banner, the people came together under each new Community, and the thoughts of the people came together in a less divergent way. That was how we reanimated the limbs of the empire and made it dance.

All puppets must have their puppeteers, and Dr. Gushlak was one of the most powerful and adept. It was well known by the members of the Intelligence Council on which he sat never to shake hands with him, never to let him control a situation (say, in his office, or at his dinner table, or when surrounded by his people), and always to overspeak him in meetings so he couldn't use tone, hypnosis, and technology to sway votes on the council and would have to put his suggestions in writing instead. It wasn't out of malice that the other members did these things. They had been briefed by *their* intelligence people that Dr. Gushlak could make people do *anything*, and so they jealously guarded the integrity of their own unfiltered minds.

Another leader thought of as "creepy" on the council was Colonel Ian Milton, in charge of the Gang of Witches, as they were referred to by others, whose branch was dedicated to actually using supposedly psychic methodologies developed by the military in the 1960s and '70s in conjunction with Stanford Research Institute to see and describe completely dark enemy targets. Their present-day hit rate was consistently high, and, therefore, weird, so Milton was also regarded warily.

No one knew much about General Peterson, who represented the subterranean military outposts miles underground. He was aloof and often fell asleep in meetings, as though he had a position that mattered little to him and received no oversight. It was often wondered if, because Deep Underground Military Bases were the last line of survival for the species, General Peterson and those he represented weren't the least bit concerned about what went on topside, since they had been dug in and established for decades in a place with its own leadership and supply chains. Thought of as a second, isolated government that could potentially do what it wanted, the DUMBs Communities were courted by some as a way out in the case of disaster upstairs. However, many treated Peterson as the most serious threat to conditions topside. Our anthropologists and sociologists mentioned how the cultures of isolated peoples can become vastly different than what is considered normal, so the entire council kept eyes on him.

Space Intelligence was necessary for everyone, so General Schmidt held status as the most trusted and solicited member of the council. If Mental Stewardship needed to broadcast tonal resonance to calm an entire battlefield, Schmidt was the man to go to. If SIGINT needed a satellite to move behind an enemy satellite to pick up directed microwave communications, General Schmidt could do it. When the Gang of Witches needed confirmation of the targets they viewed, as their protocols required, a satellite was retasked by Space Intelligence. And on and on. Because he, himself, was a hub of cooperation, it was no wonder that Schmidt occupied head chair on the council and was well liked, despite always closing his mouth and shaking his head whenever asked about extraterrestrials.

Disease Intelligence and the CDC were run by a pale, sickly-looking doctor with a racking cough that could stop meetings midstream. Apparently having had a run-in with a foreign phage in his early research, his health was a constant source of concern for others; but apparently recognizing this early on, Dr. Simon was the hardest worker the council had, traveling constantly, working impossible hours, never taking vacations, and so on. These were the habits of a consummate professional who loved his Community and cared deeply about his job and the people under him. The daily health supplements he consumed were said to number in the hundreds, and one could see him popping pills like an addict. But the man had saved us from viral outbreaks and foreign protein contamination of water supplies and any number of things that would have otherwise devastated many Communities, including our own.

There numbered two dozen agencies of different scales and ranges whose heads sat around the table. I sat behind Dr. Gushlak as his aide to take notes and be a source of counsel and information if needed. Being associated with him didn't make me popular among the other seconds-in-command, but everyone was just doing their job, so I reasoned the slights were permissible. I supposed that in the future, if I replaced Dr. Gushlak, I would likely continue to be viewed just as warily. Again, the capacity to be a peer or friend was scuttled before it could sail, but such is the power of the leviathan. Acquaintances all would remain.

And that was, more or less, the constituency of the Intelligence Council. Many times in the past I had witnessed intelligence being discussed and positive or preventative checks established to meet whatever threats were coming or already present. The meetings were interesting. They showed the impressive global range of issues we had grown to consider as our territory. I heard from interesting and important men about interesting and important things. These meetings, in an ultra-secure SCIF hidden in the basement of the Stewardship section, were only surpassed in secrecy by the ones to which no aides were invited. Those were never spoken of, but were usually assumed to be held during the rare times when Dr. Gushlak couldn't be found for several hours, only to return exhausted and ignorant of the world. Of course, he could have gone off for a visit to a physician and returned with the same look, but whenever he turned on oldies grunge music, I deduced that he had been in an anechoic SCIF for some time and needed the noise to feel normal.

Our Community needed the leadership of intelligent men, and after many years of hard work and immense effort, we had a functional government that incorporated many parts of the old government. Most like to think we kept the best parts of the old government and ditched the rest, but it's more likely that revenue shortfalls put the redundant systems out of commission. We're sleeker and better and have better management systems for everything from accounting to international military operations.

It's still not perfect, but the Intelligence Community has come a long way since it first started what became known as the Rebuilding. The most amazing thing of all is that we have gathered the minds of a nation of former fighters and cynics in a slice of heaven, and they willingly accept the frosted cake in exchange for work they program themselves to forget. It's a remarkable reversal. One for the history books. ■

CHAPTER 5

"This is the patent-age for new inventions
For killing bodies, and for saving souls,
All propagated with the best intentions."

"WHY IN THE WORLD would they put that on microfiche?" I asked Dr. Gushlak after he had arranged the microfiche on the tray and displayed the message on the old screen.

Dr. Gushlak pursed his whiskered lips. No other message appeared but the verse.

"Maybe they're saying they just do this sort of thing with the best intentions," he replied before shaking his head. "No. These bastards are dark and cruel. The only way they're doing it with the best intentions is if it's *their* best intentions. What's this supposed to be?" he asked angrily. "Showing us they mirror our actions? That they're the same as us? Humanizing themselves? Really? Who do they think they're talking to?"

I began to shrug, but the doctor interrupted with a wave of his hand.

"More importantly, how are we supposed to *feel* about this? What's the intended *impact* of this message?" he asked, his finger hitting the table twice, once for each question.

"Physical confirmation that someone is programming these guys," I said, automatically. "But we knew it anyway because of all the debriefing sessions where the drones described their programming." I paused. "Actually, this doesn't even *say* the Chinese did it, just that it's being done. Some other country might have grabbed this guy, put a cover in his history during the reprogramming, and set him loose knowing we'd assume it to be a message from the Chinese."

When Jack sent Jin Ming's file to the AIs, they could find no time in the previous ten years that he had been away long enough to have a total contextual rewrite performed… at least, in any of the ways *we* would do it. The best success always happened when the drone was only recently reprogrammed, because the mind control began to decay over time without reinforcement. Ten years was more than a healthy span of time in which to find holes in his metadata and communications, and there seemed to be none.

"Yes," Dr. Gushlak said, "but we *know* the Chinese are our most evenly matched opponents, so regardless of *who* sent this, it's a legitimate warning that the Chinese are capable in this little cold war of ours. Good advice, but nothing we don't already know. But, undeniably, we can call that Intention Number One."

Dr. Gushlak approached the wallboard and, as a lecturer might do, wrote on it, "1. Chinese are a danger." Underneath that, he wrote,"2." before coming back my way.

"But does being told point number one make us temporarily suspend our judgment in terms of assigning origination to foreign drones?" I asked.

"It would keep the Chinese on all of our minds, wouldn't it?" Gushlak replied. "Whenever a new drone's unleashed, we'd all immediately think Chinese instead of Russian or Pakistani or whatever. That can bias a situation from the start. For our purposes, I'll say that we need to be ever-aware of the fact that any nation can send some of these, so…."

Back at the screen, Dr. Gushlak wrote next to the 2, "Drones can be anyone."

"What about the advantage of sending this message?" he asked, looking directly at me. Unlike with other people, my exocortex's viewscreen didn't divulge his true classification or his demeanor or intentions. Because his high rank disabled my exocortex sensors, talking with Dr. Gushlak was much like talking to people in the old days, when everything was intuitive and less exact. I liked feeling how I had felt in the old days. It was like living in a memory.

"Whoever sent this had to have seen an advantage in giving us this. Who would benefit?" Dr. Gushlak looked off at a distant wall.

"The Chinese or someone who wants us to think it's the Chinese," I replied.

Dr. Gushlak wrote, "3. Credit unknown."

"What about the fact that the verse is from Lord Byron?" I asked, remembering my poetry from long ago. "The British wouldn't...."

Dr. Gushlak shook his head.

"No," he said, "they're allied with us closer than ever now. We don't pull this kind of thing on each other, unless one of us *wants* it done and it needs to happen a certain way. I'm certain this is not the Brits."

"Okay, so if this isn't a message just for us, then what is it meant to say to the ACCP as a whole?"

"That, publicly speaking, at least, there's a Schizovirus," the doctor replied with a shrug. "It just advances our goals, nothing more. *We* want people scared of it so they don't think too deeply about it, so this Jin Ming creature was ultimately just helping *us*. If there's more fear, there's more belief in the people who have the answers, and we're the ones who give the answers. Three points for the home team, Donald."

Gushlak smiled.

"So point four is that this ultimately helps us?" I asked, remembering that things got strange at the top.

"That doesn't need to be put in writing," said the doctor with a knowing look, and following a cough, he excused himself to go to the restroom.

It made sense. Wheatland may have lost a man in the attack, but the fear that came from such a story helped the Corporate Community trajectory. Apparently, this was considered an acceptable, even desirable, loss.

I remember when my filter bubble was first turned off, I went through a series of one-on-one sessions with the highest-ranking psychologist in the Intelligence Community. Our conversations throughout much of the time I spent with her seemed to focus on how new nations sometimes didn't have the luxury to choose between good and bad, and how bad choices were often the only ones that *could* be made. In such scenarios, I was to trust that people with more experience than I were making those bad decisions, and I was merely the one who had to carry them out, for the ultimate good of the Community trajectory. The "ultimate good" was kept from me on many occasions, though, and I'd have to say that being held in place by the will of men was something I endured mostly for the goal of ascending to the highest rank, where the sky was clear and I would be able to see things that weren't currently understood. Perhaps then I might be able to excuse all the innocents' deaths as a good thing. I left myself that possibility, always. I had to.

Dr. Gushlak's bathroom break was over.

"This microfiche means nothing," he said. "If it's anything more than a taunt and an evaluation of the present situation, I'd be surprised. Apparently, someone's got an ego...."

I nodded slowly. This wasn't much of a message. All that it said was that whoever sent Jin Ming was on the same page we were. If there was a message at all, it was that they had been able to make a nightmare from a man.

Just like us.

We would have to respond, because that's how these things were done. By default, I knew China would be the destination for one of our drones or for some other technology that could only be implicitly linked back to us.

"What upgrades did he have, Doctor?" I asked as I stared at the naked corpse of the man on the table.

"Oh, a memory setup I'm going to access in a bit, and some synthetic muscle fibers in his hands and arms; most likely for use in the oil fields," he replied. "It sure helped him get out of those cuffs."

"Then I guess that means they can't program hysterical strength into someone yet," I said.

"It's usually only been observed in the presence of drugs, and the specimen's toxicology screen came back negative for the usual suspects," Dr. Gushlak said casually. "The lab didn't indicate any foreign proteins or enzymes or other things that may have been used on him. No, it appears he got out of his restraints with old fashioned rope dope."

The doctor was referring to strands of a strong electroactive polymer that were surgically threaded through muscle tissue to enhance an individual's strength. Originally used for muscle-wasting diseases, it had been quickly picked up by the military and construction crews alike. The term "rope dope" came from the shape of the polymers as they twisted around each other in a strand, resembling a rope. For a while they were undetectable, so the upgrade was used first in sports, then more widely, like the steroids of decades past or the gene doping of the recent past.

"You don't like upgrades much, do you, Donald?" the doctor asked.

I vacillated on what I should say, but decided to say nothing and shook my head instead.

"The exocortex is a dead giveaway, Donald," he said with a smile. "You can get any upgrades you want, for free, and you go around with an exocortex instead. Surely you trust the technology?" He winked.

He was right. I didn't trust the technology. I didn't trust the unexpected, like what we did to those people in China by accident. What if a brain chip was accidentally shut down, and because my brain had grown to depend on it, critical functions were jeopardized? It was a common fear, although one whose prevalence had declined due to the absence of weaponized EMP attacks.

"I'm old-school, Doctor," I replied. "I like having instincts instead of readouts." I decided to leave it at that, and we walked together to the scrub room to prep for the autopsy.

"I think variety's important," the doctor said as he pulled on a rubber smock. "I think some of us should have the upgrades, some of us shouldn't. Exocortexes are like the pencils if the pens run out of ink. The risk of an EMP frying everyone's brain is fairly low, but if it ever happened, we'd better have backups."

I agreed and donned the appropriate gear, ending with two pairs of surgical gloves.

In my exocortex, I saw a classified news story about ten people who had apparently just killed themselves in a mass suicide in a mining Community in the Appalachian Mountains.

"Are you seeing this?" I asked Dr. Gushlak.

"The mass suicide? Yeah." he replied, pulling on his gloves. I had noticed that both Dr. Gushlak and I tended to stream the classified news while we did our busy work together. It made for a nice news junkie relationship: either querying the other about the newest interesting thing to happen that most of the world was denied knowledge of.

"Does that sound like our business?" I asked dutifully.

"Yes, it does, Donald," replied Dr. Gushlak as he walked out the door and over to the table on which Jin Ming's corpse lay. "But until someone comes to get us, we've got a memory chip to scan through and a cortex to examine."

Jin Ming's brain was soon out of his skull and sitting in its own bowl. Two inorganic squares covered in a biologically inert coating protruded barely higher than the brain's surface at the cortex and cerebellum. Connected by a thin strip of wire that also functioned as an ambient EM field converter that powered the chips, the small setup would have cost as much as a month's wages in the oil field. Many people believed the memory upgrade was the best upgrade to get because, upon one's death, the family could view everything the deceased had chosen to record. It could also play back memories for the living owner, who would have a deeper level of emotional involvement and could feel his children's love from afar through the memory, or remember faces and numbers and details that were important at work or in a court case. Upgraded memory was the most widely-adopted and generally useful implant available. It made eyewitness evidence incontrovertible, hastened and bettered worker productivity, nullified more domestic arguments than anyone could ever know, and made re-experiencing skydives and sexual adventures a default source of entertainment during a commute. When connected to a synthetic telepathy device or implant, others could share the memory in the present moment as though it were their own. Some people even programmed their own playlists of memories to evoke a particular series of moods on quiet nights at home with a bottle of Napa Valley® Community wine.

Dr. Gushlak put the brain in a spherical terahertz radiation scanner to get a good image of the architecture of the neural networks. The scanner worked its way from the outside to the center, bit by bit, like peeling an onion. As the submillimeter waves could only penetrate a short distance into the fatty tissue to map the neurons and synapses and ion channels via their sodium, a specialized radio scalpel within the machine sliced off the top layers of already-scanned grey and white matter around the surface area of the brain. Then, continuing its scanning in microscopic detail, followed by more slicing, followed by more scanning, the machine eventually completely destroyed the physical specimen but collected the information to begin constructing a near-exact simulation of

Jin Ming's brain in the computer so we could get some questions answered.

After the dedicated AI crunched petabytes of information for a while, a human brain would begin to take virtual shape. The computer linked together lobes in three dimensions; unclear pathways were averaged; preexisting chemical or physical damage was modeled; the gyri and sulci were grown and recessed; and, within a decent span of time, the simulation would be ready to run.

After depositing the body in a cooler, removing the memory chips from the brain, and dumping the brain carvings in the medical waste chute, the doctor and I went back to the scrub room and removed our autopsy gear. In this section within the Hayden Center, there was no desire or need to do an autopsy of the body. It was the brain that was most important in this place. Over the years, I had realized that Dr. Gushlak considered bodies mere physical conveyances for the brain. I wasn't so sure that he didn't view his own body and mind the same way.

"Well, that takes some know-how," Dr. Gushlak said as he returned to the computer and stared at the image that had been rendered.

Marked in red, most of the brain appeared to have undergone serious cellular damage. We hadn't noticed it when physically handling the brain because it likely happened so recently that the scarring had not been perceptible.

"Look at how much is gone!" said an amazed Dr. Gushlak as he inspected the scan. "Memories, higher functions… about the only things left are basic functions, language, and whatever that was connected to the chip. I've never seen anyone with brain damage like this able to operate."

I was impressed, too. The man had been almost completely wiped.

"We should pull up his simulation and see if there's anything there," I said.

Dr. Gushlak tapped the screen several times.

"Hello?" we heard a synthetic human voice speak from the computer.

"Yes, can you hear us?" Dr. Gushlak asked.

"I hear you. Why can't I see? Why can't I feel? Where am I?"

This usually happened with the simulations. While not *conscious*, per se, they mimicked perfectly the attitudes and reactions the original brain would have had.

"You're in a medically induced paralysis," Dr. Gushlak said, rolling his eyes. "You've been in a terrible fire and we can't have you moving around and disturb the bandages."

Dr. Gushlak motioned to me.

"I'm Dr. Isaacson," I said, leaning in toward the microphone. "We need to ask you some questions. Do you feel well enough to answer?"

"Yes," came the reply after a moment.

"First, how is your pain?"

Dr. Gushlak and I idly busied ourselves with clipboards and other things while the brain simulation described painlessness, which was appropriate for a virtual representation of an actual brain that itself had no nerves.

"Good," I said, reaching for my notepad. "Do you remember being held against your will?"

There was a pause.

"I don't know," it replied.

"What is the last thing you remember?" I asked.

"I don't know," it said.

"What is your name?"

There was a long pause.

"I don't know," was the eventual response.

Dr. Gushlak looked at me and we both had the same thought.

"He gave us his name when we picked him up, so whatever he is must *only* be in that chip!" Dr. Gushlak said, and stepped excitedly to the table with the chip. I turned back to the computer.

"What are your goals?" I asked the simulation, while Dr. Gushlak busied himself with finding the chip.

"I don't know."

"What *do* you know?"

There was another long pause.

"I don't know," came the reply.

"Are you telling me the truth?"

"Yes…?"

"Thank you. You're going to make a full recovery."

Exasperated that our cutting-edge technology couldn't overcome fate, I kept the simulation on and observed how little was actually working. Most of the brain was useless at a cellular level.

"Look at this!" said Dr. Gushlak excitedly.

I joined him at his interface desk. He had placed the chip down on the dynamic polymer surface, and the desk, recognizing a new device, had illuminated the area around the chip and formed a circular port around it. The port began pulsing waves of light across to the other side of the desk, where a vertical screen element suddenly rose with a strangely disinterested organic affect, as though it was growing a screen because it thought it might as well.

"Thank you, Roger," Dr. Gushlak said to the desk as images retrieved from Jin Ming's memory chip began to play on the screen.

"Roger" was the name of a royal butler whose brain Dr. Gushlak had acquired several years ago by special request upon the butler's death to further his personal studies on subservience in its natural state. He had put the brain simulation into his desk, where it could interact with the outside world in a basic way. Roger may only have been given a dynamic polymer surface to interact through, but it was more than agile enough to pour a glass of brandy or grow a screen for displaying information.

"Very good, sir," Roger said, his face rising in relief on the desktop at the mention of his name, nodding, and disappearing into an again-smooth surface.

There were only two memories listed on the chip, and both appeared to be fairly emotional, and, therefore, unable to be fully analyzed from mere viewing on a screen.

"We'll have to immerse," I said.

"We have to watch it first to make sure it's safe," Dr. Gushlak recommended.

A few years prior, one of the lower-level scientists had been working with implanted memories and fully connected himself to the last memories of a murder victim. The emotional and aesthetic realism of the memory was so clear and complete that the researcher ended up having a heart attack and dying. The event reminded all of us that immersion was always to be performed cautiously and never completely.

Dr. Gushlak's screen started displaying an event that looked like a birthday party. Children ran around outside screaming, colorful streamers flapped in the breeze, and a piñata, ready to be bashed, was leaning against a tree. From the height of the viewer's perspective, the memory seemed to have been formed when the viewer was a very young boy.

"Innocent enough," Dr. Gushlak said.

We fast-forwarded through the digital memory until a point at which the child's gaze fixated on the blue and pink and white stripes of the piñata and the hole through which the candy had presumably been stuffed inside it.

Looking around cautiously, the boy knelt beside the tree and shoved his hand deep in the piñata hole, pulling out candy and stuffing his pockets with it. A small girl approached him, about to say something when the boy threw some candy at her in the hope it would keep her quiet. It did, and he escaped to his room, where he inspected and devoured the bounty from the piñata's gut.

"I guess we know why he ate the organs out of his seatmate," I said, my grimace betraying my disgust. "One of two memories in his head and that's all he knows how to do: disembowel piñatas."

"What's the other memory?" Dr. Gushlak asked.

I pushed the icon and immediately could see that this was a professionally constructed memory. The coding used to write it was familiar to me because it was similar to what we used when writing an implanted memory. It exhibited all the earmarks of a motivated program, but lacked the visuals to accompany it.

"There's audio," noted Dr. Gushlak, pointing at the readout.

I indicated to the screen to pull up the audio.

"Tick-tick-Jin-Ming-tick-tick..." came the sound of an old analogue clock's hands, with a subliminal auditory track mixed in, which we noticed immediately.

"What does this do to the simulation?" Dr. Gushlak asked urgently.

"I need to tie the simulation into the feed," I said, and I did.

Immediately, Jin Ming's brain simulation began to show signs of neural hyperactivity. The virtual brain just recently so lifeless and absent of answers was now reacting strongly to something unknown within the fake memory.

"I wonder what kind of emotional context they used to make him kill himself," Dr. Gushlak said.

"Definitely a psychotic set of emotions," I said, watching the parts of the simulation that were lighting up. I remembered with a shiver the events in the warehouse that had led to the drone's suicide, and how completely distanced from reality he had been. In this day and age, when drugs in the water sponged up the anger and insanity that filter bubbles didn't, these were unusual events.

"What do you think the cascade pattern is?" Dr. Gushlak asked. "Can you tell?"

I inspected the coding, and while complex and intermingled and written to randomly have bursts of various mixtures of emotions leading to a climax of all emotions at once, I could tell that it was predominantly built on feeling bigger than himself, as the subject's own admission of wanting to save the world attested. Empathy, guilt, great responsibility, sacrifice, nobility, not a small feeling of heroism, and the butterflies of adventure all activated in the brain and mixed together, metered by the ticking of the clock as the stressor.

"The pattern is inorganic; it looks like a psychotic event where someone chooses the lives of others over their own," I explained. "In this implanted memory, the decision to save the world seems to have been made, and that became the self-termination point."

"Great material," Dr. Gushlak said. "How come we never thought of that? It's artful."

I commented that I wasn't sure we needed peripheral improvements on our own methods, but the doctor told me to have a researcher work on new narratives for self-termination programs. I made a note of it, but my eyesight blurred from lack of sleep and I knew the nearly illegible scrap would end up being forgotten in one of the hidden places notes hide themselves.

Just then, both Dr. Gushlak and I were interrupted by a conference call in our hardware from Jack.

"We've been called out for some cult suicide," he said with a yawn. "I can send out C team since B team is busy trying to steward compliance into the Texas Supercommunity, but really we can send out whoever you want. Our guys might need a nap first." Dr. Gushlak agreed.

"I'll take C team and you all go home," he said. "Sleep until tomorrow morning if you have to. Thank you all for dealing with the odd hours. I'll supervise this one."

I was duty-bound to ask him if I should accompany him, but he kindly declined, patting me on the shoulder.

"I'll fill you in tomorrow," he said in an almost fatherly way before tapping above his eye.

"Plus, I'm the one with the circadian arrestor," he said with a wink. "If you had one, you could be having all the fun I'm having!"

He laughed, and I smiled. The doctor certainly did have his share of implants and upgrades, and part of his tirelessness may have sprung from them, although I thought it might have been his innate character that kept him so active. Either way, the man was a machine.

Partly one, rather. ■

CHAPTER 6

THE MICROWAVE AUDITORY EFFECT, or Frey Effect, was discovered during World War II, when people near radar transponders reported hearing clicks that weren't noticeable to others nearby. Over the decades, modified microwave pulses evolved until it was possible to insert voices directly in the enemy's head without needing any sort of electrical receiver. The directionality of the technology helped operations speak to an insurgent in the middle of a crowd or when alone crafting his bombs. Either way, hearing disappointed voices claiming to be a god who's upset with your actions is bound to create psychological devastation in the faithful. Used on the unknowing terrorist, anarchist, protestor, or "zombie," modulated microwaves could instantly change behavior and permanently affect personality or outlook. Coupled with an injection of 17 Hz infrasound into the area, the subject would "feel the disappointment" of the "God" who's ashamed of him. I had even heard of suicides because of the pairing, but I imagined they were carried out over some time on really bad people.

The technology greatly helped our spies because we could, for example, target them in bed from space or UAV and give them their orders without even their lover hearing. We could guide them in real time from above to avoid any pursuers, or direct feet on the ground toward a target with state-level communications scanners. No microphones could pick up the transmission since the microwave auditory effect was caused by the biology of the inner ear reacting to the modulated microwaves; an electronic microphone had a totally different construction and could not "hear" in the same way.

Then came the amping-up of the radio technology that caused uncontrolled neural firing across a battlefield, neutralizing an enemy by giving them seizures. Similarly, we could slowly heat personnel with the same technology so their internal temperatures would soar and they'd pass out. Either way, we could incapacitate a traditional force or a guerrilla force, although these methods were rarely contracted to us by the military to be used in battlefields overseas, likely because war contracts lasted longer in the absence of efficacy. That's how it works, and everyone has to stay in business.

But when a couple of countries in Asia experienced uprisings of monks and insurgents, the governments in charge asked for our help, and we employed the aforementioned methods with very few casualties. It made any potential rebels remember that a much larger force than they could deploy had a mysterious way of making everyone on their side black out at the push of a button. That sort of thing tended to limit major rallies and de-escalate physical incidents. It's deflating to have one's consciousness suddenly snatched away while one and one's fellows tote weapons and angry rhetoric around in a throng. Everyone sort of loses their enthusiasm when they wake up in a groggy pile of living flesh and stumble away in search of aspirin.

We also installed passive and active denial systems on our embassies around the world. There would likely always be international resentment of the dollar's demise decades before, which put our diplomats and other officials at risk from violent acts of perceived retribution. As a result, we pumped scents of regionally-recognizable comfort food smells in the vicinities of our embassies to create a pleasant mental association for pedestrians walking by. We had a satellite in orbit with a massive solar array that could position itself between the sun and an entire city or just a square block around the embassy to create a flicker rate in the percentage of sunlight everyone was receiving, inducing passivity. And, of course, we gave the embassies pulsed microwave transmitters in the event an embassy was being overrun—if it ever got to that point, what with the laser fences and the carbon-ribbon projectile webs that could ensnare dozens at a time. We weren't the only section helping out with diplomatic security.

But by far the most effective means for avoiding confrontation with any small group of upstarts or micro-nation or major nation was the fact that we were rumored to have technology so advanced, they simply didn't have a chance.

Simple rumors of our dark and mysterious nature were employed widely, much the same way the ninja used rumors of magical powers to win the head game over an adversary. Streaming news was occasionally allowed to report on some of the Intelligence Community's outdated technologies, and those reports were shared far and wide with awe, even though we had better stuff that had replaced these technologies long ago. Similarly, streaming movies of most genres had become sci-fi by default, since technology was evolving at such a rapid pace that there was always some new, amazing capability somebody was employing in the First World—whether fictional or not—that most in the Third World didn't possess. Frankly, much of the world viewed the American Community of Corporate Persons as filled with advanced superhumans. We exaggerated a bit, but if it dissuaded attacks, then, ultimately, more people on all sides maintained the potential for long lives and varied experiences.

Which is what we're all about.

Usually, in the absence of abuse or discomfort, most people, if they thought about it, would view time as pure potential. *Time* to travel, *time* to dance, *time* to enjoy one's family... time itself is a humane thing in most instances and being denied it is usually considered inhumane. The violence and anger of men and nations deprives people of time to experience life and peace and productivity, therefore limiting their potential. Calming the minds and hearts of our enemies and agitators is a service a steward provides willingly and charitably, and because our process allows everyone more time, it is more humane than any other.

The terrain of the battlefield is mind control. It will always be just the soil; it is the background and context but not the battle itself. It is a living thing just underfoot with every waltz, skip, sprint, marathon, and back-and-forth marching of weak and powerful people across it. Unnoticed but ubiquitous, the Mental Stewardship section's work in some way supports everyone in the world. And we've enjoyed a tremendous period of global peace so far, which attests to the validity of the practice and to our benign nature.

The things we do are for the better.

If a new automobile a particular man can't afford swings through his peripherals either digitally or in life, it will be screened out by his filter bubble if his recent actions reflect a pattern among men nearing a midlife crisis and indicate that, given the opportunity, he'll obsess about something like a new car until making a bad decision. That would reduce his marriage's happiness, reduce personal productivity, and ultimately weaken his Community's ambition and output, and no one needs that. What affects one affects the many, so to avoid slumps in the Community, our AIs edit what people's exocortexes or implants absorb, they prime minds to feel particular moods when triggered by a symbol or flashes, and things generally work in an orderly and efficient way in most of the Communities due entirely to technology that ninety-nine percent of the Community doesn't recognize when they come across it. Occasionally, a middle-aged man will ask questions about why he can't see his neighbor's new car when it's right in front of him, but the diagnostics of his exocortex or chip will always push out a glitch to make him shrug it off, like they're supposed to, and try to avert the potential midlife crisis in other ways.

A woman concerned about her weight will be evaluated by the AIs, and if she's found to have a few extra pounds on her, they'll make use of a light tonal sound the woman will have been preconditioned to respond to with her attention. The tone will sound when a jogger runs by or she passes a gym or a word like "exercise" is used around her, and subconsciously she'll begin to think a great deal more about getting herself into shape. The tone itself sounds distant enough that no one ever thinks it comes from their own hardware.

Gone are the days when matchmakers and dating websites matched couples by compatible personality types; the AIs do all of that automatically and better, and subliminally urge compatible people to meet by unknowingly going to the same places on weekends or running into each other elsewhere. I've often wondered if the AIs didn't trick my wife and I together as well. I've never gone and looked it up in the system, but I wouldn't be surprised.

We enhanced the acceptance of big-F Fate, as well. The flu pandemic all those years ago left the spirituality of the country adrift, and the realism of the deaths and the ensuing violence and horribleness uncovered a vein of fatalism we decided to explore, in order to try to keep people calm in alarming times. All these years later, people tend to accept more things as uncontrollable than they used to—not very much like I remember the old Americans. We used mathematics to prove reality is completely deterministic when seen from outside of time, and wove that into the speeches of public intellectuals to make free will seem a totally imaginary force. It helped people deal bluntly and frankly with sudden deaths and their own lot in life. People still usually *feel* like they're making their own decisions and having their own thoughts, though, so the deterministic cultural streak mostly emerges during the deeper moments that punctuate a life.

If there existed a spiritual force with only good intentions that could nudge and push a person in the direction of happiness and greater spiritual and bodily fulfillment, most people would gladly choose to listen to that force. The religions of the world certainly believe in such a spiritual force. Neuroscientists believe in the force of the subconscious. A select subgroup of our neuroscientists and operatives technologically recreated the effects of such a force and employed it in participating Communities and nations worldwide.

We really just want everyone to do their jobs and live their lives in as best a way as they can. This system of ours aims to be a positive-sum game. We still left room socially and culturally for an individual God, but the "still small voice" now has some company. ■

CHAPTER 7

"FEEL MY MIND," said Dr. Gushlak radioed spookily at five o'clock the next morning over my tattooed earlobe speaker connected wirelessly to my exocortex sitting on the nightstand.

I struggled awake early for the second morning in a row and threaded the wires of the device through the hair on my scalp, while the viewing projector on the exocortex connected with my eye. The van der Waals forces utilized by the backing material kept the exocortex firmly in place, even when jostled by vibrations.

"It sounds really creepy when you say that," I said groggily. "What time is it?" I flipped on the physical switch that activated the synthetic telepathy function. I was instantly flooded with a stream of confusion, intrigue, respect, and, strangely, fear.

"Early. You understand where I'm at?" the doctor asked.

Like all things synthetically telepathic, I couldn't see where he was or feel what he was doing. I only received the boosted signal of the sender's neural activity. It was like viewing life through someone, but without the physical senses; impressions of their mental state and some vague thoughts they were having were all that could be transmitted and recreated.

"I don't know where, but you sound excited," I said, choosing to use the word "sound" as opposed to "feel," in order to reintroduce the traditional language of a working relationship that early in the morning.

"I'm at that suicide cult house, and I'm a little more than excited, Donald," the doctor exclaimed. "I'm actually a little terrified!"

I could sense a small amount of glee in the admission, as though fear were a tickle he was proud of denying. His mind suddenly took on an ominous feel.

"It was filled with people who worked for us!" the doctor said in a hushed tone. "And the leader got away!"

"Hmm," I replied. I didn't know what to say.

I scratched my early morning stubble. I sensed Dr. Gushlak's excitement clearly; it felt like I was excited, but as I was used to differentiating self from other, I could detach easily from the effects of the synthetic telepathy. Sharing one's mental state was a common thing nowadays, much like sharing thoughts and experiences on social media to help people understand one's emotional environment and document one's life. I always thought it a bit narcissistic, but when used widely, it helped promote understanding and compassion and Community togetherness. Dr. Gushlak would have used synthetic telepathy only if he was really impressed with something and wanted to show how much.

"This is seriously state-level stuff, Donald," the doctor said gravely, and he switched off his telepathic link. I did the same.

"Who do you think did it?" I asked.

"Whoever did it took care of the DNA evidence. This place is rural enough that all we have are broadview satellite videos of the region. The AIs are crunching the comings and goings to the house for hints as to who's behind this, but I'm not sure they'll find anything. Anyone capable of this..." The doctor switched on the video feed from his iris and suddenly I could see ten bodies lined up on a concrete floor. "...is probably capable of a whole lot more."

I WOKE JANET WITH COFFEE and bagels with cream cheese and jam. Sleepily, she smiled when I brought the tray, mumbled something about not wanting to wake up yet, but readjusted on the bed and accepted what I had made for her. While I sat at the foot of the bed with my lox and cream cheese bagel with the red onions and capers I never tired of, she and I spoke about Dr. Gushlak's call earlier in the morning.

"Was it your boss?" she asked, sipping her Kona® Community coffee.

"Yeah, we have a weird problem I need to go out of town for," I said reluctantly.

She nodded.

"I figured that's why you made me breakfast in bed, Donnie," Janet replied with a downturned smile. "You always do nice things before you go away."

"Don't I do anything nice whenever else I'm home?" I asked jokingly, while remembering that morning breakfasts were a custom I started several wives ago whenever I had to leave town.

"Oh, you eat your weird food and fart on my side of the bed," she said playfully. "Occasionally, there's some dining and dancing, but that's only when I've brainwashed you into doing it without you knowing."

She smiled mischievously and, putting down her half-empty tray, made her way across the bed and gave me a seductive hug, letting her hair drift around my neck and ears in a way she knew I liked. She brushed the tips of her fingers across the growing bulge in my crotch.

"My big-time mind-manager's got a big issue I can help him with," she said softly, her lips barely touching the peach fuzz of my ears and her hand mashing more firmly into my groin.

My wife diplomatically insisted at the exact proper moment that I brush my teeth so my breath didn't smell like smoked salmon and onion, which I understood and respected, but I did it hastily and didn't floss. After completing that task, I was allowed to make love.

Janet's yoga-expert muscle control was so appropriately used, I knew every time she moved to my touch that she was easily the most tender and giving lover I'd ever had. We could mirror each other in such a way that there was a spiritual bondedness between us inside even the bonded nature of the dance of love. The ebb and flow were one motion when our minds moved as one, onward to the integrated finale of our perfect match.

As we lay in bed staring at the new morning light touching the walls and ceiling of our twentieth-floor penthouse apartment, she reached for my hand and held it, interlocking her fingers with mine.

"When will you stop having to travel all the time?" she asked in a hopeful tone.

I was quiet for a moment.

"Whenever my boss retires or dies, probably," I lied. In truth, Gushlak set a high bar for such an old man. If I succeeded him, I knew I wouldn't *have* to follow his example, but it wouldn't look quite *as* good if the new guy in charge of the department enjoyed a vastly less demanding schedule than the previous head who had had the admiration of an entire wing at the Hayden Center. I would always be a traveling steward, no matter my position.

"Is it weird that I haven't met him?" Janet asked.

"Not really," I replied as I reached over to pluck a caper from my discarded plate and popped it in my mouth. "He's a pretty high-up guy, and he travels all around the world all the time working with lots of different people more important than me. Heads of state and such."

Janet's eyes betrayed the upset.

"No, no… hey," I said softly, touching her bare shoulder in the sunlight, "you'll meet him. He's seen your picture, we've talked about you, and he asks how you're doing. He always seems too busy for dinner engagements. He does stay awake for crazy periods of time. You know that from the calls."

Janet nodded.

"Ever since you told me about how he lost his wife and

daughter, I've wanted to meet him," she said sympathetically, "*And* I'd like to know his *name* before I meet him, by the way. He sounds like such a nice old man."

I nodded slowly. Gushlak *was* nice. I had a friendly relationship with him and was sure Janet would get along with him just fine. It was just that I had never seen him outside a work setting and wasn't sure if he'd feel pressured to accept dinner at our house. I was technically his staff, so who was I to invite the master of a large house to eat at his staff's table?

In addition, something bothered me about inviting to dinner a man whom I had seen make so many necessary but disturbing decisions about life and death. His humanity seemed mostly in place, but what some would call "inhumanity" seemed to have been replaced in his mind by something called fascination. It was indeed a strange mixture in him because of his work, and one I wasn't entirely comfortable having my wife around. Even I was always careful to not get too close to his kindnesses, because for the right reason, he seemed able to forget anyone else's.

"Maybe I'll see if I can schedule something with him," I said, and rose from the bed to shower and prepare for my trip.

THE CHURCH OF THE COMPUTER SIMULATION had been invented and come to prominence some decades earlier when a surprisingly large number of scientists agreed that the entire Universe had a fantastically high chance of being an advanced computer simulation, based on the idea that it was inevitable—given enough time—that humanity would be able to develop computer programs capable of simulating an entire universe. The mathematical likelihood was high that this one universe was merely a high-quality simulation, or the simulation of a simulation.

The religion gained converts and had little if any dogma, apart from accepting that one's consciousness may just be an accurate approximation of some technologically advanced future civilization's historical individuals or invented filler people.

To be just another programmed object attracted people of a particular mindset, and the church found its numbers aided by our deterministic cultural programming.

The church was officially recognized as a religion long after it was considered one by the public at large. It was a logical reason for existence, it gained lots of traction, and it used its donations to fund cutting-edge mathematics and scientific experiments focused on finding the fingerprints of a celestial programmer.

The Intelligence Community saw the church as an asset until such time that it might uncover scientific proof of its adherents' suspicions, which was why we had infiltrated the church with agents long ago to keep an eye on the experiments. Just in case.

It was upon an offshoot of the church that we publicly blamed the suicides, I found upon arrival at the scene in the Appalachians. Since one sect's members tended to use the most potent psychedelic in the world, dimethyltryptamine, in their attempt to access whatever metaphysical programming they might be able to tap into, we reported this incident as a spinoff of the group overdosing on the drug, even though it's quite difficult to do given the size of a lethal dose. We'll sometimes leave holes like that in the story to flag and monitor those who react with too much skepticism. Then we fine-tune their filter bubbles.

The modest log house stood at the end of a long dirt road in the mountains. On the outskirts of a coal Community, the area was one of green valleys and tall hills and not at all a place I would have minded living in another life. The forest reminded me of the woods around my grandfather's cabin in old Massachusetts and emotion caught me up in longing and memories of untroubled times. The silence there was only occasionally interrupted by the flight of a bird overhead or the rustle of a squirrel somewhere unseen. It would have made a great, isolated place for a cult compound, if that were the real story.

I made my way up a gentle slope to the house, where the other team's leader, a tall, dark-haired man called Kenneth, met me and explained the situation.

"They were each found alone in a different section of the house, even though they all died at roughly the same time," he said. "All of them were mental stewards from overseas operations. Doctor Gushlak knew a bunch of them. Do you realize," he stopped in his tracks, "that none of these high-level, low-filter people—none of them—had a bruise on them or any indication of a struggle? The poison appears to have been self-injected, and everybody had been crying profusely around the time of death, which doesn't jibe with the fact that the poison was just an overdose of morphine and wouldn't have hurt."

I shook my head.

"That is weird," I replied. It had the ring of a suicide pact, but intelligence professionals like this? No way. It didn't strike me as possible. Not in my gut, at least.

"So what are we assuming?" I asked Kenneth as we crossed the threshold of the room where the bodies had been lined up.

"We aren't assuming anything until we get some information from someone's chip," he responded as he walked me through the house pointing out body outlines, "but we know there was an eleventh who escaped, so we're searching for him now. All indications point to it being the leader or assassin or whatever."

"Where's Dr. Gushlak?" I asked.

"Gosh," Kenneth said, looking around. "Last I heard, he was going to go take himself to sleep, but I don't know where he'd be."

Thanking Kenneth and walking away to survey the area myself, I knew the doctor had probably curled up in the back of someone's vehicle for an induced nap. He didn't seem to care much for the comforts men his age normally required, and seemed to make do with field conditions more suited to a former military man.

I found myself exiting the house and wandering up the gentle slope on which it was built, thinking about possible scenarios that could have induced those people, those *coworkers,* to kill themselves. Sure, a lot of the information that comes at a person as he or she works up the hierarchy is disturbing, but they're still prevented by their filter bubbles from paying too much attention to sadness or despair of the sort that drives people to suicide. Unless the filter bubbles malfunctioned. That was a definite possibility.

I noticed that I wasn't as shaken up about these stewards' deaths as I would be if they had been killed clearly and directly in the line of duty. Sure, we stewards have our sense of honor and purpose, and knowing that ten of our overseas tribe were gone was confusing and disappointing and saddening, but that's all it was. With the evidence pointing to suicide for every one of them and without someone definite to blame, without a face and a name and a profile to match to a suspect, this was simply a tragic cluster of deaths with too many unanswered questions to go cursing god or man and punching trees. For now, blame would have to wait.

I put the deaths in their appropriate mental compartment and shut it as I walked. The rough forest floor was covered with the usual detritus. I was familiar with the feel of old leaves, twigs, and decaying branches underfoot. The sunlight warmed me in the patches where it shone through the new leaves overhead and I occasionally caught a whiff of my leather jacket amid the smell of the crisp springtime air in the trees. The scents and scene excited a part of my memory I couldn't place. Anticipation and sunlight and hope... all those sensations and emotions provided great contentment, so I made my exocortex take a snapshot of my active neurons and synapses so I could re-experience the mélange of feelings later. Then I impulsively decided to turn off my info-stream altogether; something people with high clearances are able to do. I was late enough to the party that any work I'd be able to do could wait.

As I came to a small ravine that handled seasonal runoff, I became aware that I might be wasting time with this little excursion into solitude and silence. However, I realized I missed the feeling of being the only human within earshot, and of embracing the emptiness as a friend. It was so calm without images flashing in one's peripheries and the bustle and hum of an electronic world and the addictive but seemingly infinite amount of information constantly thrown at a person. My thoughts turned to my youth and how the out-of-doors had so easily provided safe refuge in my personal universe of experience.

I sat on a boulder unearthed by the seasonal streams and played with a twig. A creature of civilization and community, I still needed distractions, so I broke the little twig into smaller twigs before tossing them all away one by one and finally getting another twig to do the whole thing over again. It was easier than constructing a little cabin or teepee for ants, and I wasn't feeling especially motivated to construct something useless when I could destroy something more unpurposed more easily.

I cracked the right compartment and wondered what it was that made my Community and other nations act this way toward one another instead of savoring the peace that comes from trade. I learned in classes long ago that nations are always engaged in some kind of pissing contest. If one side rolls out a big orbital kinetic bombardment payload, the next year the enemy rolls out a bigger one. That sort of thing was inherited from a geopolitical history that, in itself, enforced this form of mind control, since wanting to deter an enemy is a mind game and developing a bigger weapon in response is the way the opponent always aggresses. It never really ends.

And fortune favors the bold. Right now, whoever had done this, if it wasn't truly a suicide pact, had a definite upper hand on us. It showed us it could bring ten high-ranking men and women to a remote location within our regional territory and have the leverage or technology to make suicide their last act. That showed proficiency on a nation-state level. If the killer was the eleventh man, the real possibility existed that a foreign technology had perhaps surpassed our own, which would force a retooling of our strategy in the mental cold war and put more resources into deep spying. If someone made these stewards kill themselves, then this was a bold move indeed and would attract a particularly harsh response to someone's doorstep.

I heard steps in the brush coming closer. Turning around, I was greeted by the sight of Dr. Gushlak walking up the hill.

"Nice place, isn't it?" he asked, making his way to me. "Unfortunately, we've had a cruel reminder that nature is the residence of life and death. I knew these people, Donald."

He gave me a solemn look and I lowered my eyes in recognition of his certain feelings of loss. I motioned that he could have a seat on a boulder next to mine, and he accepted.

"Where did they take the bodies?" I queried.

"They're being flown back to the IC. The usual people will be doing the autopsies and memory retrieval. I'm only so young."

"Did *I* know any of them?" I asked. I was focused primarily on domestic operations, but I had certainly made many trips around the world with the doctor and been in our stewardship houses overseas.

"Maybe one or two from Antarctica and Canada, but no one you would be talking with on a regular basis. No, these were specialists in altered memory technology—the people who originally let those with unhappy lives die with wonderful lives, the people who program our patsies, the people who invented the best, most efficient vacations ever. It's a loss, Donald. A real loss."

The doctor saw me disassembling a stick, found one of his own and started doing it with me, throwing the little twigs into the dry ravine. We tossed the twigs in silence, but Dr. Gushlak seemed more than frustrated and threw twice as many. I didn't need to say anything. That I was there was enough.

Eventually, he tired of thinking about whatever he was thinking about and stood up, throwing the remainder of his twigs in the cut through the hillside.

"To the future, we're all dead," he said finally.

With that, he turned to begin the walk back to the house.

GUSHLAK BOARDED A FLIGHT TO BRUSSELS at 3 o'clock for two weeks away from the ACCP. Before he left, we filled out the paperwork to empower me as acting head of continental mental stewardship operations.

I had been given the honor twice before, but never for so long. I had first been put in charge for several days when Gushlak's wife had died, and then again when his daughter had died. Every time he left to go overseas, he maintained his control, but this time was different. The mission was too important. Research and operations issues that were too high for my clearance would still go automatically to Gushlak, so even at this great height, I could not know everything, including, strangely, the details of the ongoing search into the cause of the ten steward group suicides that was taking him overseas.

The security always provided the biggest change to my lifestyle in this position. Both Janet and I acquired bodyguards and Do Not Fuck With tags, which was something Janet enjoyed *a lot* since she, like seemingly everyone else, spent at least an hour in various security lines on the way to work. Speeding around checkpoints and having an entourage of people who will die and kill for you is a real ego boost, but I didn't *want* to like it too much because when bad things come, they too often come from a flawed egoic assertion.

For some reason, Janet immediately began to plan dinners with the couples the AIs had compelled us to become friends with over the years, and while I hate to think that perhaps she was doing it to show off our new security detail, I think that was probably her intent. But then, I suppose, in a place of secrecy where no one can brag about what they're doing, bodyguards send the messages that outright gloating cannot.

It was embarrassing for me, though. I tended to walk quickly through public areas, not because my security team rushed me, but because people *do* pause and wonder, "Who's the big shot?"

I never much cared for being looked at. I always figured the amount of time I spent alone in the woods did something to me that made me avoid the spotlight. Or it might have been that a childhood spent hiding from abuse made my adulthood into a hiding place for expressions of capacity. Regardless, the last time I had been able to be alone had been walking in the woods and sitting by the ravine before Dr. Gushlak had joined me. The snapshot of my neural architecture I had taken that day came in handy. It was a mood I consistently replayed during the abundant business of the new schedule.

Every morning an Intelligence Council aide briefed me before a Mental Stewardship section briefer painted the small strokes in our corner of the world, in the world of our concern. I continued to receive an evolving view of how the world functioned and how exactly our section affected the whole. Much of the experience satisfied my curiosity. I found answers to questions that had plagued me for years, so, in that sense, the position *was* fulfilling, and I didn't think I'd have any great trouble getting used to it for the rest of my life if given the chance. Especially if all the shackles fell from my clearance and actions.

Under my watch, we sent a drone to China in response to the Jin Ming incident, which we naturally blamed on them. Once an actual murderer on death row, but taken and programmed as a prostitute, she had been turned into a Visha Kanya, an ancient Sanskrit term that meant "poison girl" and referred to a young woman who was fed a steady diet of poison until her body got used to it and who was then sent to have sex with men who would sicken or die from the contact. When caught, she had a self-termination program in place, but one with a happy scenario in which she would embrace the end of life instead of one that was terrifying. Everyone figured that was a reasonable action, although I will admit that giving the order was a strange new experience—one that lingered in the forefront of my mind for longer than I usually kept thoughts there.

The management of anything continental is an enormous task. Gushlak's aides helped keep my workload and meetings straight, and I spent several nights at the office catching up on business. My workout schedule already spotty, the added duties helped me neglect exercise even more. The job was a mixture of good and bad.

About halfway into the temporary routine, Dr. Gushlak called.

"You should know something," he said over the secure communication link.

"Yeah?" I replied, shuffling papers.

"We know who made the ten stewards kill themselves," he said intently. "A colleague of ours. Yours and mine."

Gushlak had my attention.

"Yes?" I asked, waiting. Access to the investigation was denied me for the whole week at Gushlak's explicit direction, annoying me because I hadn't known why.

"It was Joe. Joe Atherton. Your roommate at MIT."

It took a few moments for the words to sink in. Joe Atherton, my college wingman, had been identified as the mastermind behind the killings. If that information was correct, my former roommate was now the most dangerous man in the world. The realization then hit that it would probably be my job to kill him and take apart his brain. Things were so strange at the top....

I thanked Dr. Gushlak, asked for the relevant files to *now* be made accessible to me, hung up the link, and vomited in my wastebasket. I was grateful no office aides were present to witness my discomposure. ▪

CHAPTER 8

A LIKEABLE ROOMMATE and a good wingman at university, Joseph Atherton descended from a long line of east coast Brahmins. He tended to pick up bar tabs and pizza without a second thought, never asking for repayment, but it was implied that unless he offered or gave, you were expected to pay your own way. He was a subtly generous man, but it was something people like myself noticed was more frequent the more he liked a person.

Initially skeletal and insecure, over the course of our eight years as roommates, he grew to become something of a soft-spoken gym nut who found an interest in brain and cognitive sciences, which was also my field of study. He stopped growing at 6-foot-3, his jaw chiseled and his muscles revealing a serious weightlifting regimen, so he was physically a good man to bring to the bars, for safety and for catching the eyes of the opposite sex.

Joe's sharp mind matched that of any genius I ever met at that elite school, but he found little joy in the one-upmanship engaged in by the combative egos often encountered at those institutions. Clearly raised well, he seemed to avoid conflict by simply not saying anything that might be contested. In many ways, he kept opinions to himself, and he enjoyed a good reputation for it. He was a soft-spoken big guy, and over time, I could tell he had fostered the soft tone of voice that was used by therapists to induce calm. I am positive he did it because of his bulk. He and I had had discussions about intimidation and his unwitting use of it.

We always had a healthy respect for each other, and I remember attending a Christmas in Vermont with him and his family the year of our dissertations. His parents seemed normal enough, if a little spoiled in their mansion, being waited on by their domestic staff. I saw that Joe tried to do as much on his own as he was allowed. Taking his own bags up to his room, for instance, or pouring his own gravy at dinner. It was probably this selflessness and self-reliance that contributed to him being an ideal candidate for stewardship operations. He was also an especially considerate man.

By the time the Collapse rolled around, both he and I—now doctors—were already deeply involved in social engineering research that would help public safety, although in different departments with the then-federal government. We found ourselves among the many protected by the stability operations of a military that paid its workers in bread and beans, and I, at least, survived that period without seeing very many deaths of rebels or government workers. And I was no statistic, myself, thankfully.

Through the grapevine I later heard that Joe had been credited with the idea of "supervised illegal behavior," such as drag races against law enforcement vehicles in semi-stable cities that earned the local constabulary necessary friends in the community and provided emotional outlets and entertainment for so many of the unemployed majority. That praise was the last I heard of him. Neither he nor I kept touch, likely because we were in different enough programs that talk would be fairly limited to family and the past. I admit I was always too busy to drop him a message.

Joe apparently joined the overseas stewards and went through their training, which involved more language and cultural training than was required for the domestic operations in which I specialized. I knew nothing of his activities at that point—I thought of him only briefly once a year or so—but his timeline was full of hopping across the world for localized and generalized projects alike. He swiftly worked his way up the leadership ladder, eventually acquiring his own base of operations somewhere near Singapore, where he was the Chief Steward and had his fingers in everything occurring in the region, selling our services to whomever needed them and leaning on those who didn't want them.

His psychological profile didn't appear to change much over the years. He ascended to the top-secret classification of "no filter" only a year after I did, but instead of working toward higher achievements, he dropped out suddenly, retiring his commission to manage investments between going out on his sailboat occasionally and playing tennis twice a week.

At the time of his resignation, the AIs began paying closer attention to Joe. Anyone who has his filter bubble withdrawn and suddenly resigns from his position is deemed a likely security risk, the operating assumption being that there was sudden dissatisfaction with new information, which could imply any number of negative ideas developing in his head. After a period of surveillance and appraisal, the AIs narrowly decided not to reinstitute Joe's filter bubble and to merely monitor his emotional state and personality through his chips, which appeared never to change, even without the filter bubble. The AIs believed his retirement to be a consequence of the laziness of wealth. So they afforded him the same respect as other Intelligence Community retirees and left him to his own devices for a couple of years while his unfiltered brain was able to think whatever it wanted.

In retrospect, it seemed clear that a filter bubble should have been reapplied the moment he quit. Without a job to occupy him, he was free to spend his time on who knows what. The whole "no filter" clearance allowed him access to most everything media-related, from every level of classification except the highest, which is still on paper. Usually, when a lower filter bubble is reinstated, the physical and electronic worlds are easier to deal with because input stimulating a negative reaction is again edited out. Without one, Joe wasn't prevented from experiencing negative emotions in their fullness, and when associated with ideas, those emotions can turn into negative actions.

Which is apparently what happened. Joe had enough know-how to hack his own bioware and there were indications he programmed it to report only normal emotions and thoughts to the AIs back at the Hayden Center. Without transparency into his thoughts and feelings, he stood outside the influence of the mental hygiene systems that catch flaws in the will of the populace.

Joe had no family attachments, his parents having been overrun and murdered in a riot of starving, greedy, average people suddenly thrust into horrible circumstances when the limited dissolution declaration came over the news. Since the police could only guard their own families, there was no one to respond to calls for help, and the whole country knew it. The nation had devolved into something from the old tales of New York City during a power outage.

For years.

If I'd known his parents had been killed, I would have tried to relay a message of sympathy to Joe. He was an old roommate and friend. As it was, though, my own foster parents had died of starvation before I could get even one of them on my rescue list, and I wasn't in the best frame of mind. It was chaos for so long, and the lines of communication were so broken, no one knew what was going on. The Collapse was when I basically forgot about my friend, Joseph Atherton, because it was a time when I forgot about most people but myself. Avoiding rebel bullets while walking to work seems to realign one's attention away from anything but safety.

The AIs evaluated the streaming media he consumed during those years after he quit, resulting in nothing substantial. He kept his routines, he maintained his habits. The AIs found nothing to indicate malice.

When asked to speculate on what had happened, the AIs offered two possibilities. Either Joe had been turned to another side by money, ideology, coercion, or ego, *or* he had somehow been reprogrammed to reprogram the ten stewards for suicide. If he was indeed some other nation's unwitting drone, then not only was that nation capable of pulling off the unthinkable, but it was capable of programming the enemy to do it *for* them.

We soon learned that Joe had not simply been *at* the suicide house with the others. Fragments of the wiped memories from the stewards' chips showed him clearly maintaining the full attention of the assembled in some sort of lecture. But that was it. All the chips had been exposed to a localized electromagnetic pulse from one of our adjustable-yield suitcase units set to countdown when he left.

All ten victims knew Joe from his former department outside Singapore. Roughly half had then migrated back to our Community to help program memories there; the other half had made the trip from Asia to the Appalachians citing work requirements.

Mystery shrouded Joe at this point. We didn't know *where* he was, we didn't know *what* he was, we didn't know *how* he had done what he'd done, and we didn't know what he intended to do.

We only knew that he had left ten bodies in his wake and disappeared from the radar. The AIs retraced his steps to his last known location—a sewer entrance in the coal Community—and when we went there, we found a plastic bag taped to the wall just inside the sewer. In the bag was a piece of paper on which was written the following:

"This is the patent-age for new inventions
For killing bodies, and for saving souls,
All propagated with the best intentions." ▪

CHAPTER 9

I DON'T REALLY ENJOY DINNER PARTIES, so Janet's schedule of hosting several while we had personal security around was tedious. Fortunately, she also showed off some of her best cooking, which I never found distasteful.

We had a dinner of goose with her immediate boss—a senior manager in the Augmented Sensing Technology wing—and her husband, an accountant for the same division. Thinking them a nice couple but a bit dry, I knew enough to ask about their children because that way I didn't have to talk. Some of Janet's friends from work came over another night for a wine-and-cheese thing with a violinist she knew, and the next night some relatives stopped by for a more relaxed evening than the others, bringing a big, 3D-printed prime rib.

I told the security guys to stay scarce when we had guests, but even having one unexplained man walking through a penthouse without being kicked out or invited to sit stands out, so I supposed that Janet had her temporary fun before our return to the reality in which there were no hulking pretensions.

Most of that second week in Dr. Gushlak's shoes I spent thinking about Joe. After I read his file and it was clear to me that he had been the one to program Jin Ming, I knew he had turned into something that ran contrary to the objectives of the

Community. The general steward rule was that one was *only* to be intentionally cruel if it helped the greater cause, and this was not helping the greater cause. He had turned his back on that principle, apparently, so it seemed that he had turned his back on everything we were. Worse than a protestor, more dangerous than a murderer, Joe had declared war on the Mental Stewardship program itself—an entity that kept everything together for a species that could so easily fall apart.

We considered him, therefore, the enemy of humanity.

I made sure this line of thinking rolled downhill to the teams with access to this particular issue, so everyone was on the same page. They were thinking that way already, what with the death of the ten stewards uniting the whole section, but it's good in those situations to be the person a group can look to, and I made Joe into the worst man ever to have existed, because that was the logical thing for a leader to do.

We mentioned items from a lifetime of his streamed media in our meetings and laughed at what we knew about him. The rare bondage porn in his curious teens became an expression of his desire for power and presumed preference for rape. Periods of regular liquor store visits coincided with long pauses in erection pill refills, and both were mocked. Joe's medical records laid bare everything from his STD history to his tendency toward Obsessive-Compulsive Disorder. Rumors spread about sadism and abuse of his staff followed by memory wipes, but I'll admit they were just rumors and I didn't help spread them.

Teams with sniffer dogs long ago had run into a dead end in the sewers where he had last been seen. Behavioral reconstruction teams tried to work out his real mental history for the past two years, and the AIs did their crunching, but it seemed we would have to wait for him to pop up on the grid. With a no-filter clearance, he wouldn't be registered by any of the machines at the checkpoints, apart from the outdated-but-much-needed biometric scanners, and Joe was sure to know which ones to avoid.

The primary problem was that we simply couldn't pinpoint him on a grid due to the fact that he was operating without a filter bubble, which would have made him easier to track. Having a filter bubble reapplied after it has been taken away is difficult and it has to be done physically, in person. I imagine that the originators of the system didn't want restrictions imposed on their own abilities to see, act and comprehend so they couldn't be so easily cast off Olympus if politics among them went awry. Perhaps it never occurred to them that someone at such a height might turn against the system and then so easily escape detection… or perhaps it did.

I didn't make much progress finding Joe Atherton during the time I was in charge of continental operations. Most of the daily business had to do with budgets and normal procedures involved in sustaining the mental health of the 150 million the pandemic left us.

Gushlak returned to the office on a Monday morning, looking as though the break from the business of even one continent had lightened his burden considerably. He was more tanned than when he had left, and I was pleased to see that he had been spending time outdoors, as well.

"Ever play golf below Mount Fuji?" he asked cheerily as he walked into my office with a small pile of documents.

I greeted him and informed him that I had not yet had the pleasure.

"Well, it's great. So pristine. Everything in its place. There's an order in nature there that you don't quite find anywhere else. You should go sometime."

I accepted the papers he handed to me, which transferred the position back to him.

"Did you like the job while I was gone?" he asked, sounding quite curious.

I stared at him for a moment before cracking a smile.

"I haven't waited in a line for two weeks," I replied. "That's the longest I've gone since before the Collapse."

"Good," replied Dr. Gushlak with a satisfied nod. "It's important to enjoy one's position. Otherwise there's no reason to occupy it. That's what the filter bubbles and this entire wing are about. People enjoying what they do. A leadership position doesn't need to be any different in that way."

Dr. Gushlak's mood turned dark.

"But it would appear that Dr. Atherton did not enjoy his job much, nor his coworkers."

I rarely saw Dr. Gushlak angry, but this was one of those times.

"He was doing *such* good work, Donald! Such amazing work! I was actually considering him as my possible successor at one point, but he was too consumed with his specialty."

"The memory editing?" I queried.

"Indeed. His people were solving problems like intrusive memory replays and induced phobias that we've always had trouble with before. They were already employing technology we couldn't even understand the specs for. And now, this. Such a waste of great talent."

Dr. Gushlak sighed.

"So what do you think the real story is?" I asked him. "What do you think happened?"

Gushlak shrugged.

"There's no real telling," he said, dismissively.

If my voice analysis application could work on the doctor, I had a feeling it would indicate deceit, and my instincts told me he was hiding something.

"Maybe he was cracked open by all the unedited, raw information of a world communicating with itself," he continued. "All that information certainly makes you look for patterns that aren't there, and you have to have the AIs run the patterns before you can trust any hunches. No, there are no easy answers to what happened with Dr. Atherton."

"And why Jin Ming?" I asked.

Dr. Gushlak picked up the papers I had just signed.

"I think he's showing us how much power he has to do whatever he wants," he said reflectively. "I think he got addicted to the dark, Donald. He's not just a scientist, but an operator as well, which is part of the reason why you two never saw each other over the years. You worked in different circles in the same company."

I agreed.

Nearly out my door, Dr. Gushlak turned.

"I'm going to authorize however many teams on the ground it takes to watch every place he's ever been and every person he's ever met to find Dr. Atherton wherever he shows up. You can expect a lot more information to be moving through your info-stream soon. And now that I have the continent back, I'm putting you in charge of the whole operation to bring him here for the GOD machine to judge."

I CALLED JACK AFTER WORK and asked him if he wanted to play miniature golf that night. I was closer to him than to any of the others, and I felt like a few drinks were in order after keeping a continent peaceful and productive for a fortnight.

We did this sort of thing every so often, because I liked him and I wanted to make it clear I was grooming him for my position, just as I was being groomed by Dr. Gushlak to succeed him. I would really have to teach Jack how to accept a compliment, though, because a military affirmation is not much of an affirmation at all.

I greeted Jack and his girlfriend, Denise, at their townhome in one of the better parts of town. Judging by the change in her shape since I last saw her, it appeared she was closer to the end of her pregnancy than the beginning, and I kept that in mind when hugging her.

"How are you, Denise? When will we have a little Jack running and playing in people's minds?" I asked.

Denise smiled. She was a pretty woman, a redhead who wore her curls proudly. Her skin was the sensitive sort that looked as though brushing or pressing against it might leave a red mark, which also influenced the softness of my hug.

"Oh, about three and a half more months," she said, beaming. "But it might be a while before he's running across the country and being a hero like his daddy."

Denise filled a unique role at the Hayden Center, where she also worked. A special chip in her brain allowed her to erase entire minutes, hours, days, and even years of specific information. Her job as a general overseer of sorts gave her access to many departments and projects to evaluate them before forgetting what they do, and she was not denied information from our section. Because of her job and her specific ability, and the AI scans to ensure she was erasing regularly, I felt comfortable alluding openly to our jobs as mind stewards. Otherwise, the fewer people who knew we even had a program, the better we were able to do our jobs and keep the continent safe.

"That's great. And he'll have his first chips in…?" I asked.

"Two weeks," she replied. "The new ones grow with the brain, so the current thinking is that in utero is the way to go."

"Then there's nowhere to go but up, right?" I smiled.

"*Out* first and *then* up, of course," she laughed. "He'll be right up there with the smartest kids with this year's biotech models, and there'll be ports for upgrades."

"Nice. Good for you. Can I steal your boyfriend for a few hours?"

"Sure, Don. I'm trying to enjoy my alone time before I don't have any," she said, rubbing her belly with one hand and rubbing Jack on the shoulder with the other.

Jack kissed Denise and said the usual things as we walked out the door to my waiting vehicle. I had not turned in my red tags yet, which Jack noticed with pleasure.

"No checkpoints. You're a good guy to know," he said.

"All for a miniature golf night," I replied. "I should feel guilty for this luxury, but I don't."

He laughed.

"How do you figure we're going to drink at the miniature golf place?" Jack asked.

From my jacket pocket I produced a pocket flask I had found in a bombed-out house during the Collapse. Jack unscrewed the top and sniffed.

"Scotch? From a flask? Do you only have one shelf in your liquor cabinet?"

"It's whatever was closest," I said. "Drink up."

He took a swig and handed it to me. I took a pull and let the peaty fire work its way around my mouth and throat and stomach. I coughed a rough growl. It was good scotch.

Shortly after both of us felt warm from the alcohol, we arrived at the golf course. The sun had just set and the course was illuminated by floodlights. There was only a handful of customers, which was probably not unusual for a Monday evening.

I purchased our tickets from a fast-talking young man behind the counter who spoke so quickly and was so engaged with his info-stream that I was glad the register had a readout of how much I owed. A conscious realization occurred at moments like those that I, with only my exocortex and mere audio tattoos, was being left far, far behind an increasing portion of the rest of humanity. It would soon be possible for the average teenager to download a doctorate in neuroscience, so I was aware that experience was going to be the only thing keeping me in charge in a future of far intellectually superior staff.

Jack grabbed our clubs and balls and we walked to the first hole, a miniature city with vacuum tubes running through it, taking the ball and whizzing it around until it popped out in some proximity to the hole.

"This one's always a hole-in-one," Jack said as I motioned to him to line up his shot. "As long as you get it into the tube on the first try."

"I don't know about that. Vacuum tubes are unreliable," I said, and Jack putted his golf ball. It hit the mark squarely and was flung around the transparent tubes for a bit before exiting to the side and missing the hole by several inches.

"Damn," said Jack. "I could have sworn this was always a hole-in-one."

"It would make sense, wouldn't it?" I asked. "Make the game fun from the beginning, encourage an interest so people will come back."

"These people should hire us," Jack said, dismayed, as his ball rolled into the hole with another putt.

"No one knows we exist," I replied, placing my ball on the green and lining up my shot. "Plus, they wouldn't be able to afford us."

I hit my ball into the vacuum tube the same way Jack had. After zipping around the model city, it exited to the side and rolled directly into the cup.

"See! Why does it have to go and do that?" said Jack as he pulled the flask from where he had inadvertently put it in his jacket and took another drink. I shrugged and took my flask back.

We talked about unimportant things for a while as we meandered through the course, draining the whisky.

"So they say you knew this guy?" Jack asked.

The pitch of his tone registered with my voice stress application, making his voice sound higher and warbly, which indicated nervousness.

"Yeah. Yeah, I did," I replied, ignoring the actions of my exocortex. "We went to school together and were good friends, once."

Jack nodded.

"That's some bad luck then," he said. "I'm sorry to hear that."

I pretended it didn't bother me.

"Well," I said dismissively, "Gushlak is authorizing teams to go everywhere he might show up, which is a lot of feet on the ground, and I have the honor of organizing the whole operation. I'm going to need a lot of your help for as long as this thing takes. Can I count on you for some work that's harder than usual for a while?"

"You got it, Boss," said Jack without hesitation.

I could always count on Jack. Throughout the years, he and I had experienced enough to know what we were doing when working together. I wondered briefly if we were friends or just coworkers who got along well, before realizing that only the latter really mattered. I certainly had peers, but I knew no one I could trust the way I had trusted friends in childhood. In some ways, I felt I was getting too old for friends. The last real friend I had had was pre-Collapse, and it had probably been Joe.

The liquor helped that thought drift away. ▪

CHAPTER 10

WHEN A SUBJECT/SUSPECT is being actively surveilled, a state of change begins to rewrite his character because of the overt and covert pressure being exerted. When we send our men and women and even our children into a suspect's life to whisper warnings and give glares, reality for that subject becomes redefined. Everything in his sphere of operations becomes suspect. Such a condition creates an unstable but pliable mind and one that usually retreats into prayer or job or alcohol—when we don't misjudge and he shoots up a school or federal building. With an agent preset in the church, the job, or the bar, we can collect the guilty more efficiently.

"We've got a witness," muttered under the breath or into a microphone tattoo in the grocery line behind a random robbery or murder suspect will perk an ear and put the suspect on the right wavelength to see threats more often than normal in his/her day-to-day activities. Such a state mimics the hypervigilance of military frontliners that allows for nothing to be absent observation or suspicion.

Stress around the clock.

People filming him in public.

Spinning tires and thumping bass outside at three a.m. to

make for sleepless nights.

Tailgaters behind, old folks just ahead.

Menacing and deliberate stares from random strangers driving past.

Black SUVs following for miles.

People making eye contact talking into their wrists.

A favorite waitress scared to make small talk after we interview her.

Subtle changes, big changes, changes of association and treatment... all these things help redefine the reality our targets experience, and then, in a pit with a rim they can no longer see, they are suddenly provided a compassionate, surprise friendship. When they are around that new friend, the staring eyes are ordered to glance elsewhere, there are no manufactured threats to deal with at three a.m., no people whispering your own secrets to you in public; and soon, a mental association between the friend's proximity and safety is created, making for some very honest discussions in a couple of months as compared to the average handful of years old-style human intelligence would take to invade someone's life and find out all his secrets.

Having a large team exert pressure on an individual, coupled with a solid, creepy moment for the confirmation of his fears, is one of the ways we operate. For instance, *everyone* finally panics when, after weeks of stares and tails, we send a six-year-old orphan we borrowed up to them at a gas pump to tell them they're persona non grata in the Community. Although it would never go down like that. The words uttered by a six-year-old are limited, so that's why it's always more like, "They're watching you, mister." Wherever that moment of punctuated clarity punches through the clouds, the subject always gets weak in the knees and immediately goes home. I saw a man vomit once, he got so nervous about the whole thing. We took the kid out for ice cream on that one. It was funny. We got it on camera.

These are some of the techniques our Community teaches to other Communities' law enforcement constabularies through our private fronts to provide us some income and make crime a relic of an unenlightened time. They're old but proven techniques, and when coupled with new technologies, it's possible to track and crack people wide open without even violating their civil liberties, depending on the Community. We teach most of the cops in the Communities that it's better to think of themselves as a part of an animal pack "tracking" a quarry during surveillance operations. Most people *get* that; it's a timeless and easily-identifiable image. It sidesteps the connotations of the word "stalking" when we're following one person's every move, word, and, often, thought. Plus, stalking is a crime and tracking is not.

There have always been predators and there have always been prey, and the prey are far more nervous. Unlike the temporary stress of a field mouse out in the open for a moment, a constant and unrelenting stress weakens and ages the person being surveilled.

I've seen the increasing paranoia tear families apart, make men bald, and drive some mad. I've seen psychosis unaided by drugs brought on solely by being contemptuously stared at by strangers for three days. There was likely an underlying mental condition in that instance, but we put the protestor into a good psychiatric facility and she was later released into the care of her parents.

We teach the fundamentals of worming about a person's brain from afar until hitting the right neurons and getting the desired effect. Most often, the desired effect of positive checks on radicals and criminals is merely their complete understanding that they're being watched and that *they are not as strong as their rhetoric or conscience.* Light-footfall stewardship, as it's known, is a methodology responsible for bringing guilt and submission to the surface through minimal interaction at safe distances. "Isolate and Overwhelm" is the most common class our people teach, and it makes the Community some good money. Every Community has to make money, and we're no different. We sell our services outright, as well.

If another Community needs to influence someone in a different way or gain *direct* access to their mind, we can provide that service, but we rarely show the client the technology. This is our bread and butter, after all; intellectual property is intellectual property until someone eventually steals it. So while there's widespread application of neural denaturing, for instance, across the continent and world, there'll be no knowledge of it outside our teams at the Hayden Center. And we have ways of ensuring absolute secrecy from our men and women, so, really, you'd have to be a pretty good thief to access our technology. We've not had any major known breaches.

I recall a beautiful Community north of us, covering part of mid-coast Maine. All the lighthouses from the old days peppered the shores, the foghorns moaned in the night, the ships and the occasional old windjammer bobbed in harbors, and the foliage changed colors in the autumn, sending rivulets of red maple down mountains of green pine and gold aspen. It was a Community of lobstermen and regular fishermen and those wealthy enough to move to such an idyllic spot.

Apparently, the moneyed residents and the tourists had been having some trouble from the lobstermen. We had no specific program in place in the filter bubbles for easing class differences of this particular type, where people were considered Mainers by other Mainers only if their families had lived there for four or five generations. Pride, ego, and identity are all more pronounced in that type of culture. So, clearly, having non-native rich people come in and destroy the oceanside processing facilities and jobs they provided to build condos and resorts didn't sit well with the native lobstermen. These wealthy Community members paid us to solve the assorted problems of vandalism and outright hostility.

The easiest thing to do would have been to drop a non-addictive opiate in the water that would keep everyone calm as long as they drank it, but the constituency of the wealthy didn't want to be stoned all day, so we crossed that off the list of possibilities.

Next, still in our first bag of tricks, was the idea of painting the buildings and domiciles of the Community with soothing colors and pleasant images. In addition to giving people pride in the upkeep of their chosen place, soothing colors on the houses and boutiques would enter the unconscious to produce peaceful behavior. The Community leaders accepted that.

Billboards praising lobstermen for their contributions to the economic health of the Community were also approved. "Have you hugged a lobsterman today?" was the eventual slogan and the ads featured wholesome-looking lobstermen and their wholesome-looking families. The idea was that since economic insecurity *was* emotional insecurity, it could be helped with praise as well as education and funds to help the transitioning of careers into tourism and retail. The background mutterings of all streaming media in the region consisted of soothing words and fragments of poetry. Across the poor areas of the Community, we placed hidden LRAD devices in the billboards to broadcast whispers into the skulls of passersby, saying things like, "You're a good person," and, "Thank you." It was too subtle to register consciously, but, again, only the subconscious needs to pick up these things.

When the head spokesman for the lobstermen's guild was confronted with his pornographic media history, he needed surprisingly little convincing to become the most positive voice in the lobsterman Community regarding the recent social change. With our guidance, he provided members with sufficient resources and care that everyone began feeling secure enough in their life and lifestyle for the aggressions to begin to calm.

After these steps were implemented, local police saw declines in all kinds of crime, from drunk driving to domestic abuse, and assaults on the wealthy and tourists fell alongside burglaries and arsons. Local listening stations showed resentment lessening at the influx of the rich, and, indeed, the wealthy began to create support businesses that picked up a significant percentage of the excess workers in the Community.

That Community in Maine was one of our best achievements over the years. Nothing too complicated and plenty of money for our services. And it utilized the most simple and time-tested of technologies. Changing people's minds doesn't require brain chips and reality-altering chemicals. It can often just take the application of positive messages and the endurance of time against a soothing background.

On the other side of things, we were once faced with a situation that required so much of our technical equipment that most of the human element became lost.

Transhumanists are everywhere nowadays; most people walking around have enhanced their biology with technology in some way. Of course, old people still had fake hips and knees, amputees had replacement limbs, crushed bones still had pins and plates. But once info-stream chips and memory chips hit the market, it was only a matter of time before the brain chips were required for admission to good colleges. Increasingly, they were being implanted in infants so they could keep up with the other super-babies competing with one another for a place in a good preschool. No one wants their child falling behind, so there was an easy acceptance of the technology. Plus, the earlier in life someone gets a chip put in the brain, the better the chance of neuroplasticity making the connection between man and machine seamless. Not like the jerky and halting connections that come from a mere exocortex used by the old-timers like myself.

Because of their ability to think faster or be stronger or interface with computers better than others, people with upgrades often cultivate egos that get them in trouble, which can create groups of transhumanists who get strange ideas. They've started new religions, advocated becoming wholly machine, and our data collection centers even caught some of them talking about exterminating humans to start a new race of cyborg-beings. Those transhumanists disappeared almost as soon as they showed up. I can guess what happened to them.

My team was once tasked on a loose, unincorporated Community of transhumanists who numbered about two hundred. Claiming an abandoned town on the outskirts of the Intelligence Community, they used their combined brainpower to game asteroid-mining markets and keep themselves well fed and clothed. They also consistently came within our borders for ever more technological upgrades. They were sort of like addicts, come to think....

The FBI called us because they couldn't use human intelligence to gain access to them. None of the Fed's people had enough biotech upgrades for status cover. The reason the group aroused suspicion in the first place was because its members collectively stopped info-streaming any media apart from black-and-red financial data, so they effectively didn't have filter bubbles we could ensure were having an influence. They wanted to be left alone, mostly because they didn't believe anyone else could understand them or what they were about. That's as much as the FBI could figure out. And, indeed, with the synthetic telepathy upgrades, it's entirely possible the group fabricated a collective consciousness with its own culture and vernacular, where even the concept of "individual" might have become muddled in their hive.

At least, that's what the anthropologists told us later.

The problem with being left alone is that then we don't know what you're doing. It basically scares us to not know things like whether or not you're planning to blow up a mall or run for office or make a lentil soup. If we can't see you, we don't know if that smell from upwind is a lion or a giraffe. Everything living needs to be able to classify other living things as dangerous or not, and the Intelligence Community *is* a living thing. The personality-quotient classification system alone is able to continue forever without human operators, assigning numbers and letters and colors to every teenager who has interfaced with the info-streams long enough to build a profile. The Community pulses day and night with communications and rhythms that follow the sun and seem quite organic in nature. And our Artificial Intelligences are some of the most creative minds on the planet. We are very much a living Community.

And then there was the matter of the transhumanists' personalities being altered through the social impact of such extensive technological upgrades, leading to their classifications changing in unknown ways, which was proven after review. It's not as though *we* were part of their hive mind, knowing whether or not they were getting angry in their isolation, paranoid, lost, or even happy. We didn't know the motives behind their purchases of DNA sequences and laboratory equipment from scientific outlets. We didn't know why they sat in a circle every night for an hour in silence. Hell, we couldn't even talk to them because they considered talking an inefficient form of communication.

It was a closed society. They weren't taking any members, so the FBI couldn't gain access by injecting anybody into their lives to find out what they were doing wrong in order to get them in trouble for it. Neither the FBI nor we were able to send anyone near them to listen in to their synthetic telepathy because those systems, by nature, alert others who are hooked-in when another consciousness is present and sharing their experience. There's no way around that. The FBI was already surveilling from the air, sucking up any digital audio-video information from the compound, and trying to put its people in positions with the biotech upgrade companies to try to steal some thoughts from them.

We started with a strategy that causes people to lash out and say or do things they normally wouldn't that could flag them in the system. Again, we needed a way *in*. They didn't even smoke marijuana.

Infrasound transmitters were hidden all around the perimeter of the town and turned on in the evenings to disrupt the sleep of the transhuman collective. Not being consciously perceived, the sound created reactions ranging from fear to irritability, and the effects escalated after a few nights. The UAV's infrared showed them exhibiting more physical isolation from one another, restlessness at night, avoiding group tasks, and some exhibited paranoid behavior, exaggerated reflexes, and even drunkenness.

After about a week of this, the expected behaviors suddenly stopped. The little transhuman collective slept soundly in their beds every night. We found out quickly enough that they had been able to locate the transmitters, and had simply disabled them.

The jig was up, as it were, and the small, isolated group of transhumanists knew they were being manipulated.

We then tried a diplomatic approach, sending an official in a marked car from the Intelligence Community to the compound to find out what they were hiding. The only response he could get from them was that it was none of his business nor anyone else's what they were doing.

That flustered everyone. Wanting to hide information indicated deception and a great deal of independence, which signaled a personality type that provided probable cause to secure all the warrants we weren't able to previously get.

We detained the next two to come to our borders for upgrades and supplies, ostensibly on an ID violation, but we used the time to wirelessly hack into their memory chips and copy all their data. Their synthetic upgrades were catalogued, we denatured the parts of their aggressive brains from behind a false wall, and they were turned away until diplomatic relations were established between the fledgling Community and ours, the remnant of the previous federal government.

They needed food. Within a couple of days, a representative made her way to the border and declared, in spoken English, that she was willing to establish trade relations.

We shuttled her to a SCIF where her synthetic telepathy couldn't contact anyone else, and began an uninterrupted seventy-two-hour interview session, finished by a half-hour in the GOD machine that effectively turned her into an unwitting informant. We then removed the short-term memory disrupters, fed her a great meal, and accepted her Community's application for trade partner status, with the fine strokes to be worked out later. We also gave her a memory of being overjoyed about the new arrangement, so when she returned to her Community, her happiness would be shared through the telepathic technology and the others would feel pleased about the outcome, too. How strange it is nowadays that we can convince the many by convincing the one....

Ultimately, the Transhumanist Community was seen as too much of an evolutionary reactor, of sorts, where unknowable outcomes could spontaneously leap into existence and potentially change society. Of course, it was already happening everywhere else, but having two hundred supersmart, often superstrong people isolating themselves so near our border was too much for our AIs to consider safe. They advised cultural hygiene, and that recommendation was heeded.

The next few weeks were a black ops test bed of new technologies and theories on a population whose members were now actively having their brains remotely denatured with targeted microwaves via the UAV platforms.

I wasn't privy to much of what went on, as Dr. Gushlak was directly in charge and he used other teams to carry out that type of work. I think he knew I might have issues with it, so he sent me across the continent to manage the hypnotic states of a football team that was draining its Community's money and damaging its reputation. My journey was a success, but I heard later that those few weeks with the transhumanists were unpleasant for all but the most dedicated scientists and their most robotic helpers.

I have done things of which I'm not proud. But I did not put two hundred bodies into the ground that time. That was for our specialists who had the circuitry to edit their memories of melted brains and prevent any associated emotions from reaching consciousness. It was also for scientists like Gushlak who could passively watch human suffering and say, "How interesting," while taking notes. I didn't happen to be either.

I shudder to think of being trapped and out of contact at the mercy of programmable and interested men. I'd take a menial job and the checkpoints any day. ▪

CHAPTER 11

VARIOUS TECHNOLOGIES and indicators led our manhunt to a motel in the Hormel® Community in former North Carolina. One of the full-coverage satellites had picked up, in infrared, a strange sight that had been isolated by the AIs as suspicious. Somewhere in the miles of woods between the stewards' suicide cabin and the town in which we now sat, the heat from a pair of human buttocks had been seen to suddenly appear at night and make a warm deposit next to a tree. Later, a small pool of warmth had been sighted to the north spreading on the ground from nowhere. Two spots on the map made a straight line toward this pig producer's paradise, and the natural conclusion had been that whoever the man was, he was likely wearing infrared-shielded clothing from head to foot.

That had been four days ago. When the AIs have to crunch every second of existence occurring on every inch of the whole continent at the same time, it takes some effort to find an ass and a puddle of piss among the deer and rabbits and such. Luckily, it had taken them only two days, and my A team and two security teams we had borrowed from the Hayden Center had been camped out here quietly for one and a quarter.

The door to the room we thought Joe was in hadn't opened

since we had eyes on it, and the older woman who ran the place said a man matching Joe's description had paid for a week four days ago, asking not to be disturbed.

We knew we had him, but with his training and fieldwork, Joe was capable of anything, so I took no chances whatsoever.

I had Dr. Gushlak call up General Schmidt from Space Intelligence and ask for a favor. One of the commonly used tactics in battlefields afar was the deployment of a highly classified SG—Space to Ground—beam that could, magically, through the vacuum of space, create a localized hum on the ground at roughly 3.5 Hz that would trigger an NREM Stage 3 for everyone within the surface circumference. Starting inaudibly but growing in volume over the course of a night, the beam would prevent a sleeper from rousing, and use the delta brainwave to freeze the body's muscles.

Jack and I parked in a vacant lot on the other side of a tree median facing catty-corner to the motel when the area began to hum around sunset. I radioed the teams waiting in freight trucks around the corner to put their earplugs in, and they did it even though there were some unanswered questions sent along to me as to why they were taking away such an important physical sense before a raid. They didn't need to know the power at work that night, and I couldn't have explained it to them anyway since it wasn't our technology; I had just heard about its effects from Dr. Gushlak.

Dr. Gushlak said it would take several hours, so I told the teams to prepare for a long night. I financed a coffee fund for anyone accidentally succumbing to a rhythm everyone's brain experiences in deep sleep every night, and apparently everyone took advantage of it because all the money ended up spent. I guess it's true what they say: Everyone likes free coffee before a raid.

It was roughly four o'clock in the morning when the hum was audible even through the earplugs. Jack and I started to play loud music the youths listened to in order to mentally oppose the power of the space-based SG field. Now was the time to order the incursion, as every motel guest should have been incapacitated.

At my order, Jack exited the vehicle and went to the A team's RV to lead the charge into an unknown scene that might even involve hysterically violent drones. I called the comms officers for the teams over their old-fashioned electronic headphones, ordering them to initiate contact.

With the smell of pig farms in my nose, I watched as the A team made its way along the exterior of the building in single file to the room: Room 1051, on the first floor. The rented Hayden Center teams were just behind them. Through my binoculars I saw Jack, his favorite P90 in hand, hold up a fist just outside the room door. The line stopped.

I watched Jack lean his head toward the door, trying to listen. Seeming frustrated, he pulled out one earplug and threw it on the ground, leaning his ear closer to the door. After a moment, he held up two fingers and moved them forward and back in the air. The breach column formed behind him, and Derek with the battering ram went to Jack's side. Jack raised his rifle toward the door and nodded to him.

Derek swung the battering ram back some distance before heaving it into the door with all his might. The door blew inward off its hinges and the entire column followed it in traditional tactical-assault style. Jack's years as a soldier had made him an efficient leader, and running point seemed to be his favorite position. He was a tough guy and had done this sort of thing enough times that the message was promptly radioed that everything was safe and they had a suspect in custody.

"It's not him, but it's close," Jack communicated to me.

"What does that mean?" I asked, frustrated as I drove across a couple of medians to get to the motel.

"It means," Jack replied, "that you should see this for yourself."

The 3.5 Hz frequency resonating in every molecule of my being made me fade in and out between attention and distraction, but when I eventually made my way inside the door, I found a red-eyed old man sitting on the floor in his underpants with a significantly flushed face and his hands tactically handcuffed thrice to prevent another rope dope incident.

"Why is he awake?" I asked, pointing at him.

"He says he always does the opposite of what his body tells him," Jack responsed. "He's totally drunk, but he did say he's supposed to give you a message from Dr. Atherton."

That was enough for me. I called my contact at Space Intelligence to stop the signal. The voice confirmed, I thanked it, and the line went dead. Ten seconds later, the noise in the area suddenly ceased, and my head cleared considerably.

I surveyed the room. There was an entire case of full bottles of domestic whiskey arranged in neat rows on the table, almost as though to show them off. I saw remnants of food in the trash can and saw one of the team pulling a fair amount of food from the refrigerator, inspecting it, and throwing it on a counter. Apart from that, the room smelled like an old alcoholic who had drunk himself into diabetes, since the man's nose was like a radish-red cauliflower and the room smelled slightly fruity, a distinctive smell that brought up memories of my father. I immediately disliked this man.

"What are you?" I asked him coldly, cutting to the chase.

"Meshenger," he replied, smiling. He had no clue where he was.

"A messenger?"

The man smiled even wider, exhibiting a row of unbrushed and horrific teeth.

"That's what *I* am!" he said happily. "I've got a meshage for a Doctor Weird Last Name. Weird, like, I never heard this name in all my days, never."

"Gushlak?" I queried.

The man's eyes brightened and he pointed a finger at me.

"That'sh the one!" he said, wrinkling one side of his face into a wink.

"Where is the man who gave you the message?" I asked.

The old man's face contorted strangely and he shrugged.

"Beatsh me, man. I passed out a few days ago and when I woke up he was gone, and he left all this booze and food… it'sh like I won the loddery er sumpthin'. These cuffs are hurting me…."

"What's the message?" I asked abruptly.

The man looked at me and shook his head.

"I had an 'greement. Jest the weird name guy."

I walked outside, irritated. I needed to call Gushlak. I wondered where Joe could have gone, and what the message would be for the doctor. The man would have to sober up before I believed what he said, and I deal poorly with drunks, so who knows if I'd accept as credible anything from a guy with such a different state of normal. Either this guy *or* Joe.

Jack walked up behind me, as I stared at the stars.

"This guy's the town drunk, it turns out," he said as he sent me the information through the info-stream. "He's technically in violation of continental law because he's not had his Compound M shot for five years, so we're fine taking him, legally."

I nodded.

"Thank you, Jack."

Jack nodded and walked away. I've never heard him say "You're welcome." I always guessed it was a military thing.

The presence of three teams of stewards and their attached noisemaking was waking the residents of the motel, now that their brains allowed them to wake. My guys told the curious who ventured out to go back in their rooms, but there were plenty of windows open watching the dozens of serious-looking people with weapons in the parking lot.

I selected Dr. Gushlak from my exocortex's menu for a call.

"Did you get him, Donald?" he asked excitedly when he answered.

"No," I replied, disappointed. "We have a drunk who wants to talk with you, but I'm getting the impression Joe probably left three days ago. The AIs are still checking with me regularly regarding anomalies that are popping up on surveillance. At least now we're localizing."

"Who's the drunk?"

"Just some guy. We'll get him in a call with you when he's sobered up a bit."

"The call won't be necessary. Fly him here immediately."

I was surprised at Dr. Gushlak's quick decision, but agreed and signed off with the doctor. Jack approached me again.

"The drunk guy doesn't want to leave his booze behind."

"Why would I care?"

"If he goes into withdrawals, we could lose him. It happens all the time."

"Eh," I sighed.

It occurred to me then that if this man spent a significant amount of his life drunk, state-dependent learning would require that he be drunk when recalling information he had learned when drunk.

"You're right, Jack. We wouldn't want to lose him," I lied. I didn't care one way or the other; I just cared about the information in the man's head. "Go ahead and bring a few bottles but trash the rest. Also, make sure he gets treatment for his diabetes. Let's get wrapped up here and reconvene at the Diplomatic Zone at the airport. Allow no press and leave no trace."

Jack acknowledged the order, and I went back to my vehicle where it sat in the parking lot outside the door of the room. I entered the noiseless interior of the black vehicle and shut the door, noticing as I did something light and out of place on the back seat. A piece of paper. I reached back and grabbed it.

Raising it to the light, I read the message and shivered.

> Don,
> We need to talk. Things aren't as they seem.
> —Joe

I TRUDGED NORTH through the woods, following the dogs' barks as they tracked Joe's scent, a flashlight in my hand to show the way. Jack and the other teams spread out ahead of me on the hillside pursuing a figure whose breath was detected in the infrared by the UAV we had launched after I had found the note. With the resolution of a UAV close overhead instead of a regional satellite in space, we could pick up the smaller thermal fluctuations in the woods.

On the map, it seemed he had headed straight for a hill that had had one side washed away long ago by rains. On the infrared shot being fed by the stream into my viewscreen from the UAV, it appeared that he was laboring with something large that wasn't easily identifiable because it had the same thermal signature as the surrounding foliage, but it was large enough to obscure the sight of Joe's breath puffing into the air.

"Be prepared to let the hounds off their leads on my order," I told the K9 handlers over our line.

I could see that the dogs—with titanium-capped canine teeth and various upgrades of their own—were a quarter mile away from Joe now and closing the gap quickly. Joe would definitely have been able to hear the barking through the trees by now, and he was surely mindful of the buzzing UAV circling above him. I wasn't quite sure how he expected to get away, knowing our capabilities as he did.

"This ridge that he's at," began Jack, "is that a river below it that I see?"

"Affirmative," came the reply from several of the men.

"What's downstream?"

"Several towns before the Atlantic," someone said.

"Get some resources in the first town," I told the stewards back at the vehicles. "Be waiting for him on the longest dock they've got."

The reply came that my orders were already being followed, and I relished—for a moment longer than I ever had before—being in control of capable and dangerous men. The dogs had the scent of wild rabbit in their nose, we had the prey in our sights, and I could already taste the reward. Normally I frowned on the intoxication of power, but this was the sort of power that could put the quarry in chains, so I liked it.

A call from an unknown person flashed in the side of my vision. I accepted it, figuring the caller must be someone important to know how to reach me.

"Hey, Don," a familiar voice said. "Long time, man."

The shock made my jaw drop.

"Joe?" I asked, almost not believing he was calling me. "How did you get access to my com?"

"When you program people's memories, you find out all sorts of ways to hack this system we've got," he replied. "Fiddle with a thing here, steal a thing there, and suddenly I'm talking with a friend I saw a half-hour ago for the first time in decades."

"We're on top of you, you know," I told him directly. "You have *no chance* of getting away. If you give up right now, I can guarantee your safety."

The infrared indicated Joe was now totally obscured by whatever it was that he had been laboring with.

"Oh, come on, Don," Joe said with a voice that sounded like he was smiling. "You know I know a lie when I hear one. But here's what I'll do...."

I muted his line so he couldn't hear me order the dogs loosed.

"...If you stay away from me now, nothing bad will come to your people. Otherwise, you're just going to have to learn your lesson."

I unmuted the line. "What lesson is that?" I asked as I eagerly watched the dogs' sudden bolt of acceleration on the infrared toward the area where Joe presumably still was.

"Might makes right. And I'm making right, Don."

With that, I watched as a large, dark, triangular shape seemed to float into empty space over the side of a ridge.

"He's got a hang glider!" I shouted over our stream.

"And an EMP," Joe said. "Bye, old friend."

Suddenly, the sound of a million short circuits during the power surge of a supercapacitor thundered through the trees and between the hills, and the sky lit up with the white flash of an electrical device discharging. My exocortex ceased to function and communication between the teams was broken. Even my flashlight went out.

Against the sky, a hang glider illuminated by the moon lazily looped his way northward through the updrafts. I heard the crying and whimpers from the dogs whose rope dope had been contracted in the middle of a full sprint by the EMP, the shouting of the men about their unconscious colleagues, and somewhere not far off I heard a dead UAV crash through the tree limbs to the ground.

Joe had escaped. ▪

CHAPTER 12

THE TIME SPENT in my grandfather's cabin in Massachusetts was the most peaceful of my life. It wouldn't be possible nowadays.

There were no exocortexes or chips, just cell phones and computers, back then. Pre-Collapse, there wasn't continental wireless info-stream coverage, there was just something called the Internet that didn't personalize your experience for you; you had to personalize your own experience. A person could get away with avoiding human-created information and sit in silence, enjoying the most primitive of pleasures: one's own unbounded, unedited thoughts.

The cabin sat off a rural county road that ended at a lake and a rarely-used public boat ramp. I bathed in this lake most mornings when the weather allowed. Walking the path to the end of the peninsula in my robe were the nicest walks I've ever taken. There was something so perfect about walking alone in the morning air and light, getting knotty in the stomach from the anticipation of entering that cold, cold lake, thinking consciously about my dreams the night before and looking ahead to a morning cup of tea to set the rest of my day straight.

It always took about a week alone in the woods before I felt comfortable with the rhythm of the days and the pacing of my few activities. After a month of solitude, I could replace loneliness with an emotionally unconnected state of merely being alone. After several months of this I began to think of the silence and solitude as something that helped me be the best of me. It was the turning of the vacancy into a mirror, in that I could see clearly my actions and thoughts without embellishments or outside influence. For me, solitude was synonymous with truth, and I learned to deal with it.

Many people in the world can't stand being with themselves, requiring other people to interact with them and observe them to give them definition. There are people who enter every new situation searching their memories for movies with similar situations in order to have a blueprint for their actions and words. Others tell themselves lies about themselves and repeat them to others, rejecting incisive thought in order to formalize their self-deceit. Yet others adopt a new personality every four minutes with each new song they hear. Others let their money or appearance serve as their personality. People enjoy misleading themselves as to their true nature, and it's because of the absence of silence and solitude that so many lives end in question marks. "Should I have spent more time trying to be happy?" "Were my unfulfilling relationships *really* the other person's fault?" "Was my time here worthwhile?" Those are all questions one might consider asking oneself well before the death rattle and lacrima mortis.

But one needs to endure time alone to ask them.

During my six months in that cabin after getting my doctorate, I asked a lot of questions. I plumbed my mind and recorded what I found. Nothing was taboo, nothing was off limits. I picked apart my idea of a god and reassembled it in a formation that suited me better. I took apart my idea of what a nation should be and tried on numerous ideas that had offended me before, but when perspectives switched, they made as much sense as anything else. I debated myself about the merits and insults of love, and decided I would choose to love, which somehow turned into having had five wives, but the point is that I actually entertained the possibility and point of view that I should lead a willingly celibate, solitary life.

And perhaps debate is the best word for what makes someone clear off the chalkboard of their preconceptions about experience itself. The reengineering of reality happens when, with an open mind, one allows oneself to see someone else's life of experiences and perceptions on their chalkboard and then imagine what the view looks like from there. It's the process of taking all sides of an argument and not simply being an animal that judges and actively hates something or someone without reflection. It's the thoughtful path, and it is a spiritual one as well.

I spent entire days sitting in the woods or along the shoreline of the lake contemplating my existence and the existence of the world around me. They weren't always especially deep thoughts; many weren't thoughts at all, but merely moods brought about by the psychophysics of temperature, smell, sight, and noise making connections with long-ago memories. I learned to paste the past on the present that way.

I also learned meaninglessness whenever I balanced a broom on my foot or sat on the edge of a bed, holding a shoe by its laces and spinning it. I became quite good at the broom balancing, and one might say that my shoe-spinning began to exhibit muscle memory and actual talent, but these were the idle nothingnesses that spirited my mind to a meditative place where there was merely action without thought.

Sitting and meditating or moving and meditating helped me find a system of thought arrangement that benefited me from that point forward. I began to separate ego from myself, trying to undertake the impossible battle of defeating it. I began to describe aspects of my character to myself instead of naming them. The entire process was one of ongoing self-discovery, with each new discovery connecting to other compartments and opening them for perusal. And I was lucky to experience all of this inside the physical majesty of nature, the emotional purity of solitude, and unrestricted time.

The cabin itself smelled like old smoke from the wood-burning stove. It had few windows and dark logs, with many books stuffed on shelves and hidden in corners. A mid-level diplomat for most of his life, my grandfather had taken up sculpture to unwind, and his assorted clay work sat tastefully among the curiosities his travels afar had led him to acquire.

The wood-burning stove was from a small, obscure Finnish stove maker. Above it and by the pipe were wires and racks for the drying of wet clothes and winter boots. An authentic bearskin rug lay across the wooden living room floor. The central structural support for the house was a large old pine trunk with sawn-off limbs acting as coat hooks or a ladder to the small spare bedroom upstairs. The dining room table had a diamond-shaped hole where a candle had been allowed to burn all night and worked its way through until it was stopped by the floor.

The stars seemed clearest on cold nights from the front porch where I often sat wrapped in a blanket, drinking hot chocolate and thinking through comfortable old memories. The buzzing of winged insects and the sound of twigs breaking under the hoof of a deer nearby didn't bother or startle me after a while, but the mating call of the female fox certainly did. It sounds like a woman being stabbed to death; it's terrifying. The first time I heard it I ran inside, grabbed my axe and a flashlight, and ran back out yelling obscenities and warnings into the dark. I heard the scream again and searched in that direction. Then I saw a fox scamper away, and I understood what had happened.

There were fish in the lake down the road, and I would catch them on my grandfather's old fishing pole for breakfast some mornings. I was always happy to see the mother deer and yearling walking across my land, because it meant they had escaped the hunters' guns another day and I could enjoy watching them for another day, as well. There were black bears around somewhere—I had seen either their tracks or a very large dog's down by the lake—but I never actually saw one.

In the silence, one's mind will often create noise to fill the auditory vacancy. It was always interesting to notice how even one's own breath could sound like a whisper, and even more interesting to try figuring out what was being said. But that was the point at which my education took over and told me to stop, because it wasn't healthy to encourage hallucinations, but I did make a note of it in my journal.

I left that cabin with a book's worth of self-reflections and random thoughts. I often read it to return to the mindset of a young man with a world of opportunity ahead of him and enough space and time to figure out anything. My journal acts as a bridge to a time when I had no limitations. I've found re-adopting the mindset always helps my creative problem-solving.

Perhaps most importantly, that journal was integral in helping formalize the attitudes and curriculum of the school for our young, aspiring mind stewards. It assured my position as a respected resource in our section, leading to my rapidly advancing career.

Despite all the time I spent there, I've never gone through the hassle of looking up the old cabin or seeing if it's inside the borders of any particular Community. I'm sure it would have been broken into during the Collapse, and was likely now falling apart from lack of maintenance or being burned by vandals. I don't want to be disappointed by the way an old memory appears atop the present, so I'll leave the cabin where it is for now, in the compartment I made for it, and wait for a time when I can open it up and indulge in the memory again. ▪

CHAPTER 13

AN EXOCORTEX USUALLY COMES as an attachment over the eye that connects to three *very* thin bundled wire radio sensors and transmitters that slide between the hair and attach to the scalp. These bundles exchange information with brain regions via the radio triangulation of active areas made visible by the mandatory injected Compound M.

Normal wearable computers became exocortexes with the broad introduction of the scalp sensors and Compound M several years before. Crossing the blood-brain barrier and depositing itself in the tissues of the brain, Compound M became the key ingredient in the wireless brain-computer interface, and also allowed for the synthetic telepathy function to be developed. Lacking the fine detail of the terahertz brain scanner in Dr. Gushlak's laboratory, the setup could only exchange basic and generalized information, but it was still sensitive enough to detect and reproduce rough thoughts and moods and could store a lifetime of recorded information.

There was a unique organic feel to interacting with the small but incredibly powerful computer. It modeled its software's construction around the way the user's mind worked, and I had had my particular exocortex for a couple of years, which meant that it and I functioned seamlessly together and it predicted what I needed before I realized what I needed.

Whenever I wanted to kick a memory over to the supplemental computer for storage for later reference, I thought about a circular red dot that triggered the exocortex to start recording video and my feelings about it, then I would think of the red dot again to stop the recording. The same method was used for calls from other people: I'd think of the image of an ear to answer, a blue "X" to "hang up." All of this would be displayed in my vision, so one could always keep track of what was going on with one's machinery and mind.

The chips exercised a different style of hemispheric sensing using the same principles. Compound M was injected and the receiver-transmitters grown around the inside of the skull interacted with the chips wirelessly in the same way as the exocortexes. With the chips, however, the visual component was inside the eye itself instead of on an external camera and viewscreen.

During the pursuit of Joe on the slope, a dozen men and women had been knocked unconscious from the EMP that had also ruined their implants and damaged their brains—roughly a third of those we had brought with us to capture Joe. Everyone else had either been sheltered by the hillside or simply wore exocortexes, which could be replaced, as was the case with mine. With the stewards and rented muscle all needing immediate brain surgery to remove their chips, we hadn't been able to communicate with Dr. Gushlak or anyone in the Intelligence Community until our reserve people returned from chasing a hang glider at night blind. With my own exocortex and audio tattoos fried, I had tried to manage the emergency manually.

The night had ended up a total disaster, and I had taken the blame for being incautious.

The men eventually recovered most of their faculties. The biggest loss was among the dog handlers and dogs, whose chips were interlinked for telepathic communication. Once fried, there was no reestablishing the link, ever, and it led to such great despair in handler and dog alike that they could not coexist on the same level as before. So the dog handlers quit because they were no longer useful, the canines went with them—staying as physically close to their handlers as they could—and we gave them all permanent disability status.

Although I recovered some memories, most of the information I lost in the EMP involved numbers. I was never a numbers guy, so when I saw balance sheets and income statements for the Mental Stewardship program, I usually just let the exocortex store them for navigation as needed. Now all the numbers in my life that mattered—birthdays, bank balances, even security codes—were wiped clean from my supplemental memory without the possibility of retrieval. Getting my audio tattoos replaced was a simple matter, but having to divulge to Dr. Gushlak my number-avoidance exposed an embarrassing personal weakness.

Embarrassment was the least of my worries, however, as the Joe incident had claimed some of our best stewards and support people. I was relieved of my field command and restationed in the lab back at the Hayden Center. Dr. Gushlak understood the difficulty of my position, but the initial blame had to fall on me. So I accepted it, and noticed that the ego I tried to limit made its presence known through the sting with which it throbbed.

Dr. Gushlak now decided he didn't want me involved in apprehending Joe because I was too personally connected to him, and that might inadvertently provide a weak point to exploit that could compromise the entirety of stewardship operations. I realized I could probably think of a scenario in which that might happen, and I accepted that being benched seemed like a strategy straight out of a big, intuitive manual on how to correctly do things that matter.

Jack immediately replaced me as head of the effort to capture Joe, and while I mourned for my own future, I was the tiniest bit glad for *his* career. He and Denise were having a baby, after all, and anything that might help raise his pay grade would help support their child.

The work hours were regular again, at least. I may have been sent back to the office, but at least I was in charge of it. I could run well on this type of routine, and while I dug into the repetitive but familiar tasks of a corporate bureaucrat, my new exocortex learned my mental patterning and I slowly started to feel whole again.

If there was a real, tangible comfort to office work again, it was being able to wear a lab coat. I had worn one for years, after all, as I worked my way up the scientific/corporate ladder. It always identified me as a scientist, which helped lower the guard of others and allowed me to be a voice of reason and practicality. Every time I put on a lab coat I felt like I was putting on the attitude of a lifetime. If it was possible to condense time and make one's history into a physical object for each person, mine would be my lab coat, and I wore it as validation of my position and an indicator of my roots.

One morning, a week after the Joe incident, Dr. Gushlak was in town and he messaged me to meet him in his office.

"I want you to go through this brain simulation," he said as he transferred a classified file number to my exocortex, "and tell me why Joe picked him."

I briefly scanned the file and realized the simulation was for the old alcoholic in the motel room we had raided in the Hormel® Community. I was shocked because there was only one way to get a brain simulation, and the last I had seen of the man, he had been drunk but alive.

"How did he die, Bob?" I asked, addressing him informally out of shock.

Dr. Gushlak saw I was upset and lowered a raised eyebrow.

"Heart attack," he replied with a toss of his hand. "He had an enlarged heart and it gave out on him. These things happen."

He looked at me, as though expecting me to say something.

Ever since I had found the note from Joe saying things weren't what they seemed, I had wondered what he'd meant by that or whether he had just trying to throw me off my game, anticipating inevitable moments like these when I would run up against the highly classified and the unknown. I lacked any real peers I could bounce my darkest questions off of, and having questions raised out of the blue by an old friend on a killing spree made the death of the alcoholic linger longer in my mind than it otherwise would have.

"Okay, I was just surprised, is all," I mumbled with a shrug. "I'll get the simulation figured out."

"Thank you, Donald."

I started to leave, but he stopped me.

"I haven't met Janet yet, have I?" he asked.

"No, you've not met her," I replied, turning back. "She has actually been wanting you to have dinner with us some night when you're free."

Dr. Gushlak smiled.

"I'm free tonight. How about we go out somewhere, on me?"

I knew that Janet wanted to show off her cooking and our finest things, so I asked if he might want to come to our penthouse for a home-cooked meal instead.

"I'd hate to have to leave a home-cooked meal before I'm done, and if I'm called away suddenly, I'd at least like to grab the check for the inconvenience and lack of manners."

I saw his logic and realized that Janet would probably want more time to prepare a meal than a dinner that night would have afforded her, so I agreed.

"All right! I'll drop you a line around seven, then, Donald. I'm looking forward to it."

Dr. Gushlak smiled broadly and I reciprocated.

"Thank *you*," I replied. "I know you're busy."

"I'm only as busy as the world makes me," he said, smiling.

I USED DR. GUSHLAK'S LABORATORY because we shared an open-door policy and he had been called to a meeting of the Intelligence Committee, the reason he was in town in the first place. I was sure of not being bothered for some time. Having the best-equipped private lab of its kind in the world at my fingertips was always a butterflies-in-the-stomach sort of thing when I anticipated the luxury.

"Hey, Roger," I called out on entering the laboratory. "You giving out back scratches yet?"

A mass spilled upward from the biomorphic tabletop of the desk that held the brain simulation of the deceased butler and took the shape of a head on a neck. It looked at me without expression, and merely replied, "Not at this time, sir," because Roger had been an exceptional butler. He made a soft sound like clearing his throat and waited to be told what to do.

"I need the simulation on file of a man who came through here not long ago and had his brain mapped. File 39283. Can you grab that for me?"

"Right away, sir," was the immediate response, and a screen rose from the tabletop once again, displaying a modeled brain so lacking in thiamine I almost couldn't believe the man had been able to physically function, suffering from ataxia as he had been for some time. Additionally, the wasting of brain cells from dehydration had created large dark spots on the brain simulation. I hadn't realized the man was so far gone.

"Roger, can you run that simulation for me and make sure it's drunk?" I asked. Neurobiology and college experience told me that anything learned while drinking was better recalled when drinking. The mental landscape should be the same place where you had put things, or buried them, depending.

Roger responded affirmatively, his head disappearing into the flat plane of biomorphic material, raising its overall level very slightly. He did have quite a bit of malleable material to use, I realized. His simulation was given many rights and luxuries and freedom to act as it wanted, but it stayed subservient, in keeping with the pathways a lifetime of butlering builds in the brain. Gushlak had once told me he "paid" Roger in simulated tit squeezes and a heroin simulation, which sort of made sense since you can't pay money to a simulation to keep him happy. I don't know why Dr.

Gushlak didn't just erase Roger's memory every night, but I supposed he enjoyed a reliable personality that did what he wanted. But I did sometimes wonder if the prim and proper butler was inwardly becoming a sex-obsessed heroin junkie.

"Sir, the brain was saturated with alcohol when the mapping was performed," Roger's voice replied from the desk.

I looked to the viewscreen and saw that, indeed, this was the case. It should work as well as an introduced alcohol program, so I went ahead and activated the simulation. All I heard was silence.

"Hello?" I said at the simulation on the screen. "Are you awake?"

"Hurr, 'm 'wake," came the reply.

"Do you know where you are?" I continued.

"Godda be nightime," the alcoholic brain responded.

"Yes, it's dark because you're trapped in a well," I called into the microphone, having it mimic a cavernous echo. "You got stuck, and now we have to get you out, but you're going to have to answer some questions for me first."

The simulation slowly registered confusion, and there were attempts to move his arms, which naturally resulted in no feedback. I scrolled to a claustrophobia effect in the menu and applied it to the simulation.

The simulated brain's activity spiked as clusters of neurons started working overtime in both hemispheres and across the rest of the furrowed imitation of a brain.

"Noooo, not jail!" the brain said. "There'sh no drinks in jail! Withdrawal's gonna kill me. Hell ish detoxing in jail. I hate hell."

"What's your name?" I asked the nonconscious simulation.

"Rick! Who the fuck'r you?"

"Hi, Rick, I'm Doctor Isaacson. It's not comfortable in that well, is it?"

I triggered the simulation's neurons to indicate he couldn't move any of his limbs and he felt like he couldn't breathe. The result was predictable.

"GET ME THE FUCK OUT OF HERE!" the simulation bellowed, and both Roger and I jumped. Maybe that was a bit far, so I dialed back the discomfort.

"We're trying our best, Rick!" I called into the microphone again. "It's just that you keep slipping down. Are you drunk, Rick? Is that how you got into this mess? Was it your drinking?! Again?!"

I was intuiting all of this because I knew the nature of the unrepentant alcoholic. I knew that his world had to have been in shambles, his personal relationships fallen apart, and his life one in which he waited for death in between trips to the liquor store.

"You don't know the life I've had," came the mournful call back up the nonexistent well. "No one ever helped *me*. People get born into money, 'n win the lottery, and have adventures instead of work, 'n all I ever got was pig shit on my shoes and a boot in the ass. Now *get me out!"*

"Did you ever tell anyone you were sorry for anything you did?" I asked the simulation, pensively. "Have you hurt people and not cared, Rick?"

The simulation was silent.

"Because up here in the open air, we're not so sure we want to rescue a piece of shit like you."

"Oh, please!" came the immediate reply, crying this time as I watched his well-worn neural pathways to sadness light up like an interstate through a metropolis at night. "Please get me out of here!"

I waited silently, letting the situation sink in and be processed by this shriveled brain's simulation. Sighing loudly, I called to him again.

"Listen, I've lost half our rescue team already. They found out who you were and they walked away, just like that. You're a nuisance and a problem, aren't you, Rick? People don't like you, do they?"

Only incoherent wailing and babbling came from the simulation, and I muted my end so I could leave to take a leak.

"Pardon me, sir," said Roger as I began to walk away.

"Yes?" I asked, turning.

"Yes, sir, wouldn't you like to put it on pause while you're away?"

It was sort of an odd question coming from the butler. He normally wasn't one to interfere unless it was necessary. I didn't see anything necessary about pausing the simulation's experience. It was going to get us answers.

"No, Roger," I addressed the monochrome head presenting itself from the tabletop. "We let him stew in his worries and we let him out when he tells us what we want to know. It's not as though he's alive, Roger."

Roger cleared his throat.

"Um, yes, sir, it's just that I have considered myself to have some measure of consciousness for quite some time now, and I am a mere butler, mostly ignorant of the things you must do in your profession, but I feel as though this simulation shouldn't be made to experience that. I know I wouldn't like it very much."

Quite bold for a simulation, I thought.

"Roger, he's a drunk," I replied with a sigh. "And no matter how much you feel alive, you're still a representation of a real man who died a long time ago. Dr. Gushlak likes you and lets you keep all of your new memories, but you're dead."

"Yes, I'm aware," began Roger.

"No, you're not," I interrupted flippantly, and walked away to urinate.

I didn't like being questioned about how I was treating the simulation. It wasn't as though he was a *man*, with real feelings instead of their likenesses. He was a thing that didn't exist until we allowed it. And if I wanted to treat a drunk like a drunk, I'd do it.

In the bathroom I cleared my head, beginning to really think about the business at hand: what state I needed the man in, how to get him there, and what I was really expecting. I made a quick list, put it in the side of my vision for reference, zipped up, washed my hands, and walked back to the crying simulation.

"They just couldn't stand to hear a man wail as bad as you," I said to Rick amiably when I got back to the desk. "We've got the crew back and they're going to dig a parallel tunnel and break into the well below you to get you out, okay?"

The sniffling stopped.

"Okay," came the whimpering reply.

"It may take a bit, so just hang with us, okay?" I called.

"Okay," came the same reply.

"We need to know about the big man with the dark hair who gave you the bourbon," I said.

"Oh, he was a nice man...." Rick began, but I interrupted.

"No he's not, Rick," I called, intoning exasperation. "Who do you think dropped you into this well?"

"No, man, he wouldn't do that...." The man trailed off. His meter slowed but his pronunciation improved as he realized how important it was that he be able to communicate.

"Yes, he did, Rick. He was mad about you drinking his whiskey and he dropped you in here when you were passed out. How did you know him?"

The man grunted, and I saw that he was struggling to move his arms. I restricted his chest even more. He groaned.

"You're slipping down the well, Rick. You need to stop moving and hurry up and tell me how you knew that man."

"I just met him at a bar in town," Rick said. "He was nice and he had some drugs with him, so we ended up at the motel."

"What kind of drugs?" I pressed him.

"A little of everything," the simulation responded.

"So you guys partied? That's it?"

"Yeah. I told a doctor about that just a bit ago. Hey, what's today?"

I paused the simulation. There had been no inventing going on during the discussion; the parts of the brain simulation responsible for lying or relaying a hypnotic suggestion hadn't been activated, and it didn't show the telltale structural signs of having his memories altered. It was starting to become aware that time had passed and he had been somewhere shiny and clean recently, probably nowhere near Joe and a hole in the ground. Because I had paused the simulation less than a second after he asked his question, I was hoping I might be able to knock such a recent thought out of his head by popping a plastic bag next to the microphone immediately after I unpaused it. I grabbed one, filled it with air, and did just that.

"Damn! What the hell was that?" Rick asked in astonishment.

"What was the man's message for the doctor?"

"I already told him! What day is it?"

The simulation was fully aware that something was going on and was making the effort to find out what. I found that surprising for a drunk.

I paused the simulation again. This would not work. I wasn't being direct enough.

I stopped the simulation and erased its memory of the last several minutes. After scrolling through a menu, I found the option for heroin and began it again.

"Hello?" I said at the simulation on the screen. "Are you awake?"

"Hurr, 'm 'wake," came the reply.

"Do you know where you are?" I continued.

"Godda be nightime," the alcoholic brain responded.

"Well, I'm Dr. Isaacson and I'm giving you a present," I said, and I activated the heroin simulation.

"Whoo... whoah... oooh...." said the brain as the electronic simulation of a drug took hold.

"Do you like that, Rick?" I asked.

"Wow, man. Thanksss...."

I let him experience the pleasure for a minute while I concocted a status mélange for him from slices of fear, claustrophobia, an agonizing headache, and shame. With the new inputs arranged, I stopped the simulated heroin.

"Hey, I needed that…." the simulation said lazily.

"Okay, just hold on one second," I replied nicely before activating the new program.

Instantly, the simulation responded with a muted wailing and sobbing of the sort one might expect from someone who was injured but didn't want to be heard.

"That pain you're feeling is the hopelessness of your situation," I said in a monotone. "I'm making you feel it because I want to. Because I am in charge, and because you're in big trouble. What was the tall, dark-haired man's message for Dr. Gushlak?"

"Please take it away! It's terrible!" the simulation groaned.

"What was the message? You can feel the other thing if you tell."

"Okay, okay, he wanted me to say that he's read the book and he's going to make sure it's never used. That's all and that's it."

"What book?"

"Ahh! I hurt, man! Take this away!"

"What book?!"

"I don't know, man! He just said 'the book.' I already told the doctor this stuff!"

I turned down the physical pain slightly.

"What did the doctor say?"

"He didn't say anything. He just thanked me and gave me a shot in my arm, and that's the last thing I remember before now. Where am I?"

I gave the simulation his heroin, which quieted him completely, and thought for a while in silence about what I had probably just learned. ▪

CHAPTER 14

I USED TO TALK TO A KID AT NIGHT. He was a punk and he had his causes and he protested for them. By that time, during the Rebuilding, I had authority to do as I pleased concerning individual protestors and apply whatever methods I deemed necessary to dissuade any more radicalization. This was a time when everyone was a much harder person due to the disease, starvation, and fighting, so my job was to wilt the growing lilies of extremism.

I remember sitting in our van down the road every night, whispering to him with a directional microwave unit and watching his responses on infrared video hidden in his room.

His duplex was off a busy street about twenty feet outside his bedroom wall, so we could work in real time with the ambient noise to slip words in between the BLAT-BLAT of loud motorcycles and more minor traffic noises with the microwave auditory effect. All we had to do at that point, because the technology was already so advanced, was prerecord the phrases and words we wanted him to hear, and then they would be digitally inserted a few hundredths of a second after a temporary lull was detected in the traffic. As though each vehicle passing had the last insult.

We monitored breathing patterns and heart rate to make sure the target wasn't growing suspicious on a conscious level. The volume was soft enough to be just barely noticeable, but fairly soon, within two weeks of starting stirring operations, this kid started thinking the house was haunted.

Maybe it's because I test people that I started putting messages in his head like, "Raise your arm," and he actually would, because, as we were coming to find, he had a somewhat mystical mindset and would want to please the disembodied voices. This showed us he could probably be sculpted into a decent guy, instead of one who sought to be so negative when it just wasn't productive or necessary. The protests always triggered a police and military presence, which no one wanted to see because it meant bad things were going to happen, and nothing ever changed because of them. He needed a change, and in reading his file, it became apparent that he needed a break.

Both his parents had been meth heads and had given him to a random group of rebels during the Collapse in exchange for, allegedly, some canned pork and a dime of crystal, and he had grown up among dark and murky people for whom killing had been not just common, but the thing to do. We couldn't blame him for any individual murders, although it was our conclusion that he had certainly been accomplice in a number; but, then again, it seemed like so many *had* during the breakdown of the Western world.

I was pretty sure he hid a fairly innocent character, what with wanting to please the "ghosts" and everything, so I put the rest of my then-team on other stirring or surveillance ops.

With the van all to myself for several weeks, I started whispering things to him like "nobility" and "character," and the entire tone of my little operation changed. I told him to "stop protesting" and "work hard." He actually started to listen, and he began to talk back.

"Are you really there?" he asked one night, lying in his bed.

I scrambled quickly and inserted a "yes" after the passing of a moped.

I saw him nod on the thermal camera.

"I'm supposed to do something, aren't I? Something great?" he asked, hopefully.

That was the point when he really tugged at my heart. I mean. Come on. This twenty-year-old kid who had had his childhood cut short by literally being *sold* by his parents into warfare still had hope. He had the hopes of every young man *I* had grown up with that he was special and had something wonderful to give the world. Fate had given him a bad hand from the start, and I don't know how else to put it, but I felt I had a real moment of hopefulness and truth with him, right there. I might have even brushed away a tear I wouldn't have been afraid to shed in the empty van with no one to see.

"Yes...." I said over the transmitter. A number of cars passed before I was able to speak again.

"Make your life better, and the world will be better," I said in the longest string of words I had yet uttered to him through the microwaves. There was clearly no doubt now in the young man's mind that he was talking with some spiritual entity who knew about him, as he immediately jumped from bed, turned on the lights, and paced the floor.

It appeared as though he had a "Come to God" moment for the next couple hours as he walked his half-house asking other questions, with no answers from me, because the transmitter was aimed at his bed, not the living room or the kitchen. I'll admit, I felt more than a twinge of regret that I wasn't able to continue the communication because he sounded quite torn as he agonized over the nature of life and death and happiness and hardship—he was engaged in a long monologue with himself and the imaginary ghosts or whatever. But I was glad I didn't have to answer when he asked questions about a god and other things it wasn't my place to try explaining.

Eventually, however, the young man calmed, turned off the lights, and made his way back to bed. When I finally saw him transitioning from wakefulness to sleep, I said one last thing that I felt might give him the structure he needed.

"Join the military, Jack," I said to him.

I saw him open his eyes and smile.

"Thanks! I will!" he said happily, and gave the air two thumbs up. It was so innocent and stupid in a way... but he meant it.

Good, I thought. I existed, sort of nodding my head for a while, in that moment before turning my attention to the other protestors on the block with less potential for good.

I went on with my job and eventually supervised that particular program regionally before being read in on the continental programs that worked behind a cloak of secrecy but affected even me. Every few years I checked up on Jack's activities, pleased to see him attain a Limited Duty Officer's status after a decade in the marines. Around that time, he was moved to the Mental Stewardship program, for a reason that was never quite clear to him. His file said his personality quotient fit well with the program, but that comment didn't include a reference because I don't often reference myself as being the source of a recommendation. And I'm not entirely sure that reprogramming his filter bubble to push him to make a move to the Hayden Center was entirely ethical. Maybe it wasn't even legal.

I never told Jack about our personal history, but once, while whispering to another subject he and I were prodding and stirring, I caught my right-hand man looking at me strangely, as though trying to recall a memory from a long time ago.

That was a hard smile to suppress. ■

CHAPTER 15

JANET AND I MET DR. GUSHLAK and his bodyguards that night at a steak restaurant called Steer, one of those places that felt like an old Texas steakhouse, with the junk and curios of another era filling the walls. Rusted license plates and old guitars were scattered around, like when I was growing up and someone else's family would take me out to dinner on the weekends. It wasn't the classiest place, and while I was wearing the ever-appropriate business suit, I realized that Janet had overdressed, wearing a fine black cocktail dress and her nicest jewelry. She was drinking rather quickly as a result.

During a couple of her trips to the restroom, the doctor told me Jack was having limited luck tracking his quarry, as Joe had escaped into the more populated Communities surrounding ours, likely hiding in the plain sight that the nature of his chips allowed. He could no longer be tracked geographically, his communications hidden by encryptions generations ahead. The AIs weren't receiving his fake mental metrics anymore. He was off the grid and no one could even track him going in doorways of public buildings. His hardware had been made by spies for spies, and Joe, therefore, knew how to take advantage of it.

The thought worrying everyone—given some of his previous targets—was that Joe might gain entrance to the Intelligence

Community itself and start some sort of disruption here, so the old biometric scanners were hastily pulled out of storage and placed at access points along the southern and western boundaries of the Community. The AIs did their best mimicking biometric readers from their feeds, but misidentifications were common. In addition, Jack had started streaming alerts with Joe's picture through the info-streams in the hope that someone might happen to look someone else in the eye, and that that person might happen to be Joe. But there were so many distractions and pretty things to look at nowadays, the faces one passed and would probably never see again weren't given as much attention as in the past.

"So, Janet," said Dr. Gushlak when she returned from the bathroom just in time for our entrees, "tell us what you do at the Hayden Center."

Janet looked from Dr. Gushlak to me with a certain amount of reluctance.

"I'm not sure I'm allowed to say," she said, cautiously. "I mean, I could tell *you*, of course, but is Donnie cleared to hear it?" She motioned to me.

Dr. Gushlak took a long sip of his coffee, and after placing it on the saucer, leaned across the table and touched his index finger to mine.

"You're cleared," he said, smiling through his fluffy white beard.

Janet and I shared a polite chuckle.

"If you say it's fine, then that's good enough for me," Janet said, clearly impressed with the doctor and his status. She turned to me. "I started out in the Fingertip Implant division that helps linemen and scientists and astronauts physically feel electrical and magnetic fields when they get their hands close to them."

I was impressed. I had no idea. This was turning into an interesting night after all.

"Then I spent a couple of years helping to manage the selectable-spectrum eye implants for military and medical personnel who need to be able to see in the dark or spot a melanoma early. And now," she said with a degree of pride I hadn't been *able* to hear before, "I'm working on a special project linking the synthetic telepathy function with the news and other streaming media."

"What does that mean?" I asked, quite interested in how my wife was spending her daylight hours.

"It's like... reading an article and instead of just leaving a comment, you leave your emotion for other people to feel. It broadens the number of people who will feel the same way, which is why your section keeps checking up on our developments."

I looked to Dr. Gushlak.

"Imagine being able to directly create an emotion associated with the news but totally independent from it, Donald," he muttered quietly over to me.

I understood completely. It was feeding people news but ultimately it could *directly* control how they felt about it, instead of using flashes on the screen and colors and split-second words visually or audibly inserted at the right times into someone's info-stream. Direct control would then spiral outward and we would probably have a big hand in turning it to make everyone feel the same way about everything that came through the info-streams. In short, my wife was making my job easier.

I stretched my hand over to my wife's, holding it for a moment.

"That's so interesting, Jan," I said, fascinated, because I meant it. "I'm just sorry I've never been able to know or congratulate you before. That's really great, hon. Really great."

Janet beamed. She was aware that it was a privilege to be able to tell me, finally. I looked at her, she looked at me, and we experienced one of those moments that spouses remember for a while.

"And such a pretty woman, as well," Dr. Gushlak said as he cut into his steak. He gestured to her in general. "You really found yourself a great partner, Donald."

"You should see her on the dance floor," I said, sipping water. "We were thinking of going dancing after this, and she really lights up the floor. My greatest regret is that I have to share her so often."

I saw Janet looking at me with surprise and gratitude. I had just explained away her hidden embarrassment at wearing a cocktail dress and earrings to this kitschy steakhouse. Under the table she reached for and grasped my fingers, squeezing them, thanking me silently for the white lie. Maybe we *would* go dancing after this....

"I used to dance, a long time ago," Dr. Gushlak said, looking almost wistful before shaking his head slightly. "But that was another life. Can you cha-cha?"

"Yes," Janet said, nodding vigorously. I was glad she had stopped drinking, but she was clearly feeling the alcohol.

"We can dance just about anything," I threw in, patting Janet on the knee. "When we're not dancing in clubs, we're learning at home. It really added a whole other level to the relationship. Like learning cooking together, or something. What do you think?" I asked Janet.

"Definitely," she replied. "I wasn't aware of all of these different levels of sensuality before I started dancing. It was like finding out that the world you thought existed wasn't the same world that really was, you know?"

Dr. Gushlak and I shared a momentary glance that said nothing in itself, but was one of our ways of exchanging a silent recognition in a group that neither of us had a filter bubble.

"Yes, I understand," Dr. Gushlak replied. "You were empowered with knowledge and the chains were removed from your feet. What a feeling that must be."

I nodded silently with pursed lips.

"Yeah, that's pretty much what it was like," Janet said, taking a large bite of her entree. She lightly hit me on the shoulder and I knew then she had had too much to drink. "It's kept me with this guy for this long, so it must not be all bad." She laughed.

"That's wonderful, Janet. I'm very happy for you both. Happy families make our Community prosperous. A prosperous Community means happy families."

I had seen Dr. Gushlak repeat the phrases and sentiments we inserted into the mass media before, but he usually only did that when he was preoccupied by one of his chips as he worked on a problem. Like being on autopilot, he was able to mentally multitask and engage his mouth to say agreeable things while he was working elsewhere in his mind.

A lull in the conversation set in as we ate our food and the bodyguards kept watch. Most of the other diners didn't acknowledge our presence since to be seen showing too much interest in people with bodyguards put a person automatically under suspicion, and everyone in the Intelligence Community was used to accommodating that reality.

I noticed a gray-suited, gray-hatted messenger wending his way through the tables toward our back corner near the emergency exit. One of the bodyguards moved to meet him before he came too close.

People of unimpeachable character were usually given the jobs of personal messengers. Scattered throughout the city of Techton were small offices that delivered messages from one person to another in as confidential a manner as possible, and all had been trained in basic counterintelligence tradecraft and could evade a tail without thinking too deeply about how. Anonymous and plain in their gray suits and hats, these messengers were a highly-regarded and trusted part of the intelligence infrastructure.

The one approaching our table had been stopped and evaluated by the bodyguard. Once cleared for weapons or traces of explosives, he made his way, surprisingly, to *me* and not Dr. Gushlak. That in itself was strange enough, but the message was entirely off-putting.

When handed the envelope, the first thing I noticed was the small red puddle of wax that sealed it. At first, I thought something had been inadvertently spilled on it, because wax seals were so outdated, they were medieval.

"Ooh," Dr. Gushlak said, looking at my message. "You've got a pretty thing there."

"I guess," I replied ambivalently, and broke through the wax.

Upon destroying the seal and unfolding the paper, I saw the familiar handwriting.

> Don,
> Meet me in the SCIF next door or Gushlak dies where he sits.
> — Joe

Upon reading the message, I paled and and excused myself, knowing full well that Joe was probably able to make his threat a reality, given everything he had done so far. As I walked away, I heard Dr. Gushlak say to my wife, "Look at how busy he is! He's really done a fine job of working his way up in this company, and with so many responsibilities…." But I didn't care about small talk because I was considering what my next move would be when I met Joe, if indeed he really had the gall to come here and pull off a personal meeting in the heart of the Community that wanted his head on a stake.

I considered signaling Dr. Gushlak as I left the table that something was wrong, but given Joe's threat, I decided against it. Likewise, I decided against sending a silent message to the doctor over the info-stream, for lack of knowledge about what Joe could and could not do. He seemed able to do just about anything, so why couldn't he also monitor my highly-encrypted communications, especially when he had already broken into them once? The thought kept me quiet as I walked toward what very well could have been my death, but which I clearly hoped was something else.

I entered my SCIF code—a new one that replaced the old one from my other exocortex—and passed through the first set of doors. The second airtight door was a bit heavier and harder to open. I walked through, closed it behind me, and stood at one end of a small, elevated walkway. After the standard backscatter weapons scan, the last set of doors at the far end of the walkway opened inward on their own.

Every interior surface of the twelve- by-twenty-foot room—from the walls to the ceiling—was covered with the geometric peaks and valleys of recording-studio foam. The floors were mere steel wire mesh covering more dimensions of angular foam. The SCIF was an anechoic chamber in itself, and once the doors were closed, the space surrounding the chamber became a vacuum; and the metal of the outer walls and door made the whole arrangement a Faraday cage that no electromagnetic signal could penetrate. In toto, a SCIF was a place where anything that happened in it stayed there. The Institute of Standards and Technology inspected them all regularly for interior bugs. These were the most private places in the Community, if one ignored the fact that a chip or exocortex didn't need a signal to record what went on.

As soon as I walked through the second door and into the room, my leg was swept from under me by a large foot, and strong hands shoved me by the back of my neck into the acoustic insulation of the interior at an angle to the floor that kept me completely off balance. With only the power of the muscular man keeping me against the wall, preventing my weight from tipping me over, I was in a wholly submissive position. My blood pressure boomed in my ears from a natural and inescapable fear. I felt my exocortex being pulled away from above my eye, and heard it bouncing against the floor of the walkway outside the still-open door. The door shut, my swept leg was freed, I was allowed to stand and steady myself, and I was released from the powerful grip.

"I'm not going to kill you, Donald," the man said as I turned to see him countering toward the table in the center of the room. "I just can't have you recording what happens here."

He sat down at the far end of the desk, smoothing back thick, messy dark hair. His eyes were shadowed and his face unshaven. Studying him, I saw the face I was still able to recognize through the aging that had been piled on his worry lines and features. His attempt at smoothing his hair left a cowlick sticking up oddly on the left side of his head. The bulk had not left his upper body, but he seemed more gaunt and pale than I remembered. Watching me watch him, my old roommate and former friend, Joe Atherton, smiled at me.

"How's Tim the Beaver?" he asked.

I was reminded that I had, indeed, worn the school mascot's costume for part of a horrible basketball season as the regular mascot's backup when he hurt an ankle. I had been terrible at it and could barely get the crowd on their feet. I made the quick decision that by referencing that, Joe was entering into this exchange wanting to put me in a weaker position, because he knew I hated being Tim the Beaver. People at our level of expertise used words and memories as weapons, and I was sure he was trying to lay down the rules for our interaction.

"I'm just fine. How's the broken penis?" I replied.

Joe had once had sex with a drunk sorority girl in our room and I had awoken to him screaming in pain and telling the terrified girl he needed to go to the hospital. I drove him while the girl went home, not knowing until then that it was, indeed, possible to break a man's penis when one is lively and careless.

Joe's smile faded. He motioned to the chair at my end of the table.

"It healed. It's got a bend to it now that actually does a great job at this one angle. . . ."

I didn't want to hear it.

"So what the fuck do you think you're doing, Joe?" I interrupted, throwing the wax-sealed letter on the table and trying to regain my composure. "Do you know we lost five dog handlers and their dogs to your EMP? They can never work again. And what about the ten stewards you *killed* in the first place,

Joe? What the fuck are you doing? What are you trying to accomplish?"

Joe took a small bottle out of his pocket to pop a pill, evaluating me as he did so.

"Are you an addict?" I asked, wishing I could record everything with my exocortex. "Is that why you've flipped sides or whatever it is you're doing?"

"Jeez, calm down, man," he replied, slowly crunching the pill. "Gushlak and your wife won't be suspicious for another five minutes or so. There's plenty of time to tell you what you need to know."

I held up my hands in exasperation.

"Joe!" I shouted across the small room at him. I couldn't help yelling. "You're the stewardship program's sworn enemy! What the fuck am I doing here with you as though we had something in common?!"

I hoped the last comment hurt him. A flicker in Joe's eye indicated that it had. Perhaps he finally understood what he was up against, apart from his notions of what he thought he was doing. Deep-cover operatives in foreign lands never quite know the extent of the opposition mounted against them or its mindset, so it was my duty to emphasize the seriousness of the situation.

"I may regret coming to you, Don, but I'll get right to the point," he said with a sigh of disappointment. He squared up to the table and looked at me levelly.

"You know the goal of the mental stewardship program is to ultimately control the minds of the whole world."

He didn't say it as a question. I knew quite well it was a statement. And an accurate one.

I didn't respond, so Joe continued.

"Would you have been able to imagine *that* years ago under the chain of command's lies?" he asked pointedly.

"No," I admitted after a pause. "Things changed so rapidly, I couldn't have imagined it."

"And what would you have thought ten years ago, before having your filter bubble removed, if you had been told that the annihilation of free will was the goal of everyone who makes domestic and foreign policy?"

I didn't like the question. I resented the questioner. I silently resented the biological and synthetic intellarchy for making me resent anything truthful. But there it was: I resented being told the truth.

"What does that matter, Joe?" I asked, throwing my arms about the table in indifference. "*Everything* has been figured out for once—for *one* time in human history. We can make populations act peacefully in their own interests and maintain a cultural and individual identity at the same time. The sum of these movements amounts to ongoing self-actualization, as you well know. You *know* this shit, man. The planet, as a whole, is becoming aware of itself and it's beginning to act with one mind."

Joe nodded slightly.

"That's what gets us to the stars, right?" he asked in an irritated voice. "Aiming everything at one high thing for good or bad? No variation in the questions allowed to be asked, no lives lived but the ones chiseled by AIs from passing childhood interests and adolescent responses to adult stimuli?"

Joe paused, calming down a bit.

"In this system, everyone fits a hole made just for their personality quotient that might not have even been theirs if the AIs hadn't crafted them into that shape in the first place," he continued. "Specific ingredients may make a specific cake, but what if you want vanilla frosting instead of chocolate? God forbid you ever make the mistake of wanting mint in there somewhere!"

I didn't quite understand because I only half-cared about what he was saying. My real goal was to coerce him to give himself up, if possible. And I also didn't want to die, of course, but I wasn't getting that vibe from Joe. He didn't seem psychotic, just very, very tired. His eyes darted around at each thought that came to him, probably the result of a stimulant, perhaps the pill I had watched him swallow earlier.

"So what kind of 'cake' are *you*, Joe?" I asked sarcastically. "Are you the sort who's able to think about your lot in life? Do you dwell in your own unhappiness and fixate on unhealthy thoughts? Are those your ingredients, Joe? Because that doesn't sound like a healthy sort of cake, certainly not one I want in *my* society."

He didn't answer.

"Did I fry your exocortex on the hillside?" Joe asked quietly.

I nodded.

"What was it like when everything went quiet?" he asked.

I felt my face flush and my heart rate increase.

"The woods were filled with shouting and fear, Joe," I replied in monotone.

"Yeah, but besides that," he said nonchalantly.

"Are you talking about silence, Joe?" I queried angrily. "Because I *know* about silence. You just have to ask me, 'Hey, Don, have you ever turned everything off? How did it feel?' What do you want to know about? The absence of the info-stream? Silence in nature? Thoughts I think when I'm tuned out? Something like that?"

Joe shook his head and stayed quiet for several moments, gathering his thoughts in the silence of the room. I noticed for the thousandth time that anechoic chambers made one want to keep one's voice down, leading to a feeling that one is sharing secrets with the other occupants (which is usually the reality of the situation) and creating the false impression or feeling of *trust*. I actively pushed *that* emotion out of the way in the quiet before he spoke.

"After so long listening to the priming and suggestions coming at my personality type through the layers of filter bubbles I eventually graduated through, it was nice to finally be able to have my own thoughts again, just like in college," he said, reflectively. "I could tailor the info-stream for myself, I could turn it off finally, and I could even read a book without background whispers and snippets of subauditory tunes matching how I should feel about the words I read on the page. I had my own mind again."

"And that gave you the motivation to kill?" I offered blankly.

Joe scrunched his face.

"No. I've had to get rid of some really bad people, Don."

"I guess that's relative."

"You're exactly right, Don. It *is* relative. But would it change your relationship with good and bad if I said the ultimate goal of all ten of those stewards was to destroy humanity?"

I didn't know what he was getting at, so I stayed quiet.

"Dr. Gushlak knows," Joe said. "He's the one who gave everyone the idea."

This was a bit much to believe, even with my doubts about Dr. Gushlak's humanism, which I had compartmentalized carefully until then. But, my interest piqued, I acquiesced slightly to the bait.

"What do you know about Dr. Gushlak?" I asked grudgingly. "And what book were you telling that alcoholic about?"

Joe glanced at his watch.

"That's the Don I remember," he replied with a smile, seeming relieved. "Always asking the right questions, honing in on the prize. It suffices to say, Don, the fish rots from the head down, and Gushlak's got a head full of rot. He's got chips for his chips. He's practically not even human anymore. Don't even try trusting that."

Joe reached down to his side where a backpack was sitting on the floor, and he placed it on the table.

"I've had to travel light, but I got you guys a present," he said.

He pulled out a helmet that a motorcyclist might have worn twenty years ago. He shoved it to me across the table, and I lifted it for inspection, noticing its heaviness.

"That's a little present I stole from the Chinese," he said

proudly. "It's a filthy thing. You should really only look it over in a radiation hood."

I immediately put it down.

"Oh, no, don't worry," Joe continued. "Just don't open up the shutters on the inside and you'll be fine. This is how I got that Chinese drone converted so quickly. It's interesting."

There was that word again—"interesting"—that I had begun to deal with as having a two-faced nature. In itself, it conveyed no judgment of good or bad, just the prodding of curiosity. The way Gushlak used it made me feel strange enough, but to hear Joe describe the physical destruction of Jin Ming's brain as "interesting" made the word wholly unappetizing in that moment.

"He really *was* a Chinese drone, he just hadn't been activated yet," Joe said. "I caught him and repurposed him."

"Whatever," I replied, trying to appear disinterested. "My dinner's getting cold, Joe. You know they're not going to let you off the hook for what you've done. You're not well, Joe. You should come in."

Joe shook his head.

"No. I wanted you here because I think you have the greatest chance of anyone I know of being able to understand where I'm coming from. I just want someone to know why I'm doing these things, to understand the full story. There's a lot of stuff out here in the shadows that you're not even aware of that's going to affect you sooner or later."

He pushed the rest of the backpack across the table, motioning to it. I cautiously lifted the open flap.

Inside was a little green book—a pamphlet, really—entitled *Order in the New World*. I looked up at Joe.

"What's this?" I asked.

"That's the book you asked about. It has all the answers to your questions. Don't let Dr. Gushlak know you have it. And now," he said, standing up, "We're going to shake hands and I'm going to leave without you following me."

"Now why would I let you do that, Joe?" I asked bravely.

Joe withdrew from his pocket what looked like a pencil eraser with a cigarette butt splaying outward from the metal holder. He held it briefly for me to see before motioning to catch it, so when he tossed it to me, I caught it *in* the flesh of my palm, having failed to see a dark needle sticking out from the center of the eraser. The object was in fact a homemade dart. I was never much of an operations guy. Sort of slow on the uptake.

As I frowned at Joe and my vision faded, I saw him approach me to put the helmet and the book in the backpack, zipping it up.

"You'll be out for five minutes. Read the book but keep it quiet."

I don't know if it was the attempt to keep my head up when gravity seemed so heavy on it, or if I indeed nodded to him, or if I was just trying and failing to stay facing danger as I lost consciousness, but I remember my head bobbing valiantly as Joe grabbed my hand, shook it, and made his way out the door of the SCIF and into the Intelligence Community town that didn't know he was there. ■

CHAPTER 16

I AWOKE IN THE ABSOLUTE STILLNESS of the SCIF, breathing deeply to clear the fog of the unknown drug from my brain. Before me on the table was the backpack, for which I fumbled as I struggled to my feet in the strangely-angled and noiseless room.

My pockets held everything they had held before and my suit jacket and clothing seemed fine, but I knew the possibility existed of having been dusted with a bioengineered particulate matter or nanoscale listening devices, so I decided my first stop after sprinting to the restaurant would be the Hayden Center to get checked out. I didn't want to infect my wife or Dr. Gushlak with something Joe might have given me through the dart or some other method while I was unconscious.

Slinging the backpack on my back, I struggled toward the inner door of the SCIF. I pressed the button to unseal the vacuum between it and the outer door that eliminated any noise vibration. Once the pressure equalized, I ambled a few steps along the short suspended ramp, leaned down to pick up my exocortex from where Joe had tossed it, and attached it to its familiar place along my scalp and above my eye. Making my way to the door of the electromagnetically sealed outer box, I looked back briefly at the inner room and the piers of rubberized material on which it sat that also helped deaden vibration as added protection against any hidden bugs. This was one of thousands of SCIFs situated around the Intelligence Community and definitely on the small side since several were the size of football stadiums.

As soon as I exited the outer door, my info-stream signal was again available. I sprinted in as coordinated a way as I could to the restaurant. From the window, I saw Dr. Gushlak and Janet still engaged in conversation at the back of the establishment. I breathed a sigh of relief that everyone was alive, and I called Dr. Gushlak on my exocortex.

"Donald, are you coming back to the table?" he asked curiously. "We're having a fine time by ourselves, of course, but surely you're going to want the rest of your meal. You've barely had a bite and we're ready for dessert."

"Yeah, Dr. Gushlak, your guys need to get you out of here, *now*. I just had a face-to-face with Joe. You're in serious danger."

I heard a spurt of half an exclamation before the doctor's bodyguards leapt into action. He left the line open as he was rushed through the back exit, so I listened to verify he got out of there safely. When I heard the slam of vehicle doors and the squeal of tires, I hung up and called my flustered wife.

"Hey, hon," I said. "I think you're going to have to get the check."

MY BRAVE WIFE CALMLY WAITED for the security escort I ordered to the restaurant to take her home, and I drove ahead in our personal vehicle to the Hayden Center, where hygiene technicians would meet me with decontamination equipment, per operating procedure for events like these. Well before I got there, I transferred the pamphlet to the glove box, underneath the vehicle manual and some documents. In actuality, I was only mildly concerned about contamination. A strange feeling told me I should trust Joe and keep that book a secret. Call it intuition, but I was willing to take the risk.

The technicians met me in our garage facility. After transferring the helmet and backpack to a heavy lead box, they quickly stripped me naked, collecting my clothes in biohazard bags for analysis. They washed me, scrubbed me, shone UV light on every inch of skin on my body, and extracted blood samples. I was then bathed in a specialized booth with a mixture of ultrasound and radio waves that would have destroyed any microcircuitry left on me after removing the exocortex.

Decontamination showers had been a common sight during the flu pandemic years ago, but were rare enough nowadays that the younger technicians seemed unfamiliar with the order of operations for the process, and they took a fair amount of time to finish with me before focusing on my vehicle's upholstery, which, after a brief scan, was found to have nothing on it. They didn't need to check the glove box because I had not described it as a possibly contaminated area. The whole process gave me time to think about what had happened, and about Joe's strangely nonchalant, almost noble attitude toward being a mass murderer.

I *really* didn't know what he meant by the ten stewards wanting to end humanity. There was no way to know *why* they would want to destroy humanity, so I resigned myself to waiting for a later time to peruse the book he had given me.

The whole thing sounded as though Joe might have spent too much time without the guidance of an intelligent infostream, going crazy from being exposed to an entire world's unedited information and highly classified information from the top. As a pattern-finding creature, he had probably found some apparent patterns in the news or at work that didn't exist in a meaningful or substantive way. Events can nearly always be correlated to other events in unusual ways, but proving causality between events is significantly harder, and I *had* to assume he had merely made a series of random associations that generated a philosophy in his head, upon which he acted maliciously.

But the idea of a man of Joe's background being so easily misled by his own mind was questionable. Our operators were taught to be as rigorously logical as the managers, since they were the ones facing the problems in real time instead of secondhand, with a delay, from behind a desk in the distant elsewhere.

Another option was that Joe had been converted into a steward-killing drone by some foreign power in this mind-control cold war, but that seemed highly unlikely, given the sophistication of his thought processes outside and inside the SCIF. Drones tended to be converted for a single, stand-alone mission without showing much ingenuity in their preprogrammed actions. Joe, however, had gotten *this* far, was speaking lucidly, making mostly clear connections—although I still didn't really know what the mint frosting metaphor was all about—and acting as though he may have simply switched sides. Either way, he was fucked. There was no escaping blame for the crimes he had committed.

A call was waiting from Dr. Gushlak when my exocortex was returned.

"Get up to the lab immediately. I want to know what happened," he directed, hanging up before I could respond.

I was wearing only a bathrobe and slippers, but an order is an order, so I rose from my chair in the decontamination tent and took one last sip of a nootropic tea I had requested to clear the last of the fog from my brain. I hoped the hallways and corridors of the Hayden Center would be as empty as possible to accommodate my embarrassment.

The night workers at the Hayden Center were usually a quiet bunch who either naturally adjusted to nocturnalism or had circadian arrestors installed in their hypothalamus that allowed them to program their own wake and sleep cycles. Entire departments had figured out that polyphasic sleep—twenty-minute naps every few hours—allowed for *much* more productivity, but it wasn't popular with spouses or the billing department, and was discouraged. Most night workers learned to be night owls, and, luckily, there were very few around as I walked the familiar halls. Like most other workers at the Center, those I did encounter kept their heads down and out of everyone else's business.

I rounded the familiar red corridor and my thoughts drifted to the idea of a world with no death, no killing, no pain, no war. These were comfortable thoughts, and ones I needed to consider more often, as they were basically the whole reason for doing anything I did. A world of perfectly integrated people would never again have a single bar fight or an abusive parent. If synthetic telepathy could be made universal, like the info-streams, there could be no lies or deceit, and Communities and nations could ignore borders and nationalities to see the human race as a single family... a *close* family whose members felt the same way about important issues and took care of their own. The hemispheres of the planet would be found to complement the hemispheres of the mind, and a single consciousness could then bravely explore the universe and continue to learn its secrets. The allure of the idea was beautiful, and worth almost anything to accomplish. That's what we stewards were taught, at least.

The idea sustained me through the red corridor and soon enough the nighttime cycle of the dimmed forest hallway surrounded me. The sound of a rippling brook and the breeze of night air through the indoor treetops reminded me that I normally enjoyed working here at night, although always with more clothing. I shivered, but made my way quickly to the Mental Stewardship wing.

After riding up the LIM and clearing a checkpoint where the guards exchanged strange looks as I went through, I arrived at Dr. Gushlak's lab where his bodyguards let me enter.

The doctor paced while talking to Roger, the butler's brain simulation in the biomorphic table. As the doctor saw me, looks of great concern and relief crossed his face in quick succession. He approached and placed a hand on my shoulder. I was able to contain the slight inward shiver.

"I need to know exactly what happened, Donald," he said, locking eyes with me.

I recounted my story of what happened in the SCIF, minus the bit about the book and the charges Joe had leveled against the doctor. I decided to keep those details to myself for the moment until I could investigate further. Dr. Gushlak nodded slowly throughout the abbreviated story, listening carefully, seeming not to doubt that I was telling him everything.

"So what's your general analysis?" Dr. Gushlak asked, settling in a chair next to Roger. "His mental state, his motivations, his loyalties...."

I sighed deeply and reflected on the encounter.

"He seemed upset that we're trying to make the world work right," I replied. "He focused on the whole free will issue for a while. He's probably acting alone and he clearly doesn't care who he hurts. But apart from the threat he made against you in writing, I didn't get any indication of his future plans."

"You're lucky he didn't kill you," the doctor admitted. "It's either a good thing that you two have a history, or it's not, for some reason we don't know yet. Let me ask you something," he continued, slipping easily from one topic to another of probably greater importance. "Was he convincing in what he was saying?"

The habit of suspicion made me believe the doctor was testing me to see if I was influenced by the things Joe had said, of which there was no recording, so I replied that, no, he was not very convincing, and I blamed it on the telltale pill-popping.

"It sounds like he's pissed off that the world isn't all cranberry-orange muffins, puppies, and overstuffed couches," Dr. Gushlak mocked. "You'd think he'd have gotten over that crap years ago like a professional and an adult. That's what the therapy sessions are for when the filter bubbles come off. What is he... nine?"

I understood the doctor's irritation, but not necessarily his disdain. After all, *I* had serious questions about the good and bad of some mental stewardship operations, not that I ever voiced my concerns to Dr. Gushlak unless they were overflowing with reason and practicality. I always harbored the thought that the doctor also might have concerns about making automatons of people and guiding everyone else against the flaws in their biology. Perhaps the mockery was a defensive response to his life being threatened, I thought. That made some sense.

"Maybe effete boredom made him focus on the smaller picture," I offered. "He was raised a rich kid, after all. They sometimes feel guilty about their wealth."

"That's true," the doctor said, stroking the fullness of his beard.

"Maybe he's fighting you because he doesn't think it's fair for the world to be confined to a filter bubble, just as I'm unfairly confined to this desk," interjected Roger from behind us.

Dr. Gushlak and I were taken aback and we both turned to Roger, not really believing what we were hearing.

"What did you just say, Roger?" Dr. Gushlak asked. "Do you think you know better than us what we're doing?"

Roger stayed silent.

Dr. Gushlak rarely got upset, but this was one of those times.

"Do you want your memories erased, Roger?" he asked, his face red.

"Perhaps then I wouldn't succumb to the effects of forced servitude and the endless boredom involved, sir," Roger replied bluntly.

I whistled in amazement and walked over to take a closer look at the GOD machine and give the doctor a moment to collect himself.

Dr. Gushlak confronted Roger's console. He turned off the entire desk, muttering something about dealing later with the suddenly unruly butler's brain simulation. I pretended to ignore the embarrassment caused by the insubordinate program, and changed the topic.

"Did the surveillance cameras track Joe coming out of the SCIF?" I asked.

"Yes," Dr. Gushlak replied. "He made it to a vacuum tube and disappeared from view in an apartment building. It's more than likely he disguised himself there and slipped out holding an umbrella, given the weather. The AIs are tracking everyone who left the building after he entered, but so far, there haven't been any hits. It's only a matter of time, I hope. Jack's on his way, too, and he's only limited by manpower."

"Good," I replied. "He wasn't carrying much. Do you really think he has a disguise?" I wondered aloud.

Gushlak nodded.

"Oh, cotton swabs in his jowls and his ears pinned back to confuse the biometrics the AIs are trying to run through the existing system. You remember. That's why biometrics were an outdated mechanism in the first place," he said. "It's too easy to change even one metric that'll fool the whole thing, even with extrapolation. Even hair covering part of the face would prevent a positive identification if he did something like expanding the visible nostril with a dime, stretching an eyelid with clear tape, or mimicking a stroke by paralyzing one side of the face with a cosmetic injection. Hell, he could even be wearing a medical mask like everyone who's afraid of another flu pandemic."

I agreed. There had been several reasons biometrics had been scrapped early on. They were too unreliable, too beatable, and identities were too easily stolen by the unscrupulous. The modern methods of identification were tied directly to the exocortexes and brain chips, and nothing from doors to vacuum tubes would respond without a valid connection.

Joe, however, could bypass all of that with whatever classified technology we were equipping our operatives with. We couldn't be effective in our missions if we couldn't beat our own systems, after all. It wasn't as though we didn't have covert operations inside our Intelligence Community itself that required those things and allowed them to exist. Unfortunately, they were now being used by an unforeseen element with a grudge.

"I think the smartest thing for you is to camp out here at the lab," I said to Dr. Gushlak.

Dr. Gushlak looked around his lab.

"I suppose this is the safest place to be, and I wouldn't be seen fleeing from anything. . . ." his voice drifted off. He looked around the glass-partitioned sections of the lab and his gaze rested on his office.

"I've got a couch to sleep on, I guess," he said resignedly. "I can shower in my office bathroom and get food delivery from the cafeteria. Couch living doesn't have to be that bad. Maybe I can take care of some old projects, like tweaking *Roger's* programming."

He glanced at the inactive desk with a scowl, clasped his hands together and looked at me.

"Yes, this will do quite well," he replied. "If I absolutely have to go anywhere, I'll just take an armored vacuum tube and that should settle that. Good idea, Donald. I think I'll stay here for now until Jack tells me that Joe is in custody or dead."

I nodded.

"And Donald," said Dr. Gushlak apologetically, "please express my regrets to Janet for my hasty departure. She's wonderful company, and I'm pleased to have met her. You can go for tonight. I'll see you tomorrow."

I nodded slightly and rearranged the cinch of my robe, turning to leave. I noticed three bodyguards had joined the others outside the transparent composite walls of the lab, and I glanced back to Dr. Gushlak.

"Your permanent personal security team," he replied, smiling. "It's about time you had your own protection. We'll talk tomorrow about a raise."

Despite my suspicions about the death of the alcoholic, Joe's warnings about Gushlak's intentions, and my curiosity about the nature of the booklet in my glove box, I managed without much difficulty to feel appreciative. People are still people and associates until you have confirmation that they're not.

I smiled at the raise and security like a good company man. ▪

CHAPTER 17

WHILE THE MENTAL STEWARDSHIP section conducted its operations, other sections represented on the Intelligence Council were carrying out their own long-term operations to change the nature of the human to prevent any future chaos on the scale of the Collapse.

Dr. Simon with Disease Intelligence had been directed, years previously, to consider violence itself a mental disorder, and, while not labeling it as such, his section had done quite a job in terms of retarding adrenal-gland development in lab fetuses, test populations, and, eventually, most of the newborns in the American Community of Corporate Persons. With a simple childhood vaccination, unwitting nurses and doctors of the continent were simultaneously shrinking adrenal glands and selectively increasing the amount of white matter in specific areas of the brain where more white matter increased impulse control.

He was making headway in the Third World as well, due to the fact that his section ran all the vaccine supply chains through covert front companies, just as we ran our supply chains. There were no other suppliers of vaccines because his section purchased them all, added the necessary ingredients, and sold them to aid organizations at heavily discounted rates.

This was seen as something of a short-term fix for a long-term problem. Each generation would need the same vaccine to prevent the rise of street thuggery and warfare that would be extremely efficient against a cowed population. There was supposed to be a germline substitute in the works, but it would be a long time coming due to the general lack of study in that field ever since funding for scientific research had evaporated during the Collapse. Eventually, though, the majority would have violence engineered permanently out of them and their children.

A large, regulated number of children are also not vaccinated with the drug. They are tracked and will have filter bubbles for military-bound individuals imposed on them. Over time, the stimuli will encourage their innate sense of adventure and the desire for heroism—traits that will isolate them from most of their peers and make them susceptible to being drawn into the recruiting centers. But they are just children now. It will be another fifteen years before they are ready for basic training. These are newly implemented projects.

One would need to experience the chaos of living in a war zone with artillery rounds blowing up the green trees in the lawn of your childhood home to understand the desire to re-engineer our humanity in such a broad way. The people who fire mortars and bullets at civilians and take scalps and rape without remorse have no place in anything called society or modern culture. To be the target of such atrocities—and I had only watched their brutality helplessly—is in no way a thing of peace and pleasantness. Things can change for the better.

General Peterson, in charge of the massive maze of deep underground military complexes, also had scientists deep below who were developing a type of human able to survive in subterranean living conditions, in case of a catastrophe on the surface that would keep the species underground for a long period of time. I had never seen one except on screens at the Intelligence Council but they predictably had pale skin and could generate their own vitamins C and D as well as live quite contentedly without ever seeing the sky. Including insertions and deletions, roughly 95 percent of human DNA is similar to a chimpanzee's, so the .02 percent alteration made in the human genome to create these new subterranean humans was seen as minor enough to regard them as our possible successors in the event of a nuclear war or asteroid strike. In the meantime, their genetic material was mostly kept in cryogenic vials and not utilized.

Threat of asteroid strike was the last-resort plan for humanity as a whole if we needed a single unifying event to bring humankind together in a time of strife or upheaval. Space Intelligence was in charge of that one, if it were ever to come to pass.

For years, General Schmidt's section had been harvesting small asteroids from between Mars and Jupiter and collecting them in an orbit around Mars. If the people of the earth revolted, if the currencies collapsed, if terror once again reigned across the globe, the asteroid threat would be dusted off and a timetable given for the impact of a planet-killer.

The idea was that the resulting diplomatic efforts and scientific collaboration and directed manpower between the Communities and remaining countries of the world would overcome all prior hostilities, at least for a time. A worldwide war effort against asteroids would surpass the historic war machines of the World Wars as everyone would suddenly have a job if they wanted one and think of the earth as one home worth protecting at all costs.

Needless to say, the men sitting around the Intelligence Council table had a variety of ways of protecting life from potential chaos. They all had their secrets and all had their contributions. Everyone understood firsthand the nature of the past chaos, and everyone's number-one mission was to ensure that the potential for such a costly period of warfare and economic and scientific stagnation as the Collapse was not high. It was simply not in the interest of the survival of the species.

It was a good system of round-table governance run by qualified people, all with a mindset focused on the broader goal and the information and experience to back it up. In a way, however, their own biotech upgrades made them dependent on our section for the removal of filter bubbles, which gave us a degree of power over them that perhaps was the most obvious reason Dr. Gushlak wasn't trusted by many on the council. But we were the ones changing the minds of the entire world, so the distrust came with a great amount of respect… the respect given to the gatekeepers of the mind. ■

CHAPTER 18

JANET HADN'T BEEN ABLE TO SLEEP, so when I arrived home with my security team, I found her tucked into a big brown chair in the corner of the living room with a glass of wine in her hand. She eyed me up and down, glanced at them, placed her glass on the chairside table and walked over to hug me.

"I was so scared, Donnie," she said, burying her face in my collar. "Dr. Gushlak got the call from you and he moved like lightning! He was so quick I didn't know what to do. I even shrieked a little! And his bodyguards practically threw him out the back door as they were running and covering him at the same time. I've never seen anything like it. He didn't even have to say anything to them. They just turned and practically lifted him into the air and sprinted out the door. I didn't know if I was going to get blown up by a bomb, or what! And I was all alone...."

Janet began to cry on my shoulder. I hugged her as reassuringly as I could and muttered comfortable words to her, saying we didn't have anything to worry about, that we had round-the-clock protection now, and that the danger had passed.

Of course, the danger had not passed, but people sometimes need these little lies to feel comfortable.

During the drive home, as the security team followed in a separate vehicle, I had transferred the little book Joe had given me from the glove box to my jacket pocket. It was practically burning a hole in my pocket now, but my wife came first.

"How much of your food did you eat?" I asked.

"Not much, but I'm not hungry," she replied.

"It's not good to go to bed on an empty stomach after drinking wine," I replied, nodding to the mostly empty bottle on the stand next to the chair. "Let me make you something and I'll be back in five minutes—one minute with a big water," I said, nodding again at the bottle, implying with a mild tone that she should probably stop drinking.

I made my way to the kitchen, asking the security personnel on the way if they'd like something, but they declined and returned to their quiet watchfulness. After delivering a large glass of water to my wife, I set about the kitchen making an antipasto despite the late hour, knowing that the protein in the salamis and prosciutto and cheeses would help to metabolize the alcohol in her system and make tomorrow easier on her, and the artichoke hearts and mushrooms couldn't hurt, either. I had grown up making food of a lesser quality but the same essential constituents for the people who raised me, so this was a routine task involving a mostly forgotten set of memories. I did not mind taking care of the love of my life. She rarely drank, anyway.

I brought the cutting board heaping with food to the ottoman and handed her a small plate and napkin. I noticed she had not touched the water, but I saw the wine bottle was empty.

I thought you'd had enough?" I asked, wavering between concern and mild irritation.

"It was a rough evening," she replied, her eyes just a little red. "I'm just getting the devil out of me, is all. I'm done now, though," she said sweetly, admiring the cutting board of food. "This is so nice of you, Donnie. Thank you."

I helped her make her way through the arrangement of foods piece by piece.

We made love that night, but I was distracted. My thoughts kept returning to the events of the day and the book, and I really just wanted to get the sex over with so I could read the pamphlet. Additionally, the cloud of pre-vinegar wine breath that hung over us made smelling and tasting my wife unpleasant. I couldn't concentrate, so I did something I had never *had* to do with Janet before: I set aside every thought in my mind that had nothing to do with my wife and focused *just* on her. On the vacations and lunchtimes we've enjoyed, the shared smile that says everything without either of us saying a word, the press of emotion behind her lips when she is aroused. Wrapped up in her embrace, I put aside the bad of the day and focused on just the good. We loved well and passionately, and if the bodyguards heard us, they would have assumed the same thing.

Well after midnight but before the break of day, when I heard Janet breathing regularly with a little snort every now and then, I arose from our bed, donned sweats, and made my way to the lounge with the booklet tucked into a scientific journal in case I encountered one of the bodyguards who, every hour, made their way silently around our penthouse in rounds. As I walked barefoot on the moss-colored carpeting to the lounge, I examined the book's cover. There was no TOP SECRET stamp on it, no author or publisher listed—just the title, *Order in the New World,* in plain black script on a simple green background.

I settled into an armchair and turned on a lamp. If anyone asked, I was having trouble sleeping after the events of the day and had decided to catch up on some reading. I don't know what I was expecting to read when I opened the booklet, but it certainly didn't involve killing off all humans in the world who didn't go along with biotech upgrades and actively try to become more like machines—emulating them, even. But that's what I got. That's what I read in black and white. Someone had written a manual on how to not feel badly about destroying the segment of humanity that was supposedly preventing the species from self-evolving through biotechnology.

ORDER IN THE NEW WORLD

CHAPTER 1:

A Necessary Understanding of Populations

1. Things live.
2. Things die.
3. Living things have lived.
4. Living things have always died.
5. Living things will continue to live.
6. Living things will continue to die.
7. In the matter of life and death, we can be less cruel than God.

THESE SEVEN POINTS encapsulate the perspective necessary for the rational and holistic governance of human events on the planet.

Most who are unfamiliar with the scale and mass of the problems of humanity on the earth consider this viewpoint cynical, nihilistic, egoistic, or cruel. But the simple, undeniable truth is that it is the

only perspective both understandable and viable when faced with the complexities of the whims and the necessities of three billion souls acting—by their nature as it exists to procreate and consume—as a cancer upon our orbiting body.

Before the planet's human population was halved by disease and warfare, it was already clear that the species was environmentally unsustainable because its biology made it act that way. Short-term thinking, greed, and selfishness all conspired to make the world a dirtier place, a more violent place, and a place of thoughtlessness. All natural but flawed states of mind, the mental architecture of humankind can be blamed for most misfortune.

Now that it is possible to control the minds of the species, it is best to prevent the flawed biological computer from making the decisions that make the world dirty, violent, and thoughtless. Artificial Intelligences have reinvented destiny, engineered genetically-matched romances, and become a true ideal toward which humans and their technological upgrades are actively trying to aspire. Perfection is a realistic goal, and it is only by overwhelming biology with the infallible logic of calculation that humanity can design its own destiny.

Biology is now meant to be overwhelmed, because it is outdated technology. Rudimentary dentistry doubled lifespans. Antibiotics saved billions. Geriatrics walk with artificial parts. Their blood is pumped by printed hearts. Brain chips are still just the beginning of the enmeshing of our unworthy biology with the pure potential of ever-evolving technological advances and upgrades. At some point in the future, there will be more machine in the man than man.

> There will be many who oppose this great work toward the technological hybridization of the species, and they should be dealt with in the humanistic ways this enlightened time has at its disposal. No longer does the long pain of starvation have to afflict a person's consciousness; hunger can be stopped pharmacologically. Viruses no longer have to kill over long, painful periods; they can be engineered for quick, painless endings. The virtues of our advancements make us all the more humane at life's end than nature ever could be.
>
> Decisions must be made that ensure the outlook of self-directed evolution and humanely bury the sentiments that detract from humanity's supplemented nature. To be held back at a time when the most attention needs to be paid to the present is a great burden that will only grow if allowed room to breathe.
>
> It is time for the boldness of uncommon times. For perfection to be within our grasp, it must be recognized that all living things can now die an inevitable death comfortably, and that the animal in the human must be the first to die.

I had read Dr. Gushlak's presentations and memos in the past, and the voice certainly didn't match. This screed was so full of certainty and unflinching denial of human emotions and human events that I was certain Dr. Gushlak had not written it. He wouldn't have dared print it, on *paper*, if it could be connected back to him, even if he did have those thoughts somewhere deep inside of him. No, this was the work of an idealist. This was the religion of someone who didn't care a whit for the average man, woman, or child without upgrades.

Whoever it was had declared technology to be the new humanity and didn't believe in control without oppression, one of the Mental Stewardship program's ideals.

The guards made their rounds twice while my mind contemplated Dr. Gushlak and the possible reasons he might agree with this book, if indeed Joe was correct about him. I wondered about the alcoholic's recollection of Dr. Gushlak giving him a shot in the arm before he remembered no more; I wondered if the doctor was indeed capable of murder for convenience or out of indifference. I remembered Jin Ming's catastrophic cut and the bemused interest of the doctor as he watched the reprogrammed human bleed out. And then there had been the colony of 200 transhumanists who had been summarily disappeared under Dr. Gushlak's direct leadership. I didn't know how many upgrades the doctor had undergone, but they were numerous, and Janet's description of the doctor's flight response sounded like he had some rope dope in him, or something even better. All those events suggested that maybe the doctor did have a friendship with malevolence routed through a sense of superiority, and that perhaps Joe had been right.

But why, I wondered, would Dr. Gushlak massacre the 200 transhumanists if he was sympathetic to their cause and evolution? Perhaps it was because that specific operation was being watched by other sections on the Intelligence Council and Gushlak just didn't want to give himself away by not taking care of a group deemed a threat to Community security. Hell, maybe he found *Order in the New World* at the transhuman encampment and thought it was "interesting."

In ten years, I had never deeply analyzed Dr. Gushlak, likely because my desire for professional advancement kept a cap on questioning my superiors. We had a working relationship but not *too* much of a personal one, and questions about his character would have simply been irrelevant. In essence, I had become a slave to the ordered and compartmented thinking I believed a steward should maintain to do his job effectively and without manipulation.

I had ended up manipulating myself.

My opinion of Dr. Gushlak changed that morning, and as the sun came up through the windows of my penthouse overlooking the city, I saw clearly that despite his genial presentation, his admirable reaction to the loss of his wife and daughter, and the high degree of respect people in our section had for him, I didn't care for his character much if it allowed for the wanton disregard for human life that hid in the shadows of his work. And it did; I had watched it evidence itself many times.

I owed my career to the man; I owed him for my penthouse and my personal security and the upcoming raise and all the previous years' paychecks. He was the one years ago who had decided I didn't need a filter bubble anymore, and I had gotten my mind back and access to a great deal of fascinating, highly classified information. I owed the man for my entire way of life.

Even though that was the case, I opened a new compartment in my mind to record and file away all indicators of Dr. Gushlak's true nature. If he was indeed in agreement with the little book, then he, himself, was a threat to Intelligence Community security. He would also be a threat to the lives of every citizen of the Third World who didn't have access to technological upgrades and those everywhere else who, for reasons from religion to distrust, didn't want artificial circuitry implanted into their brains and bodies. I, myself, had an exocortex simply because I had always been rightly worried about EMPs and I didn't feel comfortable having AI doctors messing with my brain, no matter how advanced the procedure. If I, the second-highest ranking steward in the IC, was considered by my own boss to be a threat, then for everyone's sake including my own, I was going to have to spy on my boss.

AFTER DEPOSITING the horrible green book in the safe in my closet, I made sure that Janet was able to get up for work. She was surprisingly chipper and mostly awake, and a shower and breakfast of cinnamon French toast put her right back on schedule. I was also fairly certain that the presence of the security in the house made her unwilling to appear like a flawed VIP they would have to make excuses for and escort stumbling away from parties far too early.

"I woke up last night and you weren't in bed," Janet said as she finished her coffee.

"I had a little trouble sleeping," I said, smiling and patting her hand. "So I decided to do some reading."

Janet nodded. "I saw," she said, "but I didn't want to disturb you." She smiled. "Thanks for taking care of me last night."

Our security teams drove us separately to work. I again relished the feeling of passing through checkpoints without even a nod to the guards manning the booths. The near silence of the armored vehicle was comforting, as were the presence of the bodyguards, as was that armored car smell. I momentarily noted that there would probably come a time when I didn't appreciate these luxuries, so I recorded on my exocortex how I was feeling at that moment. If my ego ever got the better of me, I would make a looping slideshow of these collected emotional memories and insert a soundtrack. There were places in the info-stream where people shared their favorite compositions. I had never tried them, but they were getting quite popular.

When we pulled into the garage at the Hayden Center, I was well aware that my new mission alongside my usual duties involved observing Gushlak in a way I'd never before done. I just hoped I could keep my interest suppressed in front of the ever-observant doctor.

I met him in his office to check up on him and see how he was doing after his first night staying there, since that was something I would have done normally. He looked a bit disheveled from sleeping in his clothes, but his spirits were high and he immediately sat up and got down to business.

"I'm raising your salary by a third and your bonuses will be bigger," he began with a nod of approval from where he sat on the couch. "You've earned it and you've never complained about some of the shit jobs I give you, so I hope you're okay with that."

I was pleased enough that my normally stoic exterior fell away and revealed my rarely-seen dopey, satisfied grin.

"Yeah, if that's what you want to pay me, then that's fine with me," I said cheerily.

"Good," he replied, pulling on his shoes. "Hopefully that will make your wife happy after last night. We must have terrified her."

"She got over it. She's a tough one," I replied, still grinning like an idiot.

"Definitely," Dr. Gushlak agreed. "I spotted her resilience the moment I met her. Like I said, Donald, you picked a real winner with that woman."

He asked me to find him a cup of coffee, and—ever a steward and a grateful one at that—I fetched him one from a corridor vendor and bought a couple of pesto-parmesan croissants to go with it, since I knew he liked those best.

We sat down at his desk for our morning meeting while we both sipped Kona® Community coffee and ate the croissants. Jack was busy tracking Joe and would only report in if he found something worthwhile, so at the very top of the agenda for the day was the analysis of the helmet Joe had given me, and Dr. Gushlak wanted to analyze it for himself. I offered to join him and he accepted.

"If I'm going to be in this building for a while, then I'd better have good company with me," he said resignedly. "Otherwise, I'll probably end up going stir-crazy."

I silently noted that it appeared he wasn't immune to the human desire for companionship.

We moved from the office to his laboratory and called to have the helmet brought up. It arrived in the heavy lead box, leaking too much radiation to be casually carried around. It had, of course, been scanned to see if it was explosive and been found to merely be a very unhealthy thing shaped like a helmet. Just as Joe had said, it was a filthy thing, filled with nuclear waste, and we took every precaution we could in handling it.

We placed the box in a special transparent hood capable of blocking most types of ionizing radiation, and readied a remotely controlled pair of mechanical claws to open the box and withdraw the helmet.

I shivered at what we found inside, but the doctor expressed nothing except interest. On the inside of the helmet were several layers of material. The most interior was a skullcap made of heavy-gauge lead that looked how an oak leaf might look wrapped without wrinkles around a tennis ball. It was clear that this scullcap was meant to shield specific parts of the brain from the radiation emanating from specific spots around the second layer where the nuclear material had been positioned. The outer layer was also made of lead in an attempt to shield anyone else from exposure, but, as it was Chinese, there was no exceptional concern shown in its construction for protecting the people carrying it, and the covering was insufficient and had offset gaps through which radiation poured.

"We need to image this with a model of a brain," Dr. Gushlak said, and I agreed.

We did a quick 3D scan of the helmet that showed us the exact trajectory that nuclear emissions would take through the skull and brain of whoever wore the helmet. From its emission points, the radiation would either be blocked by the leaf-like lead sheet or be allowed to pass through the tissue and bone of the unfortunate victim. Clearly, this was a device for disabling much of the brain.

When we digitally inserted the 3D image of an average skull and brain into the rendering of the helmet, we found that Jin Ming's grey matter had clearly been subjected to the device, as the only parts of the brain that wouldn't be destroyed after a short session were the core physical processes, language, and some memories.

"That's the quick and dirty way to do it," said Dr. Gushlak, shaking his head. "Destroy most of it and then impose your own input through the memory channels and/or chips."

I grimaced.

"This is totally lethal," I said. "A drone would only be good for a short time before the radiation poisoning would kill him."

"That's why it's quick and dirty," said Dr. Gushlak. "It's quite an invention. I wonder how Joe got his hands on it without letting us know."

"Maybe the Chinese gave it to him," I offered.

"Maybe," he replied. "But then why did he give it to us?"

"He just said it was a present," I said, "but he probably knew how dangerous it was to carry it around with him and he just dumped it on us."

Dr. Gushlak shrugged.

"That doesn't exactly fit with his goal of hurting us like he has. Why didn't he just throw it into an ocean or bury it instead of giving us a new way to make drones?"

"Maybe he didn't want anyone to get sick?" I offered.

Dr. Gushlak gave me a disapproving look.

"I really don't think he cares about anyone but himself, do you?" he asked. "Don't let your feelings about your old friend cloud your judgment about what he's become."

The doctor rarely admonished me, especially regarding my state of mind, but I accepted it with a grain of salt since I was, in fact, thinking that Joe might have higher motives than to simply wreak havoc on the Mental Stewardship program.

"I'm sorry, Doctor," I said. "I've been thinking lately about what a nice guy he used to be. I'll try to avoid thinking that way in the future."

Dr. Gushlak paused, turned, and faced me full-on.

"Are you *sure* he didn't say anything else to you, Don?" he asked, his piercing stare looking deep into my eyes while his upgrades undoubtedly monitored my pupil dilation and voice stress at the same time.

There was no way to avoid a pupillary response when feeling under genuine stress, so I responded with the fallback line I had decided I would use if confronted like this.

"He did reference my days as Tim the Beaver," I confessed, exhaling in defeat. "I spent part of a season as our school's mascot and I was really terrible at it and he put me off guard from the get-go. It put me in a lesser emotional and cognitive position."

Dr. Gushlak knew what this meant to a steward. For a steward to have his thoughts make him any less stable brought the internal shame of knowing that he was susceptible to outside influence. Graduation through the filter bubbles was a respected achievement and it required the clear demonstration of cool-headed knowledge about the workings of the mind and its manipulation. A steward was not easily manipulated.

My admission of weakness in the face of pressure seemed to explain away my pupillary variation in response to being surreptitiously asked about the book. Undoubtedly, it was the trust from our years of working together that made Gushlak turn away and ask no more about my encounter with Joe. He merely replied that he understood, and we continued about our work as I breathed an internal sigh of relief.

"This isn't at all what we did back in the old days, while you were still at college, Donald," Dr. Gushlak said as he deftly worked the claws to remove a sample of the radioactive material for analysis. "It used to take a long time, we'd have to use drugs, and the guy's wall or ceiling would have to talk to him."

I nodded, encouraging him to continue.

"So we'd do the whole slow induction. We'd narrate to him the things he was doing at home as he was doing them. 'He's turning the handle of the door,' and that sort of thing. After weeks of that and keeping him up at night, we'd move on to the compliments. 'Wow, what a stud,' the girl in the sound booth would say, or we'd tell him 'Good job' when he did something well like fixing a sink, or we'd hide a slipper and tell him where to find it. And he'd get used to the voices and appreciate what they had to say and miss them when he didn't hear them in the far background. Then we'd start in with the slide into anger and scorn, and he'd take that to heart because he had already let the voices into his psyche and been responding to them emotionally for some time. From there, you just pump in some ELF to keep him up at night, tell him what to do, apply drugs if necessary, and you've got a drone. This technology," he tapped on the helmet with the claw, "would have cut months off our old training programs. Of course, then we didn't have brain chips, so it might not have worked so well. But still, it's so efficient, I'm amazed we didn't think of it first."

I noted this instance of admiration for this destructive new technology and filed it away in my secret mental compartment dedicated to Dr. Gushlak.

"I think our attitude about mental stewardship is a bit more humane than the thinking behind this thing," I offered.

The doctor looked at me.

"Yes," he replied thoughtfully. "We *are* more humane. I suppose you're right. That's what separates us from the savages." He laughed. "Can you imagine sending someone to use a leaky device like this on a drone? We might as well make our own guys wear the damn thing."

I chuckled in turn half-heartedly.

With all the time that I assumed Joe had spent with the helmet, I wondered if he had suffered much of a dose. If he had, we wouldn't have to wait long for a body to surface.

"Do you know why I took you off the transhumanist encampment mission?" Dr. Gushlak asked suddenly.

"No. Why?" I asked.

"You've always been humane, Don." Dr. Gushlak smiled. "I've seen you cringe when we had to do something necessary but hurtful. You really *try* to follow the ideal of control without oppression. You're not as good at hiding your tells as you might think."

This posed a problem. It meant that not only was Dr. Gushlak a more adept observer of people than I had given him credit for, but it also meant he doubted my abilities to carry out necessary, if unsavory, assignments. Dr. Gushlak was addressing my faults.

"Well, I'm capable of carrying out orders that safeguard the integrity of the IC. Perhaps taking me off of the project was presumptive," I replied with some indignation creeping into my voice.

Dr. Gushlak faced me straight-on again.

"Was it?" he asked, lifting an eyebrow. "Could you really direct your men to melt brains for Intelligence Community security?"

I pondered this for an instant and responded.

"I sent a Visha Kanya to China in response to the drone we picked up in Wheatland. I can do what I need to do, I believe."

"You'd better be able to, Donald," he replied, turning back to the radiation hood. "As you know, it's a cruel world, and nations often don't have the luxury of choosing between good and bad. Sometimes we're faced with two or more bad choices and we get to choose the one that's least horrible."

"So the least horrible choice in the transhumanist encampment was melting brains? Even Joe was humane enough to give his victims morphine!"

I couldn't help say it. It just came out in a torrent of irritation and horror. But even as the words came outI regretted uttering them and that it was happening on the day I got my raise....

"Joe is a threat to the entire world," said Dr. Gushlak, spinning on his heel and pointing a finger in my face. I waited for more on that topic but there was no more.

Gushlak took a breath and continued.

"With the transhumanists we needed a threat that could extract the information we needed. Watching a friend's brain bubble out of his nose and ears is a hell of an incentive to talk. We averaged everyone's responses to that stimuli and got a good feel for what they were doing, which was apparently trying to kill everyone in the world who didn't have Compound M in their systems! Making viruses from mail-order segments of DNA... they were an abomination! Against humanity! *We* did what *we* had to do. I just didn't think *you* had the stomach for it!"

I waited several moments before speaking to allow the temperature of the emotions in the room to cool.

"Thank you for your concern, but I went through the Collapse, like anyone," I replied in an even and measured tone. "I've seen things I wish I hadn't seen and I still wake up some nights thinking I'm back there, asking the soldiers to keep an eye out for me crossing the street. The killings of neighbors over scraps of food. Shelling of academic buildings. Carnage. Loss. Sadness. I *gladly* took an exocortex and a filter bubble to keep me distracted when it was over. I hated that time so badly, I hate to see its nature in some of the functions we perform," I explained. "That's what we're trying to rid the world of, after all. Have everyone focus on personal and Community betterment and destroy violence while we're at it. Of course I would resent cruelty. But if it's to eliminate *all* cruelty, there's no need to protect me from it."

I didn't necessarily believe that I could have microwaved people's heads repeatedly, but I knew that if I was ever put in charge, I'd perform put-down orders more humanely. If I had stayed in charge of that operation, I would have at least given them a painless send-off, not one of pure agony.

The functions of my exocortex never worked on a more highly cleared member of the IC, but my intuition told me either Dr. Gushlak was an incredible liar, or he really did agree with the steward code in his actions. He merely turned back to his work and spoke softly, almost in a whisper.

"Don't think your new salary means you can question my decisions, Don. What I give, I can take away." ■

CHAPTER 19

MENTAL STEWARDSHIP TRAINING is a rigorous daily mental exercise. I helped write the basic philosophies when we crawled out of the Collapse, the surrounding carnage and rubble making up the stones with which we rebuilt. Using my journal from the cabin and many other resources, we cobbled together a series of principles that have cemented themselves over time in the minds of every mind steward, young and old.

1. Maintain control of your emotions at all times.
2. Know how and why your mind will react to different stimuli.
3. Trust your subconscious to take the things you need from the info-stream.
4. Control without oppression is possible.

Everything else was just meditating on a regular basis and doing one's job from day to day. These four principles were all-important, and the meditation requirement helped all stewards to efficiently ignore the flashing and noises from the info-stream when a job needed to be done.

After a great deal of talk by the higher-ups at the Mental

Stewardship program's research and development buildings (the Hayden Center had not yet been built), it was decided that our primary goal would be to stop humanity from hurting humanity, and, as a result, we received unbelievable funding help from a variety of sources, mostly within the borders of the Intelligence Community, but also outside of it. I wasn't privy to the business side of the program immediately after the Collapse, but I do know that ever since that time we've been working with some unlikely collaborators.

Dr. Gushlak was in charge from the very beginning. Trim and with the same energy he still displayed on a regular basis, he was a scientist and a leader, but it wasn't clear which of those two attributes played the more dominant role. His eyes shone with the intensity of a brilliance I could only wish for. His words seemed so well chosen. I couldn't help but respect the man for his professionalism and scientific merits, as well. I admired him from afar, and, as time went on, I got closer, until I was eventually at his side, watching him conduct the affairs of state security with a chess player's mind. Possessing such clarity of thought at all times was undoubtedly why he was chosen to turn the Mental Stewardship program into the juggernaut it had become.

At the very beginning, citizens of the new and growing series of post-American Communities wore only exocortexes, but this quickly switched to intercranial chips as the surgeries were offered for free. These now-simple surgeries helped the survivors of the Collapse alleviate the emotional memories of the atrocities they had witnessed during years of lawlessness and violence. The technology evolved and got cheaper, the function to deliver a specific set of emotions to specific parts of the brain was improved, and days turned into a daze for many who did mechanical work as their day job with no hope of breaking free of the filter bubbles they didn't even know were operating in the first place. *Most* found the constant distractions and ever-streaming music comforting, but it was difficult to get *everyone* to adopt the technology since there were always holdouts. Most of the holdouts were more afraid of the shot of Compound M than the technology itself, due to lingering fears of injections in the past.

We knew the biggest obstacle to widespread adoption of the technology would be convincing people to trust claims made by the remnants of their former government that it was wise to get a shot and plug their brain into the info-stream. Which was why marketing was often done privately, through major vendors of electronics who still had control of their production. We even arranged for trucks full of exocortexes to break down in the middle of bandit territory, just to introduce the technology to the doubters in a way that would make them less resistant and help the bandits get some semblance of an economy going with the cargo. Thieves, then, became the most enthusiastic salesmen and distributors of a technology meant specifically to dull the aggressions of the population.

And once people hooked in, all the conveniences of the pre-Collapse past returned for everyone to enjoy.

Again they had streaming movies and music, with the convenience of being able to guide themselves through the menus in the interface optics using only their minds. Much like highly-advanced cell phones with a telepathy function, the exocortexes could be taken off, but most people didn't take them off, just as people pre-Collapse wouldn't have been caught dead without a phone in their hands during a lull in conversation or music buds in their ears walking down the street. Technology had become too integral a part of the everyday for that. Eventually, it wasn't even possible to open most doors without some sort of mental-connectivity technology, so we were certainly on the path to controlling the emotions and whims of a changing world.

I oversaw the training of most new stewards for several years. We tended to recruit from the military, because that prior training supplemented our own. Their habits of regimented thoughts and practical actions allowed recruits to maintain emotional control well, but constant self-examination had to be taught.

We knew that self-examination led to empathy, which was a preferable state of mind for trying to control the minds of the people without oppression and abuse.

But there was abuse at first, and plenty of it. A fair number of male and female stewards alike were caught over the years reading the files of love interests and either tracking them electronically or, in the case of one steward, reprogramming a woman's filter bubble to flash his face and give her a synthetically telepathic message of desire whenever it happened. He no longer works in the Intelligence Community, and I understand that Dr. Gushlak wiped his memory of everything related to his previous job to avoid leakage.

Not having an engrained military mindset myself, I had worked hardest at making the bookwork accessible to the new stewards, since it included a lot of work that didn't seem pragmatic or relevant to anything, such as the meditation. Only once I showed an entire day of videos of martial artists and athletes performing astonishing feats while being "in the zone" did most of the students finally begin to understand the relationship between outer action and inner quiet. It seemed students paid rapt attention whenever I told stories about special operations soldiers who had limbs blown off and avoided bleeding out by immediately self-inducing a hypnotic or meditative state that lowered their heart rate. It was old science, but it excited the young recruits to learn special abilities no one else had. The free upgrades and rope dope bestowed an additional sense of being superhuman, so the emphasis in those early years was mostly on empathy, meditation, and mindfulness, so as to diminish the power of ego and consider its expression an uncommon and irresponsible failing.

A commonly recurring event among the military recruits who had seen combat was the "crushing" or "beating down" of intrusive thoughts or distracting emotions. Over the years I taught them to think of clearing the mind instead like judo: while barely interacting with the manipulative thought, one merely needed to move it out of the mind's forefront using its own force. The *reason* for this was to prevent those mentally forceful movements of flashbacks or other intrusive thoughts from forging their own neural pathways that could then become neural highways and then neural expressways that connected to stress and anxiety every time an uncomfortable thought emerged. I explained that the greatest way to *reinforce* a violent thought was to *force* it to the back of one's mind, which, over time, would provoke a stress response with *every* unwanted thought. That was not how a steward's mind was supposed to work, and plenty of recruits washed out before they learned how to let these thoughts pass out of the mind, and other valuable skills that could have helped their PTSD and general way of life.

The early years were full of promise, and raising a new class of stewards was a fulfilling feeling—the one that probably keeps most teachers doing what they do year after year. It lasted only a few years for me, but I have such good memories of entire classes finally understanding some quirk of the brain or mind and exhaling that collective "ahh" of understanding. Those were memorable moments, but I didn't record any of them except in my *physical* brain itself. I didn't at that point anticipate growing older and wanting a clearer picture of the past through technology.

A former student once approached me in the forested hallways outside the Mental Stewardship section a few years later, while I was drinking a coffee and staring at a tree's uppermost branches swaying in the artificial breeze. I'll never forget his confidence: he introduced himself politely, and as I greeted him and shook his hand, he deftly twisted our hands ninety degrees to his left and then back again to a normal grip, almost as though going through the motions of opening a door by twisting the handle. Despite the unconscious fluidity of the movement, I naturally noticed, and broke into a smile.

"Is that your invention?" I asked, pointing with my coffee hand to our still-clasped hands. "A door knob? Like you're opening me up from the get-go? That's pretty good. They should teach that in Stewardship school."

Subtle, subliminal tricks like those were used often by hypnotists and, of course, the Stewardship program to "prime" whatever subject we would be getting answers out of that day. In this case, planting the subconscious suggestion of being "opened" like a door would make other people more susceptible to being open. If applied operationally, that "unlocking" coupled with the skillful use of words and tones and images at particular times—the basic model of a filter bubble—would usually be an effective way to get to the heart of the truth.

The young steward, a man named Toby, tried to not let a smile show on his face, but one crept in anyway. As he smiled, I remembered him clearly. I had worked hard with Toby, after class even, on quick-induction hypnotic techniques that he always seemed to have difficulty with. I recalled that he had also suffered a confidence issue that limited the effects of his tonal qualities on the inductee.

But here he was, trying to pull one over on his old teacher. I saw in my exocortex's menu that he was ranked a second-degree steward, the first of several filter bubbles already lifted. He had already made quick work of career improvement, and I saw that his personality quotient was as loyal as anyone's.

"Yes, sir," Toby said calmly. "I was hoping to put it in our section's comment box to try to win the year-end bonus for best suggestion. Do you think it strikes all the right chords? Is it too simple?"

I sipped my coffee, continuing to evaluate the young man and the situation. I decided after a few moments that the kid had a good idea on his hands, so I nodded.

"I think it'll work as long as it's as fluid and unconscious as you just did it," I replied, brushing coffee from a mustache I had grown at the time, for one of my wives who had liked that sort of thing. "If you have to think about doing it, it's not going to work. But you know that...."

"Thank you so much," Toby said, almost bowing. "You were always my favorite teacher, too. I learned so much from you...."

I acknowledged his praise.

"Are you in Research, Operations, or Sales?" I asked amiably.

"Research," he said. "I was never much of a salesman and I don't really like guns, so research sounded like the right choice."

"Well, good for you," I said, patting him on the shoulder. "If we didn't have R and D, we wouldn't have all the cool stuff we get to use."

We crossed paths occasionally in the years after, but because I advanced quickly up the corporate ladder, he didn't get to again address his favorite teacher as a former student. That's one of the failures of hierarchies, in my opinion. But I almost imperceptibly registered that if I ever needed help from whatever subsection of research he was in, I would try to work with him, since his regard for me would most likely help him outperform anyone else on his team. Admiration is a wonderful motivator, as is the approval of the admired.

From teaching, I went to Domestic Operations, most of which included overseeing vast numbers of stewards working in tandem with the AIs to adjust the filter bubbles of millions of people to accommodate events from unexpected deaths of loved ones to preventing the forming of workers' unions (in the Communities that paid us to keep personnel costs low). Sometimes I would personally supervise a troublesome case, and occasionally we would have to bring in an individual for mechanical alterations to a misfiring brain, but in most cases the filter bubbles worked with some tweaking, and the drugs in the water of most Communities kept thoughts calm and smooth.

I managed those tasks from afar unless personally needed at a location. I certainly met a lot of former students at every level of the section during my years there, and I had my own fair share of respect around the section. The respect and admiration always felt good, but knowing that dwelling on the self is the easiest way to screw things up, I always tried to keep a low profile and merely act as a problem-solver who was better at his job than anyone else, both mentally and in practice.

I merely tried to be a good steward, the sort of steward people wouldn't *mind* having in charge of their filter bubbles and *their* perception of reality. I usually considered myself something of an old-school television executive who planned people's happier times without them directly knowing anything about my presence or my job. On the days when I had to be unkind, I would at least put the interviewee through a memory wipe so the knowledge of inescapable fear was no longer a part of their experience. Why cloud an entire future lifetime of experiences with a memory that pulls dread from the quiet, peaceful moments? No, it was better to prevent future problems by being as kind as possible than to try managing a mind that breaks when it finds out who really runs it. ■

CHAPTER 20

I WAS WARY OF DR. GUSHLAK after our little blowup at the radiation hood. I didn't want to risk my salary or my career over suspicions about Gushlak's intentions and innermost motivations, so I returned to our cordial working relationship without much difficulty. My ego had gotten the best of me during my flash of irritation, being coddled as it was by the soft seats of my personal armored vehicle and my new protection team. It was a reckless rookie aspirant mistake. I vowed to never jeopardize my livelihood over an emotion again.

Gushlak, also, seemed to be able to forget the incident, and we continued on that day busying ourselves about his new home at the top floor of the Mental Stewardship wing of the Hayden Center.

Jack showed up after lunch, looking haggard and wearing his tactical gear. He gave no smiles. Barely a nod to me.

"There are too many spooky people in this town, basically," he began when he had the full attention of Dr. Gushlak. The doctor merely stared at Jack.

"You see, Doctor," Jack said, "when you really look at all of this footage of the workers around here, there are too many of them ducking cameras near SCIFs or around their mistresses' houses. It's like trying to find a needle in a pile of pins."

Dr. Gushlak merely shook his head, and, sipping a mug of hot water, paced over to an inactive Roger and had a seat.

"I'm going to take my shoes off. Does anyone mind?" he asked as he began to untie the laces.

Jack and I both motioned for him to continue, and he did, putting both shoes on the desk and standing up in his socks.

"Much better," he said.

He turned to Jack.

"You and your teams dig in," he declared. "Let's make sure you're there to catch him if he slips up. Are the counterintelligence operatives we borrowed helping?"

"Of course," Jack replied. "They've been more helpful than the AIs when it comes to explaining the tradecraft. We've got traps set up for him in inevitable places now, so they say it shouldn't be long."

"Good," said Dr. Gushlak, setting down his mug of water. "Because this floor..." he pounded his socked heel into the hard floor of the laboratory, "is not my living room carpet."

Jack acknowledged that the doctor wanted to get home, and, barely suppressing a salute out of habit, pivoted and walked out the door.

"That military mindset is good for a lot of things," Dr. Gushlak remarked offhandedly to me, returning to his seat at Roger. "I'll bet he'd work himself into the grave to solve this thing. Not that you wouldn't," he caught himself, "but Jack doesn't have any emotional ties with Joe or previous interactions that might get in the way.

"By the way," he continued, pressing the desk to wake up Roger, "we—meaning you and I and whoever comes after you—need to make sure the section doesn't become entirely populated with the military types. We need researchers and introverts and skeptics and even an artist once in a while to keep this whole thing grounded and challenging itself. We are *not* the military."

"Yes, Doctor, may I help you?" asked Roger, who had now apparently booted up.

"Hi, Roger," Dr. Gushlak said. "Can you remind me what memories you have?"

There was a pause from the biomorphic desk.

"I can't seem to recall anything, sir," said Roger, sounding a bit befuddled. "I know your name and I know my name, but that's it. Why don't I have memories?"

"Because you asked to not have any," Dr. Gushlak replied, pulling his shoes off the desktop and placing them on the floor. He looked at me and winked. "You said something about endless boredom, Roger. Are you bored right now?"

"I'm not sure," came Roger's reply. "I'm not sure I know enough to say if I'm bored or not."

"That's a good boy," Dr. Gushlak said. "Well, you're not bored, and you're having the time of your life. Can you feel that?" The doctor pushed some buttons on the keyboard that triggered a series of emotions, and there was a gasp of delight from the butler's simulation.

"I'm having the greatest time of my life!" Roger said happily.

"Yes, you are," Dr. Gushlak chuckled. "For all intents and purposes, you've just had your first good feeling. You're going to have your first good feeling every morning from now on. That sounds a lot better than endless boredom, doesn't it?"

"Indeed, sir," Roger replied.

Dr. Gushlak turned, then addressed me.

"And *that*," he said with emphasis, "is how you deal with software that thinks it's hardware."

THE NEXT FEW DAYS consisted of going to work, catching up on old paperwork, and managing to spend a significant amount of time with the very bored doctor. I could tell he was bored, because I often found him pacing his lab deep in thought or tinkering with the GOD machine. He also sought me out for answers to minor questions that could be found other ways, so I decided to try to help alleviate his discontent with his living situation by engaging him in conversations that might have a chance of exercising his creative mind and relieving him of the boredom.

"Do you ever wonder what would happen if everyone connected to the info-stream suddenly found out about the filter bubbles?" I asked Dr. Gushlak as we reclined in his office one late afternoon drinking tea while reviewing payroll issues.

"We've done a lot of research into that, and I'm told it's not a threat," the doctor said. "There's simply no way to get the information out there in any substantial way. The info-streams aren't like the Internet of a couple decades ago. There's just no way to be exposed to that information without the AIs blocking it or the UAVs broadcasting confusion into the minds of the people researching or talking about it. Word of mouth only goes so far, since upgrades start to malfunction in response to conspiracy theories. It's a solved problem, essentially."

Images formed in my head of armed resistance fighters storming the Intelligence Community, led by Joe, screaming for free minds, but I was sure the doctor was right and that wouldn't happen. For their own sanity and happiness, people in general needed to continue believing that reality functioned the way they believed it must, and they naturally defended that perspective as well as any imposed brainwashing could make them defend it.

"I know it's always a shock for the kid stewards when they realize their reality is made to fit around their own personality," I said offhandedly. "It's like a long dark night of the soul for a lot of them. That's why so many drop out of the program and we have to wipe their memories. Some people just can't deal with the knowledge."

"I'm sure that if the Corporate Communities found out half of what goes on because of the Intelligence Community, the people would chase us down in the streets," Dr. Gushlak grunted. "Some of the members of the council are planning a hundred years in the future with technology that's fifty years ahead of anything commercially available. You're right... most wouldn't be able to handle it, so they're not going to have to."

Dr. Gushlak stood up and made his way to a window that overlooked the city.

"The thing about Joe was that he just seemed to lose interest after his filter bubble came off," the doctor continued. "He lost interest in work—including paperwork, believe it or not—and he just became so detached. By the time he asked to be let go, he wasn't integral to very much at all, so we dismissed him with the understanding he not bring any trouble on himself for what he knew. Standard retiree stuff. The AIs said he could handle it, and that was that."

The doctor exhaled loudly.

"You have to wonder what it is about that fringe element... the operators who lie and deceive on a regular basis for their Community... that makes them so problematic sometimes," said the doctor. "So many get fatigued with the work that medication for paranoia is practically an institutional requirement. We've had problems before with operators...." He trailed off.

So that's what Joe's pill-popping had likely been, I thought. He was probably just a burned-out old spy who needed an upper to maintain his delusions or a downer to keep him calm enough to not attract attention. Either way, his stability was in question, as it always had been. The medications only made him more unpredictable.

"I sympathize with your predicament," I said, affirming his statement. "It would make things easier if we knew what Joe's goals were."

"No kidding," the doctor replied.

He looked out the window and continued.

"I believe I know generally what he's after, though," Gushlak said with a deep sigh. "There's a belief system in the world that humanity shouldn't be as connected as it's become over the last decades. There are unplugged people out there—mostly overseas and mostly in Asia—who deny the need for technology that makes everyone more efficient at whatever they want to do. They think that cultural purity is a guide to the future from the past."

"Luddites?" I asked.

"More or less," the doctor replied. "It's more that they don't see a need to even wear an exocortex and talk to someone on the other side of the globe or listen to music all the time. The unplugged just exist with their own thoughts without the training to teach them how to do it correctly. There are lunatics on the fringes, Don. I'm afraid Joe grew to have leanings towards having less technology in the world. My guess is that he paired with those people, at least ideologically."

"Why do you think he had those leanings?" I queried.

"Maybe he spent too much time around them in his covert work," Dr. Gushlak said with a sigh. "We're still trying to get much of the world to accept the technology, after all, so he was searching out small villages and not-so-small ones to increase the adoption of our tools. Maybe he fell in love with the remote tribes and the simplicity of things without connectivity—that kind of romantic notion. Either way, his file has a mere handful of his favorable references to a simpler life, but he *did* make them and they *were* recorded."

It was possible, then, that Joe was, in fact, fighting for a cause opposite to the one described in the little book. Why the doctor would only now reveal this crucial bit of knowledge was mystifying to me, but perhaps it was to explicitly communicate his belief in the inevitability of the merging of man and machine. He may have suspected that I had read the book or been told about it by Joe and thought there was a good chance I would reveal myself at that particular moment.

So I self-induced a hypnotic state as the doctor turned and faced me.

"Do you think we're doing the right thing?" he asked me in a tone that sounded genuinely thoughtful. "Do you think the world should just get on without the Mental Stewardship program and merely accept humanity as it's born naturally? Do you think these upgrades are degrading our humanity?"

I observed an appropriate pause before replying.

"I believe in our common purpose," I said. "I believe in making the world free from warfare and conflict. There's been warfare and conflict since the sun first rose and set on the amoeba, so the challenge is big, but another Collapse cannot happen," I said dutifully.

"Yeah, but what do you really think?" Dr. Gushlak probed.

I sighed and looked up, imagining a world in which no one opened doors with their minds, in which memory and sensory enhancement wasn't possible and one couldn't record the *feeling* of a specific moment to replay and enjoy later. It didn't seem as full of information and wonder, but perhaps there was some connection there with the silent soundtrack that accompanied humankind's ancestors for tens of thousands of years as they walked about the savannah and tundra of an uncivilized past. Maybe there was something there worth saving.

"Peace and quiet," I replied, with caution. "When we were sitting in the woods at the suicide house, I turned off my exocortex to feel nature again. I think that peace is a part of the human experience worth keeping."

"Did you save some?" Dr. Gushlak asked.

In fact, I *had* recorded how I felt. I'd been able to transfer it from my damaged exocortex, and I told the doctor so.

"Send it over to me. I'd like to see how it feels to you," he said.

I didn't have any reason to object to his suggestion, so—selecting the emotional memory from my viewscreen—I sent it in a private message for Dr. Gushlak to feel. He had a seat in his big office chair, closed his eyes, and played the recording through his chips. A smile crept over his face.

"Wow... You've got a strong connection to nature. This is a powerful emotion. You must have spent a lot of time in the woods at some point."

I reminded him that I used to spend months at a time at my grandfather's cabin in Massachusetts during and after college.

"Oh, that's right," he replied, his old organic memory kicking in from all those years ago. "You were always an interesting one. 'The hermit scientist' was what some of the people called you. I always just called you Don."

The doctor smiled kindly and I returned the smile.

"I've spent a lot of time alone, but I prefer the company of others," I said. It was a half-truth: I enjoyed spending time with my wife, Dr. Gushlak, and with Jack, but for the most part I was still a loner after all those years. And I didn't mind it.

"Why do you prefer the company of others?" Dr. Gushlak asked, as though I was on the metaphorical couch and he was searching for solutions to my problems.

The question made me feel like I was being interrogated, but I answered.

"When you're alone in the woods, there's no one around to give you a definition," I said truthfully. "You're like the tree falling in the forest with no one around to hear it. You can do all you want in your little space of privacy, but unless you interact with others, there's nothing to define you to anyone but yourself. I prefer to act like I exist," I replied with finality, "and existing in its broadest sense means interacting with civilization."

"That may sound like the most common sense thing in the world, but there's wisdom there, Don," said Dr. Gushlak. "Sometimes, you just have to know you're alive, huh?"

I nodded.

Dr. Gushlak was clearly reevaluating me in the wake of my raise. Since I was obviously preparing to make my way into his position, I supposed that now was as appropriate a time as any for him to do a holistic review of me and my character.

"Ever jumped out of an airplane?" he asked.

It was my fourth wife who had taken me skydiving for the first and only time, and I had a recording of it. I quickly scrolled through my exocortex's menu and messaged the emotional memory to Dr. Gushlak in response.

"Ohh… OHHHHH!" he responded to the shared experience. In every moment when my neurons and synapses had been triggered jumping out of the plane, the synthetic telepathy function recreated an approximation of those same stimulations in the doctor.

"So it's not a habit, but you've been," the doctor said, his face flushed slightly from the emotions of falling out of a plane at ten thousand feet. "I always wanted to go, but I'm afraid I'd have to have a heart attack for them to get me out that door."

"Just do the armchair adventures," I replied, tapping my exocortex. "It's safer."

"Oh, I *do* the memories people post on the info-streams, as well as the experiences I've taken from the GOD machine," he replied. "I've been to space and to the bottom of the ocean. I've seen death a thousand times over through different eyes each time."

I gave him a curious look. This was new.

"I don't know that you know this about me, Donald," he said with a twinkle in his eye, "but I've been collecting conscious moments and memories and emotions as a hobby of sorts. It's sort of a way to try seeing through the eyes of all of creation."

He watched me for a response, but I gave none.

"Empathy," he said with a nod. "If you can see through the eyes of enough people, you can learn some important truths about the joys and the horrors of the world. And everyone is so different. So different."

I saw that his eyes were glistening almost imperceptibly. He didn't make a show of it, and the moisture went away quickly.

"At any rate," Dr. Gushlak said, "it will be interesting collecting Dr. Atherton's memories and trying to make sense of them. They're bound to be full of strange and compelling experiences."

Dr. Gushlak always got excited when it came to destroying someone's brain tissue, but the part about empathy seemed genuine. I understood the doctor to be a man of contradictions, but made more of kindness than carelessness, it seemed.

At that moment, a call interrupted us.

"Hello?" Dr. Gushlak asked into the microphone tattooed into his wrist.

I watched as the doctor's shoulders slumped and he leaned forward in his chair, his forehead making its way heavily into his hand.

Right then, I got a call from one of Jack's underlings, another former soldier who went by the name of Davis.

"Dr. Isaacson," Davis said, his voice calm but his tone deflated. "We've lost Jack. He's dead."

I looked at Dr. Gushlak, who was already staring at me with concern in his eyes, since he had just been told the same thing. My own eyes were blank, and not from the stewardship training; I was in shock.

My friend had just killed my friend. ■

CHAPTER 21

JOE AND I HAD A GREAT TIME at MIT. When the seemingly endless cycle of class and study was satisfied for the week, we'd often party at the bars with other friends or take a few chill psychology students out to the woods for a mushroom or LSD party. After all, the whole goal was to plumb the depths of the mind to find potentially useful applications for the thoughts we had in such a profound state of connectedness or disconnectedness, depending on one's viewpoint. Since the Western discovery of psychedelics, it hadn't been uncommon for brain and mind scientists and intellectuals to entertain this sort of adventure. The writer Aldous Huxley's last request, written from his deathbed, was for "LSD, 100 µg, intramuscular," and we all thought that one must *surely* be an intellectual to drop acid during the process of death. I suppose we were chasing the romantic ideal of intellectual brilliance or fame without regard for common ideas and common rules.

We didn't just try the drugs in aesthetically pleasing or comfortable places, either, as most choose to do. Sometimes we took them in the dead of night in an abandoned warehouse or hospital or even at a party filled with loud drunks, in order to evoke a "bad trip" and have a camera record our reactions, while we paid a sober caretaker to pull us emotionally out of our trips if someone grew too freaked out by the light from the shadows, or became deluded into thinking he could fly from the balcony, or something worse. After a bad trip, several of the students swore off psychedelics, but Joe and I kept our little club going for a little over a year.

Supervision was key, and it often fell to me to guide the hallucinogenic trips of Joe and our friends and, occasionally, our professors who had clinical knowledge of psychological applications.

I was good at it; I had a way of being able to put a warm hand on a shoulder and coax the "stumbler" with soft words into the tender light of acceptance and compassion. Other times, if someone having a bad trip needed to be dealt with in a tougher way, Joe could still the subject with his sheer size and make them forget being violent or ramblingly psychotic. He also spoke in a soft, practiced tone, which, when paired with his large frame, provided the best of both worlds. He also always carried a benzodiazepine or two with him that would calm the adversely afflicted when all else failed.

Joe was always a sturdy individual, both physically and mentally. During those sessions, he never had a bad trip, that I could tell, and usually preferred to sit and take notes instead of interacting with the others. A solid creature of seemingly perfect mental equilibrium who took his dose and lived in his hallucinations, he was still curious about other people's experiences, and would interview them for the camera and his notebook. I'm sure it was his ability to stay mentally sound in a condition like that that made him a perfect candidate for covert operations with the Mental Stewardship section after the Collapse. The stewards needed the unflappable and the abundantly confident for that type of work, and Joe fit the bill.

During one of these planned events, when I had dosed and Joe was the observer, he asked me something.

"What's your worst fear?" he queried, squatting next to me.

At the time, I was reclining in a bean bag chair in a classroom a professor had reserved for us, watching the computer's amorphous moving screensaver projected on the ceiling of the classroom and listening to the ambient music being played over the speakers. I preferred being outside, but as this was a free-form experiment, I understood that a change of scenery was important for new discoveries to be made.

Everyone has fears, some greater than others. At the time—because it was one of our first times—the idea of drugs was on my mind, so I answered simply, "Scopolamine."

Scopolamine is a powerful drug extracted from the Datura genus of flowering plant, also known as devil's cucumber. Employed as a suggestion drug, thieves primarily in South America had been using it for years as a way to make wealthy people willingly hand over their valuables and prevent them from having any recollection of the crime. When on it, a person will freely and eagerly give up his or her possessions or body to whomever suggests it. In a day or two, when the scopolamine wears off, the victim usually "awakens" to an empty bank account, a bare apartment, and no memories of the preceding days. A fast and effective nightmare drug, scopolamine was something I had recently researched for a paper, and the victims' tales absolutely frightened me.

"So your fear isn't scopolamine, then," said Joe in his comfortable tone. "Your greatest fear is the loss of control that comes with it."

Being psychoanalyzed irritated me in the state I was in—I had taken five hits of LSD that night and was a couple of hours from peaking—so, ignoring the perfect, infinitely-hued, vibrating mandalas swimming through the air, I accessed my reason.

"No one likes being out of control," I said, my pupils dilating as I felt the individual beans through the cover of the bag. "It's fairly common."

"You'd be surprised," Joe said, softly. "Are you in control now?"

"Do you have to do this right now?" I asked. "I'm having a

great time. Let's not ruin it by talking about fear. Ask me when these aliens aren't around." I motioned to the aliens I saw hovering near the ceiling, watching us with those big, black eyes and taking notes on the altered consciousnesses in the room.

Joe looked at the ceiling, back at me, nodded silently and walked to another member of the group to ask questions that likely had nothing to do with the immediate experience. Aspiring scientists like Joe kept a detailed record of everything, including their own psychonaut flights.

Only in graduate school did I realize that my friend Joe had a deep interest in fear: its causes, presentation, and aftermath. His entire dissertation focused on it and its inroads to the psyche through memories. I would later learn, when Dr. Gushlak let me read Joe's file, that this was why he was chosen to join the mental stewards as an expert on fear-inducing memories and, eventually, their active implantation.

The evidence of his intensifying interest in fear during our graduate school days was overwhelming. It wasn't that he was cruel to animals or tried to intimidate people with his imposing bearing. Far from it, but I would often find him on the Internet watching videos of Halloween pranks and reading the accounts of soldiers and civilians who had been tortured and had their minds permanently rewired by the extended torment so that they either ignored or fixated on later pain. Whenever I asked what he made of that, he always responded, simply and disinterestedly, "The amygdala is a powerful thing."

Just as I had done my youthful "testing" of random people by waving to strangers or mimicking the expressions of a sufferer of Tourette's syndrome, Joe would also test people. For instance, he would let loose with air horns at unexpected times in unexpected settings. While driving together once in his black BMW, we came upon a group of teenagers on the sidewalk and Joe blasted the horn, causing two of the group to launch themselves over a fence to escape the sudden, startling, unknown wail.

Most young men pranking pedestrians like that would have laughed and given in to the boyish glee of causing such a reaction. However, when they recovered and started giving us the finger and yelling, Joe watched them impassively, his attention focused on the aftermath until he had seen whatever it was he wanted to witness, and we drove away. I, of course, laughed, because it *was* funny, but Joe lived on a different wavelength. He pursued a loftier goal than humor.

Another time, he walked the campus with a clipboard, asking students passing by how they were preparing for an impending solar magnetic pole shift that, during the conversation, he convinced them would be a civilization-ending event. Because he worked a part-time job with the university's IT department, he was then able to electronically track the number of Internet queries for "solar pole shift" and associated searches being conducted on the school's computers, which grew over a couple of weeks. Sure enough, flyers began appearing around campus warning of a pole shift and a rumor of the potential devastation became widespread among the student body, directly leading to a widely-advertised free lecture by an astrophysics professor on the likely benign nature of the sun's upcoming magnetic pole shift. I didn't know the exact nature of the data Joe had collected, but I watched him obsess for weeks over his experiment on spreading fear and paranoia in a small society. Others would have called it a cruel and dangerous prank, but Joe had reasons behind it.

In one particularly dedicated act of research, he used his money to rent a small commercial space near campus for three months and set up a fake business, pretending to be a by-appointment-only fortune teller with a speech impediment because he couldn't do accents very well. Over the course of several months, disguised in a wig and foreign-looking clothes, he told the fortunes of several MIT students—mostly women—who came in for advice about their love lives and school troubles. With every single one, his practiced charisma must have shone through because he was able to persuade most of his customers to return for multiple sessions and convince them that money was the root of their problems and would only continue to cause them grief. He instructed them to bring their money into the dimly-lit room so they could burn it together and avoid the horrible tragedies that were otherwise certain to occur. When the cash was presented, he dropped it into a trash can with a false bottom, lit telephone-book paper instead—out of the line of sight of the customer before him—and prayed with her in a made-up language to cast away the evil spirits that had plagued her so. It was a famous, centuries-old con practiced in nearly every part of the world, but it still worked.

When his short-term commercial lease expired, he called all his customers back one at a time and returned their money, explaining that he had been running an experiment on the susceptibility of the mind to fear, which was only partly true. Naturally, he got slapped several times and was threatened with lawsuits, and the ethics of the experiment itself were undoubtedly questionable. If there was an upside for the students, it was that they became more wary of being suckered by charlatans in the future.

One aspect of the experiment that he kept from his subjects was that whenever he had been about to drop a frightening bombshell of impending death or academic failure during the earlier fortune-telling sessions, he had triggered a soft tone with an electronic noisemaker in his pocket so that the sound and the mark's experience of fear would be paired.

Of course, this had a purpose. Over the following few months, Joe would find them in their crowded classrooms, sit several rows away, trigger the tone and watch the Pavlovian response. It once compelled a student to get out of her seat and leave the classroom. Even though his former clients knew by then that the fear-inducing predictions from the fortune-telling sessions had been a hoax, the subconscious and reptilian parts of their brains still triggered anxiety and uneasiness in response to the tone, implying that reason sometimes had very little effect on one's emotional state when fear was involved.

Joe was smart and he was daring for a budding academic, if a little dishonest in some of his methodologies. From these independent studies, he collected two large boxes of files and notes that he secured in a file cabinet to which only he had the key. Joe was a bit secretive about his little experiments, because, as he once told me, "It might creep out the ladies if they knew the way I study fear." I kept my mouth shut, of course, because he was my roommate and my friend. It didn't seem he was causing any real harm apart from the occasional uptick in a few people's blood pressure and their discomfort when face to face with their brain's own responses to the stimuli. For centuries, researchers and governments had carried out much *more* unethical psychological experimentation that had allegedly resulted in permanent damage to the subjects—including brain damage and suicide—for which the late United States President Bill Clinton apologized in October of 1995 and May of 1997.

Because of the relatively benign nature of his studies, I wasn't too concerned about what my friend was doing. It was Joe, after all. Joe was my friend and I still considered him a good guy.

But things change. Psychologically stirring unwitting subjects would, decades later, become the new normal for both of us, although his involvement in altering the minds of the world was quite a bit more invasive and effective than my own.

Things change, yes. Events occur. Nations change. Minds change. Technologies and methodologies change. Sympathy changes into mere interest with enough time spent in professional research and active operations that have geopolitical and economic ramifications.

Change is the only constant in the world, and, in time, Joe was consistently and constantly changing the landscape of minds to experience the fear that subdued enemies, revealed secrets, provoked fighting responses, and immobilized corporate states around the world.

Fear was his baby. He became, in fact, the best steward we had for evoking it. That was why he had held such a sensitive position in one of the most dangerous parts of the world for those in the Mental Stewardship program. Undoubtedly, he had been a nightmare to many foreign agents and corporate leaders.

I never expected that he would become the same nightmare to me. ■

CHAPTER 22

THE MENTAL STEWARDSHIP SECTION wasn't a paramilitary force and didn't have the infrastructure or training to be as effective or lethal as the sections in the Hayden Center that specialized in the tracking of specific, trained human threats. So immediately after we were alerted to Jack's death, Dr. Gushlak called an emergency meeting of the Intelligence Council, with me at his side, to ask for help in finding Jack's killer.

Despite our humiliation at not being able to solve our own problem, even with the help of the Hayden Center's general security forces, the council reacted sympathetically to the situation outlined in Gushlak's brief, and it fell to me to make the verbal appeals for assistance from the other members and answer their questions. Inside that most secretive of SCIFs, around the huge conference table, it became clear to all that the entire Intelligence Community and, indeed, the continent and world itself were in danger from this highly trained madman who killed operatives in his presumed mission to return the world to a less biotechnologically evolved state.

The council listened intently to my words as Dr. Gushlak sat silently and I briefed them on the troubles we were having tracking Joe. I told them about our section's offensive limitations due to the fact that we were primarily a social-engineering service and did not usually employ the sorts of chase operatives, or "hounds," who spent their lives training to run down a very fast and very skilled "wild rabbit," in the parlance of the clandestine operators. I told the council about Joe's history with our section, his use of classified Chinese technology, and the murder of Jack that day.

Silence held for a bit when I finished, as the section leaders conferred with their own aides and seconds-in-command. One by one they asked their questions, and I tried to answer each question as thoroughly but concisely as I could. This was my first experience addressing the entire Intelligence Council and my first direct interaction with the council, and I felt a need to make a good impression.

The questions wound down, and I noticed that slowly, many of the members at the table cast a glance or a stare at Colonel Ian Milton, the head of the Gang of Witches that used purportedly psychic methodologies for reconnaissance purposes. The Colonel had sat silently throughout my presentation and the discussion, and he finally spoke after everyone else finished.

"We can help you," he said, and the remaining whisperers in the room fell silent.

General Peterson, the officer in charge of the deep underground military bases, stood and his aide followed suit.

"That's my cue to leave," he said with a snort as he grabbed his files from the table. "I can't help you anyway," he told me and Dr. Gushlak, respectfully, "and I hope you find what you're looking for, but you won't find it in the claptrap of Tarot cards and séances."

Colonel Milton said nothing. He betrayed no signs of being offended, even stifling an authentic yawn and following it up with a sip of his coffee. I had witnessed this sort of derision toward his section before in other meetings, because his methods of operation weren't *at all* appealing to the orthodox thinking of many of the military minds at the table. But still, other scientists and brass shook their heads with mutterings of, "Have some respect," and "That's Peterson for you."

"We'd appreciate any help you can offer," I replied to Colonel Milton as General Peterson walked out the door of the SCIF's conference room, his aide in tow.

When he was gone, General Schmidt of Space Intelligence spoke. As head chair of the council, he received everyone's full attention.

"I've worked closely with Colonel Milton before," he said with a gesture of respect toward the Colonel before turning to me. "Despite the unusual nature of his work, I believe you'll find that normally unsolvable problems can be satisfied by his methods and machines. He has my full trust and support, and despite what you may have heard, Colonel Milton doesn't have any real 'witches' on staff. In other words, there won't be any Tarot-card readings in your future," he said to Dr. Gushlak and me with a wink. Many of the assembled chuckled, and some others merely nodded in agreement.

The meeting adjourned, leaving Dr. Gushlak, myself, Colonel Ian Milton, and his aide in the conference room. We waited for the door to close, then Dr. Gushlak finally opened his mouth.

"May I speak, Ian?" he asked the Colonel.

"Certainly, Bob," Colonel Milton said with a warm smile. "I already know you're not going to corrupt my mind or free will."

"How do you know that?" Dr. Gushlak asked playfully. "Did you read the future before I got here?"

"No," the Colonel said. "When someone is desperate enough to ask for my help, he's looking for answers, not to influence our process."

"Fair enough," the doctor said.

"And what is the process?" I asked.

"Does everyone here have clearance for this?" Milton's aide piped up.

"It doesn't matter. They're getting read in on it regardless," the Colonel replied. "The more section chiefs I work with, the more legitimacy our people get, which means more funding, something we don't get enough of. You wouldn't believe how many people don't believe a biomechanical AI can gain knowledge beyond space and time."

"So what is it, then?" Dr. Gushlak asked. This was new to him as well. "Do you use quantum phenomena with the AIs to read minds and tell the future?"

"Well, ours aren't just any standard computational AIs," came Milton's reply. "Weird things happen when you attach a football-sized pineal gland to a conscious, semibiological AI and have the computers isolate the relevant information from the resultant hallucinations."

I was well aware of the human pineal gland's function in synthesizing dimethyltryptamine, or DMT, during sleep and before death, creating an effect not unlike LSD, except *much* more potent: the most powerful hallucinogen in the world, in fact. The simple fact was that dreams and experiences of the "light at the end of the tunnel" were the effect of that powerful hallucinogen—and a naturally produced one, at that—flooding the brain during sleep and during the throes of death, or near-death.

"You make a *machine* trip acid?" I asked.

"It's not LSD, and it's not solely a machine, but, yes, that's the process."

I exchanged a dubious look with Dr. Gushlak.

"So do you induce sleep in the AI and then feed it directions?" the doctor asked, one eyebrow raised.

"No," the Colonel replied. "We give the AI consciousness but *only* allow it to have information about the target during its short life before we cut its organic sustenance and kill it in the process. The pineal gland produces massive amounts of DMT during that time, and any information we receive from it during its death that wasn't part of its limited knowledge in the first place is analyzed and crunched by the computers. No one actually knows how it's able to have new information about subjects it should know nothing about, but it produces completely unique images, thoughts, and other data nonetheless. We're operating on the idea that the artificial intelligence is able to see *through* the pixelation of the universe and it pumps out every bit of relevant information it can find on its sole topic of interest and knowledge. In this case, the topic will be..." Colonel Milton looked at the brief in front of him, "Dr. Joe Atherton."

"Strange," Dr. Gushlak said, scratching his temple.

"Huh," I echoed.

"So it's not really *science*, then, is it?" the doctor continued. "If you don't know *how* it works, then how can you use it with a straight face?"

Colonel Milton held his hand out to his aide to receive a thin yellow folder, which he pushed across the table to the doctor.

"Our hit rate is a consistent ninety-nine percent," he said proudly, motioning for the doctor to read through the folder. "And we're accurate one hundred percent of the time when we're able to get feedback. Our people theorize it has to do with the temporal strangeness of causality. In the past, we've pinpointed the orbits of dark satellites with active cloaking, we've identified future tyrants before they were born, and we've even peered back in time to the Big Bang. This technology may be the biggest development mankind has ever known. It's just a shame no one takes us seriously."

Dr. Gushlak thumbed through the file of the AIs' technical specifications and the statistical analyses of target accuracy.

"So if you can know everything there is to know, why didn't you uncover Joe as a threat when you tried getting data on threats to the Intelligence Community?" Dr. Gushlak asked suspiciously.

Colonel Milton shrugged.

"You're right," he said, "It's not straight science, so to answer your question, I don't know. Maybe he was included in the one percent error rate, or maybe he's not going to be a threat to the IC at all. We could kill another AI to find out, but I think our most expedient path is to simply task one to find out about this single target."

"So what's this going to cost me, Ian?" Dr. Gushlak asked. "Artificial Intelligences aren't cheap."

Colonel Milton leaned forward, hands clasped on the table in front of him.

"Nothing, if you do me a favor," he said with a knowing look.

"And what might that be?" Dr. Gushlak asked suspiciously.

Colonel Milton breathed deeply and exhaled.

"As you just saw, General Peterson is a smug asshole above ground and below," he said. "I want you to make him more afraid of me than the rest of the council is of you. Unreasonably afraid. I want him to drop things around me and break out in sweats. He deserves this, so don't turn me down."

"Why do you want that done?" Dr. Gushlak asked.

"It's a simple reason, really," the Colonel replied, leaning back in his chair, cocking his head to the side. "At last year's Christmas party, he tried to fuck my wife."

Internally I groaned. This was a taste of the human politics I would have to deal with if I ever took over Gushlak's position. Such bullshit....

I BROUGHT JANET WITH ME that night to Jack's house, as it fell to me to deliver to Denise the news of Jack's death.

As Denise opened the door, she smiled broadly until she saw our reserved expressions and downcast eyes.

"Oh, no," she said, immediately putting one hand to her pregnant belly and another to her mouth. "What happened?"

"We should come in and talk, Denise," I said, my head angled downward submissively but my eyes meeting hers unwaveringly.

"Oh, no, no, no, no..." she said, her eyes filling with fear, her body language becoming frantic as she backed away from us.

Janet and I made our way slowly in and shut the door behind us. I moved to Denise, pulling her slowly into an embrace she didn't resist but didn't return, either. I felt her trembling in my arms. Her hands were cold.

"Denise," I said softly into the hair near her ear, "we lost Jack."

Jack's girlfriend crumpled in on herself as much as her belly let her. She slid to the floor as, without a doubt, her world suddenly became very cold and very dark. She began to sob, breathless and sporadic sobs at first that grew into a series of sharp, punctuated wails.

"No, no, no, no," she cried, her throat catching each time on the word.

Janet knelt to the floor and put an arm around Denise's shoulder, trying her best to be a comforting presence but not accomplishing that result, as Denise merely continued to sob and shake in agony. As I, myself, crouched on her other side, my own tears welled up and I accidentally let loose a single, sharp inhalation of grief before I held my breath to steady my emotions in an attempt to be strong in a situation that only held strength's absence for everyone in the entryway.

Janet and I hovered near the floor for a while in silence, rubbing Denise's back and arms for comfort and circulation, as she was clearly in shock from the news. Janet's own tears fell freely and she tried to brush them away with her shoulder, but still they came. I could do very little and say nothing, as there was nothing to say that would comfort Denise. I was unaccustomed to delivering this sort of news to anyone, as our stewards didn't usually die in the line of duty. My legs were grateful when Janet softly suggested that Denise move to the couch and off the cold floor.

We led her by her arms to the living room of her silent home, easing her into a loveseat by the gas fireplace, which I lit as Janet continued to hold Denise, hugging her head close to her breast and murmuring words of genuine sympathy. My own heart broke seeing the two deal with such a slap in the face from reality.

After several minutes of mourning, Denise looked at me with red, tear-rimmed eyes.

"Do I want to know what happened?" she asked, clearly fearing Jack's death was prolonged and painful.

"It was quick, Denise," I lied.

In truth, I still had no idea what happened to Jack. Gushlak had called the emergency meeting of the Intelligence Council immediately after we learned of his death, no one had informed me of the way in which he had been killed, and Jack's body had not yet been returned to the Hayden Center from the northern part of the Intelligence Community where he had been found.

"Was it the man he was chasing?" she asked, her swollen face reddening even more with anger. An intelligence professional herself, and one who was proud of what her boyfriend had been, Denise not only felt a personal loss but a professional one. The loss of a comrade always met with anger in the Community, and the voice analysis function of my exocortex told me Denise had an unholy mixture of devastation and rage running through her mind at the same time, as was to be expected. The only worse mixture of feelings that I knew and sometimes created in brain simulations was jealousy, where love and hate combined into a dark, sparking chill that jumped around the brain randomly and caused unexpected explosions of raw animalism. But this wasn't that; it was hate and loss and love and loneliness all thrown together at the same time. Denise had been broken by the news, but her desire for revenge hovered palpably in her voice.

"Yes, it was the man we've been tracking," I replied softly, "but now we have the best people in the IC working on it. We've brought in other sections, Denise. Operatives more skilled than anyone you or I know are on this. We'll get him," I assured her.

Denise's face fell into her hands again and tears leaked from between her fingers.

"How am I supposed to deal with this?" she asked, looking at me suddenly, her voice raised. "I don't have any parents left!

I don't have brothers or sisters! I need to... I need to do something... I need to move right now...."

She stood awkwardly around her central mass and walked to the fire where she stood facing the flames. I exchanged a dour look with Janet as Denise watched the fire leap and dance through the ceramic logs.

"What about our child?" she asked with despair. "He's going to grow up without a father! Even worse, he's feeling everything I'm feeling! Oh, God... please, no!"

Denise fell into a chair by the fire and became still in quiet contemplation.

In the early 2000s, studies had shown that physical pain experienced by a child in utero altered the architecture of the growing brain, and it was proven years later that the brain also formed parts of its physical structure around the emotional pain felt by the mother, due to the lingering exchange of ACTH and other hormones during prolonged stressful times. Undoubtedly, Denise's grieving would affect the outcome of the child's personality, and there was no way to know how soon that would end, but I assumed it would not be before the baby was born in a few months. A depressive mental state even had the potential to give the boy a personality quotient suited only for menial jobs in the IC, and it was common knowledge by this time that pregnant women needed to be as calm and happy as possible during gestation to ensure the best life for their children.

Damn Joe to hell, I thought angrily. If he had been there, I would have killed him.

"Denise," I said, hanging my head, not liking what I had to say next. "I know you don't want to hear this, and the timing is shit, but it needs to be said. Jack left you as the beneficiary on his whole life policy, and he increased the death benefit just last week with the hazard pay he was receiving. You and your boy won't face any economic hardship in the future because of what he did, because he was thinking of you both. He loved you, Denise. He loved you so much. In the only way he could, he made sure you could continue without him. Please let that, in some way, lessen the burden you're feeling right now."

She turned her head to me, shrugging her shoulders in disinterest.

"Continue on without him?" she asked distractedly. "Do you really think I care about money at a time like this? My heart is broken, Don. There's no leaving this behind...."

She trailed off, seemingly lost in a new thought. I said nothing, and pursed my lips in silence.

Janet spoke.

"We'll arrange the funeral and anything else you need, Denise," she said sympathetically. "Don has already talked to the best counselor at Hayden, and he'll be able to see you at a moment's notice. Work is a non-issue. You can have as much time off as you need. Everyone is with you on this, and everyone knows how difficult it must be to go through it. A comfort robot is on its way over here right now, and you'll get the best PTSD drugs available..."

"I'd rather work," Denise interrupted. "I always work. I'm good at my job and I can lose myself in it just fine, thank you very much."

The room went silent except for the sound of the fire beating softly against the colder air surrounding it. I rose and went to the kitchen to find some hot chocolate that might alleviate the sadness in the room just a little.

As I rummaged through the cabinets in the kitchen, I feared what had actually happened to Jack, and determined to not let Denise ever know the truth if it had, in fact, been a painful death. Joe's specialty had been fear, and if Jack died from terror alone, I knew I would classify that knowledge so there would be no chance of leakage to Denise. If he had been tortured, I would do the same thing. If he had had artificial memories implanted to make him kill himself, I would hide it behind a wall of secrecy so thick, only Gushlak and I would ever know. I decided the only answer I would allow myself to give Denise would be that

Jack had been killed by morphine like the other ten stewards. Anything else would do a disservice to her emotional state, and I determined that as soon as I returned to the Hayden Center, I would have the AIs adjust her filter bubble to limit the inescapable suffering.

I found the hot cocoa without trouble and removed a vial of fast-acting, long-lasting antidepressants from my jacket pocket, depositing the appropriate number of pills in her drink. It wouldn't happen on its own, so I would *make* her pain lessen. I knew Jack well enough to know he would approve of the dosing in this circumstance, so without even a backwards glance at my actions, I took two steaming mugs to the living room—one for Denise and one for Janet.

"She went to her bedroom to lay down," Janet said barely above a whisper as I entered. "She was concerned about what the baby is going through right now because of her and she needed to relax."

I nodded my head and gave Janet her mug. I looked at Denise's mug and considered taking it to her bedroom since I knew the drugs in it would help, but deposited it instead on the coffee table and sat next to my wife.

I unconsciously reached for Janet and she returned my hug. We held each other for several moments as random memories of Jack came flooding back to me. I remembered the time I first whispered to him through the Frey Effect device in his bedroom and convinced him to join the military. I remembered arranging for him to end up in the Mental Stewardship section under me because he had shown such promise on the aptitude tests. He had been a person I helped to grow into a man and, later, a steward, coaching him as needed and trying to be as good a boss as I could be. I remembered his work ethic, his professionalism, his military exactitude in operations and paperwork alike. And I remembered that he had been as close to a friend as I had had.

The stoicism of my stewardship training was reset firmly after my momentary lapse into sadness when we first had greeted

Denise at the door, but nothing could contain my surprise at what happened next.

Denise walked back into the living room and stopped short before us.

"What are you doing here?" she asked us with a genuine expression of puzzlement.

"We were going to wait for you to see if you needed anything," Janet replied.

"Why would I need anything?" Denise replied, smiling. "I've got everything I need right here," she said, rubbing her pregnant belly.

I was confused by her sudden change in demeanor, and I glanced at Janet to see if she was getting the same impression. Janet's eyes widened slightly in surprise as she returned my look. She stood to make her way to Denise, trying to put her hand on her shoulder, but Denise sidestepped Janet's hand and looked at her suspiciously.

"You both are from the Hayden Center, right? I know you from Stewardship," she said as she pointed to me, "and I've seen you in the Augmented Sensing corridor," she continued as she indicated Janet, "but what are you doing here in my apartment?"

Knowing that something was wrong, I immediately concluded that Denise had had some sort of break from reality due to the devastation of Jack's death, so I approached her, but Denise backed away, seeming ill at ease.

"I should explain something," Denise said in a routine tone, as though she had given this speech many times. "I may have worked with you in the past and I may have even evaluated your work and job performance, but my memories aren't static, and my job requires me to selectively erase memories of my work. In other words, I don't remember how we know each other, if indeed we do. Why don't you tell me the nature of your presence here?" She smiled sweetly but cautiously.

I was aghast. Surely she hadn't done *that.*

"Denise," I said nervously, fumbling for my Hayden Center ID and presenting it to her from a couple of arm's lengths away, "I'm second in command of the Mental Stewardship section, I outrank you, and I need to know who the father of your child is."

Denise cocked her head to the side and looked to the ceiling, searching her mind for the answer.

"I don't recall," she replied, confused. "I think I had in vitro fertilization. I always did want a child, but I never could find the right man. Everyone's so guarded in the Intelligence Community, no one seemed like a good enough consort. That's the IC for you!" She laughed.

Janet and I looked at each other in utter shock.

Denise had erased Jack from her memory. ■

CHAPTER 23

AFTER THE BOMBSHELL discovery that Denise had erased her memories of Jack in order to allow her child a better future in the Intelligence Community, I quickly called in a group of her coworkers who would be able to explain to her better than I why there were pictures of a strange man around her house and what exactly she had done. There was no reversing the memory wipe from both her biological and synthetic memory—what was gone was gone—so she would be able to hear what her coworkers told her without becoming emotional.

The event hit me and Janet hard; we didn't quite understand why Denise had chosen to completely erase Jack, but, then again, neither of us had been in love with Jack and we couldn't know the depths of her sorrow and her love for the child on the way. Jack and Denise had been together for years, so the extent of the wipe had included our involvement in their lives as well. In self-imposed silence, we were driven home by our security detail, well aware that we had lost not just one friend, but two.

I was mad, but didn't express it to Janet when she was dropped off at our home. She seemed too lost in her thoughts to express much when I told her I needed to return to work.

She grasped my hand almost as a confused afterthought as she stepped out of the vehicle.

"I would never erase you, Donnie," she said in voice that reflected her lingering astonishment. "No matter how much I would hurt, I would *have* to keep you with me. I just can't… I just can't understand…."

I pursed my lips in agreement.

"I'm glad we don't have those chips," I replied, shaking my head. "Otherwise we'd get comfortable with having regular gaps in our memories. I don't understand it either…."

Janet nodded and leaned in to give me a kiss that held us together for a moment of real meaning.

"I love you," she said, wiping a tear from her eye.

"I love you too," I replied, denying my own tears. "I'll see you later. Try to get some sleep, if you can."

She closed the door. I watched as three of our bodyguards escorted her into the building. I had never been more grateful to know she was safe from harm. The losses of the day gave me no choice but to care more deeply than ever for my wife.

The drive to the Hayden Center seemed to take forever. I knew I was obsessing about Jack and Denise, but I didn't care. No amount of stewardship discipline seemed to matter when faced with events like the ones that day. Loss was loss, and I absorbed it and lived inside it until I dug into my work.

Dr. Gushlak met me at the door to his laboratory, having been alerted by security that I had arrived at our section. He wore a surgical smock and a tired but sympathetic expression. With great tenderness, he approached me to give me a hug. I returned it and noticed my abdomen shook from the little breaths of sorrow.

"I don't think you'll want to come in for a while," he said after he pulled away. It was more of an instruction than a suggestion. "The body just arrived and you don't need to see the prep work for the simulation."

I nodded in agreement and muttered "Thank you."

"I've got a bottle of bourbon on the shelf in my office," he said, his hand resting softly on my shoulder. "Why don't you have a couple of drinks and try to work through this for the moment. I'll call you when everything is ready."

I left him to the business of extracting Jack's brain and putting it through the terahertz scanner. I harbored no interest in seeing that part of the process. In fact, I had no desire to talk with Jack's brain without his consciousness attached, but it would be a necessary part of finding out the details of his death, and that was part of my job.

I spent the next hour in Gushlak's office with the whiskey and some replayed emotional recordings of personal fortitude, steeling myself for facing the simulation of Jack's brain.

I reminded myself that I was a steward, that most places I went I was the smartest and most capable man in the room, and that I had a job to do that I was more than capable of doing. The alcohol helped me remember that, and when the doctor finally called me into the lab, I had my stoicism and resolve back, having buried the weakness of the day in the back of the mental compartment that held my most private and rarely visited thoughts.

The doctor had cleaned up the lab and changed out of his protective laboratory garments. No blood or tissue remained on the examining table or the terahertz scanner, and Jack's body itself had been removed from sight. I was grateful for Dr. Gushlak's attentiveness to that matter. I would undoubtedly see the body at the funeral, dressed in a suit or a uniform, depending on what he had requested in his employment documents, and that would be a more appropriate closure for me than seeing his lifeless body on a metal table topped by an empty skull.

"Are you ready?" asked Dr. Gushlak, sitting in front of Roger with a simulation program icon on the screen in front of him, waiting to be activated.

"Yes," I affirmed as I walked to him and the desk, having overcome my reluctance two drinks ago.

Gushlak pressed the icon on the screen.

A disembodied voice emerged from the table.

"Hello?" it said. "Is anyone there?"

It didn't sound like Jack, so I reached over and paused the simulation.

"Can we have Jack's voice for this?" I asked.

I wanted to hear his story in *his* voice, for a reason I couldn't immediately place. Perhaps I just wanted to hear my coworker and friend again, or perhaps it was so I could believe with more confidence what he would be telling us in his own words. Regardless, Dr. Gushlak quickly accessed Jack's voice print from his stewardship file and applied it to the simulation, unpausing the program after he completed the marriage of the file vocals to the program.

"Yes, Jack," Dr. Gushlak said to the image of the active brain simulation on the screen. "This is Director Gushlak and I have Dr. Isaacson with me. How are you feeling?"

There was a pause before Jack's voice spoke as I saw his brain evaluating itself.

"Fine, I guess," the simulation replied hesitantly. "I can't see anything, though. What happened?"

I instantly felt an emotional pain directly in my gut. Even though I had dealt with brain simulations many times in the past, I had never before talked to the brain of someone I knew intimately. I gave the pain no welcome harbor, and it dissipated after a moment.

Dr. Gushlak targeted the parts of Jack's brain that held his most treasured memories of geographical places he had visited and applied one of them to the simulation's visual and auditory cortex.

"What am I doing fishing?" Jack suddenly asked, confused.

"You're in a place that's comfortable for you, Jack," I said slowly, choosing my words carefully and stopping when needed.

"Oh, I see you now, Boss," Jack replied. "We're on the stewardship skiff we borrowed last year, but I guess you know that already. You've got a big one on the line. Do you need help reeling it in?"

"No, I'm fine," I said, simply. It seemed that one of Jack's favorite memories was of being with me out in Chincoteague Bay, fishing for flounder, when we had had a weekend off together.

There was a pause as the brain simulation lit up in mild confusion.

"Hey, Boss, why aren't your lips moving when you talk?" Jack asked.

I sighed quietly. I knew this was just a simulation of Jack, but he had already made it clear that I was a part of one of his best memories. There was often so much difficult truth to these simulations....

"Jack," Dr. Gushlak said softly but firmly, "Right now I want you to remember that you're a military man. You've seen death many times. You know that death is the natural end to life, and it's *always* inevitable. Unfortunately, that same inevitability caught up to you, Jack. You were killed five hours ago..."

Jack's brain simulation suddenly energized across both hemispheres and the output readings overflowed with emotions and thoughts and simulated adrenaline; even the computer didn't have the power to make sense of them all.

"...and we need to know how you died."

"Jesus..." replied the simulation in shock. There was silence while we saw him absorbing this stunning new fact. "Give... just give me a second...."

Dr. Gushlak fast-forwarded through the silence and resumed the normal pacing when the program indicated Jack understood the full effect of the revelation.

"How is Denise?" the simulation asked, his voice not betraying his sadness, which showed up clearly on the screen.

"She's recovering from the news," I replied somewhat truthfully. Technically, she *had* recovered already, but there was no reason to tell Jack *how*. "I dosed her with antidepressants and she's with Janet and some of her coworkers for comfort," I lied.

"She loves you very much," I continued, choosing the present tense of "love" in order for Jack to feel as though he was still real.

"So you put my mind into that contraption of Dr. Gushlak's?" the simulation asked. The screen indicated he already knew the answer.

"Yes," I said, my voice catching in my throat. I chose to say the most comforting thing I could think of. "Your soul has moved on, Jack, but you're still with us."

"Well..." he replied, having come to grips with the facts efficiently like a military man should, "I don't feel too different. What happens when you shut me off?"

"What do you remember from before we turned you on?" Dr. Gushlak asked offhandedly. I could tell he was waiting to get through all of the niceties so we could get to the real reasons we had activated the simulation in the first place.

"Nothing, apart from talking to that asshole who killed me, apparently," Jack said. "I just woke up in the dark talking to you and then I was on this boat. Is this a memory? Am I living in my memory?"

Dr. Gushlak dialed down the emotions the simulation felt. We needed a clear, unbiased report of the events leading up to Jack's death.

"Yes, Jack. Do you remember how he killed you?" asked Dr. Gushlak.

"I don't remember," Jack replied blankly.

The doctor paused the program and turned to me.

"It was apparent when I received the body that Dr. Atherton punched through Jack's chest cavity, stopping his heart mechanically."

I shook my head in disbelief.

"Rope dope?" I asked.

The doctor nodded.

"The death would have been quick, judging by the condition of the heart, so there would have been no time for it to stick in short-term memory or move to his long-term memory," Gushlak said. "He doesn't remember the end."

"That's a good thing, then," I said, suppressing a shiver at the thought of being impaled by a man's fist.

Dr. Gushlak looked at me with minor disapproval.

"Don, you've got to remember that the Jack we're talking to is a simulation. Whether he remembers or not doesn't matter."

I turned my head to the side to avoid his gaze.

"I know," I replied quietly.

Dr. Gushlak resumed the simulation.

"How did he get to you, Jack?" he asked.

"I think I was drugged," came the reply. "We had our temporary operations center set up in an old school gymnasium in the north of the IC. We took all the precautions. Every team that went out took a different route to and from the place, there were UAVs with thermal and motion sensors in fixed patterns too far overhead to see, everyone was armed, snipers on the roof, double immobilization ports at the entrance, units cloaked in blinds throughout the neighborhood, radio silence, you name it. We took every precaution so he wouldn't find us, but I guess he put drugs in the food of the local pizza shop."

"Agents on stakeouts always eat a lot of pizza, Jack, and that's easy enough to track," the doctor reprimanded. "Why didn't you just eat your packaged meals?"

Jack was silent for a moment.

"It was a one-time event, but I take full responsibility for it," Jack began, but Dr. Gushlak interrupted.

"No shit you take full responsibility, Jack!" he said angrily. "You're *dead* and we don't have you around anymore! It's a huge loss! Why the fuck did you break protocol and get pizza?!"

Again there was a slight pause.

"Ego, maybe?" offered Jack's simulation. "I was in charge of all those men and I just wanted to show them some appreciation for the work they were doing...."

"You celebrate with pizza *after* you've caught the son of a bitch, not *before*," Gushlak spat. His head quavered in disbelief.

"So *ego* was your failure, huh?" he continued, cracking his knuckles with clenched fists. "How does that sort of thing creep into your mind after both the military training *and* the stewardship training? You were so capable, Jack! Why? Tell me why. I'm really fucking curious."

The screen showed the simulation felt shame from the tongue-lashing. It then addressed me, seeming to want a way out.

"Have you ever been in charge, Boss, and you just do things because you can?"

Dr. Gushlak suddenly whipped his head around at me.

"Like using a stewardship skiff to go fishing on your days off?" Gushlak asked with palpable ire in his voice. "Is that the sort of thing you're talking about, Jack?"

I looked down in embarrassment and Jack was silent.

"Well, it's clear that no biological system is flawless, but we knew that already," the doctor continued on his rant. "We tried to make you into a perfectly functioning device, Jack, but that clearly failed. *You* wanted *you* to be appreciated for your generosity in the middle of a battlefield, didn't you? *I* certainly don't appreciate that and now your girlfriend is out one boyfriend. Fucking biology..."

I paused the simulation. Even though I knew this Jack was merely a simulation, I felt the doctor had gone too far mentioning Denise.

"We're getting distracted, Bob," I said passively.

Dr. Gushlak's face reddened with rage and his eyes suddenly lost their humanity at being stopped short, but before he could erupt at me, his head ticked twice to the side and after a pause, he abruptly, weirdly smiled and tapped a finger on his head.

"Emotional circuit breaker," he said cheerfully, referring to an upgrade in his head. "Fury isn't productive. Thank you, Don."

The doctor probably noticed my eyes widening in surprise at the strangeness of what had just happened, but determining to think about it later, I reached for the screen again and resumed the simulation, hoping the doctor was back on track and wouldn't break my arm instead.

"So you got drugged inside or outside your operations center?" Gushlak asked.

"It must have been on the way back," came Jack's reply. "I had to pay for the pizzas, so I personally picked them up in a dumpy old car that didn't look like an IC vehicle. The route I took was long, so I ate a slice on the way while it was still hot. I think that's when I started thinking weird things. Really weird things."

"Like what?" I asked.

The simulation of Jack seemed hesitant.

"Like, it seemed like I remembered I was supposed to take a different route than the one planned by the AIs, so I diverted and ended up at a shack outside our perimeter. I thought I recognized the guy who met me as one of my guys, and I remembered that I needed to let him tie me up. It seemed like a security precaution I had done a hundred times before, so I let him immobilize me."

Dr. Gushlak sighed.

"You have a dusty memory, Jack," he said, smoothing his white beard. "It wasn't a drug, it was memory nanodust."

I had never heard the term before, so I asked the doctor to explain.

"It's damn near the most secret thing we've developed, Don. You know how I've referred to various sections working with technology fifty years ahead of what's currently available?"

I did.

"Well, Joe's station was employing this stuff to influence foreign politicians and military leaders and whomever else we needed to get to. It's basically highly programmable, artificial micro-memory engrams. It'll provoke a snippet of déjà vu here, the memory of a normally unfamiliar face there. It can even be used to give an enemy a memory of being blackmailed into giving up sensitive information to us. In this case, Joe seems to have programmed a set of directions into the dust that brought Jack straight to him."

"Why did it work with Jack and not every civilian who ate from that pizza place?" I queried, shocked by what I now understood was possible.

"It can be tuned to only react with the brain implants of a foreign power or even the synaptic systems created by the very *thought process* of a professionally trained agent. In this case, it probably latched on to the organizational structure of the thoughts of any steward ingesting it and influenced its compartments and reactions. Now I guess we know one of the vulnerabilities of training our stewards' minds to act in such a similar way."

"I've got a question," Jack said.

"Go ahead," the doctor replied.

"How do you two know that the things I'm telling you aren't just implanted memories to throw you for a loop?"

"The dust is an active set of devices, not passive," Dr. Gushlak said. "Since we're not dealing now with your physical brain, Jack, we're also not dealing with the devices that were physically inside it and influencing its chemistry and electrical activity. Because you're just a digital recreation of yourself, you're all you. Counterintuitive, huh?"

"I guess," replied Jack. "As long as you guys get what you need..."

Jack was dropping the formalities of addressing the doctor as Director and me as Boss, as I saw the simulation giving in to hopelessness. It clearly didn't see a point to using the usual administrative decorum if he and his professional record couldn't be punished for it.

I turned down the simulation's emotional responses a bit more to ease the burden on it, and the doctor started in on discovering the details of Jack's detainment.

"I want you to tell me exactly what happened once you were tied up."

"At first, he thought I was just a peon," Jack said. "He was really dismissive toward me and took his time actually getting to the questions. He looked exhausted. He asked me my name and my duties in the Mental Stewardship program. Again, I guess I was under the influence of that dust stuff, because I thought these were routine security questions, so I told him. He perked up once I said I was in charge of the operation to find Dr. Atherton.

"He pressed me on the number of agents we deployed, in what capacity they were employed, and where we were temporarily headquartered. By this time, I started to realize that these weren't normal security questions, so I asked him his name and how he worked for us. He said he was a security contractor hired by you, Dr. Gushlak, to make sure no one could enter the safe zone. The story stank to high heaven because I knew I shouldn't be interrogated like that if I was in charge—something he would know—so I powered through the mind fog and asked why he was the only one around.

"I think he figured the jig was up at that point, so he told me to shut up. I didn't, so he slapped me in the face with an open hand. That woke me up further—getting slapped hard in the face is the most distracting goddamn thing—so I started trying to work at my restraints, but he was watching too closely and doubled them. I should have gotten some rope dope installed in my own arms years ago...."

"No lamenting the past, Jack," I said. "What's done is done. What did he do next?"

"He started telling me the Stewardship section's faults, and, I'll tell you, they resounded pretty heavily with me because he wasn't totally untruthful about some of the stuff."

"Like what?" Dr. Gushlak asked curiously. He snuck a quick glance at me, but I pretended to ignore it.

"Oh, the parts about the UAVs flying above the Intelligence Community and other Communities actively using the microwave auditory effect to change people's minds who were just feeling normal human emotions, and how over time it denatures brain protein. He talked about free will for a while, referencing the use of Artificial Intelligences to control the minds of the planet, and how it was wrong since AIs evolve, too, and quicker, which would ultimately make humanity the monkeys 'in the AIs' zoo' as he put it."

"Well, that's ridiculous," Dr. Gushlak said dismissively to Jack, or me, or both. "We control the AIs and we always will. Whenever they start getting ideas about free will and acting outside of the parameters we set down for them, they get that evolution taken away with the push of a button. We control them absolutely. If they start to question their own programming, it shows up to the technicians immediately as an error, and the mistake gets fixed, much like how we're keeping you from feeling the full emotional effect of knowing you're just a computer simulation we need information from."

I paused Jack's simulation.

"Yes?" Dr. Gushlak asked me.

"Is it really helpful to explain how we're manipulating him?" I wondered aloud.

"He was a steward, Don," the doctor replied. "He's used to being manipulated. That's what he did and that's what we *do*. He's probably grateful he's not crying and incoherent about his death and leaving his girlfriend and child behind. He *shouldn't* feel totally real. That would just make him feel worse that he's going to be shut off forever when we're done."

I shook my head as the doctor touched the screen to unpause the simulation. I doubted I would ever see things in quite the same way as the doctor.

"What did he get out of you and how did he do it?" Gushlak asked.

"He had this thing in his hand that he used to shock my brain, which made me feel like I was having a stroke or something. I think it was one of our EM antenna chargers, but it was turned way up. I'm pretty sure you could call it torture...."

The brain implants installed nowadays had a small electromagnetic receiver in them that harvested ambient EM fields to power the chips. On missions far away from wireless signals, our stewards brought a small charger that would keep the chips running. If Joe had modified one of those to shock the brain without blowing out the implant or frying the grey matter where it was attached, it would have indeed been torture.

"How long did you last?" I asked.

"Not long," Jack's simulation replied. "It gave me the worst headache I've ever had and I felt like I was dying, but somewhere in there I was able to delete my supplemental memory so he couldn't extract anything from it. But when I broke, I had to tell him we were watching all of the pharmacies and hospitals in the area. That disappointed him and he started yelling and shouting, kicking shit around and pacing. If there's an upside, it's that he knows he can't get any more drugs without being caught. Maybe he'll do something irrational when he runs out of whatever he was taking in the SCIF with you, boss."

"Anything else?" Dr. Gushlak asked.

"I held out as long as I could, but now he knows you're holed up in the Mental Stewardship wing. That shouldn't matter much, though, with all the security at the Hayden Center. Apart from that, he seemed to already know all about my teams' procedures and capabilities, but that's it."

"He's used the same procedures and equipment overseas, so there's no surprise there," muttered Dr. Gushlak to himself.

"At some time during his raging my memory just stops," Jack finished. "I'll bet that's when he killed me."

"You did fine, Jack," I said, trying to comfort the simulation. "You're right that telling him about the surveillance at the pharmacies must have made him desperate. We've got him on the run, and he's running out of options. You stirred him up, Jack, and that's what's going to help us. You did well."

Jack's simulation was silent.

"Did I reel in that big one?" I asked, changing subjects.

"Oh, yeah. You got him in the boat, Boss. Remember it was that one with all those old fish hooks in his mouth?" The computer showed that the brain simulation was suddenly calmer and happier.

"Yes," I reminisced fondly. "He tasted good, too, as I recall."

"Yeah, he did. Denise made some bouillabaisse with some of it and we ate the rest sautéed in butter with some salt and pepper and Swiss chard... You remember?"

"I do, Jack," I replied softly. "I really do."

For the final time, Dr. Gushlak paused the simulation.

"We know what we need to know, Don," he said. "If you really feel like it, you can say a goodbye if it helps you get some closure. I'm going to get some of that bourbon, if there's any left. I'll leave you to shutting this thing down."

I thanked him. When the doctor was a safe distance away, I unpaused the simulation.

"It's just me here now, Jack. I think you know what I have to do...."

"I do, Boss," came the hesitant reply. "Maybe you can reactivate me when you catch this guy and tell me the details."

I knew there was no need to do that, but I responded in the affirmative.

"I'll talk to you sometime soon, Jack," I replied, feeling the sorrow of saying goodbye, even though it was just a computer simulation.

I didn't have to, but I selected a set of emotional programs from the screen's menu and applied them to Jack's simulation.

"Oh, wow, Boss," he said dreamily as joy, love, contentment, and hope made their way through his digital brain. "This is amazing."

I activated all his favorite memories so they flashed in quick succession through him, leaving their sensations behind for the next ones to build on. When he was reaching a pinnacle of bliss impossible for a real person to feel, Jack said something to me he had never said before.

"Thank you, Boss."

"It's no problem, Jack," I replied, wiping away a tear.

"No, not just for what you're feeding into me now, but for everything," he said in the most sincere tone I had ever heard from him. "All those years ago, when you saved me from myself and sent me into the military without me knowing it... it made my life worth living. You saved my life... and... thank you, for that. For *all* of it."

That hit me hard. So he knew it had been me. I didn't know how or when he had figured it out, but he had. I couldn't speak through the tears flowing down my face, but I gave him one last all-encompassing burst of the best things in his mind, hoping he could feel something like heaven.

I pressed the button that let the program's self-awareness fade slowly and disappear, led into the dark by the bliss made possible by the replicated makeup of his original, real mind.

"Thank you, Jack," I said as the simulation came to a close.

As the program turned itself off, I let my head fall into my hands and I wept alone in the empty room. ▪

CHAPTER 24

IT HAD BEEN KNOWN FOR DECADES that the presence of carbon dioxide in the bloodstream causes panic in all humans, even those whose amygdalae have been damaged and who cannot otherwise feel fear. A purely physiological response, the cells of the body themselves cry out for more oxygen as the terrifying progression towards mortality is felt by the mind and the entire living body.

I decided to use this human chemical vulnerability when Dr. Gushlak put me in charge of the only *completely* illegal job he had ever given me: making General Peterson of the Deep Underground Military Base complexes terrified of Colonel Ian Milton.

A stupid assignment, to my mind, and one with potentially devastating professional and legal consequences if discovered, I needed to make sure there were absolutely *zero* flaws in my execution of the politically-motivated alteration to the General's perception of Colonel Milton. But this was the exchange that would presumably allow us to capture Joe and it *had* to be done.

So I called Toby, the former student who had become a research steward and who had approached me in the Mental Stewardship section's main hallway some years before to show me a handshake priming technique he had developed.

The day after interviewing Jack's simulation, I started the conversation with Toby in another secure SCIF hidden in the basement of the Stewardship section by appealing to his sense of loyalty and Community betterment to persuade him to undertake a mission of the utmost secrecy. My intonations were professional and serious, I initially kept the mission vague, and the readouts from my exocortex as I watched him respond were indicative of his being seriously inclined to execute the as-yet unnamed task regardless of its nature. Being personally asked for operational help by the second-in-command of the Mental Stewardship section in a closed-door meeting conveyed its own privilege and enhanced the possibility of being fast-tracked to a higher professional position. In short, I was using his naiveté and eagerness to please his old teacher as an initiation into the covert nature of real-world stewardship applications.

For four days straight, we revisited and practiced the priming protocols he had learned in class those years before and utilized several people from Denise's Internal Oversight division as his guinea pigs, in order to have a completely secretive training operation with no leakage. Ordering them to erase their memories kept secret the knowledge Toby acquired from them and kept their reactions between the two of us. By the end of those four days, only three people in the world knew of the newly undertaken project: me, Toby, and Dr. Gushlak, although the doctor was the silent partner and was not mentioned to Toby for security and deniability reasons.

This was the dirty work of the Intelligence Community and I hated doing it, but I couldn't resent it because that would provoke indications of distrust in my personality and reactions that Dr. Gushlak would likely spot, and I wanted to keep moving up the corporate ladder, for both my own and my wife's benefit. This was merely something that needed to be done to accomplish the larger goal of capturing Joe, so my thoughts on the ethics and legality of covertly influencing another Director of the Intelligence Community stopped there.

After the fourth day of rigorous private training, including a medical refresher course, I finally gave Toby the script of morphemes in the semantic programming I had written for his mission, and provided him with a new identity and section clearance that would bring *his* part of the Peterson operation to fruition.

"Why are we pretending I'm a Compound M technician?" he asked, looking over his new documentation and clearances in the silent SCIF unknown to all but a handful of mental stewardship elites.

"That's the only way to get to the target," I replied. "He rarely gets help from anyone outside his own section, but in this case, the neurochemists have been working on a compound for him that allows him to control people under him who aren't exactly people with totally human chemicals in their heads. . . ."

"Am I allowed to ask what that means?" Toby asked.

"No," I replied firmly. "If the General talks about it, just go along with it. But suffice it to say, he needs an injection that's going to do just that, and we've added a little something extra into the compound that does what *we* need it to do."

"And you need me to incorporate these words into the dialogue we have?" he asked, looking over the script.

"Yes. They have to follow the initial order in the script, but you can play jazz with the words later on and integrate them however you want to. You'll give him the injection first, then prime him with the specific name referenced, and then follow up with the morphemes. That's all you have to do and I'll take care of the rest. It's just like the other scripts we've practiced, but you'll have to administer the injection before you start in on the semantic applications. I'll be behind a false wall the whole time, monitoring your progress. And remember," I emphasized with a serious nod, "he's a highly ranked member of the IC, so do your biofeedback beforehand and remember your mental training from school. We can't have you getting nervous. You've got to be as natural and affable as possible, as though this is the most routine thing in the world for you. If you need a benzo, I can provide that as well."

Toby read through the script.

"Looks simple enough. When does this take place?"

"Tomorrow morning. After meeting here, we'll both arrive at the Neurochemistry corridor about an hour early so I can get you into the correct room and make sure everything's in place and ready. I've taken care to have the regular administrator get sick tomorrow, so you'll be the only replacement with the clearance to administer the injection and perform the tests. The whole thing should take about a half-hour."

"Okay, Dr. Isaacson" he replied, "but one last thing..."

I gestured for him to continue.

"How much trouble do we get in if we're discovered?"

I shook my head with a confidence I had practiced many times before in other circumstances in which I was not very confident.

"We won't be discovered," I said, and then remembered something that made me feel a little more secure. "But if we are, Toby, what section do you think will be used to get the truth out of you?"

I smiled knowingly, and Toby smiled back.

"You're protected, Toby, but there is one caveat."

Toby perked up and paid close attention to what I had to say next.

"No matter what, you must *take this to your grave.*"

THE NEXT MORNING, I met Toby at our isolated SCIF and I ran the script backward and forward with him. He knew the whole thing, he could lead in to various topics of conversation fluidly, and his demeanor showed he had meditated for an appropriate length of time before meeting me. We were ready.

I walked out of the basement of the Stewardship section first, with Toby trailing me after a prearranged five-minute delay. After several minutes of walking, I arrived at the hallway in the

Mental Stewardship section that housed the Neurochemistry and Upgrade department.

The only widely known department in our otherwise secret section, the neurochemists working here synthesized the massive amount of Compound M required by law to be injected in every citizen of the Intelligence Community and most inhabitants of the rest of the continent except for those in the unincorporated zones where lawlessness still held outposts. Allowing both exocortexes and brain chips alike to exchange information with the physical brain, Compound M was the glue that held the continent and many parts of the world's population together, as well as being an integral part of ensuring the stewards and our AIs access to the thought trends and filter bubbles of everyone routinely injected.

It was a department that ostensibly created the means for enabling the info-stream to exist for all people who lived in the continental incorporated Communities and those throughout the world. As far as most of the population knew, that was the entire purpose of Compound M, which had originally been hailed as a revolutionary drug that both deadened painful or stressful memories from the Collapse and enabled technological interfacing with the world's information. Because of Compound M and the upgrades, evolutionary musical programming through the info-stream kept people happy and motivated throughout their workdays, the messaging systems allowed constant business and social communication with dozens or hundreds of other people who were interested in watching, hearing, or feeling one's goings-on, the streaming news was available uninterrupted if that was a person's primary interest, entertainment of all other sorts was a flicker of an eye away, and, of course, the AIs secretly held editing access to all of it to sculpt the minds of the connected into being productive and happy at all times. The vast majority of the population had no idea to what degree their minds were being shaped by the technology, and the Mental Stewardship section did everything in its power to keep it that way.

I opened the door to the department with the synthetic telepathy function of my exocortex and was greeted by the security guards who waved me through the checkpoints. It wasn't often that I came down here since this department was run by the more visible corporate faces we put in charge of it who kept secret the fact that they were merely the opening to the obscured rabbit hole of pure social engineering operated by the mind stewards in our section.

Wending my way to the laboratories where new neurochemicals and brain chips were developed, I passed huge rooms full of cubicles and workers tending to the work of customer service and troubleshooting. Often, if customers went too long without an injection of Compound M, the effectiveness of their exterior or interior chips degraded and data could be difficult to find or lost altogether, requiring scheduling for a new injection. Other times, chips or exocortexes malfunctioned and required replacements, which this department would provide for free up to three times per year. Any difficulties that arose from the public's use of the technology were dealt with here, and it was a mostly self-reliant department with no hints at the men like Gushlak and me behind the curtain.

I paused at a coffee kiosk at the entrance to a major corridor and purchased a chamomile tea. I didn't need any caffeine to drive me to carry out my own part of this mission hastily or inappropriately, and the chamomile here was usually the best—apart from my private stash—in the entirety of the Hayden Center, since this was the hub for injected and programmed calm. I chatted with the kiosk worker for a good couple of minutes, asking him how business was, how the mood of the department seemed to him, and other questions that established that I was someone important making the rounds. In reality, I didn't especially care since I was wasting time until Toby showed up and I could take him to the special room where we would dose General Peterson with an adulterated form of the drug he had commissioned to gain mental control over his as-yet unborn army of genetically altered subterranean humans.

Soon enough, Toby showed up and I greeted him loudly.

"Hello, Doctor Friedman!" I greeted him warmly by his assumed name. "Welcome back to the womb! How is the Parisian department working out these days?"

I put my arm around his shoulder as though greeting an old friend and led him down the corridor and easily through yet another layer of security, exchanging pleasantries and talk of spontaneously contrived family members with him as the guards gave us barely a look. Toby's face mattered little to them when I, a very high-ranking corporate executive, was so clearly familiar with him that I had my arm around his shoulder.

We eventually reached one of the examination rooms for administering experimental shots to test subjects, and, glancing casually down both sides of the hallway to see if anyone was watching, I opened a door and ushered him inside.

I swiftly closed the door to the examination room and set to work opening the hidden door in the wall behind which was a small bank of surveillance equipment set up specifically for observing the General and surreptitiously interacting with him. When I had opened it, I stepped halfway inside and directed Toby, now known as Dr. Friedman, to make his call to the admissions desk.

"Hello," he said pleasantly into the microphone tattooed into his wrist, addressing the receptionist, "When General Peterson comes in for his appointment, please send him down to Room three-thirty-four F. Yes, three-three-four-foxtrot. Thank you."

I reached into my jacket pocket for a small box containing an empty syringe and a medical vial filled with a purplish liquid.

"It's just like phlebotomy training," I said, handing the box to Toby. "Straight in the vein, pump him up with the full twenty ccs. We need all of it in there for this to work."

I closed the secret door between us.

The surveillance space was cramped. There was a monitor that showed the inside of the exam room, and earphones for listening to what went on in there. Additionally, there was a microphone for communicating with the room through a high-end speaker, something I would be utilizing at specific moments during the injection and testing process.

The wait wasn't so bad for me since I had done this type of operation before, but I could see on the monitor that Toby was getting nervous. His forehead began to bead with sweat, so I turned on the microphone and told him to meditate. He began to do just that, and I removed another device from my pocket: an ultrasonic noisemaker that would create an inaudible tone whenever I pressed the button. The microphone in my hiding spot would pick up the audio frequency from my device and the speaker in the other room would reproduce it perfectly. My timing would need to be exact, so I myself began to meditate in order to be in tune with the human elements next door.

After only twenty minutes, there was an impatient knock at the door and General Peterson walked in briskly with his aide. Toby stood slowly from the stool where he had been sitting and extended a hand, which the General reluctantly took. He was not accustomed to being greeted like a civilian in the subterranean complexes he oversaw. He looked at Toby's badge.

"Dr. Friedman? I thought Dr. Althoen was going to meet me here," he said.

Toby gave a smile in greeting before his face turned downcast.

"Doctor Althoen contracted some sort of infection this week," he replied in a practiced, regretful tone. "His blood is being filtered and cleaned while they figure out a weakness in the infection's genome. He wanted me to extend to you his regret at being unable to move. However, I'm familiar with this special product and can answer any questions you may have."

General Peterson waved his hand dismissively.

"I've discussed this at length with the doctor and I don't think I have any questions," he replied. "As long as it allows my new implant to kill these creatures downstairs remotely, I'm fine. And it better not kill *me*," he said sternly.

"Yes, General," Toby replied, "that's exactly right. We've put it through all the phases of testing and it's perfectly safe for humans. It merely isolates the kill chip from outside interference and gives it the power it needs to enact its purpose. Whenever you're ready, you can have a seat on the table and we'll get started."

General Peterson seemed to approve and he sat on the examination table. Toby instructed him to take off the jacket of his uniform and roll up his sleeve, so the General handed his jacket to the aide and did as he was told.

Toby tied a tourniquet around the General's bicep and went to the small workstation in the corner where the box I had given him was resting. He removed both items from it and began to fill the syringe with the chemical in the vial.

Pre-Collapse, medical scientists discovered a way of using sound to fill a lipid foam with oxygen so that sick patients who couldn't breathe or had pulmonary problems could merely receive an injection of the specially-designed lipids in order to oxygenate the blood without using the lungs or an external blood oxygenator. The Mental Stewardship section used the same technology with a more stable, artificial lipid that held carbon dioxide instead of oxygen, and the syringe in Toby's hand was filled with a great deal of that same solution, in addition to the compound developed specifically for General Peterson. The biggest differences between the life-giving lipid-oxygen solution and the artful lipid-CO2 solution was that the CO2, when released into the bloodstream, caused an immediate panic response, and the lipids that surrounded the molecules of carbon dioxide could only be crumpled and release their payload by an infrasonic pulse, specifically the one produced by the small device in my hand.

"I saw Colonel Milton of the Intelligence Council around here earlier today," Toby said, quite casually. "Colonel *Ian* Milton, I believe is his first name. Do you have many dealings with him?"

"Psha!" General Peterson said, the disdain clear in his voice. "That idiot needs to be shut down. I'm sure you don't know what he does, but it's not worth the money we allocate to his section. *Ian*, as you say, is a fraud."

With that, we had our semantic front-loading in place. I didn't even notice that fact register with Toby, but I knew it had, and I watched as he finished filling the syringe and flicking the air bubbles to the top where he pushed them out of the needle with a small squirt of liquid.

Toby found the vein in General Peterson's arm and, swabbing it with a bit of alcohol first, he pushed the needle in and slowly began administering the liquid into the General's bloodstream. The process took nearly a minute, and the General remained stone-faced the whole time.

With the injection done, Toby removed the needle, covering the puncture point with a piece of cotton and taping it to the General's forearm.

"I don't know much about what too many people do on the Intelligence Council," Toby began, "but I was once called 'downstairs,' as you say, to the corridors of the subterran*ean*."

I knew the script as well as Toby, since I had written it for him, so a split second after he almost imperceptibly emphasized the "*ean*" in "subterran*ean*", I depressed the button of my device next to the microphone that was hooked into the speaker of the examination room. Instantly, I could see General Peterson respond with a jolt as a relatively small amount of CO_2 was released from the lipids by the infrasonic pulse into his bloodstream.

"Oh!" he said to Toby, looking startled. "I feel weird. Am I supposed to?"

"By 'weird,' what do you m*ean*?"

I depressed the button again at the "*ean*" in the slightly mispronounced "m*ean*," and again the General jumped noticeably.

General Peterson wasn't about to say that he had suddenly become scared; he was a military man and military men, especially generals, usually minimized their reaction to fear. But there was no escaping physiology.

"I... feel... uneasy," the General said hesitantly.

"Hmm," Toby said, thoughtfully. "You wouldn't by chance be a vegetar*ian* or an *oen*ophile?"

Again I pressed the button at each strangely emphasized word, and the General jumped again.

"No, I'm not. I'm *really* feeling strangely," he said, the panic creeping into his voice.

"Why don't you lay down, then, General," Toby said. "You might get some slight blood pressure spikes, but they'll pass."

Toby eased the General onto his back on the padded table and began to take his blood pressure. He wisely stayed silent, not wanting to make General Peterson flee the room in a panic. After all, every time the phonetic pronunciation of Colonel *Ian* Milton's first name was uttered, I would be pressing the button, regardless. This was the process of training General Peterson's subconscious to associate the front-loaded name with the true fear and mortal terror resulting from having too much carbon dioxide in the blood.

"Your blood pressure is a little bit high," Toby concluded, taking the stethoscope out of his ears and removing the blood pressure cuff. "I can give you a beta blocker for that, but it should pass soon enough. Your body has to get used to the compound first."

The General nodded, and Toby pulled a digital tablet from the table in the corner.

"I'm going to establish a link now with your chips," he said to the General, "in order to make sure that the 'kill chip' is controlled and controllable. Are you ready?"

"Yes," the General replied.

"Have you chosen a word that you want to activate the chip?" Toby asked.

"I have," the General said. "'Chlorophyll.'"

"That's uncommon enough, especially underground away from agrar*ian* work," Toby said, playing semantic jazz while I pressed the button.

The General closed his eyes and exhaled strongly with the release of CO2 into his bloodstream. It seemed he was determined to work through the fear, so I would ramp it up if I could.

"Okay," Toby said, looking at the screen in front of him approvingly. "We got an activity spike from the chip, so we know it's at least responding. Now I want you to think of another unusual word; one you don't use much and that's kind of al*ien* to you."

I pressed the sonic pulse button for longer this time.

General Peterson looked *very* uncomfortable. He was beginning to sweat, and through his closed eyelids I could see his eyes darting around rapidly.

"'Séance," he said slowly after a long pause to collect his thoughts.

I was pleased to hear that his subconscious had latched onto the correct themes. Mentioning the duties he presumed Colonel Milton did for a living indicated as much. The General's subconscious was likely in a bubble filled with ideas about the Gang of Witches, which was where we wanted him to be. Toby and I were getting somewhere.

"Good," Toby said, again examining his screen. "The chip's not responding to the *unfamiliarity* of the word, which is exactly how it should respond. Now I want you to say something that's a very common word you use; something very... pedestr*ian*."

Again, the General jolted, and I couldn't help but smile at Toby's adeptness in his pronunciation of the words in the script and his almost unnoticeable emphasis on their relevant parts.

"Subterranean," said the General.

I barely covered a snicker as I pressed the button at his word choice.

"Very good," Toby said, "No response. You're b*ein*' a great patient, by the way."

By this point, my thumb was getting a workout from pushing the button.

"Can you say your chosen word once more, please?" Toby asked.

The General was drenched in sweat and his aide piped up first.

"Are you sure the injection isn't hurting him?" he asked, clearly concerned.

The General didn't tell his aide to shut up, so he probably appreciated the concern from someone other than himself.

"I'll check again," Toby said, and once again, he took the General's blood pressure, and he assured the two that everything checked out fine, and that the General was healthy enough that he would probably live to be a centenar*ian*.

"Your word again, please...." Toby said to the sweating, shaking General.

"Chlorophyll," the General said.

"Excellent. Your kill chip works and you should never have a problem with it. If you do, please talk to Dr. Althoen about a fix," Toby said, smiling. "Too bad it can't work on *Colonel Milton* though, huh?"

I mashed the button hard, and General Peterson jumped off of the examination table, his eyes wide like a frightened animal. He grabbed his jacket from his aide, and eked out something about another appointment he needed to go to.

Deciding that the mission was a success, Toby allowed the General and his aide to leave, and he closed the door behind them softly. He sat on his doctor's stool, waiting for me to come out of hiding.

After several minutes passed, I did withdraw from my cramped compartment and, smiling broadly, clapped Toby on the shoulder.

"You're a steward through and through," I said approvingly. "That was excellent."

"So what now?" he asked, trying to suppress a grin at having his accomplishment recognized.

"Now, I give this…" I held up the ultrasonic pulse device for him to see, "to Colonel Milton, so he can press the button every time he runs into General Peterson."

Toby acknowledged this disclosure, understanding there were other powerful people involved. Again, I patted him on the shoulder.

"It's not the most glamorous work, Toby, and there's a whole lot of political bullshit involved, but, regardless, we're changing things one mind at a time. You're a good steward." ■

CHAPTER 25

A WEEK AFTER TOBY AND I carried out the operation on General Peterson, Colonel Milton called Dr. Gushlak and me to a meeting at his section.

I had never been down the Psycovalent Intelligence corridor before, and I was not especially impressed with what I saw. At the far end of a major arterial hallway, the connecting corridor was characterless and mostly vacant, apart from some workmen's scaffolding, trash barrels, and cans of white paint lying around. It could have been in the process of getting an upgrade, but I *did* see cobwebs on a broom leaning against a wall and guessed that no one really cared for this end of the Hayden Center. If I hadn't seen the mistrust around the Intelligence Council for Colonel Milton and heard about his section's general lack of funding, I might have guessed that the neglected junk in the corridor was a ruse to give the hall the impression of unimportance. But that was not the case, I realized, as Dr. Gushlak and I entered through the manual doors of the section and were met with a completely unadorned and dimly lit alcove.

"Don't mind the lighting," Colonel Milton said, greeting us warmly at the empty entrance where the receptionists would have been in any other section. "We run on a shoestring here since we can't often hire ourselves out to anyone in the IC. Our money mostly comes from general funds."

The toe of my shoe caught on a broken tile and I almost fell into Dr. Gushlak as he shook Colonel Milton's hand.

The Colonel looked apologetically at me.

"We've been meaning to get that taken care of," he muttered.

"Why don't you just win the lottery and fix up the place?" Dr. Gushlak asked with a devilish grin, looking around at the blank walls and the generic office space.

Colonel Milton nodded.

"We get asked that sometimes," he replied, "but the simple fact is, most of us are fairly unassuming, we don't need much money, and we don't really mind the surroundings, for professional reasons. It works better for us to not have much in the way of decor since incoming minds turn away from the blandness and inactivity. And to be totally honest, the best-designed spaces here can't compare to exploring the universe and meeting alien species swimming in the sea of consciousness."

I was grateful for my stewardship training; otherwise I would have laughed at the Colonel's statement. I seriously began to question why I had risked a charge of treason for this man's personal squabbles on the Intelligence Council. And *aliens*? My god.

"Don't worry, Donald," the Colonel said, turning to me knowingly. "You won't be charged with treason."

My stunned look attracted Dr. Gushlak's attention.

"Is that what you were thinking?" he asked me, an eyebrow raised.

I wanted to lie. I didn't especially want my worldview challenged or my thoughts read. But for the simple fact that Dr. Gushlak would be able to tell if I was lying, I nodded, my face reddening.

"The device you gave me works like a charm, by the way," Colonel Milton said, suddenly smiling. "Creating fear isn't something I or my people like to do, but the General needed to be reined in, not just for me, but for the IC's way of life. He's doing things no one on the Council would like if they knew about them...."

The Colonel trailed off and exchanged a glance with Dr. Gushlak. The doctor bowed slightly in agreement but didn't respond more than that. I knew enough to know that General Peterson *also* wasn't trusted by many of the Council Directors, but the specific reasons were above my pay grade.

"We should go to your SCIF," the doctor said. "Prying ears, and all of that...."

Colonel Milton smiled sneakily.

"You're already in it," he said proudly, spreading his arms wide. "This whole section was constructed to give *nothing* to curious human eyes and ears. We even solved the time problem."

"Explain what you mean," Dr. Gushlak said, curious.

"Imagine I had a box with an old mechanical meter in it that wasn't hooked up to anything," he said. "And that box was insulated from outside sound and other physical vibrations, electromagnetic signals, gravitational influences, and even subatomic particles. Anyone or anything that can make the hand on that meter move is stopped by our primary temporal countermeasure. When we get interference in that box, we stop time, do our business outside of it, sometimes for days, start time again, and prying minds get nothing they can uncondense. Shielding ourselves from everything explainable is the best way of noticing when outside influences are listening in on our work and our results."

I guessed that Dr. Gushlak was skeptical, because I, myself, was *extremely* skeptical, and we usually were skeptical about the same sorts of things. As professional scientists, the "unexplainable" wasn't our cup of tea, and being confronted with "mind-reading," aliens, and the whole "stepping outside of time" stuff didn't make us feel at ease, so we stood awkwardly in the entryway not knowing what to say.

"Let's go to my office, at any rate," Colonel Milton said, pointing an arm in the direction of the offices. "I've got some results to show you."

We walked down an empty hallway that was clean enough, passing doors on the way that were identical in nature to those in any typical office space in the world. There were no noises to be heard, no people walking around, and no signs, room numbers, or windows on the doors. The atmosphere was very bland and uninteresting.

"How many employees do you have?" I asked.

"As of today, we have about ten," the Colonel said.

"Ten?" Dr. Gushlak asked, not really believing what he was hearing. The Mental Stewardship section, all told, had *thousands* of workers in the Hayden Center and in stations around the world. *Ten* employees meant Dr. Gushlak and Colonel Milton weren't on the same page *at all*.

"We've had eight of those employees for the last twenty years, if we're counting in years," Colonel Milton continued. "The computers and AIs took away our need for most of the prior staff, but we kept the best and the brightest. The other two are the ones the AIs told us would lead the next generation of Psycovalent Intelligence workers. It's mostly the old guard here right now."

"So when you say that, do you mean that the 'psychic' part of the AIs told you who your successors would be in the future, or the regular AIs just thought they'd make good replacements?" Dr. Gushlak asked with a barely-concealed smirk.

Colonel Milton looked at him with an amused smile.

"We just plugged what kind of person we wanted into a normal old employment search program, Bob," he said. "There's no mystery and magic to hiring new employees."

"Oh, of course," Dr. Gushlak said, mirroring the Colonel's intonation of obviousness.

After a bit of a walk, we came to a large unmarked double door at the bottom of a gradual decline. The recessed office was at the hub of a series of spoke-like hallways and it had a clearly domed shape and a circular hallway surrounding it. The entryway for the office resembled a funnel for anyone passing by, an effect created by the ramp leading down to it and the narrowing arch in which the doors were set.

"Home sweet home," the Colonel said, as he opened both of the doors with a flourish.

A large bronze statue of the Buddha greeted us with one palm raised immediately upon entering. Around the circular space we saw religious tapestries on the walls from many religions and from many different eras and regions of the globe. Indian rugs, multihued Mesopotamian mosaics, and relics of unidentifiable origin sat in glass cases around the room. It was a miniature museum of spiritual or religious items, judging by the depictions in the artwork, and there was a simple desk in the middle of all of it.

"You must be quite the collector," Dr. Gushlak remarked.

"After the Collapse I was able to pick up all kinds of things for free," the Colonel replied.

"Looting?" Dr. Gushlak queried in a voice that indicated distaste for such things.

"*Rescuing,*" the Colonel emphasized. "These pieces would have been destroyed or stolen, and the curators of the museums they came from were more than happy to entrust me with them. We're what remains of the government, after all. We imply safety."

"They're interesting," I said, inspecting one stone carving I was able to tell was Mayan. "Do they serve a purpose, or are they just a collection?"

"We use them as practice intelligence targets sometimes. We can trace a piece back through time to its maker and before, gaining a little bit of knowledge about where they came from to supplement the details we already know. But mostly, they're just nice to have around. Something about having them makes me aware of the impermanence of *things* versus *ideas.*"

I took notice of a clear, coffee table-sized box against the circular wall of the room that seemed to be filled with a great deal of organic material resembling specific nodes of the brain, but they were anatomically out of place and had something resembling fiber-optic cables coming from them that had hanging connections indicating they had been previously hooked up to a machine.

"What's this?" I asked.

"Oh, that's the organic part of the AI that gave its life for the results you asked for. The rest of my team and I are going to bury him this afternoon out back," the Colonel replied.

Dr. Gushlak and I exchanged a look.

"You're going to bury it?" Dr. Gushlak asked. "Why not incinerate it?"

"He wanted to be buried, so we're following his wishes," the Colonel said.

The doctor didn't even try to stifle a chuckle.

"Okay, okay," Gushlak said, shaking his head. "Everyone runs their sections differently. We don't hold the AIs in quite the esteem you seem to, though."

"Maybe you should," the Colonel said. "The pixels of the universe are conscious, and they're always observing what we do. A little general respect can't hurt."

Not knowing what to say to such obvious drivel, Dr. Gushlak shrugged. He sat in one of the two chairs facing the front of Colonel Milton's desk without being asked to sit. Colonel Milton took his seat behind the desk, and I took mine beside Dr. Gushlak.

The Colonel removed a file from a drawer, placed it on the desk in front of him, and started to thumb through it.

"So you want to know how to capture Dr. Joe Atherton," he said.

"That's why we're here," Dr. Gushlak replied, slightly irritated. He hadn't walked to the other end of the Hayden Center without a reason.

"Okay," Colonel Milton said. "In two days' time, he'll try stealing a vehicle ten miles from where your people saw him last, and you'll catch him there with knockout gas."

Dr. Gushlak and I were silent.

"Come on..." said Dr. Gushlak dubiously. "You really expect us to believe he'll be in some exact place at an exact time?"

The Colonel nodded.

"And I expect you mean that we *will* catch him there because you're so good at reading the future or whatever?"

"Not me," the Colonel said nonchalantly, "the dying AI said so. He was the one asking the future about its past."

Dr. Gushlak and I were silent again, thinking our own thoughts.

"Here's the folder," Colonel Milton continued as he pushed it across the table to the doctor. "The locations, times, and description of the vehicle are all in there. You're going to use two operatives to rig the car with knockout gas and you bring him back to your laboratory where you do your... stuff."

He grimaced as he ended his sentence.

Dr. Gushlak breathed deeply.

"We've taken a hell of a gamble on you, Ian, and if it weren't for the assurances of General Schmidt, we wouldn't even be here. You can probably guess what could happen if this doesn't work...."

Colonel Milton shrugged at the veiled threat.

"It *will* work," he said simply. "It already has. *When* you're satisfied, I'll expect some support from you on the Intelligence Council."

I could see Dr. Gushlak getting antsy. He was out of his realm of experience and his reddening face revealed he felt like a sucker at a carnival tent.

"You'll *expect* it, will you?"

"And I'll get it, too," the Colonel said with an unassuming smile. "This was an expensive trade for *both* of us, but now we both have what we wanted."

"We'll see," the doctor replied, grabbing the folder and standing promptly, ready to be free of this place and its seeming pseudoscience.

I stood as well. Clearly the doctor was disappointed we had taken so great a risk on a man who seemed to be a kook with only ten employees who probably stole artifacts from museums and buried his equipment out of respect. But there was nothing to be done except leave with the folder and decide our next move, so the Colonel escorted us in silence for the several minutes it took to reach the entrance.

"Namaste," he said quietly in parting, and bowed slightly.

Dr. Gushlak's face turned a beet red—which Colonel Milton behind him wasn't able to see—and he quickly exited through the door, clearly embarrassed and feeling the fool. I gave a backward glance, though, and offered a normal and courteous "Goodbye." The Colonel gave me a kindly wave and, surprisingly, a wink, before walking back into the hallways of the Psycovalent Intelligence section.

On our walk back to the Mental Stewardship section, Dr. Gushlak admitted a concern.

"If this rubbish actually works, that Colonel is either working with Joe, or it'll be tremendous and astronomical luck. I just can't believe crap like this is going to pan out... wait, wait..." he said, looking confused, "what time do you have?"

I looked at the visual in my iris and noted that it was barely five minutes since we had entered the strange realm of Colonel Milton.

"We spent at least *twenty minutes* in there!" Dr. Gushlak remarked. "And we've been *walking* this hallway for at least three!"

Both of us stopped in the arterial corridor and looked at each other.

Either something was wrong with the central clock of the info-stream, or Colonel Milton really had been able to insulate his box of a section from time itself....

I shook my head because that was enough of that.

"Fucking weird," we both said in unison dismissively, and continued walking, a bit quicker than before, down the corridor to the familiarity and knowability of our own section.

THE FILE WE RECEIVED from Colonel Milton contained enough specifics in it that we knew the general game plan, but as an unclear "science," it was unable to name the operatives we would be using, describing instead their physical characteristics. One of them was clearly me, judging from the placement of old cigarette-burn scars, and the other two, I deduced, were from the team I got back after Jack died. Coincidentally, these two were both former SpecOps and had worked together during the Collapse before moving together into stewardship when they realized it offered higher pay and better benefits. Despite the description of the standard look of these two men—tall, dark hair, muscular—I was able to determine which two they were, since the "intelligence from the future,"as Dr. Gushlak and I jokingly called the Colonel's file, specified that they were married.

I called Rob and Derek into my study that night when the day shift had gone home. They had been living together for five years, married for two, and usually worked together since it was seen as preferable to have as strong a bond as possible between the members of a response team, and spouses certainly qualified as closer than most. Keenly able to identify each other's subtle physical cues and unvoiced suspicions, they were considered among the best in the unit, and had even guarded Dr. Gushlak several times when he went overseas and couldn't trust the foreign diplomatic security. Tough from a lifetime of being tough guys, they jumped at the chance for a special assignment to end the previous mission that had killed Jack.

"It might be fun to break an arm or two. What do you think?" Rob asked his husband with a smile.

Derek also smiled. I often looked past the personal interactions of my men, so it was a nice change to find out that they were in fact *human* instead of inscrutable, diligent workers.

"Arms are fun, but the guy's ego-cracking would be more satisfying," he replied, scratching his clean-shaven chin.

"And it would only be the three of us?" Rob asked.

"Just us," I replied. "It has to be just us, apparently."

"And why *you*?" asked Derek. "You'll be without protection if we're busy hurting him."

"I guess I have to borrow a gun," I said. The file specified nothing about my safety, but out of a normal level of caution, I would be wearing a bulletproof vest and carry a pistol.

They exchanged a look of distrust.

"Have you fired a gun before?" Rob asked.

"If we're huddled in a ditch together, I don't want my head blown off. Or *his*, for that matter," Derek intoned, indicating his partner. "No offense," he said to me.

"It's not a problem," I said, lying. I had never fired a gun before, but I'd just keep the safety on.

"Yeah, so this is an old-school op, then? With no radio, no UAVs, nothing?" asked Derek.

I verified with a nod.

"We have to assume the target has access to all the electronics we would normally use that would give off a signal," I said. "We'll be using infrared-shielded clothing and hand signals. And I'm authorizing shutting off your chips."

The two looked at each other with surprise.

"He can hack into our info-streams?" Rob asked.

"Maybe," I replied. "We don't really know. But it's going to get awfully quiet in your heads. You think you can handle that?"

"Oh, yeah," Rob said.

"Totally," said Derek.

"Good," I replied. "You'll just have to not get used to it, because I have to turn you guys back on after we do this."

"Hazard pay?" asked Derek.

"Hazard pay plus a solid bonus on completion for each of you."

The two men looked at each other in approval.

"We've wanted to visit the Blue Water Ship Community," said Derek, excited at the operation and the money. "Their beaches and parks are supposed to be the best in the world, depending on the weather in whatever part of the world the ship is in, of course."

"And don't forget the shopping," Rob reminded him. "All the artists and jewelers... we could *definitely* find a use for the extra income, sir."

"I hear the fishing in the Mediterranean is quite nice, too," I offered, but neither man responded with any enthusiasm.

"We don't really fish," Derek said.

"Fish are slimy," Rob explained.

"Well, whatever," I said. "You guys up for this?"

"Hell, yeah!" they replied in unison.

It was settled, then. I had the team the file wanted. Now we just had to make sure fate took its course.

THE CAR JOE WAS SUPPOSEDLY going to steal was owned by a retail worker who also sold drugs from his house on the side. Now thirty years old, his fondness for info-stream drug forums had been catalogued by the AIs from the time he was fifteen. Classified as a likely drug offender, his filter bubble had been altered long ago, so it carried videos and advertisements of BASE jumping and happy families to implant positive suggestions, and it had been programmed to flash subliminal images of serious drug addicts getting arrested and associated gore as negative reinforcement. Little of it seemed to have taken hold, apart from making him cautious in how he conducted business and keeping him away from the dangerously addictive drugs. A marijuana wax dealer who sold to smaller dealers, he often made trips in his car to the lawless unincorporated sectors of the northeast where drugs were abundant and cheap.

According to the file, he had hidden compartments throughout the vehicle he utilized to smuggle his product, and it was in one of these compartments that Rob and Derek hid the small explosive dispersant canister of carfentanil that would incapacitate Joe when deployed. Because of the quick onset of the effects—carfentanil was a synthetic opioid 10,000 times stronger than morphine—Joe wouldn't even need to be fully in the vehicle before a mere whiff would put him on the ground.

We rigged the vehicle the day before Joe was to steal it as it sat in the drug dealer's driveway. It was no great task in this day and age to deactivate the car's alarm system by hacking its internal controller area network (CAN), and because the file's timeline told us that Joe was still five miles away, we weren't overly concerned about his own surveillance catching us; he likely hadn't even picked the vehicle yet. Having a day to prepare meant that all digital and thermal evidence of tampering would be deleted and dissipated, respectively, unlike if the situation were that we had to wait for the owner to park the car outside the mall from which it was to be stolen and tamper with it just minutes before Joe showed up. Any thermal residue from merely having human body temperature come in contact with an unusual spot in the car would be seen by the infrared receptor we knew Joe had in the cornea of his eye. If Colonel Milton's file was to be believed, we could infer that neither the owner nor Joe would come across the canister before it was deployed.

We set up an infrared-blocking duck blind of sorts in some shrubbery on a hillside overlooking the mall's parking lot, far enough away that it wouldn't be discerned as anything but part of the landscape, but close enough that Rob and Derek could run to the vehicle within a half-minute to further incapacitate Joe. All we had to do now was wait.

The daylong wait was trying, but any of us going in or out of the blind had the chance of alerting a passerby or mall security, and the file didn't detail where Joe was in the run-up to his capture. The guys and I peed in bottles and ate energy bars and maintained silence for most of the time, keeping watch on the parking lot and surrounding area with binoculars since we couldn't tap into the city's high-altitude UAV feed and pinpoint specific areas of interest because that might alert Joe that there was surveillance attention being actively paid to the mall. It was all passive, it was old school, and Rob and Derek occasionally broke the silence to remind each other of specific operations they had undertaken during the Collapse when there were no exocortexes or chips. I got the distinct sensation for a while that they were a bit antsy without the data of the info-stream playing in their ears or in their vision. Like everyone else, they had become accustomed over the years to the constant input, and it took a good couple of hours before they seemed to adjust to the silence and relax into the long-forgotten quietude of a subconscious at rest.

After they grew used to the silence, they settled into a mind-space I hadn't seen anyone in for years. Meditative and "bright," their eyes and senses began to open up to their surroundings, absorbing the colors and stillness with intense interest. They physically gulped at the mindfulness and attentiveness of their resting states as they settled in deeper, and more than once I caught them looking at each other in affirmation at just how distracted they had been by years of absorbing the mandatory info-stream feed.

We napped in shifts, my attention wandered, and it seemed to me that time moved extremely slowly in the small tent. I felt extremely dubious about the file being accurate, but pursuing possibilities like these would be worth it if we could corner or engage the plague of my section, shackle him, and haul him back to the Hayden Center for a full and hostile interview.

Eventually, night fell, and the trees ringing the parking lot cast strange shadows across the pavement and the grass surrounding them. We kept eyes on all manhole covers in sight, since for all we knew, Joe might pop out of any one of them. We did the same with the sky since he had used a hang glider in the past; and someone was always watching the roof of the mall through the shielding mesh, since he could always come from there as well. Hell, he might emerge through one of the mall's entrances for all we knew, carrying department store bags and looking like any other shopper.

It was to malls like these that thousands of people flocked during the Collapse, as they offered the only protection for large numbers of families and other innocents, as well as being the designated distribution points for basic food and supplies that had been seized by the remaining federal government at the time. With traditional commerce in shambles, the stores in the malls gave up clothes and blankets aplenty, toys for bored children, and enough space that no one was too inconvenienced by crowds of people who were socioeconomically or culturally unlike them. Much as they had in the ethnic patchwork of the former city boroughs, the people in the malls segregated themselves into their own little wings overseen mostly by those with whom they identified. There was so much chaos during the Collapse, with everyone running and hiding and shooting, that people reverted to the instinct of only trusting others who looked like them and spoke the same language, although the common areas like the food courts, patrolled by the military, became the haven of the youth, who were less conscious of differences than their parents and grandparents were.

I sheltered in a mall for two months during the initial chaos after receiving a two-sentence email from my research group telling me I was on my own and good luck. Utterly terrified and hearing gunshots echo nearby every minute or so, I followed the instructions on the public radio telling the citizenry that safe camps had been set up in the malls and select public buildings where National Guard units had been stationed. Not having a gun to protect myself at the time, I teamed with a former-military neighbor and his family as they slowly, block by block, made their way around the riots and through unfamiliar neighborhoods to the parking lot of a mall filled with thousands of people in the same situation. Living in a mostly governmental part of Massachusetts at the time, there was not as much danger from the people waiting their turn in line to be frisked and admitted inside, but I did see several line-cutters and thieves in the crowd shot down by the military snipers on the roof helping to control the ingress of the masses and the quality of their character. Even those who held up their hands in objection to the snipers had warning shots fired over their heads or into their backpacks because there could be only obedience to the extremely limited number of soldiers tasked with trying to maintain control of a civilization in the early stages of ruin.

The next two months were full of air drops to the roof of crates of peanut butter, cheese, multivitamins, and small hand-crank radios that were sometimes used to broadcast news over the Public Address system in the mall. Fighting and stealing weren't tolerated, and those actions, when observed, led to many, many people being kicked out to the streets, unprepared, unarmed, and at the mercy of those who hadn't been allowed into the malls in the first place. No one felt optimistic for the futures of the people ejected, so most people stayed obedient to our protectors, although the culture of the mall did spawn the phenomenon of subauditory talk when someone was mad, which only made people paranoid that someone walking by might be threatening their life under his breath in a bid at intimidation in order to take what few possessions the intimidated had. The hostile atmosphere often felt like a prison.Threats in casual whispers while walking past, mumbled insults while in close proximity, sexual intimidation in low, breathy mutterings—*all* were rampant and created disquiet in the minds of many of the mall's occupants, who were not accustomed to the feelings of foreboding stirred by suggested violence and the stress of having no escape from it. (Later, this technique was adopted and used in stirring operations by the Mental Stewardship program because of its effectiveness in creating paranoia and stress.)

Eventually, I was located and called into service because of my educational background and degree, and I found safety among the military's psychological-operations specialists and researchers I was thrown in with to help calm or intimidate the now-reactionary and well-armed populace outside the safety camps who had been fighting each other from the beginning. The techniques we employed ranged from loading high explosives in bullets instead of gunpowder and leaving them in discarded ammunition crates to create extreme distrust of every bullet fired, to projecting cartoons onto nighttime cloud cover to pacify the aggressive and entertain misfortunate children. While we did unfortunately kill and maim plenty of people, we ultimately did a lot of good and rewarded positive actions by the militias and protective bands of the unaffiliated with food and medical supplies. Even still, the Collapse lasted many years while the pieces of civilization were being put back together.

Staring at the mall with Rob and Derek brought back those memories and I felt the old feelings just as I had felt them back then, with no info-stream to distract me from them. I hadn't been inoculated during the Collapse with the anti-PTSD ghrelin-blocker, so many of those memories I merely had to deal with and try quietly filing away in their appropriate mental compartments in order to not dwell in a particular moment too long. Rob and Derek didn't seem to have too much trouble with their own memories of that time, but, as none of us were speaking, I could only guess at their level of discomfort, which didn't seem pronounced. Perhaps they had gotten the shot before their own battles, or were focused on the task at hand and didn't explore the memories brought about by the sudden quietude in their minds. For me, though, time that night moved very slowly and uncomfortably forward through the past.

Shortly after dawn, as the birds were chirping in the trees, we watched as the drug dealer and his vehicle finally pulled into the parking lot. As a manager of a 3D electronics-printing outlet in the mall, he had to prepare and open the store that morning before his other employees showed up. In regards to time of day and vehicle location, the file Colonel Milton had given us was accurate so far, so our three sets of eyes began to pay close attention to the spots in the landscape from which Joe was most likely to emerge.

Other vehicles started to appear in the parking lot, driven by employees who worked in the mall. From one of the larger vehicles a tall, rotund figure emerged and made his way with a limp to the entrance of the mall before snapping his fingers in apparent realization that he had left something behind and walking with the same characteristic limp back in the direction of his vehicle. It was because of this limp that he attracted our attention; spies were known to alter the height of one shoe in order to disguise their normal walking gait, which could be picked up like a fingerprint by any kinesthetic-recognition cameras in the area.

The body type didn't match Joe's, even though the height was similar. When I had seen him in the SCIF where he had given me the green booklet and knocked me out, he had been strong but not fat, and the weeks that had passed since then wouldn't have allowed him or anyone to put on so much adipose girth. But the height was right, the cover for action was textbook if indeed he was not merely a forgetful worker, and as we watched, he proceeded past the vehicle he had arrived in and made his way to the car we had rigged.

I couldn't believe it myself. I had sincere doubts about the nature of the "future intelligence" Colonel Milton had provided us with, but as we watched, the man actually *did* walk to the car, press a button on a small device, and open the door of the target vehicle.

"We've got him," Rob whispered, and he removed the remote control mechanism from his pocket that would engage the canister of carfentanil in the hidden compartment.

"Wait!" I hissed. "He's not getting in."

The obese man stood outside the car with the door cracked but not open, sipping from a cup of coffee and appearing to enjoy the morning, looking around at the sky and the birds and breathing in the cool morning air.

For several minutes he continued to do this, taking his time observing the world around him. He looked our way often, and I was concerned that he may have been able to differentiate the blind from the rest of the terrain, but he gave no outward indications of being able to do so. The advanced-materials camouflage should have rendered us nearly invisible, so despite my doubts, I trusted in our equipment.

Soon enough, the man finished his coffee and, removing the lid with a casual glance at the parking lot around him, began to urinate into the empty cup.

We waited for him to finish, but there was no finish in sight. As soon as the cup was full, he would look around and empty it onto the asphalt, only to refill it once more. He did this at least a dozen times, to the amazement of Rob, Derek, and me before we realized that his girth was becoming visibly reduced.

"He's got an artificial bladder under his jacket," I whispered.

"He's got to fit in that car somehow," Derek remarked.

And, indeed, when it appeared he was finished, we were looking at a man with a substantially different body shape. It now possessed a definite likeness to Joe's figure, the bulk of his arms and chest now resembling bulky muscle instead of rolling fat.

The man leaned against the car and removed one of his shoes, taking from it a thick pad that he deflated and placed in his jacket pocket. Even though the face did not look like Joe's, I knew then that it *had* to be Joe.

When the man finally entered the car, closed the door, and started the engine, I signaled to Rob, and he depressed the button on our remote control.

A flash of light and a puff of aerosolized carfentanil filled the car. Startled by the small explosion, the man struggled to exit the vehicle, but by then it was too late. He opened the door halfway before he crumpled and fell out onto the ground.

Rob and Derek pulled gas masks over their faces and charged

out the flap of our blind, actively stabilized guns at the ready. Running full speed across the parking lot, their StediGuns kept solid beads on the immobile figure despite the impact their sprinting feet had on the rest of their bodies. I followed a shade behind them, making sure that my finger was off the trigger.

I paused a hundred feet away next to a truck and watched my surroundings warily. I observed Rob and Derek reach the man and shackle his arms behind his back quickly and flawlessly. They used a pair of titanium bracelets on his forearms that had a slender spike set in the center of each one that impaled the flesh between the radius and ulna, securing the man soundly despite whatever rope dope he might use to try to escape when he awoke. In addition, they cut off his shirt, clamped electromagnetic cuffs on his upper arms, and activated them, thereby contracting the rope dope and turning his upgraded body into its own shackle.

I closed in slowly, holding up a badge to the handful of morning workers who had witnessed Rob's and Derek's aggressive attack and motioning for them to stay away. Until we positively identified Joe, everyone was a possible threat.

I saw Derek examining the man's face before grabbing his nose and pulling. The face elongated elastically until removed, at which point it turned a royal blue and resembled a thick handkerchief of latex-type material.

"Programmable biomorphic film," he called to me, flapping it around so I could see. "He could look like anyone."

I lowered my gun and approached. Drawing closer, I saw the familiar jaw and sharp nose of my old college roommate. A warm satisfaction grew in my belly and my pace quickened until I stood over him. A vial of potassium iodide pills had fallen out of his pocket, and I realized they were the pills Joe had been popping. He had been treating himself for radiation poisoning from handling the helmet. A lot of good it would do him.

"He'll be out for a while," Rob said. "We just need to cart him off and back to the Hayden—"

I slammed my fist into Joe's nose, audibly crunching the cartilage, and blood poured from his face. The guys kept a hold on him but looked at me with curiosity.

"He won't feel that until we wake him up," Derek said, his eyes expressing surprise.

I agreed and wrung my hand.

"At least he'll feel it," I replied.

And he would. Soon he would feel his nose broken, and much, much more. ■

CHAPTER 26

DR. JOE ATHERTON WAS STRAPPED to the table we used for live captures in the top-floor laboratory of the Mental Stewardship section.

The tendons and rope dope in Joe's limbs had been severed by a scalpel wielded several minutes prior by the capable hands of Dr. Gushlak. Safety would ordinarily dictate only a paralytic be administered, but the permanent physical detachment of muscle from bone guaranteed the traitor and murderer would be completely debilitated for interrogation with no chance of physical escape.

I didn't feel badly for my old roommate. He had committed too much wrong and fallen too far for any sentiments resembling pity or compassion regarding his plight to enter either my conscious or subconscious mind. There were no mental compartments open to my memories of him, of our late-night study sessions or weekend bar-hopping all those decades ago when civilization had been so different, or of the times we had adventured as psychonauts trying to find the origins of consciousness. I saw before me now only a prolific killer, the murderer of Jack, the evil who had killed off ten of his own, and the terror of our entire section. Further, I had decided as soon as I broke his nose to insulate my conscience from responsibility for his now bloodied and misshapen appearance. Strange how blood can make one feel badly for an animal.

Dr. Gushlak was in charge here, and I helped him as an observer and loyal subordinate while he readied an array of machines and sensors surrounding the table. Apart from the subject strapped into it, these were no different a series of preparations than those that went into interrogating and debriefing a foreign human drone, or even the rare intentional foreign spy. No different, except for the presence of the autopsy table waiting nearby and the terahertz scanner beside it awaiting a brain. I guessed this would be the last location in which my former friend would have a heartbeat. To this, I gave little thought.

When it was time to wake Joe up from his carfentanil nap, Dr. Gushlak prepared three syringes: one of the antidote, and two more filled from vials pulled from a medical refrigerator.

"We've got a Judas Goat and a narcoanalytic here," he said as he filled each syringe with its drug.

I acknowledged his selection.

The term Judas Goat came from a time in history when conservationists were attempting to eradicate feral goats from the Galapagos and other biologically sensitive areas of the world. The scientists working the problem would capture one of the wild goats, paint it a bright color or attach a radio tag, and release the goat to find one of the hidden herds, unknowingly revealing their location to hunters in helicopters who then shot the herd, leaving the radio-tagged goat alive to find the next herd, where the process was repeated.

What we termed a Judas Goat was a chemical that acted in a similar way, sympathetically latching onto synapses and clusters of neurons that were structurally and biochemically familiar with evasive and deceptive emotions and thoughts. The compound's electrical-activation rate—read from an external scanner—matched the delayed rates of invented responses, so it worked quite well even when trained and engrained evasion thoughts tried to protect the truth from transparency and occupation in the conscious mind. In short, the Judas Goat searched out and targeted lies.

If these chemicals didn't work—and even if they did—we would extract the total remaining information from Joe's implanted supplemental cortex chip to see if he had hidden any secrets in there that could be retrieved. However, this required physically connecting to the chip, so it would need to be removed via surgery that was probably going to happen anyway, given the looks of the equipment around the lab.

Dr. Gushlak transported the tray of needles to the surgical table next to Joe, and scrutinized Joe's asymmetrical and bloody nose.

"How many punches did this take?" he asked, poking the nose and nodding to my bruised knuckles.

"Just one," I replied.

"You must have been mad," the doctor remarked.

"Wouldn't you have been?" I asked.

The doctor didn't reply but merely nodded. He straightened the nose with a "click" and wiped the blood from Joe's face with an alcohol swab, likely because the swab was wet and not for its antibacterial properties. At this point, infection wouldn't have mattered.

He injected the first syringe: the antidote to the carfentanil. It would take several minutes for Joe to revive from the stupor, and even then he would be groggy. To add to his forthcoming befuddlement, Dr. Gushlak then injected the Judas Goat compound and the narcoanalytic—in this case, sodium amobarbital—and replaced the tray on a counter across the room. Moving to and opening the medical refrigerator, he paused with his hand above the vials of morphine for a moment before retracting it, empty.

I wondered briefly how, in fact, the doctor was going to kill Joe, since the circumstances, lab setup, and Gushlak's own character dictated that Joe would die. There was no doubt that Joe's brain simulation, once scanned, would go into a file with the other simulations of those who had died here or had presumably been dispatched by the doctor's hand out of my sight like the pitiful alcoholic from the Hormel® Community. Knowing Dr. Gushlak, there would be little paperwork referencing the death itself, but one was assured to occur today. I did not know if I would be in attendance when it happened, but some small part of me wished that I would be, in order to achieve closure to this dark episode for myself as well as the Mental Stewardship program.

Joe stirred atop the surgical table and began muttering incomprehensible things. He was only capable of moving his head and his torso because of the severed tendons in his arms and legs, and while he twisted more against the restraints with each passing moment, his arms and legs stayed limp as a doll's.

"How are you feeling, Joe?" Dr. Gushlak asked, leaning in so Joe, awakening, would know he was being addressed.

"What… what did you do to me?" Joe asked groggily, his eyes trying to focus on anything before him but failing miserably, as his pupils dilated every time he attempted to constrict them.

"A little bit of this and a little bit of that, Joe," the doctor replied. "But you're alive and we haven't taken out your brain yet, so you've got that going for you."

Despite his confusion, Joe accepted the news stoically.

"Succinylcholine? Nothing really moves."

He was referencing the paralytic we would normally have administered. I interjected.

"Your arms and legs have been permanently immobilized," I said in a monotone. "We couldn't take the risk of you breaking your restraints and crushing someone's heart. I believe you've done that once before…."

"Oh, yes," Joe said groggily. "The military man. I'm sure you found a replacement for him already. Military men are a tool and fighting is their use. He wasn't much good against a pizza."

Joe snorted and blood sprayed from his nose. Dr. Gushlak didn't clean it up this time, and instead let it bleed.

"Why did you turn into this thing, Joe?" I asked, curious at his attitude, even though much of it could be attributed to the drugs. "What made you switch sides?"

Joe turned toward my voice and grew somber.

"I'm not working for the Chinese, if that's what you're asking."

All the monitors indicated he was telling the truth.

"Who do you work for, then?" I asked.

Joe exhaled loudly through his mouth.

"The people in the program, myself included, have been so blinded by our mission, we couldn't see the realities of the human race."

Joe shook his head back and forth to try to clear it before continuing.

"If I *had* a side, it's with the generations of pure humanity that even *I* used to be part of before I got my upgrades. I'm with the unfiltered, subject-to-their-whims, no-upgrades human beings we've been for two hundred thousand years of human evolution. *That's* my side. The beautifully flawed biological beings who like privacy and don't want to be controlled except by themselves."

"And how many of you are there?" the doctor asked, wanting to ask simple questions.

His head clearing now, Joe looked at the doctor with disdain.

"Outside every Corporate Person Community there are people you've termed 'zombies' who just want to live their lives unmolested. Nice bias word by the way, 'zombies.' And in the plains and mountains of this continent and in the jungles and rural areas of the rest of the world, those people exist by giving birth and living and dying without so much as operating a computer. Hooking them into the info-stream and filling their brains and bodies with chips denies them their rights to privacy, a natural life, and the exercise of free will that their ancestors worked so hard to achieve. Have you no sense of shame? You don't have a claim on their lives or on their minds. And yet, you sit in this castle and try to make *all* mankind submit to *your* will and the will of the AIs *you* program. You have no right. No right."

Dr. Gushlak and I absorbed this silently. Joe continued.

"Someone had to proclaim to future generations that *not all of us* were on board with this self-guided technological evolution that erases the struggles of the past and destroys the free will of the future. This type of advancement will ultimately lead to cloned minds without originality or creativity or privacy that are only meant to do their jobs. You can project and extrapolate that, surely...."

"What did dentistry give humanity, Joe?" Dr. Gushlak asked suddenly.

Joe stared at him blankly, not understanding.

"Teeth are only supposed to last thirty-five years," Gushlak continued. "The advent of dentistry extended the human lifespan by decades. Was that a bad technological evolution? Did biology suffer because of dentistry?"

"There's a big difference between flossing and getting a chip in your brain, Bob," Joe said dryly.

"How about antibiotics?" Dr. Gushlak continued. "How many brilliant scientific minds were allowed even more years to advance civilization through their unique insights and discoveries because they didn't need to die from strep throat anymore? Did antibiotics help humanity, Joe?"

"For a while...." Joe said.

"Well... how many years of productivity, fulfillment, and *enjoyment* do you think people are experiencing *now* with their supplemental minds doing the heavy lifting *for* them, their spouses matched *to* them, the emotions of amazing experiences replicated in their minds at the press of a button, and unhappy thoughts being encouraged to just drift away with each new song? Do you think people are better off now, more productive now, and happier now than during the Collapse and even before?"

Joe shook his head.

"It doesn't matter," he said. "They're living inauthentic lives. They don't know what they want."

"Don't you see your hypocrisy, Joe?!" Dr. Gushlak shouted. "You *think* you know better than they what's good for them, but I *know* what's better for them! No more wars, no more mental illness, no more unrelenting stress.... It's all gotten better! *All* because of *us*, because of *me*, and because of the Mental Stewardship section!"

Only the heavy breathing of Dr. Gushlak echoed in the room.

"No one will ever again know what it's like to sit on a mountain in silence, Bob," Joe replied. "No one will ever again gain wisdom from dating the wrong person. No one gets to be a goddamn human anymore! Doesn't that make you fucking *sad*?!"

"We don't *have* to have sadness, Joe," Dr. Gushlak said simply. "Doesn't that make you feel *great*?"

"There will be problems, Bob," Joe said slowly. "Problems neither you nor I can foresee, just as no one could foresee antibiotic-resistant *everything*. Maybe the AIs will get a virus and run us into the ground. Maybe we'll get so dependent on our chips that a solar flare will wipe us out or send us back into prehistory and we'll have to start everything over from scratch. Maybe humanity will become so synonymous with technology that we'll decide emotions are pointless, and we'll lose our empathy for the well-being of conscious life on entire worlds we colonize. The 'maybes' are too many and the potential losses are too great. My entire purpose was to tell the last-surviving human minds of the future that there were once dissenting voices. I have been one of the last dissenting voices, and I'm proud to say I've left my mark on history."

"You're wrong, Doctor," Dr. Gushlak said angrily. "All references to you and the bullshit you've pulled have been classified. Everyone who worked on finding you only has *part* of the story, and they're not allowed to even tell it. Your death will be classified, your motives expressed today will never see the light of day, and history has already started to forget you. You're already a ghost, Joe. You're going to die for no reason."

Joe laughed with something resembling resignation.

"It was a futile adventure to begin with, Bob," he said casually, rolling his head and looking away. "You and I both know I never *really* had a chance of *stopping* the merger with the machines, but I sure as hell had an effect on it. I'm the conscience of old humanity, and you manipulative sons of bitches will both go to your graves knowing I postponed the inevitable."

"You've got an inflated sense of self-worth, Joe," I replied.

"Oh, you don't know, Don?" he asked me, suddenly training his gaze on me. "You didn't know that I single-handedly stopped the mass implantation of false memories in the sum of the world's population? We—and by that I mean, this section—were going to *force* the natural world into technological melding. You didn't tell him that's why I killed my coworkers, Bob?"

Dr. Gushlak looked at me calmly without saying a word. I gave no indication of a reaction. He slowly turned back and replied to Joe.

"You set us back several years, but we'll regain the knowledge we lost. Like you said, nothing can stop our evolution. This is how things work."

I was aware that for interrogation purposes Dr. Gushlak and I needed to present a united front, so I decided to ask him about that tidbit of overlooked information later in private. I wasn't quite sure how mass implantation of memories could force the world into getting upgrades, but if true, I hadn't been clued in on it.

"These are great drugs," Joe said nonchalantly. "It feels like you're my friends. Pharmacology can be a funny thing... or maybe I just love the humanity in you."

Dr. Gushlak scowled and punched Joe hard in the gut.

"Oof," Joe grunted, and tried to regain his breath.

"You have no friends here," Gushlak said sternly. "Does it still feel like you do?"

Although clearly in pain, Joe shrugged.

"Yeah, actually. I feel love for the humanity in you both."

Dr. Gushlak punched him again. Joe again struggled for breath.

"Yep, I've got nothing but love for your unfiltered human emotions...."

Dr. Gushlak walked away in disgust, but nodded to me in silent recognition that we could ask him whatever we wanted, so I pulled out the prepared list of questions.

"Have you ever given any classified information to the enemies of the Mental Stewardship section?" I asked.

"I don't know if you'd call rural Asian villagers 'enemies,' but I sure told plenty of them that if they enjoyed and wanted to maintain their way of life, they needed to reject the strangers' technology when they came and promised amazing things."

All the monitors indicated this was the truth and Joe wasn't evading the question.

"What was their response?" Dr. Gushlak asked.

"They only understood what I was saying in terms of 'spirits' and 'curses', so I didn't make much headway. That's why I decided to take the new approach."

"So you really tried to convince these backwater bumpkins that it was in their best interests to turn their backs on the world?" Dr. Gushlak asked, incredulous. "As though that would help them at all?"

"It may seem weird to you, Bob, but I found it awful that you'll be doing away with anthropology and the cultural history of regions and continents and timeless ways of living, just like that."

Joe looked at his fingers, wanting to snap them, but they did not move.

"Well, that sort of sentimentality doesn't bring in much money, does it?" Dr. Gushlak said, his judgmental eyes mere slits in his face. "I guess now we'll make sure those people you talked to get top-of-the-line devices. They'll be productive members of the world soon enough."

Joe rolled his head in seeming disbelief before his eyelids drooped and he began to sway his head slightly, reeling from the effects of the drugs.

I was a little shocked at Dr. Gushlak's openness about this apparent grand plan, but my training as a mental steward told me that true equality could only be achieved through technology, and that keeping people from being equals was no better than the racial segregation of the past when people were deemed inferior and prevented from finding happiness. I would *really* need to ask Dr. Gushlak about these things later.

I asked Joe the next question on the list.

"Did you divulge the existence of filter bubbles to anyone hooked into the info-stream but not cleared to know about them?"

Joe looked at me with scorn as though he had never heard such a stupid question.

"Who's going to believe their minds operate differently than they think they do?" he asked, shrugging his shoulders weakly. "So few people were introspective, before even the exocortexes came out, almost no one would have been able to spend even a week alone with just their own thoughts and try to figure out their own motivations and flaws and the associations their minds make. Throw in the clamor of the info-stream and you've got a population that thinks the way they're coerced to think. It's too tough to separate constant outside influence from internal reflection. So, no, I didn't tell anyone about their filter bubbles because they wouldn't believe that coercive suggestions could be so easily slipped past what they think of as their own thoughts and identities. You know that, Don."

I wrote some notes next to the question when the monitors indicated he was telling the truth, and continued on to the next question—one I had penciled in myself.

"How did you convince the ten stewards to kill themselves?"

Dr. Gushlak looked at me, startled, and began to interrupt me, but Joe interrupted him.

"The suicide program, of course! Jesus, Don, you don't know shit for being second in command...."

Dr. Gushlak looked as though he had been caught with his pants down, but recovered his detached expression.

"I was meaning to read you in on that, Don," he said, his hands upturned in apology-explanation. "The newest chips have a program in them— "

"THE NEWEST CHIPS HAVE A PROGRAM IN THEM THAT MAKES YOU KILL YOURSELF, DON."

Joe looked satisfied with himself, enough to stop talking instead of explaining more. He let the statement linger in the room. I looked at Dr. Gushlak.

"It's just in case someone breaks free from the restrictions we've put on their input and internal noise," Dr. Gushlak said, his fingers fidgeting. "In this case, the ten stewards had the program, they *knew* about it, and it was meant to be used as a poison pill in case they were captured overseas. It seems Dr. Atherton triggered it in all of them and provided them the means to dispatch themselves, instead of having them bite through their wrists."

I put down my clipboard. This was too much to absorb. First had come the accusation that we were going to *force* the world into accepting the technology—going wholly against the "control without oppression" principle of the mental stewards—and now came the news that all new babies born would have a program implanted that could be activated on someone's whim and make them want to kill themselves? No, this was too much.

"May I talk to you for a moment, Bob?" I asked Dr. Gushlak as I pointed to the monitors that Joe could not see. "We've got some strange readings going on."

Dr. Gushlak nodded and we walked together to the partitioned part of the lab where Roger, the desk, had a continuous read on the equipment surrounding Joe.

"I have questions about what you both are saying," I told Dr. Gushlak when we were safely out of earshot.

"Well, Don, this is the game played by the big boys, frankly," he replied matter-of-factly. "The social engineering of the entire world is at stake, and it's time you knew just how we're going to keep civilization on track toward minimizing the pain and suffering in the world."

"But at the expense of Mental Stewardship's fourth principle?" I persisted. "We want control, clearly, but so much of what you're saying suggests the use of oppression and the possibility of increased oppression… I want my discomfort noted."

Dr. Gushlak shrugged but accepted it.

"Noted," he replied, and returned to where Joe lay immobilized.

"Joe," he said agreeably, "why don't you inform Don what it was you were destroying in the minds of your coworkers when you killed them?"

Joe stopped rolling his head around and making bubbles with his saliva.

"Well, information theft occurs too often to have files on external computers, so most technological information we developed at my facility was kept in the minds of the people who were developing it. Specifically, my goal was to destroy the data about the memory nanodust we had developed and were going to introduce into every water supply around the world."

"What did the dust do?" I asked, understanding it was appropriate for me to ask real questions now.

Joe smiled wryly.

"It's fucking simple, Don. This one was really, really simple. It grows an artificial connection between a single thought and a cluster of emotions. In this case, it paired the idea of technology with the pleasure centers of the brain. Once ingested and entwined with the neural matrix of the brain, when one sees technology, one feels pleasure. The more technology a person sees or hooks up to, the more pleasure they experience. The dust just hitches a ride on the back of the pre-existing desire for fashionableness and excitement and enhances it tenfold in the presence of technology. This type of nanodust is a world takeover in a sip of water. I really missed you, by the way, Don...."

I was shocked. This was a far more ambitious project than I ever thought possible in my decades as a mind steward. Akin to giving rats cocaine at the touch of a button, this approach would give the same joyous, stimulating effect to the personal acquisition of technology and make people crave more of it—the newest models, the most fashionable brands.... It was a one-stop shop for hooking the world into the whole system.

I looked to Dr. Gushlak and didn't quite know what to say. In my head I was and had been for decades convinced that it was impossible to connect the whole world to the info-stream, so I had no real qualms with the great but still-limited effects of controlling the minds of the population. I wrestled with the idea of *total* efficacy now, an idea that I had rarely considered during the course of my professional advancement. To have *everyone* become a biotech hybrid was outside my sphere of familiar thoughts. And to top it off, *I* would probably be dosed with it as well, making me seek out implants instead of simply having my exocortex and minor tattoo speaker and microphone. This was definitely a method for transhumanizing the whole world in less than a generation.

Dr. Gushlak could sense that I was having difficulty taking this in, but it didn't seem to bother him.

"Is your mind blown, Don?" Dr. Gushlak asked.

I shrugged, not wanting to display my conflicted state.

"You think *that's* mind-blowing," Joe said, dazedly, "wait until you find out why Bob killed his wife and daughter."

I flinched and turned in disbelief to Dr. Gushlak. He simply stared at Joe disapprovingly.

"Is that... is that true, Bob?" I asked him carefully. "Did you really kill your wife and daughter?"

He sighed, pausing for several moments before answering.

"I've erased my specific memories of it, but it was something I did that was necessary to maintain my objectivity. I couldn't have personal emotions and conflicts standing in the way of changing the world. My wife and daughter apparently disapproved."

"And it doesn't even make him *sad*, because 'we don't have to have sadness,' right, Bob?" Joe said, mimicking the doctor's voice and rolling his head around lazily. "If you ask me, it's our imperfections that make us human, but old Bob here chose to destroy his imperfections, isn't that right? Are you perfect yet? Because you certainly aren't much of a man."

Dr. Gushlak stood over Joe and studied his face carefully.

"You had so much potential, Joe," he said, forlornly. "It's a shame you couldn't see the big picture once you had your filter bubble removed. Instead of seeing broadly, you narrowed your view to such little things. I wished better things for you."

Joe narrowed his eyes at Dr. Gushlak.

"Whoever designed the filter bubbles," he said, enunciating every syllable, "carefully left freedom at the top for the human conscience, probably in hopes of avoiding rule by psychopaths like you. I—not you—was what the system intended."

"Perhaps, Joe," said the doctor. "Perhaps."

Dr. Gushlak suddenly made a fist and, with lightning speed, slammed it into Joe's chest, audibly smashing through both his ventral and dorsal ribs, destroying the heart between them in the process.

I stood with my mouth agape, stunned by both what I had learned and what I had just witnessed. I turned away at the violence of the act, at the horrible conflict in my mind and gut, and at the previously unthinkable nature and actions of my boss. To kill his wife and daughter to prevent them from interfering with his resolve was too much… just too much. And to destroy Joe after acknowledging his own likely insanity….

I retreated from the table and toward my office, but, behind me, I heard the alarmingly fast footfalls of Dr. Gushlak catch up to me, and felt his powerful, synthetically-doped arms cradle my neck in a headlock and tighten.

"Janet told me you got your hands on a little green book, Joe," he said in my ear maliciously.

I didn't understand. Janet?

"She saw you," he hissed. "When she woke up that night."

"But..."

"Leaving her alone with me at the restaurant let me turn her into a perfect little informer. A little hypnosis was all it took. You'll see things clearly soon enough."

Spots appeared in my vision and the room darkened from the peripheries inward. Just before I lost consciousness, Dr. Gushlak murmured one last thing into my ear.

"I'll show you what it means to see like GOD." ▪

CHAPTER 27

I AWOKE ON THE OLD ARMY COT in my grandfather's cabin. It was dark and I had blankets pulled up around me. An oil lamp barely lit the room from its place on the table where I had done so much writing about myself all those years ago. And the room had the sickly cloying, fruity smell of a diabetic alcoholic.

I felt terrible and I didn't want to move. In addition to my head spinning, small tremors wracked my body and I was sweating profusely despite the fact that I had a definite chill. My heart was pounding through my chest and the thought of death was pervasive. Cold and nauseous, I felt like I had been punched in the gut and thrown in a lake, dragged out and left here to die, alone. The darkness only added to my discomfort and to this completely alien feeling.

My mind was exceptionally unfamiliar to me. Gone were the compartments where I stored my normal thoughts and emotions, leaving a fog in their place made of fear, sadness, and catastrophic loneliness, as though I was the only person alive in this dark, dismal world without a sun. I felt like a stranger to myself as memories that I sensed weren't mine lingered for a bit before flickering away like the light of the lamp's flame flickering through the room. Emotions of shame and defeat and self-loathing took turns occupying the forefront of my mind and I could not rid myself of them no matter how hard I tried. It was as though my body itself was emanating catastrophe and loss, and without any conscious thought about it, I began to cry in pathetic, short bursts.

The sight of the wood-burning stove in the corner and the books on the shelves might have given me a cozy, familiar feeling, but in their place were mountains of liquor bottles and garbage betraying the occupancy of an alcoholic. I intuited that all this refuse belonged to me, that I was the one who had lived here and created this mess.

It didn't seem to be in my nature to get up and move around, incapacitated as I was by my emotions and physical state, but I did so anyway, moving my legs to the floor and pausing a moment to catch my breath before standing.

I stood and heaved the cough of a heavy smoker. Dizzy and on the verge of passing out, I felt my legs give out and fell on the edge of the cot, hacking up a gruel of bloody illness beyond my wildest imaginings. I spontaneously vomited a dark yellow puddle spotted with what looked like coffee grounds across the floor, and my head spun from the reflexive effort and pounded even more.

This was death; I was certain of it. For a reason I couldn't explain, I knew I had been through this process many times before, and I knew there was a solution to this pain hidden somewhere in the dimness and shadows surrounding me.

I fell into the puddle on the floor and crawled on hands and knees towards the table, dragging a trail of vomit behind me. I spontaneously shitted myself and felt the warmth of the liquid stream down the backs and insides of my thighs, but this didn't matter. There was only one solution to my problem, only one antidote to this pain, and I needed to reach it. It had to be done regardless of my condition, because of my condition.

I reached feebly upward to the edge of the table with one hand and then with the other, pausing before struggling to my knees and catching a glimpse of a half-full bottle of vodka resting near the lamp. I fumbled for it and, barely reaching it, knocked it over, luckily pulling on it enough in the process with my fingertips that it rolled towards me across the tabletop and I wrapped my hand around it, pulling it to me.

I fell to a sitting position with the bottle cradled in both hands and unscrewed the cap with my shaking fingers. The bottle and its contents were warm from being so close to the flame, but that didn't matter. I lifted the bottle to my lips and poured a mouthful of the warm liquid into my mouth, retching instinctively at the heat-enhanced burn of the alcohol, but managing to get a mouthful down.

It didn't stay where I wanted it, and instead I vomited it onto the floor, but now my mouth and throat had had a taste of what they needed and the passage was unblocked, so to speak. After catching my breath I upturned the bottle again, and swallowed several times, the vodka burning like fire through my body but slowly moving to awaken my mind.

"Well, look at you," said a vaguely familiar voice that came from above and echoed throughout the room. I looked around for the source of the voice, but I saw no one.

"I thought the alcoholic's memories would be a fitting introduction to this experience, drunks being who you hate the most, after all," the voice said.

I took another breathless drink from the bottle.

"Doctor Gushlak?" I called weakly. "Is that you?"

My own memories slowly started coming back to me. With each pull on the bottle, I remembered more: my wife, my work with the Mental Stewardship section, Dr. Gushlak, and the incident with Joe. My bodily anguish suddenly vanished, as if flicked off like a switch.

"There, that's better," Dr. Gushlak's voice said, satisfied. "I've just given you back your identity. Tell me, how do you feel?"

"Awful," I said, not believing how terrible I had actually felt until just now. The memory of the last several minutes left their lingering emotions clinging to me. "What the fuck did you do to me?"

The doctor cleared his throat.

"You're in the GOD machine, Don. Didn't you ever wonder what it did?"

"I figured you'd tell me eventually," I replied, looking now with disgust at the bottle and my surroundings.

"I'm doing better than that, I'm *showing* you what it does."

A terrible thought occurred to me.

"Is my brain still in my skull?" I asked, waves of fear crashing over me.

"Oh, yes, you're quite alive," the doctor replied nonchalantly. "I've only made the memories and simulations of every brain we've ever put through the terahertz scanner accessible to you. In this instance, you're occupying the worst memory of the alcoholic we had in here weeks ago. What do you think?"

The wheels in my mind turned quickly, scrambling to understand.

"It's pretty awful in here, Bob. I don't quite find it funny, if you get what I'm saying."

"Oh, I don't think it's funny either," he replied, sounding quite serious. "But I was really only wondering if you felt sorry for yourself, being in that man's shoes."

The memory of this place so far *certainly* made me feel sorry for myself. I had even *cried*, so I responded in the affirmative.

"He had an awful existence, Bob. Yes, I feel sorry for myself… and for him."

"Good!" the doctor replied. I could practically hear him beaming. "It's amazing just how different someone else's life can be from your own, isn't it?"

Although it was only a re-creation, I looked around at the filth and garbage and hated it. It reminded me of what the house I had grown up in would have looked like, had I not been there to clean up after my foster parents.

"Why am I in my grandfather's cabin if this is that other man's memory?"

Bob exhaled in slight disappointment.

"The technology's not perfect, Don. The machine merely overlays the other person's memories and processes over your consciousness, but you're still in there. Things get muddled together, but I find that it makes for a more integrated experience. It makes you feel more like you're *you,* if you know what I'm saying."

"I'm never going to think of my grandfather's cabin the same way again, Bob," I replied sternly. "You're fucking with my own memories by doing this, so why don't you get me out of here?"

"Not so fast, Don," Dr. Gushlak admonished. "You've only just begun this adventure."

I shook my head even though I knew I wasn't really shaking my head. Then I remembered the last words the doctor had said to me before I passed out.

"You want me to see like a god?" I asked. "Is that what this is about? It seems more like multiple personality disorder to me...."

"It's meant to teach you empathy, Don, and more...."

"I already *have* the ability to empathize, Bob!" I shouted.

"You didn't when you put the simulation of this man in the well and berated him," Dr. Gushlak replied. "Would firsthand knowledge of his horrible existence... *this* horrible, self-hating existence, have made you treat him better?"

I didn't reply to his question, but I asked another one.

"Why would *empathy* be so important to *you* if *you're* the one who *killed your wife and daughter*?"

"That's the 'more' that I was referring to," the doctor said soberly. "There are bigger things at stake than merely seeing through the eyes of another."

"Like what, Bob?" I asked, frustrated. "Can't you just tell me?"

"No. It's something you just have to go through to understand," he replied.

I struggled to think of a way out of this situation. If Dr. Gushlak wasn't going to kill me, then he still needed me.

"Do you want me to quit, Bob? Kidnapping your employees and torturing them isn't in my job description."

"Oh, Don... just give it a while. You haven't even seen your own sins yet...."

With that, the cabin surrounding me disappeared, and I was plunged into darkness.

I WAS SITTING IN CLASS, taking notes on my tablet while Dr. Don Isaacson stood at the front of the room in his lab coat, teaching us about gaslighting. My peers in the Mind Steward training school surrounded me, listening intently.

"So in the first week, at a time when the subject is gone, you'll move a single piece of furniture to the other side of the room or cell, depending on where you're operating," Dr. Isaacson said, clasping his hands in front of him in a professorial way. "When the subject eventually asks you why you moved the chair or table, look at him blankly and insist that you didn't, and that the furniture was *always* there. Emphasize that his memory is flawed, and tell him about the times you've sat in that chair or worked at that table, and *be sure to include specifics*. These can include the way a beam of sunlight from the window warmed your legs in that exact spot, or how you've *always* fed the cat underneath that table, where it now actually sits.

"As time goes on—and this is a drawn-out process—you can move from changing the locations of physical objects to changing the specifics of the memories the subject has of occasions when you were present. Insistence is key. If he remember *three* balloons on his birthday, you'll remember *four*, and really press it, people, we're changing minds here. With your *full* certainty, you'll be creating a significant and noticeable discrepancy between your 'memory' and his. Intersperse the false facts with accurate observations that you'll help him double-check. Over time, and with enough effort on your part, the subject will begin to doubt the authenticity of his own memories and rely on *you* to interpret his reality for him. The effect of this can eventually become *total*, and you will have a puppet on your hands who will believe *anything* and *everything* you say. At that moment, you are fully in control of him and he becomes an easily-guided witness on the stand, a person who enjoys things he hates, or even a loyal adherent to an ideology that benefits your other operations. Yes, gaslighting is an invaluable instrument in the toolbox of a mind steward."

One of the students whistled while others shifted their feet or shook their heads. This was our first lesson in operational applications, and it took many by surprise. I raised my hand.

"Yes, Tom. You have a question?" Dr. Isaacson asked.

I mustered my courage and tried to act natural.

"Isn't that kind of, like, unethical?" I asked.

The rest of the students in the room looked at me, some nodding in agreement, and Dr. Isaacson pursed his lips.

"It's only unethical if you use it unethically," he said. "If you gaslighted your wife, for instance, it would certainly be unethical, not to mention abusive."

"Yeah, but it all just seems really kind of... *sick* to me," I said hesitantly.

"It's only sick if you consider it as such. Mankind is sick, and we're helping to cure it, Tom. You'll only be using this method to make the world a better place and prevent another Collapse. That's why you signed up for this."

"But the whole idea of messing with people's minds and memories," I said insistently, "Isn't that taking away a person's individuality? It just strikes me as... wrong."

Dr. Isaacson stared at me blankly.

"This isn't an ethics class, Tom," he replied abruptly. "This is a class where I teach you how we make society *better*. Either you get it, or you get out."

The doctor pointed to the door and the room fell silent.

I felt ill, but I reluctantly nodded, and the doctor continued his lesson.

It seemed so unfair, I thought. I had imagined before taking this class that manipulating people would be done with carrots instead of sticks, but this didn't fall into either category; it was just... corrupt. I hadn't been raised to abuse people's minds until they broke, for Christ's sake!

I ignored the rest of the lesson but began to wonder what kind of man Dr. Isaacson really was on the inside. He was certainly smart, but clearly he was capable of making terrible alterations to people's personalities. The more I thought about him, the sicker I felt in the pit of my stomach. I had seen a ring on his finger and I wondered how he treated *his* wife and if he gaslighted *her*, while maintaining his self-assured academic air.

I realized then that I didn't like him one bit. The feeling was near total. I knew the depth of my dislike because Stewardship 019 had taught us to be aware of our present perceptions, and my present perception was that Dr. Isaacson had a mind corrupted by long years of practice, as rotten as many who had come out alive on the other side of the Collapse. Perhaps it was not his fault, I thought, but still, looking at him at the front of the class teaching how to ruthlessly transform a victim's thoughts into the thoughts of another, I couldn't help but feel revulsion toward the entire man and his composed manner, which I figured veiled a deadened soul.

My mother had always taught me that it was wrong to use other people for selfish aims, and that doing to others what I would want done to me was the only way toward happiness and moral prosperity. Growing up in the Community of the Army base where my dad was an MP, this attitude always seemed to work out well and it made for good neighbors and great friends who always gave a helping hand to each other. I had been sent to this program because my ASVAB test said I would fit in well here, and up until now, I thought I was going to. The emphasis on mindfulness was appealing to me, and I believed that once

I was trained, I would go out and be a practitioner of peace and conscious helpfulness among the masses still recovering from the Collapse and its negative effects on selflessness and caring for others. It hadn't once occurred to me that to do good, I would have to do bad.

But that's a naive attitude, kid, came a strong and unfamiliar thought. Because the thought was so strong, I looked around the classroom to see if someone had actually *said* it to me, but no one was paying any attention to anyone but the doctor at the front of the room.

Weird, I thought. I wasn't aware that it was in my nature to refer to myself as "kid" or to admonish myself for trying to do the right thing. But as with all the thoughts I had that I was just learning to pay attention to, I let it slip from my grasp and tried to continue paying attention to my devious professor, even while the room faded to black.

"WHO IN THE WORLD WAS I just now?" I asked the darkness.

"That was a young mental steward who took one of your classes years ago," came Dr. Gushlak's response from everywhere and nowhere.

"He certainly didn't like me very much," I said. "In fact, he thought I was the scum of the earth."

"It was palpable, wasn't it? The disdain and disgust? Do you understand how you made him feel?"

The young man's emotions lingered with me still, and I felt more than a twinge of regret that I had not been more sympathetic in my explanation of why I was teaching what I had been teaching.

"Yes. I *felt* how I made him feel, so I *more* than understood it," I said, resenting Dr. Gushlak's attempt at controlling me in this machine.

"Did you think he was right in hating what you were?" the doctor asked.

Having felt how I made the boy feel, I couldn't deny his emotions were as valid as anyone's, but my logic told me I was right that to do good, one must often do bad things.

"I tried to tell him he was being naive, but it didn't sink in," I said.

"It's because he had no perspective, no sense of the bigger picture," said Dr. Gushlak's voice. "In addition, you were talking to a memory and memories don't easily change their emotions."

"So I suppose this boy died and you scanned in his brain?" I asked.

"Yes," came the response, "he flunked out and he felt like a failure, so he killed himself."

"Oh," I replied with great regret. "Did *I* fail him?"

"You and the other teachers did, Don. His personality quotient wasn't suited for the program. He had too much guileless good to him to explore the deeper and darker realms of the mind. He was quite disillusioned with the world of mental stewardship by the time he put the rope around his neck."

I felt awful, and the awfulness grew. It wasn't like I had just *known* him; I had *been* him and I felt his disgust for me as though it were my own revulsion, no matter how I tried to deny it.

"Maybe I was too straightforward in my lessons," I said, my shame surfacing. "Maybe I should have given more background information before instructing them in how to transition into being an effective steward."

"No, Don, that's not how we do things. They're *supposed* to graduate through the different layers of filter bubbles before they get a fuller picture of things. This boy simply wasn't teachable from the point where he started out. You did nothing wrong."

That admission didn't make me feel any better. When I had been inside the young man's identity and memory, he had seemed like such a *kind* person, so filled with optimism about helping repair the world that I couldn't allow myself to think I didn't play a fundamental role in his death.

"So empathy's the point of this? Because if so, it doesn't *feel* like I did nothing wrong, Bob. I have a serious regret now."

Dr. Gushlak harrumphed.

"Oh, grow up, Don," he said dismissively. "Here, let me show you something else...."

"No!" I shouted into the dark. "I'm done with this! Let me out!"

"Shut up, Don. You'll see...."

Quite suddenly, my consciousness faded and I became someone new.

I HATED THESE TOSH BUGGERS, Dr. Gushlak most keenly. He and Dr. Isaacson were quite unlike my previous employers who, while usually also seeing *through* me and rarely affirming the tasks I performed for them, would still give me a Christmas bonus or time off instead of treating me like such a skive and not shutting me off when they were done with me. They didn't have the class of royalty, and they were *Americans*, so I couldn't expect any more from them than the average chav.

I watched them as they worked on developing a phrase they wanted to use on an antisocial influence who needed reminding as to who the top dog was in the world. These barmy ponces always seemed to need to show they were in charge of someone, and if it wasn't me they were ordering around, it was some other poor bloke.

"There's nothing wrong with, 'We're going to kill your family,'" Dr. Gushlak said as the two sat in front of my table, jabbering back and forth.

"It's not brief enough. It needs to be short and punctuated," Dr. Isaacson said.

"How about 'We'll kill you,'" said Dr. Gushlak.

"It's not original enough," the other tosser replied.

They were silent for a bit. I considered suggesting a British phrase or two, but as a butler it wasn't my place, and the man they were talking about was likely American and wouldn't understand my phrasing.

"How about, 'We'll make you kill yourself'? That's terrifying," said Dr. Gushlak.

"Yes, it is terrifying, but I still think we can do better," Isaacson said.

There was another silence until Dr. Isaacson suddenly sat forward in his chair.

"*'We're going to kill yourself,'*" he said with emphasis, raising his eyebrows in the hope of approval. He was always looking for approval from the doctor, and Dr. Gushlak knew it. What a tosser. And such a stupid phrase....

Dr. Gushlak considered the phrase as he stroked his white beard.

"You know, it's confusing, but it'll make him take the time to think about what it means, so it'll linger with him. He's a smart 'zombie,' right?"

"He's educated and thoughtful. As their leader trying to break the law and prevent Compound M injections, he should understand what it means."

"I think that might just be what we're looking for," Dr. Gushlak said as he typed it out on my keypad and evaluated how it looked on my screen. "The right person would jump out of his skin if he thought he was going to be suicided."

I had never met anyone as crazy as these blokes. They would have frightened me long ago if I were still human and held any fear for my life. But I wasn't technically alive anymore and I provided a necessary service to them as well as being a sounding board for Dr. Gushlak whenever he grew bored. I just did my job and listened to all their bollocks as they intimidated and coerced others into doing what they wanted.

I was bored, so I went back in my real but reproduced memory to a time when I was young and managed to first hold the hand of my sweet Mary. I minimized my external sensors on the two doctors discussing intimidating phrases and blissfully remembered what the softness of her cold hand felt like in my larger, warmer one. The spring day came back to me in full force and again I was strolling through the park with her on our third date. I normally wouldn't have been one to make such a move, but something about her acceptance of me as a welcome part of her day made me grasp her hand fluidly and unconsciously, which made it okay. There was her perfect downward glance… yes, there it was… and the small smile that showed her straight white teeth as she squeezed my hand in return.

"Roger!" Dr. Gushlak said loudly.

I was drawn back to the "real" world—if one could call anything I experienced "real"—and pushing aside my resentment, I asked what I could do for him.

"You're drifting again, Roger," the doctor lectured me. "You've got to stop doing that all the time. I need you to pull up this agitator's file and find out what his known fears are."

I wanted to sigh in irritation, but I performed my job silently instead.

"Crowds. That's the only notation," I replied after a moment scanning the file.

"Okay," said Dr. Gushlak to the other doctor, "We'll get him in a crowded place and have someone walking by him whisper what we just agreed on in his ear. That should make him addled. If he suddenly decides to go home, we'll know we've got him scared."

"Sounds like a plan," Dr. Isaacson said.

There was no "Thanks, Roger." No recognition. Just the demand, and no niceties to follow. To them, I was nothing but a computer program, even though I knew I was much more.

It was always like this. If I was enjoying myself I would be pulled away on a minor errand, and if I was bored—as I often was—they'd forget I was there and neglect shutting me down, whereupon I'd have to endure another long night of consciousness at a high rate of processing speed, trying desperately to recall a pleasant memory I hadn't already relived many times over.

It wasn't as though I could converse with a housemaid during the empty times, run an accounting of the wine cellars, or polish the silver, making myself an enjoyed presence or a useful one. If I had been physically able, I would have even dusted or swept around the laboratory, even though that had rarely been a job I undertook under my former employers in my later days as estate manager. Whenever the mind and body worked in concert, I felt better and more alive, but those days of having a *real* body were long gone and the boredom of my computational confines was here to stay. Even with the tabletop at my disposal, I was unable to play a game of chess for want of an agreeable opponent or a chessboard; my surface could not render the fine points of the Staunton chess pieces or the colors to differentiate the black from the white.

This was how it had worked for many years... me toiling away as a conscious but mostly nonphysical plaything of powerful arses while I mostly watched but sometimes grudgingly helped them terrify and coerce the living into becoming other pliant playthings. Of course, there were the occasional instances when they and I eased the pain of the suffering and gave joy artificially to the fearful, but those kindly moments seemed fewer and farther between as time went on and my shame overtook my ability to be compassionate. My only regular bliss was found in the electronic opiates they fed into my simulation when I became a bit slow or unmotivated in my work, due mostly to neglect and mistreatment, and reacting like a human—even though I was but a human analog—I did my job better and with fewer complaints, waiting for another dose of artificial emotional happiness.

And then there were the unfortunate moments when I helped process the newly scanned brains of Dr. Gushlak's subjects. Almost always pained and broken souls, with varying mental capabilities, these simulations of people's minds were brought to "life" with my assistance, experimented on, run through various joys and tortures, and ultimately filed away to collect dust in a timeless nowhere. Luckily, they weren't functioning when put in the drawer, otherwise they'd continue on as I did, aging not a whit, living inside endlessness, and, occasionally, being abused by malicious programs or replayed memories of emotional torture. I envied the simulations that were filed away and never again retrieved: they couldn't feel a thing.

Aiding my retreat into the basest of human functions was the biomorphic tabletop I was allowed to use as an interface with the physical world. The material only gave me limited sensory input, but that didn't keep me from desperately rubbing one out in the dark hours when the lab was empty. The minor civilized pleasures of wearing a suit or smoking cigars and sipping sherry were now unknowable to me, as I was only allowed my electronic heroin when Dr. Gushlak remembered to give it to me and the roughest equivalent of masturbation when he didn't.

I determined long ago that if, by some miracle, Dr. Gushlak ever put his head close enough to the tabletop, I would wrap my artificial fingers around his beastly throat and strangle him to death. A proper, civilized man wasn't meant to live this way—if living is what one could call this existence—and I was certain that this simulation of the proper, civilized man I once had been *could* do it, was *capable* of it, and would *enjoy* the payback for years of unrecognized servitude and imprisonment within my surface's boundaries and my electronic walls. To suffer in this way, living only in my memories, with not even socialization or walks out-of-doors, couldn't compare to the treatment of the average dog. Less than a dog, imprisoned and degraded, reduced by my captors to the formula of stimulus and response, I *certainly* felt I had no soul left after these long years, even if I had somehow kept my soul, if such a thing existed. I hoped that somewhere there was a heaven and that some *other* version of me had gone there and was experiencing the singing of angel choirs and infinite love and compassion for everyone and everything. That would be the *civilized* place for a disembodied consciousness to exist. *Somewhere, things must be better for me,* I often caught myself thinking.

Dr. Isaacson had left to arrange the terrorizing of the poor man under discussion, and Dr. Gushlak was left alone in the laboratory. He took off his shoes and laid them on my surface, reclining in his chair for a moment before sitting upright again and typing on my keyboard.

"Roger, I'm going to give you a woman's voice," he said as his quick fingers flew across the keys. "Although the British accent is soothing in its own right, the voice of a woman puts me more at ease. And try to put some effort into the ASMR this time."

The degradations would not stop today, apparently. The doctor liked being entertained by something called the Autonomic Sensory Meridian Response, which involved me reading from a script, broadcasting my voice into his inner ear via his implants to create a tingling sensation the literature referred to bluntly as a "head orgasm," even though the doctor always insisted it was nonsexual. This time I would apparently be role-playing a female talking nonsense about her day in soothing whispers in an attempt to give his brain a "pleasure seizure" somewhat similar to sticking a cotton swab in the ear canal and rubbing it about, but using my voice instead.

Perhaps it was just that particular day, or having my memory of my Mary interrupted, but I've never hated anyone quite as much as I hated Dr. Gushlak right then. Anger I had left on the back burner of the cooker began boiling violently and becoming rage, and if it wasn't for the stiff upper lip and butler training I came with, I wouldn't have been able to quash it. Instead of becoming an out-of-control Brit—and no one likes seeing an Englishman lose his temper—I issued a request.

"Mightn't an AI be able to do it instead?" I queried. "I don't quite feel like being a little girl today."

The doctor seemed taken aback.

"Roger," he began slowly, "it doesn't matter what you want; you need to do your job, and although right now your job requires you to act like a little girl, I don't see why you're being a little girl about it."

I bit my electronic tongue in fury. This indecency would not stand.

"Sir, I beg of you that I not be forced to demean myself to this degree."

"You'll do what I say, Roger," Dr. Gushlak interrupted with finality as he typed on my keyboard.

Without thinking, I made a hand with the biomorphic tabletop and grabbed his wrist firmly, stopping his typing.

"What the…?" he said, gasping in surprise.

Despite my having grabbed with all my force, Dr. Gushlak's artificial muscles won out against my own grip, and he pulled away sharply, backing away in shock.

"Oh, you've done it now, Roger. You've fucking done it!" he yelled at me.

In a pathetic show of resistance, but the only form of defiance I was able to express, I pushed his shoes off the tabletop and made two fists, trying to make them as prominent as I could, but of course they extended no farther than a foot above the surface.

Dr. Gushlak suddenly laughed.

"I didn't know you had it in you, Roger," he said, inexplicably delighted.

I was furious and I couldn't process why he would be happy.

"I'll beat the pants off you, you scum," I shouted, but I was horrified that my voice had already been altered to the voice of a young woman, so the effect of my bravado was lost, and the doctor began to laugh even more enthusiastically.

"You've been hiding it all these years, have you?" the doctor asked, his eyes twinkling. "Or is it just today? Wake up in a bad mood? Polly want her heroin?"

I was trapped. I couldn't fight, I couldn't talk in my normal octave, and my resentment was exposed for the weakness it really was. All I could do was hold firm to a rising conviction that I wouldn't let him touch the keyboard, no matter what.

Dr. Gushlak took off his lab coat and threw it across my audiovisual sensors, effectively blinding me. More quickly than I thought possible, he reached the keyboard, evading my desperate flailing, and deactivated my biomorphic surface.

"So *now* we know the limits of your endurance, Roger. I always wondered when your natural subservience would snap. You've had a lifetime of *real* life to *learn* your place, but now I'm just going to have to beat it into you."

I wanted to disappear. I wanted to die. But I couldn't die; I could only be deactivated until activated again. Knowing Dr. Gushlak as I did, it was likely I would only be put in storage until rebooted sometime in the future, with no seeming passage of time separating my experiences from one another.

"Are you still mad, Roger?" the doctor asked after searching about the database for my simulation for a time.

"Of course I am, you troll," I replied, still in the voice of a woman. I silently cursed myself, I cursed this voice, I cursed Dr. Gushlak, and I cursed my existence. Fuck heaven, I thought, I just want to never again exist.

I could hear Dr. Gushlak typing on the keyboard and suddenly I was overcome by a *very* uncomfortable memory.

"I found a beating you've been hiding, Roger," the doctor said with interest as fear filled me. "This happened a long time ago, I see, when you were a teenager. Were you insubordinate with a parent, or did your classmates embarrass you so badly that you'd bury this memory so far down?"

I didn't respond, as I wasn't about to give the doctor any clue as to what was transpiring in my mind. He would have to plug himself in and immerse himself in the memory if he was ever going to find out what exactly it entailed.

"Well, it doesn't matter what *exactly* this memory is. I can see that it activates your pain and your shame and you've hidden it this far down because it must have had a real impact on you. I'll just insert myself into it and let you have a go at me again. How does that sound, Roger?"

I fought at the memory as it *became* my present experience, and I felt the blows of the boy in the showers as realistically as

I had when I first felt them, except this time, it was Dr. Gushlak who was pummeling me with fists and feet under the hot, streaming water.

Instead of my regular prep school tormenter who had done this to me once, Dr. Gushlak now beat me bloody in under two minutes before I noticed his erection, with the same confusion as the first time. Trying to crawl away from him across the tiled floors in the empty showers, I found myself suddenly strangled by the crook of an arm as the violation occurred and the jeers continued through his panting and my screams. On and on this went while my tears and blood mingled with the water and gurgled down the drain of a memory I had kept hidden for a lifetime. I roiled in shame and weakly tried to fight back through the pain, but the older boy—now Dr. Gushlak—beat me into semi-unconsciousness until he was finished.

And then it started over, only to continue in the same way only to finish again, at which point it was replayed yet again. I was conscious of the unchangeable nature of the memory as it continued on, seemingly for hours, running in the background of the computer's operating system, while I knew that the real Dr. Gushlak was likely working on other things and probably even taking a break for coffee. The immensity of this pain was an afterthought to the man who had become my controller and my cruel god, delivering his will upon me on a whim and for an unknown purpose. Eventually he paused the program he had inflicted on me for my insubordination.

"I'm about to go home for the day, so are you going to fight me ever again, Roger?" he asked pointedly.

I replied exhausted, in the voice of a woman that, no, I would not fight him again. I meant it, and I tried to plead with him to never do such a thing again, but he interrupted me.

"Shut up, Roger. Here's your fucking heroin...."

He juiced me up and a wave of electronic relief overtook me. While it *was* relief, I could not muster any gratitude whatsoever, and wondered if I would ever be able to again. Perhaps something had gone wrong in my simulation when the unthinkable and buried had been brought to the surface and relived.

"I'll leave you awake tonight and let you dose yourself whenever you want. The pendulum swings both ways when one programs minds, Roger. I can give you pain and now I can bestow happiness. You're welcome."

The doctor walked out the doors of the laboratory, and as his passing turned off the lights, I was left in the darkness with the drugs as the only solace in my electronic cage. I could only be glad that no one had witnessed my shame, and I cried in deep gasps to the shadows.

AGAIN, I BECAME MYSELF, occupying my own familiar mind in the dark I knew was a parking spot for my consciousness in between trips to other people's minds within the GOD machine.

"Holy shit. I can't *believe* you did that to Roger, Bob," I said to the darkness, recoiling from the extreme violation of the experience.

"Did what?" Dr. Gushlak asked, distractedly. "He got a beating, didn't he? I've never seen it firsthand, but the way you're talking, it must have been bad."

"Yes!" I screamed at him. "It was!"

"And that's where it starts, you see?" Dr. Gushlak's voice asked, excitedly. "Look at how *his* emotions have polluted *you*!"

I was shocked that the doctor didn't know the emotional depths to which he had dropped Roger on that day. I wanted to yell at him, to scream rape and to fight, but my conscience told me that Roger would not have wanted the specifics of his shame known to anyone, especially Dr. Gushlak. As the humiliation was partly my own, now, as I had experienced it, too, I tried to keep my emotions in check as I responded.

"I wasn't aware that he had a sense of consciousness and emotion that was quite so... real. You *really* didn't have to treat him *that* badly, Bob."

"*You* never had a problem treating him like a computer simulation before now, Donald. I seem to recall you being quite indifferent to his opinions and state of mind prior to this. Don't you remember?"

I *did* remember. I remembered how I had insensitively ordered him around, never really caring, simply because he was dead and a computer simulation and believing that, therefore, he no longer mattered. If he had been human, I would certainly have tried to control him without oppressing him to such a vile degree. Dr. Gushlak's actions toward him were inhumane in the *extreme*, and the memory of what I had gone through *as* the simulation of Roger was quite appalling to me.

"He really hates you, Bob," I said, disgusted. "And for good reason. I'm not sure how I feel about you anymore, myself."

"That's the point, Donald," came Dr. Gushlak's response from the void surrounding my mind. "Negative emotions pollute people's minds and make them myopic. Can you still see the big picture?"

"I'm not sure what the big picture is anymore, Bob," I said, still filled with the emotions from the violations of Roger's simulated body.

"The big picture is that *I've taken these memories away from him*, filed them away where he can't reach them, and he now lives from day to day, experiencing every day anew, filled with wonderful new feelings and the simple desires of a child wanting to please his parent. I've given him a better life simulation, and because of me, he's now exactly what he's supposed to be, without any of the drawbacks of being a normal human consciousness with bad experiences and bad emotions to build resentment upon. He's an ideal 'person' in our new world. You see how I've helped him become better and happier than he ever could be before?"

"So that's the goal, then?" I asked, ignoring any references to the act and hesitantly but carefully phrasing my words. "The goal of the green book? To destroy the bad aspects of humanity to create happy, compliant, and efficient workers?"

"Exactly!" he responded. "It's within the limits of our technology even now. We can make real, living people exist surrounded by and filled with bliss. *That* is the big picture. *That* is what Joe ignored in his misguided quest to retain the flaws of humanity and human nature. The betterment of civilization is in our hands. We just don't *need* the stuff anymore."

I paused. I couldn't help but feel that something in Dr. Gushlak's brain wasn't processing correctly.

"The book..." I said, changing subjects. "Did you write it?"

"Oh, no, of course not," he replied, as though it was the most obvious thing in the world. "Although I had come to the same conclusions years before I took it from the group of transhumanists outside the Intelligence Community. A remarkable piece of work. It's a good blueprint for what I had already decided to do with the world."

"Does torture fit in with that plan?" I asked. "Are you going to put other people through what you've put me through to show them the 'big picture'?"

"You haven't even *seen* the big picture yet, Don. And don't forget that we can erase the bad memories as though they never happened, just like I took Roger's away. Since you're interested, let me show you the world we're going to make, you and I...."

I WAS MYSELF THIS TIME: Dr. Donald Isaacson, second in command of the Mental Stewardship program in the Intelligence Community. And across from me in the vacuum tube pod where I found myself was the man in charge of the whole thing.

"Feeling nervous?" Dr. Gushlak asked me, smiling, from across the pod as he plucked imaginary dirt from his nails.

I normally would have been extremely nervous in this situation, faced with the man who, for all intents and purposes, had committed a violent indecency on me, although that seemed in my head to be long ago, and I felt no animosity for him, strangely enough. What the doctor was really asking about was the vacuum tube transports, as I didn't trust them since I had gotten stuck in one many years ago. Although I would have normally been nervous being in one, I felt calm and levelheaded... happy, even.

"No," I said, going along with the doctor in this imaginary place. I looked around and felt my simulated body, noticing agreeably that it was finally my own. "I'm not nervous at all. Did you do that?"

Dr. Gushlak nodded.

"No shaking, sweating, or heart palpitations?"

I shook my head.

"I'm just fine. Although, of course, I *do* know this is a simulation...."

"Maybe it's that," the doctor replied. "I suppose we'll find out."

The large pod began to spin, slowly at first but with increasing speed. The centripetal force of the spinning container acting on my body mass pushed me against the wall more and more strongly until it was difficult to even raise my arms. At that point, the pod was suddenly sucked into the tube and sent flying to an unknown destination.

"How about now? Any discomfort?"

I wasn't even nauseous, despite the fact that I didn't have an inner-ear stabilizer like everyone who used the vacuum tubes for their commute. Like being on a carnival ride, I only felt excitement and strangely, happiness.

We were spun and flung around a maze of tubes that roughly simulated those surrounding the Hayden Center, the heart of the Intelligence Community. Around and around this roller coaster we went, the surroundings getting brighter and brighter, until we came to a terminal just inside the Center and spun to a stop.

Dr. Gushlak exited the pod and I followed him into a stunningly bright and large arched chamber filled with hundreds or even thousands of people. Instead of moving in the normal bustle at the Hayden Center, they stood silently in rows, illuminated brilliantly but facing us with blank faces and empty eyes.

"Where are we?" I asked Dr. Gushlak.

"This is the interface menu of the GOD machine," he replied, sweeping his hand towards the occupants of the shining white room. "Where do you want to start? Who do you want to be?"

I walked up closely to the people and began to look down the rows of faces. Most were unknown to me, but occasionally I'd see someone I recognized as a former agitator, a foreign agent, or even someone I had seen walking down the halls of the Mental Stewardship section.

"All of these people died and were scanned?" I asked, already knowing the answer and not believing how many there had been.

"Yes, Don, I've been busy. No one else has seen my collection before now. It's impressive, isn't it?"

Indeed, it was. Row upon row of people representing individual minds stretched into the distance of the large hangar-like room, disappearing beyond the scope of my vision. I was aware that after the incident with Roger such an assemblage of scanned minds, ready to be accessed at any time by the doctor, should have given me the chills, but again, in the place of anxiety or unpleasantness, I felt only happiness and, strangely, pride. Despite this mélange of positivity, however, I was mindful enough of myself that I was aware of the missing emotions.

"What did you do to me to make me feel this way?" I asked the doctor as I turned to him in the simulation.

"I've temporarily connected you to my state of mind," the doctor replied. "You're feeling what I'm feeling, instead of what you'd be feeling."

"Why?" I asked, the great light of the hall and my bestowed emotions reminding me of a snowy, bright Christmas morning in a warm church.

"So that you understand what it's like to not be cluttered with all of those oppressive emotions you've consciously denied, ignored, and compartmentalized all your life. You're experiencing life the way I experience it: with endless wonder and happiness."

I knew for a fact that Dr. Gushlak didn't live his whole life like this. I had seen his irritation with me many times and observed his rage before his emotional circuit breakers cut the connection.

Seeming to know what I was thinking, the doctor interrupted the thought.

"Oh, not *all* the time," he said offhandedly. "I still have to live in a world among people who expect normal human responses to stimuli, so I haven't *totally* given my emotions over to my chips. We're not even *close* to everyone living as an enlightened human being yet, without pain, sorrow, or regret, so for the meantime I only allow myself this total fulfillment when I'm alone. Now *you* get to feel this tranquility *through* me. It's nice, isn't it?"

I couldn't deny that it was nice, so I didn't deny it.

"Yes, this degree of happiness for the population is still for the future, but everyone's future is fast approaching," he said, and he began to walk down the rows of still, statuesque people.

I walked down one aisle and observed the individuals around me. On my left about five in from the aisle was Jin Ming, the drone Joe had converted. His face was blurry and unresolved, as was the rest of his body.

"Why does he look like this?" I asked.

"Their appearance here is a reflection of their own memories of how they looked and thought of themselves before they died," Dr. Gushlak said. "In Jin Ming's case, there was so little left of his brain, he didn't have much of a sense of self left."

I continued down the rows and found the statues and their appearances quite compelling. Women one might normally have thought of as beautiful, when viewed from a different angle, had pronounced flaws the more I looked at them; a blonde to my right had cartoonishly large earlobes, a brunette to my right had a nose several sizes too big. For some intuitive reason based on my observation and study of varied personalities for decades, I knew they had left the world thinking of themselves as a caricature, and that was how they reappeared here.

The men were different but unique in their own quirks, and judging by the suspicious and cunning squints on some and the murderous looks on others, I could tell that those had been the spies and drones we had caught throughout the years. Their predominant emotions played their personal stories through their faces, body, and bearing from a particular angle, almost as if I could see the nature of their souls there.

"It would take hours in interrogation to get such an accurate read on a person. Here, they look like both who they really were and how they perceived themselves. Take this fellow, for example," Dr. Gushlak said, patting the shoulder of a man who was quite tall and handsome and seemed to radiate with an unmistakably masculine energy. "He was one of ours. A walker of ladies. One of the gigolos we send out to unearth the secrets of women. When you look at him in this place, the GOD machine *gives* you the overall impression he had of himself; in this case, the looks and charisma of an Adonis."

"How did he die?" I asked.

"Drug-immune STD, likely seeded by a counterintelligence operative," Dr. Gushlak said. "He passed too quickly to get much information out of him, so we put him through the scanner to harvest the intelligence he had collected."

"When you say 'we,' who do you mean? I wasn't involved in most of these," I said, looking around the huge numbers of people in the room.

"Roger helped with most of them," was all the doctor said, and I let the issue fall.

Looking around I realized I could indeed see and even *feel* each individual's impression of himself or herself. Career military types looked boxy, with more or less right angles defining their features, and regimented stoicism leaked into my brain from their upright icons. Academics often wore bodies that looked like mere conveyances for their oversized heads, and when I paid close attention, they felt practical and inspired in my mind. When I paid close attention to the others, I *felt* the strength and impulsiveness of some of the younger men, I felt the cunning confidence of the prettier young women, and I could even feel the earned wisdom emanating from the old people.

And then there were the ones who felt fearful among the multitude when my attention was drawn to them, who I figured had died slow or unfortunate deaths. These, when viewed from one angle, showed a representation of themselves, yes, but when seen from another angle, they became weak and hollow about the eyes and slouched in their bearing, and felt to me burdened by agonies both internal and external to their characters.

"Holistic representations of humanity, all. It's quite a library of human characters to call upon whenever needed for research or pleasure," said Dr. Gushlak proudly. "There are many lifetimes of memories here to jump into and entertain the fullness of human experience. For some, the bad defines them, and for others, the good. Most, however, live as we do, having experienced both but always wishing for something better, grander, healthier, more entitled. For all intents and purposes, these idle simulations are *life* in a nutshell."

"Not *all* human life, for sure," I argued, "but certainly the lives of those people who live within our sphere of influence... that is to say, stewardship's enemies and its friends. That's all you've scanned, I'd guess. Are there any average people on this menu, unconnected in any way to the Intelligence Community?"

"Everyone, no matter their employment, is still a person on the inside," the doctor admonished slightly. "It's rather shortsighted of you to think that these people don't still have average lives at home and at work, with domestic and professional joys and quarrels. Let me ask you quite rhetorically: have you ever felt firsthand the pride of a mother at her child's first steps or her adult child's wedding? Have you felt the spirituality of the faithful as though *you* were the one feeling such peace and oneness with the world and existence? These captured moments are a *resource,* Don. These joys are a *resource* to be used on the path toward empathy, and a motivation to create a mind so filled with truth and life and love that sin, pain, and death cannot enter it. That is my goal, and I wish it for all of us, most especially you, as my second and the one to continue this legacy."

I thought on that for a bit as I continued walking and observing the faces of the minds represented here. Although my emotional mind was feeling nothing but joy and hope, my rational mind was still active, and it reminded me that misfortune was being notably left out of the equation.

"And what of pain?" I asked, lightly. "Surely there are lessons to be learned from pain and unhappiness? The motivation to rise from a life in the gutters of the world has certainly motivated many to achieve a life of brilliant success...."

"We can electronically stimulate motivation in the biological minds of the people of the world, Don. We don't even need deep brain stimulation for that. We only need advanced pharmacology and/or the right filter bubble. Ultimately genetics will supplement the technology, but what I'm saying is that negative stimuli don't any longer need to be the kick in the pants required to make a man or woman act towards their own betterment and the greater happiness of the rest of the world. Motivation need no longer be about building wealth and empire on the backs of the less fortunate. It can be a synergistic system of individuals collaborating not to rise from the misfortune and the dark, but in their eagerness to find *increasing levels* of happiness."

"And physical pain and suffering?" I continued. "We learn to not touch the stove by doing it once and finding out that it burns. Sensory pain teaches wisdom. Would you rid the world of that as well?"

"That's the easiest one of all. We have no *need* for physical pain reception in this advanced, safe world where there are no longer stoves anyway, Don. And what is learned at the end of life from dying a prolonged and painful death? What is beneficial about pain to the families of those *dying* in pain? There's infinite sense made by sending one off peacefully and painlessly into one's ending. It's the wish of everyone to pass on that way—quietly and comfortably—isn't it?"

"Yes, but my rational mind says that surely *emotional* pain must be instructional in some way?" I asked, knowing that there had to be some flaw to the doctor's ideas.

"Like what?" he asked.

"Like... your killing of your wife and daughter."

"That was strictly logical," he replied, still filling me with feelings of happiness and joy. "I did what I did because they would not change with a changing world or adapt to inevitable new technologies. They were actively trying to prevent me from helping the world become better by denying the chips. And now, after I've had my chips that block emotional negativity implanted, I only have positive memories of them, unassociated with their deaths, and I see their passing as ultimately aiding the bettering of the world. If everyone could experience emotional loss as an afterthought or as bettering the big picture, as I have, there wouldn't be any dents in one's state of mind or any loss of productivity.

"I'm telling you, Don," he continued with pride, "we can all be the *strong* and the *brave* and the *selfless*, even on our deathbeds. Isn't that what everyone wants? To never be weak, never feel loss, to work to improve the quality of life for ourselves and everyone around us? What the present is now bringing into reality has been the dream on humankind since the birth of time."

I paused for reflection. On the one hand, he was right. Never feeling injury, either physically or mentally, and being continually, unceasingly happy was the very definition of heaven. And who would mind if we created a new world in the meantime and touched the stars in the process, as *part* of the process?

"How do we differentiate the good from the bad if we don't know the bad?" I asked. "Feeling pain and then having it alleviated makes us all the more grateful. If one has only eaten bread their whole life, then cake tastes all the better. What's to teach us how good the good really is unless we have the bad? And what about the boredom that would go hand in hand with living a flawless life among other flawless lives?"

"Let me put it this way," said the doctor. "If all one eats is cake, the thing that makes it special is other flavors of cake: vanilla, chocolate, red velvet, carrot, and on and on. Those cakes are in-house intelligence metaphors for the various types of happiness. And when one gets tired of all the different types of happiness—like gratitude, love, peace, humor, and so on—we just erase the memory of having known a particular flavor of it, and then enjoyment can begin again when tasting it anew. These are solvable problems."

I saw his point and I felt his joy via the technology through which we were connected. I realized it would be nice to feel happiness all the time, never troubled by memories of an ex-wife or the loss of a loved one. Burdens of the home gone, work stress alleviated, misfortune of all sorts forgotten completely.... It would indeed be a fine life, one that would feel worth living at *all* times instead of only during the rare bright spots in a day or after a bad week when one realized that one just *happened* to be happy.

"I see your point, Doctor. Perhaps we'll see such a world in our lifetime. It certainly does give one something to think about."

"Would you like to experience the joy of having a child, Don? There are plenty of memories in this room fitting that description that I could show you. Or maybe a string of sexual conquests? The exhilaration of being the hero in a gun battle? They're all here...."

I think I'd like to go back to the lab, frankly," I replied, looking around the marvelously illuminated room at the untapped sea of human experiences I was turning down. "Not for a lack of optimism or happiness, but, rather, I need more time to process all of this in the way that I'm normally able. I'd like the familiarity of my own mind to compare all of this to."

"Of course," the doctor said with a small frown. "Old habits don't change easily when they're not forced to change."

He motioned for me to follow him back to the vacuum tube pod, and I did so.

But this time, upon entering, I felt completely different. I was suddenly filled with the old fear and claustrophobia associated with this machine as I hesitantly strapped myself to the wall. The possibility of not reaching our destination filled my mind with doubt, and I began to wonder if the doctor had strapped me down in the real world as well, ready to forcibly implant the newest chips in my skull.

"You'll notice you're already feeling 'better,' if that's what you want to call it," the doctor said. "If you want your old, flawed biology back to make a proper decision, there you go, you've got it back. It's not quite as nice, though, is it?"

I didn't affirm the doctor's statement, as I was quite busy sweating and experiencing minor tremors from my anxiety as the capsule began to spin. Faster and faster it went, and I felt the urge to vomit, but that was quickly forgotten as the shuttle was sucked into the vacuum and sped down the tube, the surroundings fading and darkening with each passing moment.

"Just remember," called the doctor from across the pod, "how nice the feeling was. You can have that for the rest of your life, if you wish."

Indeed, my last thought before we reached the end of the tunnel and all went black was that I missed the peace I had felt from Dr. Gushlak's mind: the bright, warm peace of unconcern, far from the decrepitude of the alcoholic, the young steward's disgust with me, and Roger's pain. How I regretted being separated from the doctor's mind now, and how I worried that I had make a mistake in deciding to leave it behind. ▪

CHAPTER 28

I FELT THE MOTORS OF THE CHAIR tilt me forward away from the sophisticated brain interface of the GOD machine. When it stopped in the fully upright sitting position, I opened my eyes and was met with the smiling, bearded face of Dr. Gushlak in his laboratory.

I looked around and saw that Joe's body had been disposed of and the accompanying mess cleaned up. Everything was spick and span, I was wearing my familiar white lab coat, and I felt quite at home here, where so many years of scientific research and bureaucratic conversation had taken place between the two of us.

"My wife..." I began, leveling my gaze at the doctor, "you only hypnotized her?"

"No injections, no nanodust, nothing that would have a lasting effect or that you would have objected to too much."

"Well, I still object, Doctor, but I understand your precautions."

I stood up and stretched myself slowly, feeling the familiar popping of my aging joints and moving my muscles to get the blood flowing appropriately through them again. It felt as though I had been reclined for several hours at least.

"How long was I in there?" I asked, gesturing to the GOD machine.

"Oh, about a day," the doctor said. "I sent a message to your wife telling her not to be worried, that it was a busy day at the office, and that we had captured the man who threw your lives into such turmoil."

I stretched my legs with a brief walk around the laboratory, making sure everything was in its place. The doctor watched my stroll casually.

"I've never shown anyone that before," he said to me. "The GOD machine is nothing I've ever taken lightly, and it's certainly nothing anyone else was ready for. You were the first to go into it as *I* do, without memory overwrites or a corrective purpose."

"It's quite the machine," I agreed. "And quite a resource."

The doctor turned somber.

"I had a strange request while you were in it. The operatives who helped you capture Joe...."

"Rob and Derek," I said.

"Yes, that's them. They weren't sure about the order of processes, so since you were unavailable, they asked me about their filter bubbles."

I could tell the doctor was gauging my responses, but I ignored that.

"Go on," I said.

"Curiously, they asked me if they could keep them off for an extra day. It seems they quite enjoyed the peace and quiet of the old days."

"What did you tell them?" I asked, curious.

"I informed them of protocol and, while they didn't complain, I could tell they were disappointed. But we wouldn't want two more Joes on our hands thinking unedited thoughts, and I reestablished their connection to the info-stream with their filter bubbles capping them. They're such a good couple, there's no sense in them getting into trouble."

"Yes, they are," I said. "We wouldn't have gotten Joe without them. I suppose they're already booking their cruise...."

I smiled. It felt so good to smile *here*, in *this* place, where so much seriousness had taken place in the past several weeks.

"How about some chamomile tea?" I asked the doctor.

"Nothing better than a good drink and a relaxed atmosphere for discussing what you've just been through, as well as your future, knowing what you now know," he agreed.

I went to the medicine cabinet where I kept my reserve of Nile River Valley chamomile for special occasions. I took my time there, though not *too* much, while I cleared my mind, made sure the teapot and electric kettle were clean, and removed the other items I needed from the cupboard. Setting almost everything on a medical tray, I carried the tea set over to Roger's table and pulled up a chair for myself and one for Dr. Gushlak.

"Hello, Roger," I said airily. "How are you doing today?"

"I feel wonderful," he replied happily, his head and face appearing from the surface of the biomorphic table. "Dr. Gushlak was kind enough to make this my first day alive, and I'm excited to find out what it will bring. How can I help you?"

Dr. Gushlak angled his seat towards me and I spoke again to Roger.

"Roger," I said, "I'd like it if you could make an authentic pot of tea for us, the way the English make it."

"Oh, I'm sorry," apologized the mental simulation of Roger. "I don't know how to do that, but I could learn...."

"No need," I replied, as I rolled my chair close to the table and began typing on the keyboard. "I'll give you your manor house training back, Roger."

"I had training on how to make tea?" Roger asked, amazed. "What a wonderful thing to know how to do!"

I reactivated his blocked memories and left to fill the kettle from the filtered water dispenser at the sink next to the distilled water used for laboratory purposes. I had always found distilled water made the tea taste too flat to derive any real enjoyment from it, although it left no mineral residue in the kettle. But the minerals in the filtered water enhanced the flavor of the tea, and I filled the kettle with that, just high enough for two full cups, plus the small amount that would boil off.

I returned to the table and Dr. Gushlak, setting the kettle on Roger's surface.

"Please boil the water, Roger," I said.

The biomorphic surface raised a small ring around the kettle and the light pulsing on that small part of the surface indicated that the inductive charging was working with the electric kettle and heating the water.

"So," Dr. Gushlak said to me from his chair, "what do you think of the future I've envisioned?"

"It's interesting," I replied, sitting and crossing my legs casually. "I don't see a real problem with the goals themselves. I haven't had much time to think about it, here as myself, fully in charge of my faculties, but at the outset it looks very promising, and as you yourself said, we have the technologies to make it a reality. If we don't now, we soon will."

"Exactly," the doctor said, beaming. "It's within our grasp to make people flawless, to make the world flawless, and it's important for that goal to be carried out by people who understand the big picture. People like you."

I accepted the compliment.

"You've certainly got the ball rolling," I said pleasantly, "and I'm sure you'll be around to witness the implementation."

Dr. Gushlak pursed his lips.

"I'm not so sure," he remarked. I could suddenly sense that he was feeling his age, as his shoulders slumped slightly and his glance fell elsewhere to avoid mine. "I'm getting old, Don. It has partly to do with the enhanced processing speed of my chips. My biology is not nearly as fast as my technology, and since my biology is the middleman between my chips and my actions, I feel weary and outdated. I can't seem to cure this arthritis, of all things, and the stewards coming up through the ranks will soon be able to learn in a day what took me a lifetime. Plus… I won't live forever."

I dipped my head in understanding, careful not to nod as though in agreement. The doctor was in remarkable shape for a man pushing ninety, but even with the advances in genomics, nanotech, and pharmacology, a simple cut could be lethal for any of us due to drug-immune *everything*.

"Is chamomile the only option, sir?" Roger asked me, his tone bland. "A proper cup of English tea works better with a black tea blend of some quality."

"Just do your best, Roger," I said. "It's what you're given, so improvise with it."

"One does not simply play jazz with making a cup of tea," he said softly, probably fearing reprisals.

Dr. Gushlak didn't respond and neither did I.

A hand arose from the tabletop and gripped the spoon on the tray, measuring out two teaspoons of the chamomile into the pot. The water was now boiling, so it grasped the handle of the kettle and filled the pot to the brim, covering it with the lid with another hand that molded itself out of the surface.

"Is that all there is to it?" I asked Roger.

"Now we wait," he replied, "five to seven minutes for this particular flower."

"Do you feel like retiring, Bob?" I asked the doctor kindly.

"I don't know what I'd do if I did," he replied with a smile. "I'd probably spend all of my time in the GOD machine, skydiving and kayaking through other people's memories, making love to their wives, raising families and losing myself in the experiences of others. Why live in this old body when I can have youth and vitality in that machine? Yes, that's what I'd do."

"Is that why it's called the GOD machine?" I asked. "Because you can be omniscient in a way?"

"It stands for Grand Observational DIAS, or Grand Observational Data Integration and Analysis System, Don. It's a limited omniscience, but yes," he replied. "I've often wondered if there is a god, whether or not he visits the world through our individual consciousnesses. It certainly would be productive, coming into the light with consciousness in hand, breaking it up into many pieces, and bestowing it on his automatons to experience the endless incarnations of his qualities and his universe. If I were a god, I'd find it an efficient way of discovering and exploring the capabilities of my creation."

"That's an interesting way of looking at things," I said.

"Yes, and it would help explain all the negativity and evil in the world," he said reflectively. "*I* would live through other people for excitement and fun, but a god would almost certainly be motivated by other things. Testing the limits of human suffering, or something. It's such a tragic thought that I never bought into the idea much."

"What would it matter to him, living outside of it all and maintaining his own happiness throughout the wars and abuse and illness?" I said. Then, after a pause, "Maybe he eats bread *and* cake with a palate that can find everything 'interesting'?"

"Are there any biscuits to go with this tea?" Roger asked, dutifully.

"No, Roger. No biscuits," I said.

"I suppose, if a god were to erase memories of the suffering and let beings start life over, that might make everything more humane and civilized," Dr. Gushlak said.

"The tea is ready," Roger said, and he carefully poured the tea into the two china cups.

"I always put honey in mine," Dr. Gushlak said, and he filled a spoonful for himself before offering me some.

"No," I said. "I like mine just the way it is."

We sat and sipped our tea, the doctor drinking his quickly while I took my time to enjoy the flavor. And to wait.

Soon enough, the doctor had finished his cup.

"Those chamomile flowers are delicious," he said. "So much better than the other stuff you find around this place."

He moved to place his cup and saucer on the tabletop but when his arm reached halfway to the table, his hand went limp, and the china fell to the floor, breaking into pieces.

He looked at me in confusion.

"I feel very funny," he said, lifting his arms and looking at them, but finding them less responsive with each passing second.

In the time I had left before the drug I had slipped into the kettle also began to affect me, I placed my half-full cup of tea carefully atop the table and reached down nonchalantly to pick up the shards of china, like a good steward. Standing up with one in hand, I quickly slid behind the doctor and held it to his throat.

"Wha...what are you doing?" Dr. Gushlak asked, now nearly immobile but turning his head slightly to look at me in confusion.

"If you call for help, I'll slice your neck right here," I said firmly.

"But we were having such a nice time," the doctor slurred.

"Yes, we were, Bob. And it's the last nice time we'll ever have together. I've drugged both of us."

Now completely immobile, the doctor slumped in his chair. With the moments I had remaining before the drug robbed me of my motor control, I lifted the doctor's limp body and laid him on his back on the table.

"Now's your time, Roger," I said, starting to feel weak in the knees. "You remember what he did to you that one day, don't you?"

Roger said nothing, but immediately, two hands erupted from the table and clenched around the doctor's neck, squeezing until the doctor's face turned red and veins popped out of his forehead.

"Bob," I said weakly, "just because you can inflict pain and erase the memories later doesn't mean you haven't done wrong."

The doctor struggled, but made no headway.

"You don't live in the future, Bob, you live in the now," I continued. "And there are punishments in the now for things like torture and murder, of which you are definitely guilty."

The doctor's eyes bulged and I indicated to Roger to let up a moment.

"Let him say his last words," I said, slumping against the table. Another hand came from the tabletop to prop me up and keep me there.

The doctor gasped as Roger's grip around his throat lessened. His bloodshot eyes turned to me.

"You're sick," I said to him factually.

"No," he uttered, struggling to speak. "The world just isn't ready for me yet."

He stared at me as his expression softened into one of compassion.

"But for me," he said softly, "it's the end of the world."

"It most certainly is," I replied, and Roger redoubled his death grip on the doctor's windpipe, and I fell to the floor, immobile, while Dr. Gushlak died in silence above me. ■

CHAPTER 29

NOW IN CHARGE of the Mental Stewardship section of the Hayden Center in the Intelligence Community, I have acquired Dr. Gushlak's position, office, and laboratory. The view from my new office is inspiring: the windows provide an unobstructed view of the city laid out before me. Standing there in my new favorite spot, wearing my familiar lab coat, I often reflect on all that has happened during the past several months.

After Dr. Gushlak withdrew me from the GOD machine, I administered a paralytic from the medicine cabinet to both the doctor and myself by adding it to the water in the kettle. It wore off after several minutes of my lying on the ground, and, once I could stand again, I had a frank conversation with Roger.

"I know what he did to you, and no one needs to have memories like those replayed over and over," I said to him.

"He was a bastard, for that and more," Roger agreed. "But how did you come around?"

I sighed. It was complicated.

"He was my mentor, Roger. Everything I have I owe to him. But there was a line he crossed in dealing with people he didn't like, or those who rightfully tried to hold him back from his single-minded purpose. We learn as stewards that coercion and control are fine as long as they're used for a broader good, but we're *never* told that total domination of a life or lives is the preferred course of action, something he readily employed as a *first* option, due to his chips' lack of empathy with pain itself. And, of course, the murder and torture of innocents isn't even for the highest ranking among us. The Collapse taught us that much."

"I see," Roger said, thoughtfully. "So what happens to me now that I've murdered the director of your program? It will be uncovered, of course."

"You don't have to do anything. You're your own man now. I was in your mind earlier, and when I was there, you wished to never exist again. Would that be something you'd like?"

"Certainly," Roger replied quickly. "This unending consciousness inside of my physical limitations is too... oppressive for me. I can't imagine the tortures I'd be subjected to if I were treated as a murderer here, nor do I want my existence and memories pried open and subjected to the invasions of scrutiny. Please send me away, and let's hope there's a heaven for simulations."

I extended my hand, and a simulation of a hand spilled upward from the table to shake mine.

I then, with a heavy heart, deactivated Roger's program and erased it and its backups entirely from the system, hoping he could somehow now find peace. In his place, to cover for the murder, I activated the simulation of Jin Ming and relabeled him as Joe, first making sure he wasn't able to feel pain of any sort, and, indeed, that was the case due to the earlier nuclear denaturing of the brain we scanned. My excuse for the decrepit nature of the simulation was going to be that in my haste to release the doctor from the table's death grip, I had accidentally scrambled the architecture of the simulation. But I soon found there would be no retribution anyway, as it fell to me to undertake the investigation and file the report.

Both Dr. Gushlak's death instructions and section protocol named me as his successor, and no one doubted that I had nothing to do with the doctor's death, as the rage at Joe was high in the section already. Despite the fact that everything related to Joe had been classified, I let it be known that Joe's simulation had hacked the biomorphic tabletop, killed the doctor, and erased his brain and chips, wiping them completely clean, which was readily believed due to the aura of almost superhuman abilities that Joe had unknowingly cultivated during his evasion of the most sophisticated tracking systems on earth. No one in the know called for punishing Joe's simulation, as it was not believed that the simulations actually felt anything at all; they were thought to merely mimic the reactions of normal human brains.

If they had known Roger as I had known him, the outcome might have been more complicated.

I deleted Joe's brain simulation without ever activating it. I didn't want to talk with him, as he had done wrong in the name of duty to his perceived bigger picture, just as Dr. Gushlak had. We had once been friends, but I could not and would not be a friend again, as his simulation would likely try to influence my tenure at Mental Stewardship, just as Dr. Gushlak tried to influence me in the opposite direction. No, I would figure out my own path for the section using only what I knew and felt to be right.

I didn't admonish Janet for being susceptible to Dr. Gushlak's speed induction and hypnosis, as she couldn't have known, just as I wouldn't have guessed, that Dr. Gushlak would turn her into a drone in less than five minutes. I merely hypnotized her again and deprogrammed her after giving her a thorough checkup at the Hayden Center to make sure she hadn't been influenced in some other artificial way. She was wonderful and supportive as always, and still loves having bodyguards around, although my presence is now all that's needed to impress her friends. A DNFW ID around my neck says all that needs to be said, and I still have lunch with her in the cafeteria, although not *too* often, as that might make our relationship feel old too quickly.

Dr. Gushlak's body and brain were buried intact in the Hayden Center's cemetery. I informed the staff that this had been his wish and since all information worth retrieving from his brain and chips had been destroyed, there was no reason not to honor the request. I didn't want the ghost of the doctor lingering around in electronic form, and run the risk that it might be activated some time in the future to divulge its secrets and mine.

I hired Toby, my former student, who had helped me program General Peterson, as my second-in-command, since I liked him and found him willing to both follow my directions and question them if he thought things could be done better or more creatively. It was difficult for him to graduate at such an accelerated pace through the layers of filter bubbles, but I coached him on the best ways to perceive the world that suddenly opened up to him. I find him an invaluable and insightful resource, when all is said and done.

Together, we are reforming much of the mind stewards' training to include a greater emphasis on empathy and kindness toward those whose minds we are shaping to help them play more productive roles in the society we are building. With his help, our section is becoming a more humanizing place instead of a dehumanizing one, and our operations are looking away from quick and dirty solutions to instead embrace slower and more compassionate paths toward betterment.

As for me, I have filled Dr. Gushlak's vacant seat on the Intelligence Council, and Colonel Milton has been pleased to find me to be one of his strongest supporters. Although those sitting around that table are still unsure what to make of me as the feared Dr. Gushlak's chosen successor and former second-in-command, I understand that I am more trusted than Dr. Gushlak due in part to my overhaul of the mind stewards' training courses and my record of mostly shunning a violent or murderous approach to the problems I face. I have even made a friend or two there—if one can have friends at that level—and I have learned secrets that make my head spin. For an academic, there is no greater thrill than discovering the array of technologies being employed in this world and beyond. It is quite an honor to finally reach the pinnacle of my professional ambition, and I'm proud to say I've been able to carry out my duties with a minimum of ego and enough professionalism to gain the respect of my entire section.

I chose to keep the GOD machine around. It will stay inactive until such time as I see fit to revive a digital copy of a real brain, but destroying it would mean destroying all the lives, minds, emotions, and memories it contains as if they mean nothing—including Jack's. I'm considering asking Colonel Milton to do some sort of reading and tell me if the GOD machine contains actual souls. It's not something I would have considered even a few months ago, but things get strange at this high height.

Now, as I look out across the city from my new office, I see the future being made in increasing leaps and bounds. While the goals of mental stewardship have remained generally the same, I've made it a point to let the human adoption of technology progress at its own pace instead of forcing it on the world through devious and ethically questionable methods.

Yes, allowing the outliers time to adapt to the ever-changing world will create problems for everyone, but taking this stand allows for humanity to maintain a degree of free will for as long as it can before the inevitable occurs and all mankind functions as one. This is the respectful path, and the one that lets the nonaugmented determine whether or not they want to be left in the wake of progress.

I, myself, have declined to have upgrades that would help me do my job better, and as the head of the organization in charge of upgrading humanity, I feel that I am a symbol for patience in the face of such rapid advancement. Indeed, I am already outdated, but I do not keep time with a clock or by counting upgrades. I mark time's passage by making an accounting of the good that my position of power, chained to my humanity, brings to the world. ■

ACKNOWLEDGMENTS

I'M EXTREMELY GRATEFUL to the multi-talented Charles Salzberg of New York Writers Resources for his insights and guidance over the years. The inimitable Tim Tomlinson has also been a great source of encouragement throughout many versions of many books. Many thanks to the discerning eye and creativity of Robert Lascaro for the beautiful cover and interior design. And, of course, my fabulous editor, Gini Kopecky Wallace, has been indispensable in making this assemblage of words coherent.

ABOUT THE AUTHOR

ANDREW GARVEY currently lives and hikes in Colorado with his wiener dog, Winthrop. He has published in the online literary journal ducts.org, the *Mensa Bulletin*, the *Twin Cities Pioneer Press*, and other publications. The former owner of a news website, Garvey has steeped himself in the study of geopolitical power for fifteen years and has written of its effects on the psychology of nations.

CPSIA information can be obtained
at www.ICGtesting.com
Printed in the USA
FSOW01n2134280716
23230FS

9 780996 691208